PIONEERS

PIONEERS

by

PHILLIP MANN

LONDON
VICTOR GOLLANCZ LTD
1988

First published in Great Britain 1988
by Victor Gollancz Ltd
14 Henrietta Street, London WC2E 8QJ

© Phillip Mann 1988

British Library Cataloguing in Publication Data
Mann, Phillip
  Pioneers.
  I. Title
  823[F]

ISBN 0-575-04281-8

Typeset by Centracet
and printed in Great Britain by
St Edmundsbury Press Ltd, Bury St Edmunds, Suffolk

For David Carnegie
and Pauline Neale

and

not forgetting
Kate and Ian.

PART 1

Awakening

1

I am still just waking up.

I slip from dozing to a blinking wakefulness and back to dozing again with barely any awareness of the transition. Friends from the past have visited me, Bonniface and Lindis calling greetings and recalling past adventures . . . and that is clearly impossible, but I feel warmth and ease and everything is normal, just as it should be.

Three days ago I was as inert as a statue, prone and stiff on the sea bed. Now, if I am not fully conscious, I am at least mobile and washed and sitting in our small kitchen waiting patiently while my body comes fully alive.

Three days ago I broke through the warm surface jelly of my sleeping tank, and when my face was dry and completely clear I took my first shallow tentative breath. Then, when I was breathing easily, my fingers fluttered and that motion set in full train all the complex wake-up procedures. The door covering my tub slid back and I tasted for the first time for many years the dry sterile air of the ship. The blue jelly deliquesced and drained away, for purification, leaving me high, dry and naked. Supported at the neck, head and back I was sat up by the auto-nurse and then my eyes opened. I climbed out under my own motivation and made my way to the dispensary where revival drugs were waiting. The drugs help, but there is really no substitute for movement for knitting together the sleeping body, and we are trained to stump about on numb legs and slap our hands and sing.

I remember my trainer. "Sing," he said.

"Sing what?" said I.

"Sing any old thing," he said.

And that was what I did. This time I sang an old song about

a drunken sailor and I beat out the rhythm on the walls until I was sore.

Not that I remember all the details of my waking. One never does, any more than a full-human can remember the moment of birth, but I have watched films of my waking and the pattern never changes.

Now I sit, drink cordial and wait. The thought of solid food makes me feel sick. But soon I will get the urge to chew and then I will raid the larder.

Ariadne is still asleep. I checked her on my first day. She was rising slowly. The tip of her nose had just broken the surface. Today her chin is a dimple on the surface and I can see her face. Her breasts and thighs and the tops of her arms are like pale islands of sand rising from the sea. I give her another few hours to her first breath. And I am amused at myself. I desire her already and that is a very good sign. My psyche at its deepest levels is alive and clattering. And she will be surprised. Normally she is the first to awake. Once she predated me by over three weeks. That was terrible. I awoke to find her prim and poised. It was months before our rhythms came into phase properly. She will be glad to find me there and we will wake up together, sleepy and amorous and with only the peering stars outside for company.

After watching Ariadne come gently alive I performed a grim task. It is one of the responsibilities of the first awake.

Beyond our long-sleep chamber there is a small room where the temperature never rises above freezing. When the door is opened, dim blue lights come on which seem to make the air even colder. In the room are two coffers and above each of them dangles an auto-nurse. Inside the coffers, waiting at a point just below life, are clones of Ariadne and myself.

It is an education in courage to look down at the dead sleeping face of yourself, suspended a few inches below the fluids which sluice round the body massaging it. The clones have no dreams. They are as lively as bricks. But they wait, ready in case one of us has an accident.

Each time, before and after the long sleep we must check them. Of course alarm bells would clamour if something were wrong and the auto-nurse would be far wiser than us in coping with a catastrophe; but we are required to check.

I am pleased to report that all is well.

I must have dozed again for I see that thirteen hours have disappeared somewhere. Ariadne is breathing. She will be with me in (say) five hours . . . seven at the outside.

Being more awake now, I am beginning to ask questions, such as why am I doing this? Writing my thoughts. Trying to describe things. I have no easy answer. Such an activity was not part of our training. In fact I know of no other member of a Pioneer rescue team who has ever lifted a pencil other than to fill in report forms or perhaps doodle.

The truth is, I suspect, that there was a contamination in my gene balance. No, that is a bad way to put it. Not contamination. An irregularity perhaps. A kink in the chain. Something so insignificant or innocent-seeming that it escaped all detection. I find that a nice thought. It gives me a fingerhold on individuality . . . though I am not sure that I regard individuality as a virtue. It is something that I observe in full-humans.

There, my mind is running on. There is a strangeness about words on paper. I do not know what is going to come next and at the moment I am not worried. In my mind I see the words like bubbles coming to the surface of a liquid. Something causes those bubbles. I want to discover that cause.

Apart from my waking first, this awakening has not been quite like the others. Not only do I feel more alive . . . more me . . . but I awoke with an extraordinary dream that will not leave me. I have already mentioned that dozing dream of friends, well this dream was different. I was climbing a mountain (I have climbed many mountains) and behind me was climbing a full-human that I seemed to know. We were climbing up an almost sheer face of grey stone and had reached that point in a climb at which a mountain seems to have a personality of its own which is pitted against you. I looked up and saw that we still had a long way to go, that there was an overhang coming which would require all our strength and courage. I explored with my fingers up the sheer face. I found a crevice and worked my blunt fingers into it. I made sure my purchase was firm and then called to my companion below that I was moving up. He looked up at me and his face under his helmet was dusty and streaked with sweat. He nodded. Then I lifted. Having great strength in my arms I was able to lift myself bodily until my face was above the crevice and I could see a ledge which ran like a diagonal pathway directly across the stone face. With one reach I had my arm over the ledge. A pull and I was over cleanly (no small stones dislodged) and found myself lying on a comfortable sandy path.

I squirmed round and offered my arm to my companion who was spread along the cliff holding with toe and finger. He could not quite reach my hand. I saw him transfer all his weight to his left foot and then reach with his right hand. He brushed my fingers and then his toehold flaked away and he fell. The rope jerked as it ran out of slack and I saw him spinning like a spider at the end of its thread.

All would have been well, but in my hands the rope turned to clay and parted. He did not fall immediately but hung there in space staring up at me. He called something strange. He said, "You're almost human, but not quite." And then he fell, turning over and over like a scrap of paper.

I don't remember waking from this dream, but of course I did. I glided from sleep and found myself stretched on my bunk gripping the bar. Those words have stayed with me though I cannot remember my companion's face. "You're almost human, but not quite."

Even as I write those words I feel a stillness. They carry more meaning than I understand. I am still very dozy.

Anyway. Today must be a day for memories. My mind is off again. I am thinking about stillness and I remember a full-human I once worked with. He was an evil man in many ways. The kind of man who laughs when you cut yourself and then starts to tell you about the time he injured himself. But I quite liked him. At least he was nearly as big as me and that pleased me as I don't like taking orders from small men. But we were working out from San Francisco Write-Off, about forty miles inland. I was very young then. It was only some twenty or so years since my first waking.

Someone in the South Pacific Safety had picked up a radio call and we were investigating. It was a slow jog, working our way down the old roads, cutting a path. Anyway, in the long nights this human and I would talk. He'd led an interesting life, always in trouble, and he had lots of stories of the olden days, as he called them. He meant the days before the Catastrophe. Once he'd been in prison and he described what it was like to stand in a court of law and hear your life picked apart in graceless dry phrases. . . .Isn't that strange, I can remember his words but not his name. . . .He told me how the conceits that gave his life glamour were drained of their essence. He told me that when he saw his life unwound like a bandage that still bears the marks of bloody sores, he felt a great stillness.

That is what I feel as I face that unpleasant truth. Stillness. For it is a truth that I am not quite human, but almost.

When he had finished speaking my nameless companion just sat brooding. I suppose when you can truly see yourself there is not much more to be said after all. Silence is best.

But am I jealous of the full-humans? Have *I* been brooding on that? And if so, for how long? Centuries probably. I have just heard the doors on Ariadne's sleeping tub roll back.

I have watched Ariadne limber herself out of her coffer. It is a long time since I have seen her do this. Sitting upright she slid her arms along the bars which run along the side of the tank and pulled herself forwards. The auto-nurse helped. Her legs bent at the knees as they slid over the edge of the support platform and then she sat for several minutes, her feet flat on the floor, gathering her strength. She had not registered that I was already awake. Her eyes were open but gazed vacantly. She was dozing. Then she pulled herself to her feet and tried to

13

walk. Her legs did not know what to do and she slewed round on her heels and had to catch herself and lift herself upright with the strength of her arms. Next she worked her toes on one foot and the leg inched forwards. It seemed painful and I wanted to help, but I didn't. We must all learn alone and she would not have thanked me for my strong arm. Slowly she advanced one foot and then the next.

Gradually she worked her way out of our long-sleep chamber and into the short corridor which leads into the kitchen. I backed out of the way and heaved myself up the pull-pole for I didn't want her to see me. I could still hear her. Slide, pause. Slide, pause. Then she came into the full light of the kitchen and squinted.

I was glad to see a pinkness was mounting into her face. Her hair, black as the wing of a raven, stood out round her head in ringlets, stiffened by the drying solution in which we had floated. I have seen pictures of the old enchantress Medusa and she never looked so fierce or fateful as my sleepwalking Ariadne.

Ariadne did not look up. With arms advanced she felt her way down the passage to the dispensary and washing rooms. I knew that I would not see her again for several hours.

Though I know Ariadne as well as I know my own hands, I am still startled by her beauty. I recognize the fine hand of the genetic engineer who planned us to be a pair. I know that full-humans find her attractive. I have seen men at the spaceport on the moon pause in their stride when they see her. I have intercepted many a would-be lover at the moment of his advance. I have noticed that women also want to get close to her. It is as though beauty were a magnet that draws full-humans after it. Perhaps a technician who stared at her own wrinkled face or falling hair tried to design in Ariadne an ageless, beguiling face. What did they design for me?

She is tall, for a woman, and her shoulders are broad; a necessary adaptation to her job. She is built to carry me, should that ever be necessary. The eyes that stare into you are a startling green and her hair is a mass of curls, which tumble

14

down over her shoulders. When she wakes in the morning, she brushes her hair while she sits naked in the bed beside me, and her hair falls into patterns. Sometimes, playfully she brushes my stark fur. She is supple too, in ways that I am not. She can sit cross-legged and with her back straight for hours. She can press her head between her knees. She can cross her legs behind her neck. When she does this she achieves a deformity which I find unpleasant but which makes her laugh. Imagine that, a beautiful woman naked and with her legs crossed behind her head, supporting herself on her hands and laughing. Am I not right when I say that Ariadne is beguiling?

She is also fearless. She is a woman to have at your side when trouble shows its face. More than once her speed of reaction has saved me when we have landed on some rogue world. And she has fought by my side in drinking places when we have been set upon by gangs of full-humans. There is no other woman I would have close to me whether in bed or battle. But what she thinks of me I hardly know. We have never discussed ourselves. What I am doing now, writing down my random thoughts, is the closest either of us has ever come to introspection. She accepts me. I am what is. I am the way things are meant to be. In all the ways that matter, she is totally faithful to me.

I observe that our brains differ in interesting ways. All part of the plan I suppose. Ariadne is more logical than I and can weigh up a situation in moments where I become stranded in contradiction. The price that she pays for her logic is that she is predictable. I am the one that improvises. I am the one that does the unexpected.

Today seems to be a day for questions. Here are some more. Given that Ariadne has beauty, brains and near-immortality, why is she not more happy? Given that I have a beautiful woman at my side, excitement in my work and abundant energy, why am I not contented? Perhaps the questions have different answers. Perhaps they have the same answer.

When I get the chance I must ask Ariadne if she dreams. I have never asked her that. I have never been curious until now.

I have moved out of the kitchen and up to the control deck of our ship. I want to be alone for a bit longer. Before I left I heard the shower start and that is a sure sign that Ariadne is waking up quickly . . . making up for lost time.

Here on the control deck I am surrounded by buzz and hum. I can hear the machines talking to one another, but what they are saying I do not know. Everything seems to be well. And if it were not . . .? Well, I doubt there is much I could do. The ship is its own world. Given luck it could rattle on to eternity. I sit in my swivel chair with its magnetic harness and tilt back until I can see the main view-screen which shows our destination. High and to the left of the screen is a dull red sun. I presume that our trajectory will intersect that sun and that the planet named La Plage is somewhere out there in the darkness. The name means nothing, unfortunately. The names were chosen at random. When Pioneer Murray was hurled into space, some eighteen generations ago, it was already decided that whatever world he happened upon, its name would be La Plage.

We are slowing quickly. Two g's, I am told by one of the machines. We will be strong when we make landfall. But we have several weeks yet.

Apparently we encountered interstellar grit shortly after dropping into this space and received some damage. That has now been repaired but there is a polite request for me to do some more permanent repairs in the third sector hangar. A servopipe has been sheared and this has affected the hoist capacity of the crane. Well. Well. Every journey there is something, some small maintenance problem. I think such problems are built into the circuitry to give us something to do during the long days when we are fully awake and mobile and waiting for landfall.

The air in here smells awful. It is cycled up from below without passing through the normal filters. An economy, I

16

presume. You see, when we are asleep, only the cabins, kitchen and long-sleep areas are supplied with air. The rest of the ship pumps to vacuum. The machines that run the ship prefer it that way. Air is corrosive.

I do not like the control cabin. I do not feel at ease here. The electronic jabber makes my teeth tickle after I have been here for a while. But I recognize that the style of genius that made these wise-idiot machines that protect us without cause or conscience, also created me and Ariadne.

Are we more machine than man?

That is a hideous question. It has the face of death. For if we are more machine than man, why give us life? Why give us consciousness?

What manner of creator would it be who gave us consciousness only so that we could be aware of our own futility?

I retreat from these thoughts and wonder what is happening to me. I long for Ariadne's strong arms. I long to be *there*, nuzzling deep, strong in fang and fur, oblivious of the stars and their courses; just me, simple, a not-quite-but-almost human, alive. That is the main thing, ALIVE.

2

I have not told Ariadne what I am about.

I hid in the large cupboard which houses our silver survival suits, and held the door just a fraction ajar. I watched her when she came back from the shower and was glad to see that she was walking far more easily. She still held the guide rails but that was for balance only. Into her hair she had twisted one of the long-spined fan shells which we gathered when we were on High Jinks. I was pleased to see that she was already taking care with her appearance. That again is a good sign of a healthy awakening.

She paused in the kitchen and looked at the open container of juice I had left on the table. I could see her logical brain fighting to comprehend what she saw. The can should not have been there. It certainly was not there when we entered the long sleep. How had it got there? Had she opened it while dozing? Has Angelo already . . .

She turned, partly bracing herself on her arms, and set off to our long-sleep chamber.

When she had gone I crept out of the cupboard and sat down at the table as though nothing had happened. I took the can of juice in my hand. I heard her mutter something when she found my sleeping tank completely unfolded and then I heard her begin to come back.

She paused at the entrance and stared at me blankly and then her face broke into a smile which seemed to make the cabin brighter. "Angelo, you rogue. You beat me this time. Am I very late?"

"No. Three days." I hope my smile warmed her. I stood up and crossed to her, put my arm round her and lifted her and carried her to the central table where I sat her in her chair.

"Can I get you anything?"

She shook her head and the curls began to work loose from

the prongs of the fan shell. I selected another can of juice for myself and settled down at the table opposite her.

"Three days."

I nodded.

"Have you enjoyed your peace? I always like the quiet time. What have you been doing?"

"Nothing."

"Ah."

I watched her drift away into a doze. Her pupils contracted and she stared through me, through the ship, through space and time into the world of dreams and memories.

She slept for seven hours, her arms resting along the table, and awoke with a great yawn. She stretched with her arms stiff above her head and her breasts lifted and the nipples rose. Her eyes were clear and sharp and she stood with amazing speed and flexed her fingers. She was coming awake quicker than I and had almost caught me up.

"I think I'll try a juice. Get the bladder working. Then some real exercise. Have you eaten yet?"

I passed her a can of juice. "Not yet."

"Three days and not yet eaten! You are as lazy as a whale. You woke up too soon. Have you checked your auto-nurse? Remember to check before we set off back. I'll check it for you." She finished her juice with a slurping sound and then tossed the plastic container into the disposal unit which chewed it and then spat the fragments out into space. "Come on, sleepy-head. Let's swim. That'll bring you round."

"I've been thinking."

"Ah. Well, a swim will do you the world of good. Come on."

Our ship has a small centrifugal swimming pool. True. I know these things are considered a great luxury but to us they are part of our necessary equipment. Swimming is one of the gentlest and surest ways of coming awake after the long sleep. It is massage and the water is like a womb . . . or so I am told. Sometimes we sleep in the water, lolling like dead frogs, with our arms spread. Ariadne is especially beautiful to me then. The salts in the water

19

bring a glow to her skin and the slap of the waves make her electric against me. Sometimes she holds my tawny arm, nuzzling and biting by turns. It is all part of waking up.

We swam, throwing a ball back and forth between us and diving down to retrieve weights from the bottom. I slapped the water with my arms and made a tent of spray over Ariadne and she dived at me, butting with her arms and sinking me like a torpedoed leviathan.

After about half an hour she needed to doze again and I was not surprised. I thought she had come awake too quickly. I left her there, draped in a net, with her dark hair waving round her head.

When she awoke she was sad. That again is normal. After every long sleep there is a period of depression while our emotions sort themselves out. A technician on Earth once explained it to me thus. When we begin a long sleep we enter an ideal world where everything is directed to contentment and satisfaction. Our bodies and minds are purified in sleep. When we awake after a long sleep we re-enter the impure world and that is a shock. Colours are less vivid. Actions are less meaningful. Thoughts are more muddled. And all of this leads to depression. Then the mind sorts itself out, decides to accept the nearest and most pressing reality, and we adjust. We make the best of what we have. For myself, I am glad that I cannot remember most of my dreams. I think they would make life intolerable. The only dream I can remember is the waking dream on the mountain . . . and that is different. That is trying to explain something.

Ariadne came to me directly from the pool. She was still wet as she lay down beside me in our cabin. Following an instinct that I suspect is as old as life itself, warmth found warmth, rhythm matched rhythm and we slipped into an easy lovemaking which rolled depression into a ball and tossed it into a corner like old clothes.

And when we awoke we felt happier.

*

20

We have spent our first full day together sitting in one of the view-bubbles which is the next best thing to sitting in space itself. We are surrounded by blazing stars except where the dark bulk of our ship blocks them out. The ship glimmers along its lines and planes where it reflects the starshine.

We have sat without talking, touching intimately, for space is a frightening and menacing companion when viewed in its vastness. And we are so small.

Ariadne has caught up with me as regards waking up and we are both eating. (I am already suffering bowel cramps.)

In our silence as we face the stars we doze lightly and the real world and the world of our minds flow together into a new amalgam. We see memories of our earlier life . . . especially painful ones . . . for those are the ones that need to be faced if we are to cope with the great darkness of our waking.

Soon our work will begin in earnest. Soon, too soon, the laze of our awakening will end and we will become what we are meant to be, an effective double unit, able to kill, able to cope with horrors, amoral as a knife.

Our destination lies before us already looming large. The ship's sensors are out, grappling to find La Plage. Somewhere out there is the planet: big, small, gassy or hard. We do not know. And on that planet resides a speck of life, a Pioneer, sent out generations earlier, and we will bring it back, no matter how.

3

We are two weeks out from the long sleep now, and fully awake. I have read through my early pages and in the light of full reason find them amusing. When I began to write down my thoughts I hoped that I would be able to write something every day. But that has not been possible. Some days I have had no thoughts. Some days I have had thoughts but no words, or the words have cancelled one another out. I have told Ariadne what I am doing but have not asked her to read my pages. I must add that she has not asked to read them either. When I told her she laughed. She says that she has never seen a homunculus write before . . . and that is probably true. But I am learned, and the writing gives me pleasure, and so far has done me no harm that I can see. I suspect though that my two and two will not always add up to Ariadne's four.

Sometime I will talk to her about the full-humans. I would like to know what she thinks. But for the moment we are approaching action stations. La Plage is before us.

It turns beneath us like a pearl. It is a ball of ice. I wonder what Pioneer Murray thought as he gazed down at it eighteen generations ago.

I imagine his heart sank . . . though he was programmed to take delight in adversity. Perhaps as his ship lowered he thought about the greatness of Earth for which he was a standard-bearer. I prefer that thought. I do not like the idea of a man landing in despondency so far from home.

We do not know what we will find though we know that he is still alive. His beacon which circles this world every two hours is putting out a strong life signal . . . and that signal, many light years hence, will find its way to Earth. But eighteen generations is a long time. Given his ability for rapid evolution he could by now have turned into anything. We might even find a sentient ice cube. I am being humorous.

Each hour we drop lower. The white face of La Plage fills all our view-screens. We can see the white and grey hills and the ice-braced mountains. We stare at the rough-backed glaciers that worm their way across the marginal plateau. The landscape marches slowly past us as though on a conveyor belt.

La Plage. I have looked up the meaning of the name in the catalogue: it means The Beach. The full-humans who sent Pioneer Murray on his way and chose the name for his planet would see an irony. The name summons up ideas of warmth and ease and children playing and the murmur of the sea.

La Plage. I look down at the black seas and the giant icebergs miles high and the storms which crawl like lizards, and I wonder.

We are over the equator of this frozen world and we will surely find our Pioneer here.

We wait, Ariadne and I. Our ship has all its antennae spread. We are a great eye looking into the world. We are waiting for a call bell. Below is an island. I try to think as the Pioneer did, seeking that first landing, looking for the place which would give the maximum chance of survival. An island is always a good haven except on a world with three moons. And even as I write this the bell sounds, the print-out machines begin to chatter, data flows in patterns and systems become alive throughout the whole ship.

We have found him. We have found a pocket of warmth, a pin-point of life which makes the temperature graphs soar.

We can see only a grim stony island with valleys of frost. But our ship can see life.

This is all until later. Now I set my book aside. Ariadne is calling.

4

We have saved him.

Pioneer Murray is below now in deep sleep. I am pleased to say that he looks human. He twitches like a monkey as his body relaxes. Soon he will be ready for the long haul and Ariadne and I will enter the Pioneer sleep chamber with him, and prepare him for the journey back to Earth.

I want to write about this rescue.

A storm blew up as we lowered and we burned up fuel just to remain in one place above the stony island. Clouds built up round us and we saw our ship cope with massive discharges of electricity.

Granules of snow, as dry and abrasive as sand, were hurled into our cone of light and rasped over the ship. The snow was like pouring white smoke. We saw it build round our windows and then slide and boil and evaporate as our ship transformed a fraction of its inertia into heat.

High stone cliffs grew above us as we lowered into a valley. Neither Ariadne nor I have much experience of cold worlds and we stared out of the view-ports at the plumes of snow which lifted and were whipped away by the wind as we touched the ice of the valley floor. We began a controlled slide, riding the slush down the narrow valley, towards a brilliant point of green. We came to a halt facing a low dome. There we sank into the ice until all that remained above the surface was our view-port.

The ship informed us that its automatic systems had brought us as close as they could and that now it was up to us. All about us the slush began to congeal. The temperature outside was twenty degrees centigrade below zero.

I was fascinated by the dome. It looked so brittle and its green light sent eerie shadows on to the plane of ice. I have never seen one of the domes in full operation before. The other Pioneers that Ariadne and I have rescued have all moved beyond their domes within one generation of landing. But on this world that was out of the question. It was not merely a matter of temperature. Pioneers could adapt to the cold, but the atmosphere was a mixture of hydrogen and nitrogen with very little free oxygen. Adaptation to this planet would have required a more radical change than most Pioneers can achieve.

If you want a symbol to express the proud optimism of Earth that sent the Pioneers out, you could do worse than choose the All Environment Survival Dome. Survival domes are master-pieces of the same genetic engineering that produced the Pioneers and myself and Ariadne and all the other rescue teams. Each dome is made of laminates of plastic sheet, but within the laminates are incorporated living membranes. These membranes are programmed with one simple instruction: to maintain an even temperature on one of their surfaces. Thus they whiten in brilliant sunshine, fluoresce in the dark, become super-dense insulators when cold winds blow and breathe when all temperatures are in balance. As a true living organism, they feed on whatever energy they find about them, be it the light of a sun or the impact of hail stones. Alas, like so much else which belongs to the olden times, the secret of how to construct survival domes was lost at the time of the Catastrophe.

"We'll edge in closer," said Ariadne and activated the cupped fins which extended along the whole undercarriage of our ship. Slowly the fins pushed forwards into the packed snow. Then they opened, dug deep, and pulled, dragging us like a grounded whale towards the dome.

We approached as close as we dared. The last thing we wanted was to puncture the skin of the dome. When we were about forty yards from it Ariadne anchored the ship. We towered over the fragile dome like a great black crab ready to devour a tasty morsel. Sensors aboard our ship had finally located the remains of the Pioneer's own ship. It was buried several hundred metres beneath us, crushed to half its original size. Luck was on our side in that we could see rising not far from us the crossed stanchions of the dome's airlock.

As we looked at them we both saw something move against the stiff skin of the dome. It was impossible to see clearly. It could have been a man, but my impression was that what we saw was an animal which reared up against the wall and swung its blunt head back and forth. I have seen a bear move thus. Then it dropped to the ground and was lost to us.

"Do you think that could have been him?" I asked.

But Ariadne only shrugged. She has never been one for speculation. For myself . . . well, the adaptability of the Pioneers has never failed to amaze me. Though I thought it was an animal, I could be wrong. I remembered our first rescue mission. There the Pioneer had grown a thick scaly skin, almost a carapace, to protect him from the incessant sandstorms which swept his selected planet. He crawled on all fours and made a tolerable living, and was jovial when found. He accepted with equanimity his return to Earth but died within days of arrival. Not all rescues are so easy. Ariadne and I have been lucky so far, but other Pioneer Rescuers have brought back tales of embodiments of ferocity. We never know. There is no way of knowing what we will find when we make planetfall.

"Why bother with guesswork," said Ariadne, the practical. "Let us break out the Worm and go and see."

The Worm. The Worm would interest you if you have never seen one of our rescue ships. It is one of the few adaptations that have been made to our ships since the days of the Pioneers. I do not know what the technicians call it, but the Worm is the name we give to the mobile and supple extension to the nose of our ship. At its tip are drill bits and behind them airlock connection clips. Fully extended the Worm can reach several hundred yards. It can bore and burrow in any direction and provides us with safe passage to any dome or cave or under-water lair.

We set the Worm in motion and watched it chew its way right up to the airlock. Then Ariadne and I donned our silver contact suits and ran through the catechism of safety. Checking power, checking medicine, checking weapons, checking radio. . . . By the time we had finished, the Worm had located the dome's airlock and made its connections and was ready for use.

Entrance to the Worm leads directly from the main control room via a space-resistant airlock. In the unlikely event that the Worm was torn from its roots in our ship, the ship could still take off, leaving the Worm behind it.

We passed through the circular doorway and the powerful space doors hissed shut behind us. Ariadne led the way down the Worm's segmented corridor.

We were not surprised to discover that the dome's airlock mechanism was frozen solid on our side and rusted inside the dome. While domes can remain efficient indefinitely, mechanisms are mechanisms and this one gave every appearance of never having been used. Its lubricants had turned to black dust.

We crouched down beside the dome's airlock and studied it. The pearly green light which shone through the plates made our silver suits glow and our hands were the colour of leaves. We prepared for our first difficult manoeuvre. With our visors down and breathing units sealed I bored a tiny hole through the airlock door and inserted an atmospheric probe. Once inside the dome the probe opened like a flower. It read everything: humidity, atmosphere composition, toxicity, radio-activity, temperature . . . and much to our surprise informed us that the atmosphere inside the dome was completely benign.

This is not usually the case. I remember Bonniface and Amsterdame once telling about the dome they entered on Symphony. They were attempting to rescue Pioneer Lusang. Symphony was a methane world and the Pioneer had established his dome like a blister on the side of a hill. Within the closed dome, constant mutation had created a toxic environment. The Pioneer had evolved with his world and was completely at home but the atmosphere would have choked Amsterdame and Bonniface within seconds. They did not bother to try and bring him back to Earth. They would have

27

had to bring his entire dome as well as tons of the spongy rock he now fed on. They resealed the dome and left him to live out his life.

That was not our situation. We had nothing to do but enter.

Ariadne gave me the word and I began to cut through the airlock walls, forcing back the stiff living plastic and opening an oval which finally blew in on us with a gentle whoosh.

The pressure stabilized almost immediately and we released our helmets and felt the warm moist air on our faces and smelt the soil and the rich aroma of ferns. It was the smell of Earth, beautiful and fertile, and so different from the antiseptic air of our ship.

"Is this what the Earth once smelled like all over?" I asked, and Ariadne flashed one of her rare smiles . . . rare that is when we are on business.

We stepped through and down. Ariadne first, me covering, staring at the motionless green jungle, ready for any movement. But nothing moved. The world inside the dome was still and silent. No whisper of the driving snow which poured over the outside of the dome reached its interior. Of the creature that we had seen rear against the wall there was no sign.

The earth was soft and fibrous and we made no sound as we landed. We did not have to step far and I estimated that some two or three feet of soil separated us from the true base of the dome.

In the silence we studied the trees and bushes which pressed us back against the walls of the dome. I saw the leaves of the ash and elm, and the tight pink flowers and dark green leaves of manuka. There was something which might have been a rhododendron with its tight fist of flowers just about to unfurl. Beneath the trees the shadows were black. I noticed that all the plants seemed to have undergone a tropical transformation. The leaves were generally larger and more spade-shaped as though ready to cup the rain. The elm had gained prickles. Rising from the grass were mushrooms and blue crocus flowers which looked set to catch insects.

Both Ariadne and I stood very still. The stable environment of a dome can react with ferocity when disturbed. We were both aware that more than one rescue team had been lost when it stumbled against vegetable sentience. We did not wish to add our names to that list.

Nothing moved except one of the blue flowers which nodded as water dripped from a stooping branch into its flared cup.

"Off you go," said Ariadne. "Walk with care. I have you covered, but keep talking. Describe everything as you go."

This was standard procedure. Many a life has been saved by knowing what fate befell a partner, and we were well trained.

Ariadne squatted down with her back against the torn airlock and watched me as I began to wade into the vegetation. The ground sloped down slightly away from the dome and after a few paces the grass and flowers were well above my knees. There were vines snaking through the undergrowth which caught at my boots. I also felt the rasp of thorns along my silver suit. I was in no danger (our suits are designed to withstand the pincers of crabs and the teeth of snakes) except to my face. I stopped and lowered my visor. Close to me was one of the blue flowers and I experimented by stroking its exposed stamens. The stamens exuded a gummy substance and writhed about my finger and tried to draw it within the blue trumpet. Then the trumpet closed. I pulled my finger free but so great was the adhesion that I tore the head off the flower. I had to wipe it free on my suit.

"Get a move on," said Ariadne. "Our orders are to disrupt the biosphere of a Pioneer as little as possible, not mutilate it."

I moved on and ducked under the first low branches of the prickly elm. The sweet smell of gum was very close and for the first time I heard the buzz of insects. Hanging from one of the branches was a white shape like the skin of a sheep. It was a nest and round it teemed thousands of bright red and yellow wasps. I warned Ariadne and advised her to put her visor up. The sweet smell came from the nest. I gave it a wide berth.

Further under the trees (I was out of sight of Ariadne by now) I came to a trellis of wattle. There seemed no way round it and so I broke through and the sound was like thunder in my ears. If the Pioneer were hereabouts he would surely know that something was coming.

Beyond the trellis was a clearing of bright yellow-green grass. I kept well under the shadows of the trees and called up Ariadne. "I think you'd better join me. I've come to one of his fields. Hey, the grass here is closely cropped. No animals in sight. As far as I can see the field is circular and it looks like an orchard begins on the other side. A bit straggly."

"Keep under cover. I'm coming up."

I waited in the undergrowth and never took my eyes off the clearing.

Pioneer domes are deceptive. They are not large. At most they cover only forty or fifty acres, but when you are in one, especially if it is filled with vegetation, the dimensions feel immense. You can easily get lost. Another strange property of the dome is their light. The outside world can hardly be seen. To look out through a dome is like looking through frosted glass and the woven plastic fibre sheets glow palely. From my position under the trees, the sky looked an infinity away and was a uniform pearly white.

Ariadne arrived quietly, gliding through the shadows. I have always admired her stealth. We settled silently and watched.

Across the clearing ferns moved and a low shrub twitched. Ariadne gripped my arm and pointed. We saw the bushes move again and then a blunt triangular head with curling horns poked out into the clearing. It sniffed the air and snickered. Perhaps some odour of us had reached it. Then the whole animal advanced.

It was not the Pioneer. I could not tell what it was. The head was that of a sheep or goat, but there the similarity ended. The rest of the body was that of a pig except that it was covered with ginger-brown fur. The head was low slung, like a rhinoceros and the whole creature moved with the springy assurance of great physical strength. I imagined that if such a creature charged and was impaled on a spear, it would, like a wild boar, continue running until the spear tore through its back, and it

30

jammed on the crosspiece. I have seen such beasts in Aotearoa and the way the people of that land catch them.

The animal ambled fully into the clearing. If it was aware of us it certainly was not perturbed by our presence. It began peacefully to crop the grass with a sideways tearing motion of its giant head.

"Natural mutation would not produce that," murmured Ariadne. "He's been trying his hand at genetic engineering. Cover me. I'm going for a closer look."

She stood up and walked slowly into the clearing.

I settled the creature into the cross-hairs of my gun and stepped the power of its charge higher. If the creature offered so much as a threatening gambol I would lift that head from its shoulders.

Ariadne advanced, her arms at her sides, and when she came close the beast lowered its head and forelegs to the ground like a dog that is waiting for a stick to be thrown. She went right up to it and its back was about on a level with her shoulders. She began to stroke it, digging her fingers into its rough fur and dragging them talon-like. I heard the beast snicker with pleasure. Then it rolled over on the ground away from Ariadne and squirmed and worked its legs in the air.

Ariadne has a way with animals, I have often noticed it. I believe she could sit in a cage of snakes and charm them and emerge without so much as a nip.

Her voice whispered in my head. "Come on. It's harmless but don't move too quickly. Let's get a move on and find him. I'm starting to get a bad feeling about this place. Strange things have happened here."

When I approached, the creature rolled over smartly and stood up. It growled and a black tongue darted from its lips. I bent down and tore some grass and offered it to it. The creature ambled close and sniffed the grass with its large moist nostrils. Then it spoke. "Graaaas," it said. The word was distinct. "Graaaas." And then it turned away and went back to its feeding as though we no longer existed.

Rarely have I seen Ariadne stumped for words, but her eyebrows were two question marks and her mouth an O. She tells me that I looked surprised too.

Our delay with the beast had made us vulnerable and we hurried to the end of the clearing and into the orchard. This was in its own way as strange as the animal we had just met. Here were fruit trees that carried fruit and blossom at the same time. There were plums as big as apples and apples as big as pumpkins. They rested on the ground in the shade, huge and red. A black vine twisted from the ground and bore blue and green grapes. I picked a peach and it had a rind as hard as a walnut.

"More tampering," observed Ariadne.

We met other animals under the fruit trees. One resembled a cat but was only as large as a mouse. It had made its home in one of the rotton apples. There was an old horse that was blind and which sported a single horn. I am familiar with the stories of the unicorn and it seemed to me that this was what the Pioneer had tried to create. I rubbed my hand along its back and it shivered and I think tried to speak though all it accomplished was a grunting. We saw a scaly creature which clung to the bark of the trees and scampered high into the branches when we tried to touch it. There were more insects in the orchard too. One I remember particularly was a butterfly. It was a giant with brilliant red and green markings on its wings. It flapped into the air when we approached and we saw that it had been feeding on the carcase of some small red-blooded creature.

Strange but I felt a harmony in this world, in this closed dome world. A dome always reflects the mentality of a Pioneer from the way he orders his vegetable garden to the way he sets out his stock. Everything is a message revealing the psyche. What we had seen so far seemed to me to represent balance and harmony.

Ariadne urged us on though I would have been content to move slowly under the fruit trees enjoying the warmth and

32

fecundity. I was interested to observe that Ariadne was not comfortable here. I have seen her cope with massive deformity as on some of our other rescues. But here the minor illogicality of the species seemed to unsettle her.

If I had been a Pioneer I would have been happy to create a dome like this. I wonder what kind of a dome Ariadne would make. I must remember to ask her that question sometime.

Leading from the orchard we found a well-trodden path. From the dung which stood in mounds we judged this track to be the spoor of the beast we had seen in the field. It led round a stand of rubber trees and up a low hill. We were now at the centre of the dome.

I stayed in the stand of trees while Ariadne scouted ahead. She crawled up the hill and peered over its top. Then she waved for me to come up and join her. We looked down on to the standard configuration of Pioneer hut, yard and outbuildings. It was all laid out completely in accordance with the Pioneer's manual, and all looked very familiar. The hut and farm buildings were prefabricated units and could be erected by one man in a day. They had the friendly look of wood but were in reality sheets of ferro-plastic and every joint was chemically sealed. The roofs were sloped and gabled and the windows were set high. The main hut was joined to two outbuildings to form an open square which was closed only by a small fence.

Evidence of the Pioneer was everywhere from the pink-flowered clematis which climbed up the walls to the well-tended vegetable garden. The main door to the Pioneer's hut stood open and hairy chickens were wandering in and out.

Ariadne drew my attention to the outbuilding opposite the main house. It had windows but all the shutters were closed. The back of the building had been adapted and we could see the dull silver coils of a refrigeration unit. On the roof was positioned a black umbrella-shaped unit which looked to me like an energy-conversion antenna.

"We'll look in there first. You go. I'll cover the house," said Ariadne and motioned me with her arm.

I dropped back down the hill and circled round until I found a low hedge which led right to the corner of the hut near where the refrigeration coils emerged. I worked my way along the hedge-line until I could stand up against the wall. I tried the window nearest me but it was closed inside.

"Any movement?"

"No."

"Right. I'm going in through the door." I set my gun to burn and sidled round into the small courtyard. I straddled the fence and hoped that the chickens would not set up a hullabaloo. They paid me no attention at all. Within seconds I was at the door. I listened but there was no sound except the quiet hum of the refrigeration plant. I tried the handle but the door was locked and so I burned it, melting the ferro-plastic. And when I pushed, the door swung open easily.

Inside the hut it was dark; there was no Pioneer. The room was a laboratory. In one corner was a hatchery with eggs laid out neatly. Some chicks had just hatched and were flopping about drunkenly. A shallow refrigerator occupied one whole wall. Inside were jars, each neatly labelled. It was a sperm bank. Covering the third wall and jutting out into the room was a tank which glowed a deep cherry red. There was movement inside the tank. I crossed and looked down into it and found myself staring at a foetus. I think it was a horse, but it had hands and while I looked it kicked and groped with its thumb up to its mouth.

"Anything?" Ariadne's voice sounded close and loud in my ears.

"No Pioneer. This is his workshop. This is where he has been experimenting."

"Good. Cover me. I'm coming straight down the hill and into his house. There's been no movement. I don't think he's home. Unless he's sleeping. And if he is we're in luck. Let me know when you are in position."

I opened the window that faced on to the courtyard. I had a clear view of the Pioneer's hut. "Ready."

I glanced up the hill and saw Ariadne break cover and come down the hill and over the fence and straight to the Pioneer's door. She paused and then entered, her gun advanced. I listened for a shot.

Nothing and then Ariadne's voice whispering, "Nothing here. Come across."

Inside the hut the bed was neatly made and the pans and skillet were scrubbed. There was a fresh smell of wood oil. In the centre was a table. It was set for *two* people, complete with knives, forks, spoons and, an unexpected refinement this, woven place mats.

Ariadne smiled when she saw this. "He's got an imaginary mate," she said.

We were standing looking at the table when we heard the chanting. It came from outside, beyond the hut, in the part we had not explored.

"One and one is two. Two and two is four. Four and four is . . ." The voice that was speaking was guttural and harsh and the speaker was having obvious difficulty in shaping the words.

Silently Ariadne and I crossed to the window. We saw a short stretch of grass leading down to a pond and crouched beside the pond were two figures. One was the Pioneer, bald and stooped and brown as old leather. He was holding a stick and pointing at numbers scratched in the mud.

The other was . . . well, my first thought was that it was a horse. Its head was long with large glossy eyes. But then I saw its arms which were mostly human with long slim fingers. It was back on its furry haunches and its hind feet were cloven. This was the creature that was speaking. It was simply an older version of the creature I had seen in the laboratory.

"Sixteen and sixteen is – "

It must have heard us, or else it sensed us, for it stopped and turned its unblinking gaze upon us. The Pioneer stood up and shouted something, but I did not hear. Ariadne and I fired together. I felled the beast. It toppled like a statue and then slumped. Ariadne, no doubt thinking about the job in hand, felled the Pioneer and he staggered and then collapsed backwards into the mud, still clutching his stick.

The search was over. We stood for a time staring down at the two creatures, both breathing deeply and snoring in their drugged sleep. Finally we lifted the Pioneer and placed him in a survival sack and zipped it close about him. He was very light. I knew I would have no difficulty carrying him back to our ship.

"What about this?" I said, nodding to the spread, inert form of the half-horse, half-man.

"It will recover," said Ariadne. "Leave it to the world it knows. It is not a child of Earth."

5

And now Pioneer Murray is stored. We have begun the slow step-down procedures which will prepare him for the long sleep. We allowed him to wake once, briefly, to make sure that his mind had cleared, and he stared at us, at first in disbelief, and then he smiled and called us his children. Then we sent him into an easy sleep. We will keep him steady while we make tests to see if he is harbouring any parasites or diseases. That will take a few days. Afterwards we will take him deeper, watching his reactions, until his consciousness is a tiny point of tranquil light.

Ariadne has been using her skill to create dreams for him. It is a big unknown for us and always a matter of chance for no two people are the same even if adapted. But we know he loved life and loved creating things and his dreams will centre on that. We will also give him dreams of floating. Such dreams give assurance of one's place in time. The psychologists on Earth maintain that floating and swimming bring calm to the most primitive parts of our brain.

We have brought some of his things. The quilt from his bed. The woven place mats. His knife and fork. His sandals.

When I had carried him back to the ship and settled him, we began a systematic survey of his dome. We have photographed everything and taken samples of all the flora.

His creature woke up while we were taking samples of the water. It started following us round, saying, "Where? Where? Where?" until finally I could stand it no longer and I put it to sleep.

We left all systems working smoothly except the laboratory. I killed the foetus by switching off its artificial womb and then I buried it. All the sperm samples we decided to bring back with us. The chicks I set free and then closed down the

37

incubator. We did not want to leave any machinery working which might break down and cause a fire. All other energy systems in the dome are passive and have no danger of a spark.

Then, when we had finished, we carefully closed the tear in the airlock and withdrew. With luck life will hold on there indefinitely. The dome will not break down unless earthquake or avalanche or meteor storm damage it. Perhaps intelligence will thrive. Perhaps a species, flora or fauna, will evolve that is able to survive on that harsh world.

Such speculation has no end.

When we had withdrawn the Worm, we backed our ship out slowly so as not to create subsidence. We began to crawl up the valley to a suitable launching place where we would not endanger the dome. The last I saw of the dome it was a gleaming green beacon which was quickly lost in the teeming snow. The storm was still raging and I have no doubt that all that now remains to show that we were once there is a depression in the snow above which howl the freezing winds.

We are now holding steady orbit above La Plage. I have just been to check Pioneer Murray and he is resting like a baby which, curiously, he resembles.

I have been studying his tattoos which are on the inside of each arm. They give all the data on Pioneer Murray. He belongs to an earlier era of experiment than either Ariadne or I. He was once a man, a full-human! There, isn't that dazzling. He was one of the first four or five Pioneers sent out.

So, I now know the name of his mother and father. She was Alma and he was Alexander. And were they proud of their son? And what led him to apply for special Pioneer training? Did he know what it meant? He was thirteen when he joined the Pioneer Programme, not even a man. Poor boy.

The Murray family were clear of all congenital defects such as epilepsy and varicose veins. Young Master Murray had not even had one of his teeth filled.

Indeed I can find nothing exceptional about him, except his health, and his strange first name. He was called Raoul. Raoul

Murray. The name sounds like the kind of noise I make when I am drunk.

He qualified among the top ten per cent of his year and that meant that he was destined for Pioneership rather than an administrative post. His intelligence was estimated at 130 with an inclination to abstract reasoning and a flair for engineering. Eyes, grey. Hair, sandy. Skin, white. Height, 1.890m. Personality, controlled extrovert.

He blasted into space just ten days after his twenty-first birthday.

That was over 600 years ago.

I have taken the plunge and shown the pages I have written to Ariadne. She read them in her steady studious fashion, sometimes returning to the top of a page to read again, while I sat by nervous and staring out of the view-port at the diminishing planet called La Plage. Two days ago we moved out of orbit and began the slow acceleration back to Earth. Within the next day or so we will begin getting ready for the long sleep. That is on both our minds. Though our ship is accelerating, from day to day you can really notice no difference.

When she had finished she stood the pages on end and plumped them straight and looked at me. Her eyes were merry. "Well, what a clever creature I have for a companion! Why did you begin this?"

I think I shrugged. I was not expecting this question, though it is a good question. "I think I started because I was not satisfied. I was worried by my waking up. There are things I want to sort out."

"You are worried by what you are?"

"Yes."

"Oh. You think too much. I have told you before. But why then have you not described yourself? You have described me and Pioneer Murray. Why not yourself? Are you ashamed? I think you are beautiful."

"I don't know. It never occurred to me. I mean, you don't think to describe yourself. You know yourself."

"Well, I think you should. Your readers would be interested. Tell them you have the mind of a lawyer housed in the body of an ape. That will interest them, whoever they are. Who are you writing this for anyway?"

"Myself."

"Mmm. I doubt that." She handed the pages back to me. "You have taken too much trouble. Where will your story end?"

"I don't know."

"I like stories that have an end, not just a purpose. You should think about that."

I thanked her.

I think I am disappointed by her reaction though I have no reason to be. I wonder what I hoped to gain from showing her these pages? Her approval? Perhaps. Though that is a strange thing. Why should I need approval for the truth? Questions. Questions. I will follow Ariadne's suggestion and describe myself and see where that leads.

I am called Angelo. That is the only name I have. I was made many years ago, though I cannot remember my making. My first memories are of myself as I am now. Ariadne has likened me to an ape. That is something of a joke between us, though it is a comparison that has been made before, insultingly, by full-humans. It is the kind of name that is called from a crowd and can be directed at myself or one of my true confrères such as Bonniface, Larum, Lindis, Kingi and Raven. Perhaps I will write more about them later.

I am like an ape . . . a gorilla . . . a ginger gorilla, though I have a human nose, brow, forehead and chin. Nevertheless I know I am frightening to look at.

My strength is in my shoulders and arms and in my low-slung pelvis. You would find it hard to knock me down even if you were taller than me, which is unlikely. My legs are like stumps of trees and widely spread so that I walk with a rolling gait. Most of my body is covered with fur. Why I am covered with fur I do not know. The fur serves no function that I can

40

see . . . unless it is to make me feel inferior. No, that is silly, but I will let the sentence stand. Like Ariadne, I was created to do one special job: to bring the Pioneers back. I have often wondered why Ariadne was created so beautiful and me so . . . strange. But there we are. In my work is my pride. Earth no longer sends out full-humans to do its work. Full-humans are too valuable since the Catastrophe and few of them have the stamina for deep space. But I am the last of my kind too. They no longer know how to make us. We are, in our confined way, unique.

Do you have the picture? Whoever *you* are? Well, there is one other thing you should know and which may make me real to you. My right arm is normal and I can hold a pen or work a computer or fire a gun. But my left arm is a claw with three closing talons. In all that matters I am completely ambidextrous, but my left arm is the most sensitive.

I am not ashamed of myself. I may have the body of an ape but I have the mind of a lawyer and something more besides.

Let me put it this way. If ever you were in a fight with me and Ariadne, you might be able to guess how Ariadne would react but I am the one you should watch. For I can improvise.

The days are slipping past and we have begun the slow preparations for our long sleep. Just now I am sitting at the view-port and I can no longer see La Plage. We are again in the hands of our computers and they have asked us to return their part of the ship to full vacuum. We have complied.

I stare out at the stars. An old poet once wrote that he felt heartened by the stars of home. For myself all stars seem equally alien whether viewed from Earth or from the depths of space. To put that more positively, I feel equally at home wherever I am in the galaxy, and I have visited some distant parts in the course of my work.

6

Delay. Delay. Delay.

Something has gone wrong with the navigation computers, and our acceleration has been stilled. We are drifting without spin and have no idea how long it will be before things come back to normal. By now we should have been well into our sleep preparations . . . but we have suspended the sleep programme.

Neither of us is worried. We have had such delays before. The computers are very thorough in a mindless way and when they uncover an error they begin a random check as well as a sequential check. When we get the all clear, we will know that the whole ship from saline monitors to airlocks has been scrutinized. Repairs can take a while. Once we were delayed two months. Two friends of ours, Amsterdame and Bonniface, were once delayed for over four years and you know, when they landed back on earth they looked older.

If worst comes to worst we can pilot our way home at our present speed. Of course, that will take over 1,000 years. Ariadne and I will not survive the trip in our present bodies but I believe Pioneer Murray would.

The computers have just advised us that we shall be here for some weeks. They want me to go outside and do some minor repairs. I shall enjoy that not only because I like drifting with just a back pack and magnetic boots, but also because in a naïve way my repairs will be a triumph of the biological over the mechanical. I know that this is wrong in essence for the computers have only rudimentary self-consciousness and certainly do not have the wit to be competitive. But their communications can seem brutally patronizing; they are members of an elite club who chat only in numbers and abstractions.

However, one consequence of this delay is that we shall have to wake up Pioneer Raoul Murray. Our life-support systems are geared to constant acceleration or deceleration (which amount to the same thing anyway) and do not function effectively during long periods of free fall. This will be a tricky business and will require all our tact. The Pioneer will experience the classic Frog and Prince paradox; he will not know whether he is the dreamer or the dreamed. Ariadne is about it now, slowly lifting him to consciousness.

We have him out of his bath and tucked in a comfortable berth. We know he can hear and we are playing him music from the time when he was alive on Earth. Now nature can take its course. There is nothing wrong with him physically and his body will decide when to wake him up fully.

He is watched over every minute by one of the auto-nurses who monitor us when we are in the long sleep. We will be warned when he stirs.

7

I have let a week go by . . . I do not know, even now what to write . . . what I should say. I am more confused that ever. That at least is a fact.

Pioneer Murray is awake and with us. That is another fact.

I want to write. Everything is there. Anger and laughter are rolled up together.

Damn and blast Pioneer Murray. I want to kill him. I want to take his bald little head between hand and claw and crush it and see if he smiles then.

But I know I won't.

No. I'll don my spacesuit and take a walk and find some other bit of our spaceship's plumbing that I can break so that I can repair it. Silly eh? Silly ape.

He calls me chimp . . .

But that's not all.

Where were we? We were in free fall.

I will tell you about free fall.

Free fall is a wondrous state with many levels. First there is the silly level where you walk on the ceiling and blow bubbles of water and enjoy the intimacy of a vacuum lavatory. Then there is the level of skill where you aim yourself at a doorway and bullet through without touching the sides or throw a pencil straight to your partner's hand. Beyond that there are 101 joys . . . but the greatest joy of all is in making love. It would take me a book to describe it . . . and even then I couldn't.

There is something about free fall that stimulates the sexual appetites. Why, I do not know. Perhaps the psychiatrists can fathom it. But take my word for it, it is true.

You dream of floating. Your skin becomes electric. You want to punch and scratch and bite and sprawl . . . at least I do

44

and so does Ariadne. . . . You want to be sucked out of your everyday gravity self and fired up to the stars. And the wonderful thing is that you have this magnificent strength. There is nothing you cannot do. No position is impossible. There is no top or bottom, just a round of coiling delight.

Well, Ariadne and I were in free fall, waiting for Pioneer Murray to wake up. We were at our table, anchored for once, and Ariadne was cleaning my claw. She likes doing that and I like the homeliness as she washes the dirt from under my talons and polishes the smooth, creamy ivory. She holds my arm on her lap, firm between her legs and I lay back staring up at her beautiful curly hair which billows round her head. She likes me to flex the claw, sliding the talons into and out of their sheath the way a bear does. Sometimes she likes me to nip her gently while she holds the giant claw with both hands. Oh, we have an easy understanding at such times . . . an easy intimacy and nothing can go wrong where there is trust.

There is nothing cruel in our lovemaking though to hear us go at it you might think we were committing murder. Anyway, Ariadne breathed on my claw and kissed it and drew my arm up to her neck. Within seconds we were floating, drifting together, bumping into the conduits that run along the ceiling and then pushing off and gliding over the floor.

She was magnificent in her passion and drove her fingers into my fur and held to me tightly with her lips and legs.

We came together crushed against one of the high food lockers and at the end we drifted apart like fish . . . and only then did I become aware of the alarm bell. I do not know how long it had been ringing, but I rolled over in space and found myself staring at Pioneer Murray who was standing in the doorway. He looked ridiculous: thin, brown and bald and standing naked except for a pair of my magnetic boots which came up above his knees. Standing out from his thighs was an erection which would not have disgraced that old god Priapus. He was staring at Ariadne.

It was a stare of disbelief. Once I saw a man whose hand was

45

severed by a propeller before his eyes. He stared at the stump in the same way.

Ariadne became aware of him and with a yelp pushed herself across the room to where her wrap was floating and with a swirl clothed herself.

The Pioneer watched her and then disconcertingly yawned the kind of yawn which stretches the whole body. He seemed to slump in the air and his feet slipped out of my boots and left the ground but his erection remained like something that was trying to escape him. Ariadne and I angled down and took him by the arms and guided him, floating on his back, back to his bed. He was already asleep when we tucked him in and set magnetic clasps about him. Then we switched off the auto-nurse which had never ceased its clamour.

Back in the kitchen Ariadne looked at me, full-faced and brazen. "Do you think he saw us?"

"Certainly he saw us. I've no idea how long he was there."

"Well it probably did him good." She grinned.

"Judging by his state, I think it did him no harm at all," said I, having no inkling of what was to come. "He may well have been a virgin when he blasted off from Earth . . . may never have seen a naked women."

"Poor man. Do you think he was trying to make a woman when he made that horse thing?"

"Possibly."

"Why did they send them out alone? That seems needlessly cruel."

"I don't know."

"After self preservation, sex is our strongest drive," she said, quoting a manual we both know. "Poor man. He looked so helpless . . ."

"Yes."

". . . driven by an instinct he does not understand."

"Yes."

Ariadne never fails to amaze me. Her face was flushed and her eyes were bright. She was responding to the idea in her own words and we spent the next few hours cozy and close in

46

the privacy of our own quarters. As I said, free fall stimulates the appetite.

After the sleep period we visited Pioneer Murray in his bed and found him wide awake and sitting with his knees drawn up to his chest. He had aready been fed by the auto-nurse. He seemed in complete command of his faculties.

"Who are you?" he asked, directing his question towards Ariadne.

"We came to rescue you and bring you back to Earth. We are from Earth."

"Ah." He relaxed and thought for a few moments. "I thought perhaps I was dreaming when I saw you last night. I have had so many dreams." He lay silent for many minutes and then he sneaked a glance at me and then spoke again to Ariadne. "Who is the ape?"

"He is called Angelo and he helped to save you."

"Angelo!" I saw the face of Pioneer Murray break into a wrinkled grin and then he laughed outright. "Angelo. Do the monkeys give themselves airs now?"

Ariadne saw me become restless when he said this and she quietened me with a gesture. "Angelo is a man, just as you are."

The Pioneer turned his eyes on me and I found myself disquieted by the hardness of his gaze. "Two and two makes . . .?" he asked.

"Four." I answered involuntarily and then wanted to bite the words back.

"Four and four makes . . .?"

I stood up and left the revival room. I fear I would have reached out and squeezed his scrawny throat if I had stayed.

Ariadne found me a few minutes later in the kitchen sucking on a juice can. "He's just a boy," she said. "A silly boy who does not know what he is talking about. He needs to grow up. Have pity on him. Leave him to me. Go and do your mending outside."

I left her to it. I wished her well in her dealings with this 600-year-old baby and donned my spacesuit.

Once outside the ship I felt better. The stars are clean and space is an implacable foe pitted against all life. It asks no quarter and gives none. One slip and you are dead with your blood boiling. I stumped round the outside of the ship and found the broken conduit. I saw the scratch lines along our hull where the ice of La Plage had scored us.

Methodically I filled in the deepest grooves with a ferro-carbon amalgam and then set about the tufted hairs of the broken cables. Blue matches blue. Green matches green. Yellow matches yellow. The repair was not complicated, but I gave it my best attention. What I was repairing was a back-up system to a back-up system . . . sensors which monitor hull stress I believe. Carefully I wrapped the individual cables and joined them and then tucked them back under their housing. I covered the seam with the same amalgam and watched it set to a smooth slate grey. I was glad of the work.

Then I went for a "walk" round the ship, pulling myself hand over hand and jetting from fin to fin. I stood for a while in the dark particle vents and looked out at a circle of stars which turned slowly. I thought about Pioneer Murray. Ariadne was right, he was just a boy. He'd never had a chance to grow emotionally. I determined not to let myself be angered by him but to try and help him. And Ariadne . . . how lucky I was to have such a mate . . . wise, compassionate, fun.

I made my way back to the airlock feeling tranquil and restored and when I got inside I found them fucking.

That is the word I mean.

I could hardly believe my ears as I drifted down the corridor to the survival room. Then I could not believe my eyes. She was astride him, riding him, and I saw his clenched-up face, brown amid her black curls. I saw it all. At first I thought of rape, but it was not rape. In any case, the man that could rape Ariadne has not been born or made and there are those who have tried.

I backed off. I did not know what to do. I was embarrassed and then I was ashamed.

I did not wait to see their climax but closed the door quietly and made my way to the kitchen and there anchored myself at the table.

It was there that Ariadne found me about half an hour later.

"You saw?"

I nodded.

"Good."

Then she pulled herself through the opening that leads to the showers.

I had time to think.

I don't think I am programmed to feel jealousy. Certainly if he had tried to hurt her I would have stopped him, and I don't think simple fidelity comes into it. So what did I feel? Injured pride? Insult by comparison? Invaded? Vaguely I wondered if I was experiencing one of the darker sides of love. To love is to be open to pain . . . and yet you can't help loving can you? This one thought gave me hope. Was I in love with Ariadne? Am I? Am I?

I had never thought of this before. We were a team. Ariadne and Angelo. Like Raven and Lattisbourne or Kingi and Elf or Bonniface and Amsterdame or . . . the rest. We were made to function together . . . and now something new had entered the equation.

I am sure our makers would have accepted with equanimity any degree of promiscuity so long as it did not prejudice our effectiveness.

Bah! What a stuffy sentence! I am too kind to them. What I mean is they didn't give a damn about our feelings. We were conditioned to make love because any human organism that is denied natural sexual outlets becomes either apathetic or vicious. So where did the caring arise?

I think about my comrade Larum. He is built like me but his fur is striped like a tiger. What would Larum do if he caught Silver in the arms of a Pioneer? I know the answer. He would sit down and watch. I think Larum was our maker's ideal and I am the deviant. That is why I am writing. That is why I am thinking. That is why I am hurting and that is why with one part of my mind I would like to pluck Pioneer Murray apart and toss him into space. But I won't. The other side of my programming forbids me.

But as I sat at that table, listening to the roar of the shower, I felt closer to the human . . . and I know I could have wept.

Ape man. Made man. Programmed worker. I thought about Pioneer Murray, slung into space before his beard was fully grown. He may have been born of a human mother . . . but I am more of a man.

Ariadne came back from the shower still shiny with water. She shook her hair and drops of water span from her head and dashed against the wall and hung like small beads of glass.

"When I said 'good' I didn't mean 'good', I only meant that I was glad you knew, but I'm sorry you came upon us that way. I was going to tell you."

I was interested to observe that she was having trouble explaining. If I had one fear it was that Ariadne would demonstrate the same cold passion that I have observed in Larum and Silver. What a tragedy it would be to love someone who was incapable of love and could only offer passion. We have never talked much, Ariadne and I. Perhaps now we will begin talking.

"And what state is Pioneer Murray in now?" I asked. "Tired out?"

"Whacked. He hasn't worked so hard in years."

I found myself smiling. Damn and blast. Smiling.

Ariadne sat down opposite me. "Are you hurt?"

I nodded. "But I am trying to understand too."

"There is nothing to understand."

"Why did you take him inside you?"

She paused, staring at me. "Curiosity partly. Partly pity. I wanted to wake him up. He didn't know what was happening to him. He didn't know how to kiss. He was a grounded fish."

50

"And was it nice?"

"Nice? It was like cleaning a baby's bottom."

That stopped me. "Do you mean it wasn't nice?"

"No. Just that it was necessary. He couldn't cope with himself. I brought him some relief. I think I hurt him a bit too." She grinned. "You know me."

"And what do you feel now?"

She thought. "Nothing."

"Nothing? You can't feel nothing. He's been on you. In you. You can't feel nothing!"

Her eyes flashed. "I can. I do. You don't know what I can feel. You are not a woman."

I was about to ask her what she felt about me, but I didn't. In the corridor we heard the clump clump of Pioneer Murray as he moved towards the kitchen, wearing no doubt my boots. He came into the kitchen and saw me. "Ah, so the chimp's returned," he said.

Silently I donned my spacesuit and walked outside.

8

He follows her like a puppy dog and she treats him like a child.

Once he tried to order me to get him something and I towered over him and growled and that made him think twice.

Ariadne watches both of us with a detached, smiling equanimity. I think she knows exactly what she is doing.

I have heard him ask her to go with him but she has refused. I don't think her refusal has much to do with me. Well not directly. I think she is guiding him towards maturity. He is a spoilt boy who has been King of the Castle for too long.

Tonight we played chess. Apparently it is a game he likes and used to play alone against his computer on La Plage. First he challenged Ariadne but she does not like such games. "Play Angelo," she said.

Though I have not played often I am a good player. I beat him easily.

I used my claw to move the pieces. I saw his eyes grow round as saucers when I lifted the pawns by the head and placed them delicately.

He is a bad loser and went to bed in a huff.

He still needs a lot of sleep and that is understandable. But one up to the chimp, I think.

When we had tucked him down, Ariadne suggested a swim. I liked the idea as I had been hoping for a chance to talk to her in a relaxed way. The emergence of Pioneer Murray has thrown our normally peaceful schedule into confusion. We are not natural about him and we guard our privacy. These ships are not designed for three restless people.

Swimming in free fall is impossible and I contacted the guidance computers and asked them to give us a bit of spin to hold the water in the pool.

They agreed. Repairs are almost complete and final checking is in progress. They gave us moon-equivalent gravity which means that the water sloshes like soup and if you dive, the splash goes up to the ceiling and cascades down like an umbrella. But at least we could swim.

Since our last really private conversation, one question had been dwelling on my mind: What does Ariadne feel for me?

It is a very simple question, though I doubt that before this present journey I would ever have thought to ask it. But now it matters to me. Of course, I realized that Ariadne might decline to answer.

We swam. Ariadne dived and paddled after her own fashion. I wallowed after mine. She seemed preoccupied and I decided not to press the question, but then she swam over to me and launched herself up on to my chest. "There's something I've been wanting to say to you, Angelo."

"Go ahead."

"Well, I've been thinking about how I took the Pioneer and how you reacted. I could have managed everything better, couldn't I? And then I began to think how I would have felt if it had been one of the female Pioneers we had rescued and I'd come in from the dark and caught you swiving her . . . what would I have felt?"

"What would you have felt?"

"I don't know. I don't have a word for it. But I wouldn't have been indifferent."

"Oh."

We both became quiet and I swam gently with Ariadne clasped round my chest.

"What do you feel for me?" I asked softly almost afraid of my own question.

"I think you are magnificent," she said. Those were her very words. "I think you are magnificent. Other men give me pleasure. I enjoyed the Pioneer in a clinical, athletic way, but you are the only one can drive me crazy. No. No. Hush. I want to say these things to you. Sometimes you make me want to climb up the walls with desire. Sometimes I want to climb into your skin and curl up. I never knew how much I needed you until I saw that I had hurt you. Don't be hurt by me. There is only you."

"Do you love me?"

"Love is a word I can't use. Love is a word we shouldn't use. Love is not part of our make-up."

"No."

"None of this should be happening."

"No."

"I can't help what I am."

"No . . ."

"But wherever I turn I see you. I have come to realize that. Is it just our programming?"

"No."

We drifted apart and swam separate for a while and then bumped together again. Ariadne swam beside me. "I shall take the Pioneer one more time before we settle him down for the long sleep. I will tell you when. You can watch if you like."

"No."

"As you like. So long as you understand. With him I am helping him to grow up. All women do that for men. But with you I am Ariadne. Equal and different."

Even now, though I have thought over her words many times, I am not sure I understand what she means. But I am sure that she knows. And for the time being that is good enough for me.

We climbed out of the pool and drifted back to our sleeping chamber, and there, much to my disgust, I fell immediately asleep. No, not quite immediately. I remember I asked her one more question, had she ever wiped a baby's bottom. "No," she said, "but I would like to."

Things are better now. Clearer. And Pioneer Murray is changing his ways.

Last night I slugged him again at chess and when he started to get petulant I laughed at him and told him he was a fool.

He looked at me with his nose all wrinkled up and then began to storm out. But he stopped, came back and sat down by me. "Can I tell you something?" he asked.

"Of course."

"In confidence." He looked about furtively to make sure that Ariadne was nowhere about, and then he whispered, "Listen, Chimp. I think I am falling in love with Ariadne."

I burst out laughing.

"I'm serious."

"No you're not."

"Eh?"

"Go and find someone your own age. Wait till you see some of the Pioneer women we've rescued. They'll eat you up."

I thought he was going to stamp his foot and depart. But he didn't. He just deflated before my eyes. "I don't understand you two," he said finally. "I keep thinking you are primitive. But you're not, are you. You are the future. My future . . . and you're not even fully human. You don't seem to understand human feelings. Human pride."

"Yes we do."

He sat for a while thinking, rubbing his shiny bald head with his fingers. Then we played another game of chess and I let him beat me. He sat back beaming. "How long before we set off back to Earth?"

"Very soon."

"Good. I've got a lot of living to do, haven't I?" And then he went off to bed humming.

Who says we know nothing about human feelings and human pride?

In the middle of the night I was awakened by the auto-nurse. Pioneer Murray was restless and up and about. It was my turn to babysit. I left Ariadne sleeping and turned out.

I found him crying. He was sitting alone at the kitchen table with his head in his hands and his shoulders were heaving. I sat down opposite him and stretched my claw across and over his shoulders and rocked him gently. "What is troubling you?"

"Everything. I don't know what I am or who I am. Everything I knew and loved is back there, lost." The words were broken. "So much is lost."

"Ah . . . you are thinking about your creature, your Houyhnhnm. I have told you. It still lives."

"It will not survive without me."

I shrugged at that. I didn't know what to say. He looked at me with watery, accusing eyes.

"It won't you know. It'll die. It'll die of grief. And it was learning so fast."

"You can have more pets when you get back to Earth," I said, trying to help.

"Pets," he said, flaring angrily. "That was not a pet. That was a better and gentler creature than you are."

I made no comment. I could see his hurt. He needed to break out, lash out possibly. A dam was breaking in him.

"I spent years working to make that creature . . . and then you came. You have no idea what loneliness is until you have spent centuries with only your shadow for company."

"We came to bring you back to Earth."

"You should have left me alone."

"La Plage was a cruel planet. You would never have been able to leave your dome."

"I did not want to leave it. The place I lived was home. La Plage – " he spat. "That is what I think of La Plage." He lapsed into silence.

"Tell me about your arrival there," I said, hoping to deflect his mood.

"It was many years ago."

"Try to remember."

"La Plage. Ha. I knew the planet was useless as soon as I saw it. I knew that a monstrous mistake had been made. I looked down searching for greenness, but there was nothing. . . .I knew there was nothing I could do. I couldn't reprogramme the computers. They were as stupid as the

56

computers aboard this ship. They had been told to seek out a world and they had found La Plage. Something had gone wrong with them . . . they were programmed to find planets which approximated somewhat to Earth. Well I suppose it is about the same size. I knew that I was equipped to adapt, but I needed to be given a fighting chance. Whoever programmed the computers was guessing. I can't forgive that.

"Anyway, down we went, me screaming and threatening to put a hammer through any circuitry I could find. But they locked me in my survival pod and there was no damage I could do.

"You know, just before we plunged into that white atmosphere I saw my ship eject the beacon satellite. It went tumbling away from us on its own orbit. That was my last link with Earth. Pitiful eh? Hands long since dead had made that satellite and now it was out of my grasp. I could have wept then, but I didn't. Such feelings had been beaten out of me in the labs back on Earth. I could no more weep than I could feel despair. I was not made to be defeated. I could actually feel my body begin to respond to challenge. I was helpless before my optimism. It was like an alien thing inside me which grew and took me over. In defiance of reason and common sense I was hopeful. I was prepared to plough snow. Just think what I could have accomplished if I'd been given a proper world!"

I nodded.

"I could have worked miracles. Did any of my fellow Pioneers make easy landfall?"

"Some. Most found difficulties. Worlds like Earth are not common."

"I thought so. The Pioneer Programme was rotten at its heart. A great publicity exercise, not sufficiently planned. A gesture. A sacrifice. We were the – "

"Go on with your story."

"Hmm . . . well, there I was skimming through clouds of dust and ice. I surveyed the world and then found that little island where I decided to set up camp. I christened it Gibraltar because it was a rock. We came down into a valley, dropped below the peaks and skidded on snow and slush. It was night-time. There was no storm and the peaks all about me in the starlight looked like paintings.

"I decided to start things moving. All I had to do was pull the right levers and watch. The engineers at least had done a good job. Everything worked smoothly. It was like one of the practice sessions back on Earth. A great cartouche flopped from the side of the ship and rolled away from us. Explosive charges broke the seals and it split apart and the dome began to inflate. It was like an animal. It flexed and spread as the gases were pumped into it. I saw it grow to its full shape and then anchor into the ground. It burned the snow with crackling blue electrical discharges and then, when the water refroze, it was set like a bubble trapped in glass.

"Trolleys emerged from a port in my ship's side. They had sensors in front like an insect's antennae, but they moved like sheep following one another. They nosed and jockeyed about and eventually found their way to the airlock and trundled into the dome. Each one carried my supplies which they deposited carefully on the snow inside the dome before coming back for more.

"I did nothing. Gradually, stage by methodical stage, my ship was emptied, and after three weeks the operation was complete and there was no reason for me to stay. I donned my survival suit. It was like the ones you have. I climbed aboard one of the trolleys and it carried me over the snow and through the airlock.

"Life on La Plage began. I wasn't unhappy. I was busy. I got the hut up first and then I covered the whole of the floor of the dome with carbon matting. The air screens began to function and within five days I could breathe without my mask.

"Then what did I do? I made tons of sythosoil and got my first seedlings going. That was a special moment! The first living plants on that barren world began to grow. I started with beans. I watched those seeds every day. I watched them swell and crack open and the first tender shoot appear and begin to struggle up to the light. I talked to the plants. Gave them names. They were my first comrades.

"Came the day I had my first home-grown meal. I was beginning to win. After the beans I started grass, planted my first trees, put down flowers and then enlivened my first hive. Every day there was something different . . . new shoots, a splash of colour . . . wherever I went I could make things grow. Can you imagine that?"

"You make it sound wonderful."

"It was. It was. I lived for the day. I didn't think about the past or the future. But, you know, even in those early days, I think I had given up any idea of trying to live outside my dome. It wasn't so much that La Plage was an impossible planet . . . who knows I might have been able . . . I knew a lot about controlled evolution . . . but I found myself completely bound up with the life-processes of Earth. Perhaps they got something wrong when they hammered me into shape. All I know is that what existed outside those grey and milky walls ceased to matter for me. I felt no compulsion to hibernate while my body adapted.

"I had some scares though. Once my dome was completely covered with snow and I thought it was going to break. I poured all my spare power into the dome trying to melt the snow. I succeeded in making a shell of ice over the whole dome. It was like a second skin, and that carried the weight. Lucky eh? We were buried for over five years."

"Did you ever think about Earth?"

"Oh, I thought about it. But it was like a memory of a dream and completely unimportant to me."

"Weren't you lonely, even then?"

"No, not at first. Loneliness came later. You don't feel lonely when you've got a purpose. And besides, I had the animals. All the embryos survived, except the deer. Oh and the dogs . . . they survived but they died as puppies. I never found out why. I often used to think about the dogs. I would have liked to have a dog about me . . . mmm . . . a dog or a woman."

59

"Ariadne and I were talking about that. We wondered why you were sent out alone, without a companion."

"Yes. Why? It doesn't make any sense does it? But that was the way it was. I used to think it was a political decision . . . they didn't want rival dynasties being set up. Our job as Pioneers was to make the worlds fit for human colonies, find out what worked and what didn't, make the first cut in the alien soil. But really I don't know. When I left Earth I knew nothing about women. They weren't part of my training. Perhaps my trainers hoped that all my lust for sex would be channelled into work. Perhaps they thought that all the adaptation we might have to go through would render childbearing impossible. I could have evolved in any number of different ways if I'd had a different environment, couldn't I?"

I nodded.

"I bet you've seen many strange things that were once Pioneers."

I nodded again.

"Who knows, if I'd had plenty of trees to swing on I might even have become a chimp."

"You should be so lucky," said I, glad that his humour had returned.

"No . . . they sent us out alone into the dark. . . .It wasn't so bad really . . . I didn't miss a companion for many years. But it was a cruel decision all the same. You are the lucky ones. You hunt in pairs. You have a wonderful woman beside you."

As he said this Ariadne joined us.

"Who has a wonderful woman beside him?" she asked.

"Chimp does. I've been telling him about my early days on La Plage."

Ariadne sat down with us. "Were you trying to make a woman when you made that talking horse?"

"Yes." He looked at her as though expecting her to comment but she remained silent. "Well, something like a woman. I don't know. A companion. The passing of the years had become terrible to me. I had grown to hate death. You see I

60

wouldn't die. I'm made of leather and hickory. I wouldn't die unless I killed myself, which I can't do, or unless the dome collapsed. But the animals each had their natural life span and died just when I was growing to depend on them. I used to talk to them all the time, and I was sure they understood me and I tried to read their minds. And then one day I'd find them stretched out or they'd wander slowly off into the trees and not come back. I saw an eternity of mourning in front of me. So I decided to take a hand. I had noticed mutations occurring in the plants . . . I decided to create my own mutations."

He sat back and spread his hands along the table.

"It was pretty hit and miss really. I knew enough about genetics to get started but beyond that I improvised. But I had a lab and plenty of specimens and time was on my side." He held his hand out in front of my eyes and pointed to his first and second fingers. "You see those. They were my first triumph. I managed to regrow them. I took a year but I did it. They got cut off but I didn't sew them back on, I regrew them. See, they look younger than the rest of me, don't they?" He was right – the two fingers were pinker and less wrinkled. "I kept notes of all my experiments. I suppose you brought my notes. Yes, well. I created plenty of monstrosities. . . . Most didn't survive and I recycled them. . . .Some lasted a week . . . others seemed quite happy to hump about. But it was the brain I needed to develop. I started using cultures from my own body. Then I discovered that the horse had plenty of cranial space and I managed to get some rudimentary speech organs into its throat. I remember the day of the first word. I taught it my name, Murray . . . and then there was no looking back. Each generation improved. Aaach."

He balled his fists and banged them down on the table. "If you hadn't come I would have succeeded you know. I would. I would have made a human. It might not have looked very pretty to your eyes . . ." His gaze strayed to me. "But then again . . ." He was not being humorous this time. His voice was bitter. "What do I have to look forward to? You took away the only world I knew. I don't want to be here."

61

Ariadne reached out and put her arms round the Pioneer. At the same time she motioned with her head for me to leave.

I did so.

I went for a swim.

Pioneers are like children.

9

Five hours until the thrust starts and we shall be on our way. Ariadne has hold of my claw and I am writing this with difficulty. But I do not mind. She has talked non-stop since she came back from "settling" the Pioneer and I want to record some of the things she has told me. Apparently when they got back to the Pioneer's bunk they did not make love . . . at least not immediately. He became obsessed with telling her about the Earth he had known. That is, the planet as it was before the Catastrophe.

Facts and dates do not make history, that is certain. That young boy, Master Raoul, grew up during the last Golden Age before he became Pioneer Murray. Apparently he was selected for the Pioneer Project before he was born! While in the womb genetic manipulation began. The foetus was retarded in certain ways, strengthened in others. He was born normally and grew up with his mother to the age of six. Then he was taken into a special institute and educated along with other potential Pioneers. We know some of their names. There was Aldus, the first of the Pioneers. He was brought back by our friends Bonniface and Amsterdame. When I saw Aldus he was a porcupine. He had grown spines to protect him from the fleshy Tumuloes which were the intelligent and hungry life forms among which he had lived. Pioneer Murray remembered him as a gangly youth with a passion for cricket.

There was Rip whom I have heard about but who has never been found.

There was Indira who was brought back by Lindis and Tui on their first expedition. She now lives at the Pioneer Centre on Aotearoa where she wallows in the hot pools.

There were Erika and Li whose beacons stopped centuries ago and who must be presumed dead.

There was Klein who was rescued by Kingi and Elf. Klein did not survive the long sleep home.

There was Sean who was found by Larum and Silver living in a water paradise where he had managed to domesticate the fish.

Those were all Raoul Murray's classmates. Of the other Pioneers who left Earth after him and whom we have rescued he has no knowledge. But at least he knows that there are others like him waiting for him at the end of the long journey home. He was pleased with that. Ariadne did not tell him that the world he knew is long gone and that the only reason we had rescued him was because Earth has need of his genetic stock.

He will find that out soon enough.

Our ship is very quiet. The countdown is in progress. Only two hours to go.

Of course, we do not know what to expect when we get back. Two generations out. Two generations back. It is a long time. When we left things were not so good. Only Aotearoa and parts of Australia and the Pacific islands had been reoccupied. The great lethargy which afflicted so many of the full-humans had not been overcome. Perhaps things are better now. We will know at the end of the long sleep. Perhaps the Pioneers will have begun to cooperate.

Pioneer Murray told Ariadne about the last few days before he left Earth. He was taken to visit the main centres of the world's civilization. He talked about a city that had water for streets and long narrow boats. There *was* such a city and I have seen pictures of it but I cannot remember its name. He talked about a country called China where stone warriors marched up from the soil and where a long wall stretched for miles. He walked in New York in the chasms between buildings and bought things in shops. He saw paintings in Old Paris and London and travelled on a railway which dived under the earth. He talked about the millions of people who swept into and out of the cities each day.

64

Millions of people. How different the world when he wakes up. He knows nothing of the disease which attacked the full-humans' immune system . . . or the cure which was almost as bad as the disease and left people sterile. He knows nothing of the wars that flared briefly and violently as ageing populations became desperate. I know little of history – we were not taught history – but I did hear that one nation, hoping to hold the world to ransom for its fertile resources, threatened to explode bombs over Antarctica; and then, when it was ignored, did explode those bombs.

I will not tell him about these things. They would only confuse him and he would have more questions than I have answers. But in a real sense we are all children of the Catastrophe. That one decade in which the Golden Age ended has shaped all our lives.

So, Pioneer Murray has a great deal to learn.

The countdown is well advanced. Only minutes to go. Thinking about the past has saddened me. There is something changing in me. I am curious about the past, curious too about the future. Do we have a future, Ariadne and I? I hope so. I shall discuss this with Bonniface and Lindis and Larum if they are on Earth when we get home.

Here we are, the final countdown. The computers are speaking to us.

Fourteen, thirteen . . .

I have my arms round Ariadne.

Ten, nine . . .

The ship has started to shudder.

Five, four . . .

We are looking out at the turning stars.

Two, one . . .

We feel the gentlest push. Outside the blue light is glowing round the acceleration vents. We are on our way again. We are on our way home.

10

Life is normal. We have rebegun the preparations for the long sleep. Pioneer Murray is already in his jelly. He floats naked and with his arms drooping above his chest. The clear tubes which carry air to his lungs and draw away his wastes have hardly moved and his brain rhythms are gentle and deep. I too am ready for the long sleep. This journey has been a long one, and stressful. My awakening, for such I call it, I date from the time I first picked up pencil and wrote. I have discovered much about myself and about Ariadne, but I need the long sleep to clear my mind.

Ariadne and I have just checked the clones. All's well . . .

The days are slipping past, seemingly quicker and quicker, and my mind is hazy. All I know is that we are well advanced in our preparations for the long sleep. Such things cannot be rushed. The body and mind must be closed down slowly. For the mind the rule is: think quietly and avoid dispute. For the body we have drugs.

Each day I dwell on those things which bring pleasure and I think if you could see me you would say I was smiling. As regards the mind I am my own master and I will not enter the final stage of sleep until I know that my path will be shining and my awakening wholesome. I have a private ritual which I will now share. I try to become as content as a calm sea upon which the sun plays. I think of rock pools teeming with life and the slow pull and release of the tides. When that rhythm is established I can let my eroticism flow . . .

Ariadne's preparations are similar but what she creates for herself in her dreams I do not know. In any case, the quality of dreams can never be communicated.

The body is much harder to control than the mind. That is

66

surprising, isn't it? We take drugs. Each day we take a prescribed number of pills and give ourselves injections, gradually altering our metabolism. We take pills to make our skins oily. We take pills to restrict the growth of nails and hair. We store medication in our fat. We have an inhalant which helps us regularize our automatic motor functions.

Last night Ariadne and I could not make love. We tried and we came close to climax, but then our bodies deserted us. We both faded at the same time . . . and that is a good sign really. It means that our rhythms are matched and that if all is well, we will sleep within days of one another.

Ariadne is asleep.

Last night we sat holding hands. I dozed in my chair in front of the view-screen, and when I awoke she was gone. Now she lies in jelly. Her face is very beautiful and composed.

I see that before she left she closed down the front part of the ship. All that remains alight is my small living area, the kitchen and the corridor into the sleep chamber.

Through my window I can see a blue phosphorescence. We are a black javelin trapped in a halo of light.

It is time. My body is heavy and my fur is soft. I can already hear the waves break on a sun drenched shore and the hiss of lather . . .

I can see darkness and infinity and both are beautiful. I will climb into my chamber and the warm jelly will receive me and seek out every pore and follicle.

I write my last words and leave my book on the table.

Good night.

PART 2

The Homecoming

1

"Are you awake Angelo? Come on. There is something you must see." I could feel Ariadne's fingers grating in the fur on my neck, massaging me awake. I wanted to sleep. My legs were heavy and my mouth felt as though a cat had slept there. But I responded. Somewhere in the deep recesses of my brain I realized that Ariadne would not rush my awakening without good cause.

I stumbled along the companionway behind her and up the pull-poles and on to the main control deck where the computers were wittering like a tree of cicadas.

"Now look," she said, pushing me down into a chair. The view-screen, which covered almost the entire wall, came alive like moonlight on rippling water. Then it blackened and in the blackness I saw a yellow shape that slowly came into focus like something that is raised from beneath the sea.

Saturn.

It hung like an ornament cut from jade.

Its rings, diagonal to us, scythed into space to the very edges of our view-screen. The planet seemed so close, so solid, that at first, being drowsy, I thought that Ariadne was playing some trick on me and dangling something in front of me. But it was no trick.

While I watched, the giant planet moved against the stars and a bright point of light grew about its northern rim. I watched the sun rise over Saturn. And I stayed watching until the sun became a muddy pool of light behind the rings.

Dozy as I was I realized that what I was seeing was extraordinary. Normally when we come back from a rescue mission we regain consciousness about a hundred lems from the sun which puts us within the orbit of Uranus. But we approach from all directions and never before have I heard of a rescue

71

team coming close to the orbit of Saturn let alone actually seeing the mighty planet.

It was swinging away from us. Sol was beyond. We asked the computers to identify Earth and they obliged, magnifying a faint point of light far down on the screen. Earth.

"Come on, philosopher. I thought that would wake you up. You didn't want to miss it, did you?"

"No," I growled (my tongue still felt gummy). "Thank you."

"There is work to do. Earth is alive and kicking. Chrono has been asking for you."

"What does he want?"

"I think he has news. But he was very guarded." She looked at me with her head on one side as though I were at some strange angle. "You are awake, aren't you? Try some solid food today. That will bring you round."

"How long have you been awake?"

"Almost five days, Chimp."

"Aaagh. And how is our favourite Pioneer?"

"Still asleep but well. There are no signs of any disturbance. He has grown hair on his head."

"Oh?"

"Come and have some food. Then you can look at him."

I was not sure that I wanted food or to look at Pioneer Murray but Ariadne was irresistible and minutes later I found myself gagging on the first solids that my stomach had coped with for two generations.

Pioneer Murray looked younger. The fluids had all drained away and Ariadne had instructed the auto-nurse to cut his hair and shave him. Now he lay high and dry with a stiff stubble beard and the hair of a page boy. All his hair has been saved as it will help with analysis later. He slept on his back with his hands, open-thumbed, encircling his penis.

"How vulnerable he looks," I said.

"He is vulnerable. Come away, Angelo," said Ariadne and led me away by the hand.

*

72

Chrono is one of us. A prototype. I have never seen him but I gather he is now as fat as ten men. He has his own satellite high above the moon and he welcomes every Pioneer rescue team that returns to home, to Earth. I have been told that he never sleeps.

Whatever.

His official function is to serve as a living beacon. Once he monitored all the traffic between Earth and the moon and the inner planets. He kept a careful eye on all the flotsam and jetsam that turned in Earth's wide backyard. Now he only has us rescue teams to care about as we are the only space travellers.

He gives us news that will help us.

Feeling better after some real food and more optimistic after our brush with Saturn, I contacted Chrono and was pleased to hear his calm, academic, matter-of-fact voice.

"It is nice to hear you again, Angelo. Ariadne tells me you had no trouble, no *significant* trouble, I should say. And your Pioneer is well?"

"He is well."

"Good. You will be pleased to know that I have you in constant hold and that your pathway is clear. I intend to bring you round the moon. You will pass close to Earth but you will not be making a landing."

"Why is that?"

"New regulations. Much has happened. Worst was an epidemic affecting the bone marrow. Many died before the virus was identified and a cure found. But now Pioneers are not allowed to land directly on Earth."

"Aha. The Pioneer Programme was blamed."

"You have guessed it."

"Was a virus brought back: I didn't think anything could lurk undetected during the long sleep?"

"I don't think so. I think it was just another mutation spreading from the time of the Catastrophe. But someone has to be blamed. Tread carefully when you eventually make

73

planetfall, both you and Ariadne. You are a dwindling number."

"Go on."

"Lindis and Tui crashed on the moon sixty-two years ago. That is my reason for wanting to take you round there. The wreckage is spread wide. I imagine you would like to see it for old time's sake."

"Yes. They are dead?"

"Nothing survived."

"How? I mean . . . were they homing? Was there an error?"

"I had their course steady, but then something failed. They started to spin and when they tried to correct the spin they dived straight into the side of a crater."

"Lindis and Tui."

"They were homing. They asked about you. They were hoping for a reunion. They knew you were far out."

"Does Ariadne know?"

"I haven't told her. Our first conversation was all technical matters."

"Take us slowly round the moon, Chrono. Lindis was like a brother to me."

"I know."

"So what will happen? How will we land?"

"You will be guided to an old cargo torus. It has been adapted. There the Pioneer will be off-loaded. You will remain six months in quarantine."

"Six months?"

"I have said."

"But . . ."

"I have no authority in such matters. Make your complaints to the Space Council, such as it is. See if they will speak to you."

I suppose I was silent for several minutes absorbing what Chrono had told me and perhaps more importantly, what he had not told me – merely hinted at. "So, things on Earth are not much improved?"

"Some things are improved. A reclamation team is established in India. Part of the horn of Africa is again supporting crops. The high plateau of Peru is occupied again. But the Pioneer Programme has foundered."

"Tell me."

"Semen taken from Pioneer Caesar was found to be fertile but it led to monstrosities. Clones were taken from Aimee, Napoleon and Arthur and they deformed. The genetic changes introduced into them as part of the Pioneer Programme have proved to be irreversible. What is more, some of the Pioneers are refusing to help. They are the only ones who know some of the old secrets and they are keeping quiet. There is even word that one or two of the Pioneers held at Moon Base have been killed during experiments."

"Hell."

"There is desperation. So take care. There is great interest in your Pioneer. Murray, isn't it?"

"Yes. Raoul Murray. He was one of the early ones. Maybe you remember him?"

"I do."

"He is a difficult man."

"Then I wish him well. Warn him."

"We will. Anything else?"

"A great deal, but most of it you must find out for yourself. I think you will find a qualitative difference in your reception. Be on your guard."

"Thanks for the warning. One last thing. Who else is on Earth just now? Are we the only team?"

"Oh no. You will have a grand reunion. Bonniface and Amsterdame returned twelve months ago. They are awaiting assignment but their ship is damaged. Repairs take longer these days. Larum and Silver are prospecting in New Antarctica – a krill farm I believe. Kingi and Elf's ship is on Moon Base. It was taken out of commission when they returned and they were sent home by cargo carrier. Only Raven and Lattisbourne returned in one piece. At present they are prospecting in the No-Go zones of Old Europe. I believe Kingi and Elf are with

75

them. No doubt they will all gather at the Aotearoa Pioneer Settlement when they know you have returned."

"Perhaps one day you will join us."

"Perhaps one day."

"Take good care of us, Chrono."

"I have only had the one accident. There will be no others. Keep your guidance computers on standby. I will speak to you again when you reach the moon."

That was all. Chrono does not use unnecessary words. I have never known him to be wrong. We must be careful.

Later I described our conversation to Ariadne and explained my fears. She listened gravely. When I had finished she shook her mane of dark curls. "I can explain it in one word," she said. "Intelligence. The Earth is getting stupider."

"What is intelligence?" I asked.

She smiled at me as if to say, do not try to trap me. "As I see it intelligence has two main attributes: the ability to see a problem before it presents itself and the ability to take proper action. Earth is failing on both counts. Chrono is right, we must be on our guard."

There we left the matter. I was still too dozy. I could not hold thoughts together for more than half an hour at a stretch. I went to lie down. But before I left I looked out through the view-screen again. We are well past Saturn. It is plunging on into the darkness and the Earth is swinging round the sun to meet us.

2

Ariadne has been deeply affected by the news of Tui and Lindis' deaths. I find it hard to describe her emotion. At times it is like anger; she storms about, finding fault with everything including me. At other times she is distant and coldly efficient, like a robot that does its job indifferent to praise or blame. But last night she sat down and read my pages from beginning to end and then insisted on adding a sentence of her own: "What do words weigh when set against the death of a friend?"

You see, she is even angry about my notebook.

But that will pass. I follow her shifts in mood with great interest. In a strange way which I cannot yet fathom, her hurting has drawn her closer to me. At night she holds me fiercely and drives her face into my fur. She has told me that Tui was her only friend among the women. That surprises me for they never seemed close. She has also said that she thinks their death was not an accident.

On that I have no comment. I know our ships are growing old but I have no reason to think of sabotage. Who would gain? But I think we shall both be careful in our checking before our next assignment.

Now the Earth and the moon are close. We can see the blue of Earth's seas and the white of clouds. I have a strange fantasy that if our ship foundered at this very moment I could walk my way down to its surface. We are still slowing at 1.5 g's and this has made us strong and slim. Soon we shall enter Earth's shadow and then we shall dip behind the moon.

The moon has its own beauty. It is like stretched vellum on which some untidy scribe has spattered ink and made circular doodles. It is stained brown and dark brown and grey. We have just passed over Moon Base which, with its white and green and pink domes, looks like eggs buried in the sand.

Now we are moving to the "dark" side where Lindis and Tui crashed.

The evidence is all before us. They must have crashed at a very oblique angle as their track is like a long claw mark which stretches over many hundreds of miles. Their ship lies crumpled and open at the foot of a crater wall. Where they struck the crater is broken and the explosion has left debris all over. Chrono is right, no one could have survived that impact, but surely something could have been done?

I can see the pink insulation of the inner hull. Released from the containing pressure of the ship, it has spread like the intestines of a worm and straddles mountain and valley.

The black fins still seem to be intact. We can see where they tumbled top over bottom, leaving footprints in the sand until they rolled to the bottom of a low stony hill.

That is all. Somewhere down there lie the remains of our friends.

I have no other words.

I wonder what Amsterdame and Bonniface know of this.

3

We are in quarantine; that is now official, and we are turning in high orbit above the moon. When they came aboard they neutralized our drive computers so that even if we tried to make a break for it we couldn't.

Poor Ariadne is sitting opposite me with hollow cheeks. She is wearing a beret she has fashioned out of oddments, and that helps. I am wearing overalls.

It is not the prospect of quarantine that disturbs us. We are both still shaken by the ordeal we have undergone in the last few hours.

I have just spoken with a certain Major de Beer of the Medical Defence Corps. I protested about our treatment and he had the grace to say he was sorry for any inconvenience and hoped that we understood that serious problems required serious measures and that inevitably a few feathers would be ruffled.

Feathers ruffled! I flexed my stunted claw before his eyes and then broke contact. So here we shall sit for six months and hope that when that time is elapsed, they release us.

But I will tell the story in order.

When we had left Lindis and Tui's graveyard we went on round the moon. As soon as we began to rise above Moon Base a guidance ray nabbed us and took control of our trajectory. We were ordered to rendezvous with an old cargo torus, just as Chrono had warned us. We lifted and matched orbit and just as we were closing with the torus beneath us, I was ordered outside.

"Why?" I asked.

"To check that all the locking dogs close securely."

"But – "

"Outside immediately."

So out I had to go. I knew, as did they, that all dockings are automatic. We have sensors and computer line links and pneumatic support rods all to make sure that no one has to go outside during a docking manoeuvre.

I thought about this as I pushed gently away from our ship and watched the safety rope pay out behind me.

Below, the torus was like a great inflated rubber ring which turned slowly.

Our ship jockeyed with delicate whispers of power until it had matched orbit and spin. Then the Worm snaked out and groped about until it found the torus' airlock. I saw the magnetic locks flex and anchor and the soft rubber air-seals expand as atmospheric equilibrium was established.

Dutifully I jetted over and inspected each lock. They were all secure as I knew they would be. And had they not been, what could I have done? Hammer them into place? Shift the inertia of the whole spaceship with my hands? Silly.

My suspicion was that they wanted me out of the way. And I was right. After seeing where Lindis and Tui crashed I was very much on my guard and not a little frightened. Hanging out there in the blackness in my silver survival suit I was vulnerable from any angle. At any moment I expected to see the blue glimmer of our particle engines coming alive. They would have scorched me and sent me tumbling to God knows where.

But nothing. I was simply out of the way.

After I had checked each of the locking dogs I drifted up the side of the torus and anchored myself at one of the windows. It was dirty inside. I could see the long curving green avenue of the hydroponics tanks and the tyre-scarred ramps where cargo had once been stored. New prefabricated units had been welded into place and the welding connections had not even been painted. People were there, loping round the walkways of the torus. They were moving a great inflated plastic tent, shifting it close to where the Worm was locked. An isolation tent for the Pioneer, I guessed.

"Get away from the window. Return to your ship immediately," a voice cracked in my ears.

I waved, hoping whoever had spotted me was still watching and then detached and jetted back to the dark hulk of our ship.

They kept me waiting outside the airlock for over thirty minutes before letting me inside. I had only two minutes breathing left when the airlock slid open and I was able to scramble inside.

Pioneer Murray was gone, evacuated while still asleep into the torus.

I found that the ship was occupied. Men and women in green uniforms and wearing clumsy-looking air filters stood guard over me while I stripped off my spacesuit. Ariadne was nowhere to be seen.

Then they ordered me to strip off my underclothes. With guns on me I was made to lie down on one of the tables in our medical bay and I felt the clamps of the auto-nurse close about my arms, thighs and ankles.

Only then did I start to resist.

Why did I leave it so long?

No answer. I suppose I didn't know what was happening. The initiative was not with me.

I called for Ariadne. I asked where she was. No answer. And the more I struggled the tighter the auto-nurse held me until I lay still, panting.

Then they shaved me. I could feel the electric clippers running up my skin under my fur and I saw the fur peel away. It was immediately sucked up by a vacuum tube.

They were not careful. Several times the clippers dug into me and I felt a warm dampness which could only be blood though the pain was not great.

A doctor (I suppose it was a doctor) took samples of my blood and someone scraped inside my mouth. I felt my claw manipulated and a sharp pain as the great hooked horns were cut back to the quick. Mercifully, the auto-nurse, always attuned to pain, sprayed anaesthetic gas into my nostrils and I saw the room spin as darkness closed over me.

*

81

That is all I remember.

I awoke with a stranger looking down at me. I tried to hit that alien face but my arms were like tubes of lead.

"Angelo. They've gone. We're drifting."

The voice I knew. My mind readjusted itself. I saw the fine nose and the full lips, the eyes that stared at me. "Ariadne?"

"Me."

"What have they done to you?"

"No worse to me than to you."

I levered myself up on to my elbows and looked at her. They had shaved her head. Where once had been rich dark curls there was now only a scratched greyness. All her body hair was gone and her skin was pinched and bruised. "My poor darling."

"Save your pity for yourself."

Truth. I hardly know myself. I am still strong but I am naked in a way that I can not describe, I am hairless as a frog. I cannot bear to look at myself in the mirror.

"Why have they done this?"

"It is called a sanitary precaution."

"And now we are drifting?"

"Yes."

"Where?"

"Above the moon. We are stable. A Major de Beer is waiting to speak to you."

"Where is he?"

"Relax. Not here. On the moon. He is in charge of the Medical Defence Corps."

"I'll kill him."

"He is on the moon. Relax. Talk to him. Be polite. Find out as much as you can."

"Why wouldn't he talk to you?"

"I refused."

So here we are. Six months or more to wait. I have rubbed my hand on my arm and can feel the beginnings of stubble. Perhaps in six months we shall be our old selves again.

Ariadne doubts that. Time will tell.

4

Ariadne has decided to take a long sleep.

After mooching round the ship for one whole day, taking showers, picking at her food, swimming, scrubbing at imaginary stains in our kitchen, she has now retreated into our long-sleep chamber and activated the auto-nurse.

She has advised me to do the same. "You'll do yourself no good sitting at the table waiting for your claw to grow. Come on. We can be asleep in three days."

I didn't want to. And I told her so. I intend to stay awake. I haven't explained my reasons to her but the fact is I don't trust them. I intend to barricade the ship when she is asleep. We can last out here indefinitely. If they want to get rid of us they will have to shoot us out of the sky. I am an angry creature now and each day I shall measure my fur and I shall swim and take pride in the length of my arms.

I have discovered something else. I can still make contact with Chrono. We have to be careful. We time our conversations for when there is maximum static from the sun and Earth. But at least I have an ear to the world outside and that makes me feel less lonely.

There is more.

I have made, I think, an important decision. I have decided to write about some of our rescues . . . or one of them at least. You see, I am still worried about who or what I am and I find it easier to dwell on that question when Ariadne is not about. Each rescue has taught me something. I have both saved life and destroyed life; both actions make me think.

I have decided to write about the events on Jeupardi and our attempted rescue of Pioneer Jinks. That mission was the first time we consciously lied to the officials back on Earth. If you have ever read the official report you will know that Jeupardi was occupied by creatures like ants. You will also know that we could find no trace of Pioneer Jinks; that all evidence of her and her ship had vanished and that the bleeping life satellite was presumed to be malfunctioning.

None of this is true.

Forget the official report. It was a lie concocted by Ariadne and myself because we were afraid to tell the truth. Pioneer Jinks was not dead when we arrived on Jeupardi. We killed her.

Let me explain.

5

Ants.

Jeupardi was infested with ants. Beyond whatever lived in the sea and the vegetation, these were the only native life form we encountered. They were huge by the standards of earth. The smallest we saw was about the size of a young German Shepherd dog.

No doubt an entomologist would correct me for it is dangerous to judge non-earthly species by the things that we know. But they looked like ants: they had long feelers which they banged on the ground in front of them and they tore their food with mandibles and stared with domed shiny black eyes.

From the cool of space, Jeupardi looked like a world of islands and green seas. When we dropped lower we could see that the islands were all joined up by long narrow causeways. Ariadne likened the world to a ball held in a brown net, and that is how I remember it.

We expected to find the Pioneer easily but the planet was so full of life that we could find no clear focus. We began a slow analysis, working from the poles but all our instruments could show us were teaming motes of life. There was no sign of a dome.

We quickly detected patterns of agriculture and that gave us hope. But the whole of the planet was cultivated from the poles to the equator. Thin bands of green ran down the centre of each causeway and expanded to blobs of green on each island.

We transmitted and listened on all frequencies but there were no radio calls coming from the planet, yet still the life satellite high above the planet sent out its plaintive bleeping showing that Pioneer Jinks was still alive.

"No alternative but to take a closer look," said Ariadne, and she guided our ship down until it hung only a few yards above the sea making the green water churn to lather.

Creating as little disturbance as possible we drifted over the seas and islands. Our slow journey gave us at least an opportunity to study the inhabitants of this land. We quickly discovered that all the ants were not alike. Physically they seemed alike, just as men are basically alike, but they had differences of colour. Some were bright crimson, others were the colour of wine. One group I remember was black as coal with red spots on their heads and gaster. As we passed over their fields they reared up and waved their feelers at us like old men waving their fists. We noticed that groups of different colours did not mix. On the causeways were what I can only describe as border posts. Masses of the ants faced one another, crawling three deep, and once we saw a full-scale battle erupt with each side battling to gain or protect only a few yards of territory. They died in their hundreds until the battle raged only on top of the corpses of fallen comrades. For no obvious reason they suddenly stopped fighting and each side began to jettison its dead into the sea. When the causeway was clear, the two armies settled back to a tense staring with their antennae only feet apart.

It was Ariadne who realized that the causeways were artificial though when she pointed it out I wondered why I had not seen this before. They were made of earth and stones with steep sides and a flat top where fifty or so ants could stand side by side. On every causeway was a border post. Sometimes a border post would open to allow a long chain of ants in single file to pass through. They carried food. With leaves and berries held in their mandibles they advanced, brushing against the feelers of the guard ants.

Crops. The crops at different latitudes were all different. In the colder latitudes berries seemed to predominate. These gradually gave way to maize. In the hot central latitude where the seas were shallow we saw small, earth-dyked lagoons where creatures like shrimps thrashed the water. We also saw fruits like bananas growing in giant hands and broad fleshy-leaved shrubs. Here were the biggest surface ants we saw. They were brown and striped and mottled. They were about the size of cows.

Though we scoured the islands we found no sign of Pioneer Jinks.

"There is no alternative, Angelo," said Ariadne. "We shall have to land and parley with them."

"How do you parley with an ant?"

She shrugged and then smiled. "I'm sure you'll find a way."

There was one group of islands which was considerably larger than any others. The different atolls looked like part of the rim of a vast submerged volcano. Here we had noticed a structure of ramparts which enclosed dark caves which led underground. This seemed the most clear evidence of civilization and so we determined to land there.

Our instructions concerning landing in alien environments are very specific. Basically we have to land without causing major disruption. On Jeupardi this was impossible. The cultivated fields extended to within a few yards of the sea and continued up to the lower slopes of the ramparts. We cruised for a while above the island and then lowered on to one of the wide avenues which divided the crops. This was one of the main roads used by the ants and we saw them scatter into the fields and up to the ramparts as our shadow lowered. Inevitably some crops were crushed and the nose of our ship gouged a channel in the side of the earth ramparts.

No sooner had we landed than the ants began to scamper all over us. They bit and worried the hard steel of our communications antennae. They clogged the jet vents. They obscured the view-screen so that all we could see of the outside world was a mass of legs and feelers and writhing bulbous gaster.

There was no danger to us or to the ship; disquieting only was the realization that the ants were trying to devour us without thought of caution.

"And you want me to go and talk to them?" I asked Ariadne.

"We have to find the Pioneer."

I took charge of the ship and ordered the computers to work our way backwards into the sea. We slid into the water like an alligator and watched the waves clean the ants from the ship's skin. They could not swim and fish that looked like jaws with tails picked them off and crunched them as they thrashed in the water.

Then we crawled up on to the land again. And again we were engulfed. The ants threw themselves at us in a frenzy, scrambling over one another in their eagerness to bite at our cold metal.

In all we retreated into the water some five times before the ants learned to keep their distance. The final time we emerged from the sea they fell back before us beating their feelers on the ground in unison. That was frightening. The onslaughts we could take, but now they seemed possessed by a common mind.

"Meet them now, Angelo. Use your arms like feelers. Perhaps they will recognize you. Perhaps they will fall back and worship you."

I smiled at Ariadne's irony as I strapped my survival suit tight about me. It was a standing joke among the Pioneer rescue teams that we came as gods and departed as kidnappers. There were many reports of alien species worshipping our ships.

"I think not," I replied. "Be ready to drag me in if they overpower me. Keep close contact. Get me aboard if I start to sound strange."

"Will do."

We both knew what I meant. If a group mind was in operation out there then I was vulnerable to a takeover. I have never been mastered by an alien brain but I have met those who have. Larum for instance, when he and Silver were rescuing Sean, found himself in the middle of a vast flock of birds. He tried to fly with them and ran round in circles flapping his arms and crying because he could not join their great migration. "It was like the compulsion you can feel to jump off high buildings," was the way he described it to me. "You know it will end in disaster but you can't help yourself. You want to do it. And if the pressure is too great, you do it. Thank God I was on the ground."

So, the group mind has great power. Let no one underestimate it.

With my suit firm and supple about me I checked my pistol and then secured my helmet. I felt the cool air waft about my face as the valves opened.

The diaphragm in the nose of our ship went through its complex motions and opened. There was no need to use the Worm and I stepped over its neatly folded pleats and down a few steps and on to the brown surface of the planet.

The ants still beating their feelers in unison drew back from in front of me.

Then suddenly they stopped.

Staring into so many black alien eyes I felt my fur try to stand on end inside my survival suit. Willing myself to action, I raised my arms above my head and then brought them down and forwards in an imitation of the ants' motion.

They regarded me stonily. I repeated the gesture once, twice, three times, and saw not a flicker of recognition from any of them. I took a pace forwards and was about to raise my arms again when without a sound they charged. I was pinned back against the side of the ship with mandibles snipping at my arms, neck and head.

The strength of the ants surprised me and I flailed about with my claw while trying to get room to draw my pistol. They were all over me, climbing on my shoulders and on my helmet. I heard Ariadne's voice in my ears. "Freeze. I'm covering you," and then the ants began to explode. Ariadne stood in the doorway to our ship firing. When my arms were free I managed to loose my pistol and together we cut into the ranks of ants. Still firing I retreated up the steps and then, as suddenly as the ants had charged they fell back and withdrew into the fields.

"Now what?" muttered Aridane.

"Regrouping," I offered.

"Mmm. Possibly."

89

"I don't think I made much impression with my sign language."

"Well, you got a reaction. And they had a chance to look at you. That's the main thing. They've probably realized that you are of the same species as Pioneer Jinks. Did they hurt you?"

"No. But I wouldn't have given much for my chances if they'd got to work on the helmet clamps."

"Mmm. They don't seem particularly intelligent. Brute force we can cope with. Watch out, something's happening."

Both Ariadne and I saw movement at the same moment. It was high on one of the ramparts where a dark hole led underground. Thin white feelers were tapping round the cave and slowly emerging.

The feelers were very long and reached halfway down to our ship before the main body began to appear. It was a giant white ant. It had white globes for eyes and by its movements I judged it to be completely blind. It shuffled out on to the rampart above us and groped in the air before rubbing its feelers together. Immediately we heard a drumming and hundreds of the black ants emerged from the fields beating their antennae on the ground. They advanced to within several yards of our ship and then settled still.

"Now we're getting somewhere," said Ariadne.

Moving carefully, testing every foothold with its long delicate feelers, the white ant advanced down the earth slope in front of our ship. Its legs were triple-jointed and adorned with stiff white hairs like frost. It walked with the same care as a spider, quite unlike the swift scurrying run of the dark ants. Earth dislodged by the ant fell on the waiting ones beneath but they never moved.

At the bottom of the slope it lifted its gaster and secreted a milky substance which slopped to the ground. The small dark ants broke ranks and began to devour the sickly mess. The white ant stood still until the ground was completely clear and then it stepped towards us. It reached with one of its antennae and began to tap along the ship exploring the vents and the stubby radio masts and the plates of the heat shield.

"It is looking for you," whispered Ariadne and as she spoke the ant withdrew its feeler and then dabbed out again much closer to us.

"Shall I burn it?" I asked.

"Of course not. Let it find you. Don't worry. I have it covered. One wrong move and I'll burn it to a stump."

She retreated behind me and I stepped out and braced myself directly in the path of the questing feeler. It found my foot first and I think it must have sensed heat for I saw the end of the feeler pucker and its fine hairs turned in on themselves like a sea anemone that is disturbed. After a few moments it opened again and the other feeler raced through the sky and touched my shoulder. Inside my survival suit I could hardly feel anything. I watched the feelers move. They could have been dusting cobwebs. The ant explored my helmet and shoulders and legs and outstretched arm which held my pistol. I was half afraid that the gentle pressure might make me fire inadvertently. But there was no way I was going to shift my aim from the pleated fold between the white bulbs of its eyes.

I do not know for how long I had to endure its tapping, but finally it withdrew its feelers and squatted with them pointing straight up into the air. It worked its mandibles back and forth slowly, nipping the air. I had the impression it was ruminating. I wonder if it had any sense of the danger that surrounded it as it sat quietly. Just one quick move and I think Ariadne and I would have fired together.

And of course, when it did move, both of us were caught off guard. It straightened its legs lifting its abdomen high and it banged its feelers together with an audible snap. Immediately the small ants scattered. Most ran into the fields; some scrabbled at the earth rampart and tumbled back unable to find purchase; a few ran directly into the sea where waiting jaws received them; one or two ran at our ship and tried to bite it. So that there would be no misunderstanding we burned them, scything through the narrow necks that joined the head to the alitrunk. They dropped and kicked and lay still.

When all the small ants were gone the great white ant began

91

to walk stiffly backwards with its feelers weaving patterns in the air. It dug its feet into the ground and began to climb. When it was halfway up to the dark hole on the top of the rampart it stopped.

"It wants me to go with it."

"Yes. I don't think you should. I don't trust it."

"Don't worry. Nor do I."

"Well what then?"

We stood in indecision for several minutes during which time the white ant became very agitated and beat its feelers on the hillside. Two more white ants struggled out of the hole above it and reached down with their antennae until they were all joined.

"Got it," said Ariadne. "They're trying to communicate. They've joined forces. They're trying to communicate with us, control us the same way they control the dark ants. Can you feel anything?"

I thought. I wondered. I tried to imagine what an ant thought would be like in the mind of a human. But there was nothing, or at most a mild revulsion. "Well, they're not communicating with me. I can see them and smell them and that's all."

Ariadne nodded. "Me too."

At the top of the rampart the ants continued their dance.

"Do you think the Worm would reach up there?" I asked.

"No. What are you thinking?"

"I'm thinking we've got to make a move. I'm thinking I'd better follow them. But I want the ship right behind me."

"What!"

"Inside the hill are tunnels and caverns. No doubt we'll cause a lot of damage. But I'm not walking in there alone. We'll cut a hole in the side of their hill and then move in. I'll walk in front of the Worm. You guide the ship."

"What if the whole hill caves in? We'd be buried."

"I think we could dig our way out. But do you have a better plan?"

Ariadne was silent. "OK. Well, let's give it a go."

*

Our ships are not built for warfare and we carry few guns. Our weapons are strictly defensive. We have a dab ray generator for shifting small asteroids; a few bombs; a small particle cannon and sundry handguns. We also possess two of the most powerful generators ever developed which together can lift us smoothly from a 3g world. On balance, not having seen any advanced technology on Jeupardi, I felt we had the advantage.

I closed and secured the front opening. Then I lined up the dab ray on a point about a third of the way up the hill. Through the view-screen I watched the white ants dance and scramble back inside their hole when I applied mild heat.

You must understand, I had no desire to hurt the giant ants. The imperative acting upon me then was to find the Pioneer and bring her back. All our ethical drives stemmed from that one simple order. Were I again on Jeupardi, feeling as I do now, I wonder what I would do.

The dab ray works in pulses which eventually shake matter to dust. Heat is an unavoidable by-product. Ariadne and I watched as the small circle of hillside began to waver and puffs of smoke erupted into the air. The earth burned and blackened. The small stones began to glow a muddy red. Sparks showered upwards as the deeper rocks cracked and splintered.

Suddenly half the hillside gave way and tumbled in an avalanche. The small stones and soil swept down in waves and covered the front of our ship. When the dust cleared we could see a vast cavern. A great white ant which must have been sheltering behind the rock wall tumbled forwards in a confusion of legs and feelers. We saw it vaporized as it entered the field of the dab ray which was now focused on emptiness.

I cut the ray and watched. Inside the cavern there was no movement.

"We've been lucky," said Ariadne, "I thought we would have to burn our way in for hours. That must be one of the main chambers."

We waited while the rocks cooled and then fed power to the

93

cupped fins that run beneath our ship. The ship lifted slightly, lurched as it established equilibrium and then began to crawl into the dark opening.

In front of us and curving down to the left was a long passage. Its sides were glossy and smooth where the bodies of countless ants had rubbed against it. Waiting for us, its abdomen raised and its mandibles open, was a giant white ant.

Whether this was one of the ants we had seen on the upper ramparts I could not tell. But its size within the confines of the passage was daunting. Ariadne switched on our lights and the ant stared into their brilliance without flinching. The light had one curious effect. The ant's skin was translucent and we could see through to the cartilage which supported its strong muscles. We could see the glands like veined shadows through which it secreted. The beast was quite magnificent and I found my attention held by it as we trundled close.

We bumped its feelers which were thrust out straight in front of it and the creature reared and placed its forelegs on the front of our ship.

Ariadne brought the ship to a halt. We were almost entirely within the cavern. The giant ant seemed to be waiting for something. For five minutes or so it stood like a creature made from glass and then it slowly lowered its gaster until it was turned under its legs. It loosed a secretion which spattered the front of the ship where the Worm door opens.

Then it stepped delicately back, turned and walked slowly down the tunnel into the earth.

Ariadne and I held a brief conference. We decided to bring the ship to full alert. The computers chattered and blinked to one another, estimating the relative density of the surrounding material, creating an echo graph of the chambers and tunnels, calculating the odds of our survival if the roof should suddenly cave in. It was not a comforting picture, but not without hope either. Those of our sensors which could be withdrawn into our ship were retracted. Those which would be scraped away as we

94

moved through the tunnel were isolated and their functions redeployed.

"They're enjoying this," said Ariadne, referring to the computers as the spaceship transformed itself into a mole.

"Remember," I said, "that we don't even know whether Pioneer Jinks is down there. We may be on this planet for years delving into all the hills."

"She's down there. This will be one of the greatest rescues of all time. I know it."

I kept the rest of my doubts to myself.

Eventually when the navigation computers were ready we began to inch forwards. Our ship was at least four times longer than any of the white ants which we had seen and possessed none of their flexibility. The dab ray, boosted to maximum power, shaved the tunnel walls widening the passage so that we could manoeuvre. Behind us, keeping a respectful distance, came thousands of the small dark ants.

The cavern did not grow narrower but twisted downwards. We passed side channels and entered high domed chambers where piles of rotting vegetation were heaped up against the walls. Once or twice we saw white ants which had climbed up the walls and now hung suspended above us, their long feelers trailing down and brushing over us.

The rotting vegetation over which scurried worker ants was a slippery mulch and once we came to a halt unable to find purchase until we had dug down to solid rock. Heaps of decaying leaves tumbled down on to us. The dab ray burned a path and filled the cavern with opaque steam.

Finally though the tunnel levelled and after a few more twists we came to a majestic cavern. It was natural, not ant-made, and long heavy stalagmites joined the floor to the roof like columns of frozen lather. We crunched over the rock and came to a halt half submerged in a pool of black water.

The lights from our ship played round the walls. There were white ants everywhere. Nets in which were gathered clusters of pale, watery-looking eggs hung down from the roof. We watched one of the white ants tending the eggs. It extruded a glossy cord from its gaster and attached the cord to the roof. Other ants joined it and wove a web. A pale maggot squirmed into the net and began laying eggs.

"Life continues," observed Ariadne, "despite us."

Curiously, that gave me hope. "You know, the only ants that have attacked us are the dark ones, the small ones on the surface. And their attack was a mindless reflex," I said. "I doubt if they could stop themselves attacking us, even if they had wanted to."

Ariadne sniffed. "I still don't trust them. I can't understand them."

And that of course was the truth.

"Come on, we're supposed to be finding Pioneer Jinks aren't we? Well, let's find her and get the hell out of here. I'm starting to feel this place is like a tomb."

Our lights continued playing round the walls but there was nothing to be seen except the festoons of eggs and the attendant white ants.

One white ant, perhaps the one we had been following when we entered the cavern, stepped down to us and rapped on the ship with its antennae. Our ship growled and scrabbled but was unable to move forwards. The ant moved away up the rock face to a natural fissure and there secured itself and its feelers whipped in the air. I had the foolish impression that it was beckoning us.

Our ship stopped lurching and churning the water and the computers started to chatter. Ariadne attended to them while I kept my eye on the giant ant. After a few moments she rejoined me. "They say there is no cause for alarm. They can get us out, but if they activate the main drive to lift us, the temperature in here – " she gestured out to the cavern – "will go up to about 1,000 degrees. Do we want that?"

"That will kill the Pioneer if she is near here."

"Yes. That is why they have delayed."

"Tell them to hold. I'm going out to take a look."

"Angelo – "

96

"I'll use the Worm to get as high as I can. You see where that ant is now, up on that ledge. I'll go up there first. Don't worry. I'll carry the cannon with me. If one of them comes close I'll stunt its antennae. You take care of the rest."

Ariadne looked at me strangely, her head on one side and her dark curls tumbling over her shoulder. "Are you sure they aren't getting to you? That's probably just what they want."

I shrugged. "Maybe. Maybe not. Who can tell with creatures like these? Perhaps we are attributing them with too much cunning. Are there any signs of the Pioneer?"

Ariadne moved back to the computers.

In front of me the large white ant continued its waving while high above a team of ants calmly continued weaving.

"They say the life patterns are very confused as there is so much going on in here, but, yes, there are different rhythms, there is something that could be a heartbeat, but it is very slow. They can not tell whether it is human or not."

"What's its focus?"

"Up there where your pet ant is. Seems like there's a chamber up there. Very smooth. Water-formed. Many ants moving. They can't tell much more."

"So I'll go and take a look."

I checked my survival suit and helmet. I strapped an auxiliary power pack on to my shoulders and then hoisted the cannon into its special harness. At maximum power the cannon could generate a particle beam which could shred just about anything within its range. Normally the cannon are used at low power to scale crustacea and plants off the shell of our ship after a long period on land or in the sea. But they could be a most fierce weapon.

Ariadne got the Worm working. It flexed and rose from the water and began to nose its way up the stone walls. It reached the lip of the fissure and snaked over. The ant retreated before it. No doubt it had never encountered an antenna quite so long and hard.

The Worm reached its full extension well over the edge of

97

the fissure and there it locked and settled. I began to climb inside it, stepping up its segments, leaning forwards to compensate for the weight of the cannon. Ariadne was close behind me. At the top we came to the last airlock door . . . I hesitated before pressing the switch which would open the door to the outside.

Ariadne touched my helmet and her fingers were crossed. Her voice boomed loud in my ears. "Take care, Angelo."

"Keep me covered."

"I will. Just give me time to get back down to the controls." She began to climb back down.

"And Ariadne, one thing. If anything happens, sever contact with the Worm. Don't be heroic. Look after – "

"Oh shut up. If anything happens to you I'll come out firing even if I bring the roof down."

There we are. I remember that conversation. I remember thinking that that was no way for a Pioneer Rescuer to talk. Perhaps in some ways Ariadne was in advance of me in her emotions if not in her understanding. When I look back there are so many clues to our present state that I wonder I never saw them before.

I waited while Ariadne retreated down the Worm and when I next heard her voice telling me that she was sitting in front of the dab ray controls, I pressed the release switch. The door slid open and I stared out into greyness. The giant ant was a long way in front of me. Looking back I could see the long silver tube of the Worm where it curved down to our ship. The lights which blazed from our ship turned everything to black and white.

I switched on my body lights and stepped over the rim of the Worm. In front of me the shadows reared. I found myself on a narrow pathway which sloped gently downwards into darkness. It was a gallery and the wall on my right was smooth and rippled, a sure sign that water had once flowed here. Above me stalactites hung down and from their tips dripped water

98

which dribbled away in a steady cataract down to the chamber floor.

Far in front of me the ant waited, forced almost down on to its knees by the low ceiling.

Holding the cannon firmly I advanced towards the ant and it retreated before me. It backed into a wide high chamber and there waited for me.

"Ariadne, I'm on a ledge and there's a chamber beyond. Come to the top of the Worm but stay inside. Put the computers on automatic."

"Yes boss."

The next time she spoke she was close behind me standing in the doorway of the Worm.

I moved on. The gallery sloped downwards and opened like a funnel into the chamber. The white ant continued to retreat keeping about fifty yards from me. I was aware of a misty phosphorescence about me and switched out my lights. Everything became a ghostly green. I have seen such before. Millions of tiny insects, clustered on the walls and roof, were shining.

I walked on carefully. In front of me the ant rounded a turning and all I could see were the tips of its feelers glimmering in the soft light.

I switched my lights on again. I had no desire to be caught in an ambush. I tuned the cannon to low power and scorched the feelers and saw them withdraw instantly.

Cautiously I worked round the corner and found myself facing a pink-grey boulder.

It was alive.

The ant had withdrawn, but I was hardly concerned with it anymore, for as I moved round the boulder I became aware of human features on it. There were eyes which blinked and stared up into the darkness. The mouth and nose had grown together and the teeth had grown outwards. They had become crude mandibles and even as I watched they opened sideways and then sliced together again.

I turned and as I did so my lights travelled down the body to reveal a vast and bloated giant. It lay on its back. The arms had

99

not grown and were little more than frills stuck on to the creature's sides. But the stomach was an open wound. As I watched, the giant white ant stepped up on to the body and dipped its head into the stomach. It appeared to drink. I walked beside the torso and found that the legs were as stunted as the arms. They looked silly and pathetic, dangling down from the bloated buttocks.

Other ants were in attendance and they paid no attention to me. They wandered over the body, cleaning its wastes, nibbling at the creases in its skin, and carrying balls of food up to its mouth.

I could not see into the stomach and I did not want to.

I had found Pioneer Jinks and I could guess the rest.

The ant which had led us down into these catacombs reared up on the chest and watched me as I made my way back towards the head. I kept it in the cross-hairs of the cannon but it did not seem in any mood to attack. After eating it seemed drugged and its feelers drooped, lying along the chest and over the shoulders.

I came to the head and was horrified when the eyes (I presume both of them) turned down to me and stared sightlessly through me. The look could have been one of suffering. I could have fired with the cannon, but I didn't.

Instead I hurried round the vast head and entered the gallery which led back to the Worm.

Minutes later I was back inside our ship and we were grinding our way back up the twisting path towards the hole in the hillside. Ariadne had a hundred questions, but I could answer none of them. It was not until we had lifted off and were back in the clean darkness of space above the planet that I could begin to speak.

"The true alien is unknowable. I can no more put myself in the ant mind than it can in mine. I hold on to the fact that in leading us down into the cavern, the giant white ant was trying to show us something. Perhaps it was saying, 'Look to what good use we have put your fellow.' Perhaps it thought that when we saw how useful Pioneer Jinks was that we would offer ourselves. Perhaps it thought that we were another gift from a friendly heaven, or providence, or whatever. But it didn't want *us* to die anymore than it wanted Jinks to die."

"Perhaps by showing us that Jinks was still alive it was trying to buy us off from killing all the worker ants," said Ariadne.

"Perhaps. But I doubt that," I replied. "I don't think death enters into their way of looking at things, anymore than we think about the dead cells we slough off when we scratch our heads."

Ariadne was silent for a while and then she shuddered. "Poor Jinks. How long has she been suffering?"

"A long time. But I don't think she was hurting. My guess is that she had tried to adapt . . . tried to become one of them . . . tried to become their leader. Isn't that what the Pioneers were supposed to do when they encountered an alien population? Perhaps she succeeded. Her juices obviously provided most excellent food."

"Don't."

"That has to be faced."

"No it doesn't. Be careful, Angelo. Morality stretched too widely becomes no morality. Do not forget that we are grown from human stock. That defines our humanity."

"But . . ."

"But what? If you don't agree then go down there and join Jinks. Because that is the only way the ants will accept you."

We fell silent. Eventually Ariadne stood up and dug her fingers into my fur. "Something in you admires them, doesn't it? You are too much in love with absolutes. How long do you think it would take us to domesticate an ant? Eh? I'll tell you. About as long as it would take them to allow us to live in peace and grow to a ripe old age."

I sighed. "Perhaps you are right."

"Perhaps. Perhaps. Perhaps, perhaps."

That made me laugh. "You *are* right."

"But we still have one question." Ariadne was very serious

101

and held me by both ears while she stared into my face. "What do we do about Pioneer Jinks?"

"I don't know."

"I do. We are going to kill her. In this I speak as a woman."

"Perhaps she is happy."

Ariadne hit me. It was a stinging blow jabbed from close quarters with a balled fist. It tore my lips against my teeth. I tasted blood.

"We are going to kill her."

We made three passes over the island to make sure that we had the height and speed right. Then, on the fourth pass, we opened the lower cargo bays where we would normally have stored the Pioneer's possessions and dropped the first of our bombs. It detonated above the hill and created a pillar of dust which rose in a mushroom cloud into the sky. Our second bomb dug into the hill creating a crater.

And when the smoke and dust had cleared we dropped our third bomb which turned the crater into a bubbling bed of lava. Almost the entire island sank and the waves washed over the great stain.

"And what do the white ants think of us now?" asked Ariadne as we swung into higher orbit and prepared to depart. "Perhaps they admire us."

We concocted our story while getting ready for the long sleep before the leap for home. As far as the computers were concerned we had done everything we could to find the Pioneer including placing ourselves in considerable danger. We explained the use of the bombs as a prophylactic measure, but really we had no need to be cautious. Few questions were asked.

Once it was certain that Pioneer Jinks was dead, Ariadne relaxed. She seemed to have more time for speculative thinking. We realized how little we had really accomplished. We should have found out exactly what was going on down there. Why had Pioneer Jinks grown into an almighty torso? Had she

102

tried to adapt? My own belief was that she had become a food factory for the ants. I even speculated that the white ants had gained their dominance from drinking her secretions. Maybe, as Ariadne said, such questions had no answer, though stranger things have been known.

But there we are. Jeupardi grew smaller day by day until it was just another point of bright light among many others.

We were younger then. In my own mind I have no doubt that that planet is still out there somewhere and that life continues pretty much as it always has. Perhaps there is one species of giant white ant less in the universe.

Perhaps not.

But we shall never go back to find out. Of that I am sure.

6

There, the story of Jeupardi is told. And I am surprised that it has taken me so long. The weeks have sped past and I have to confess that I have been very slow and have found the telling difficult. I noticed that I would rather do anything than sit down and face the facts of those days.

I have swum every day. I have worked in the gym until I could only crawl to bed. But I am glad to report that my fur is growing back thicker than ever. My claw is slow. I have had to treat it several times. After the clipping it became septic and I lost one whole nail. Now I think all is well.

Ariadne is regaining her beauty. I spend part of each day with her, looking down into the tank where she sleeps. Her hair has grown back and is curly but it has changed colour and she will wake up to find herself more ginger than black. What she will make of that I do not know. Already she is rising.

Chrono tells me that Pioneer Murray has been a great success. I can believe that. He is cooperating with the genetic regeneration programme. Maybe he wants to father a whole new generation. Time will tell. Chrono informs me that there has been such optimism before.

The Pioneer Programme has gone into recess for the time being, it seems. I think the space authorities are waiting to see how things work out with Pioneer Murray before sending any more of us out into space. It seems that Kingi and Elf's ship is a write-off. They suffered damage on a high gravity planet while rescuing Pioneer Olympia. They were lucky to arrive home in one piece. At the present rate of progress I think it will be several years before a new ship can be commissioned.

New ship. There are no new ships. What I mean is that one of the old ships from the moon fleet will have to be refurbished.

104

Raven and Lattisbourne have been sent to the Far North on a reclamation survey. Apparently their ship was not severely damaged and they are now in the Far North, cruising the coasts of Old Europe, looking for surviving pockets of life. I have heard it is very beautiful there now with miles of dark forests. But I doubt they will find civilization such as we understand it. There have been no lights seen in Old Europe for several hundred years. Kingi and Elf are with them as co-workers.

Larum and Silver have been sent to the southern ice continent. They are investigating an old krill farm. No word has been heard from them for some months.

Of all our friends only Bonniface and Amsterdame are still at the Pioneer Centre on Aotearoa. They and some of the old Pioneers are planning a party for us. The message they sent to us is, "Come on down. The water is lovely." I can believe them. No doubt they are keeping themselves fit in the hot pools.

7

Today I took a trip outside.

During yesterday I became aware of a bumping and scraping along our hull. Outside I found the cause. We have attracted a lot of rubbish that has been ditched in space over the years. Most of it is small: buttons, broken plastic containers, sani-bags and the like. But there was an old spacesuit of the type used many hundreds of years ago. How that came to be outside I don't know. I thought at first it was occupied. But no, it was unzipped and empty. It must have been bumping round us for a few weeks as it was scratched and part of its harness was tangled in one of the antennae.

I cut it adrift and pushed it away into space. It tumbled away from me like a stiff toy. God knows where it will end up. In the sun eventually, I suppose.

Whatever became of that plan to shoot all our rubbish into the sun?

Anyway, I busied myself for several hours, catching rubbish. Most of it I bagged and threw away in the general direction of the moon.

I found a lot of dust and grit which held to us like iron filings on a magnet. It suddenly occurred to me that much of this dust may have come from the time that Lindis and Tui crashed. A crash like that would have sent a lot of material into space to drift round the moon for centuries before settling again like a grey pall. I have collected a bag of the dust and I shall bury that when we get back to Earth. I also found a white pebble shaped like a triangle. I shall make that into a pendant and give it to Ariadne. A memento of Tui.

8

Chrono tells me that he has monitored a communication that indicates our quarantine is to be lifted on schedule. A medical team will dock with us in a few days.

They will not shave me again. I have removed a few components from the auto-nurse. I shall refuse to move from our sleeping area. I shall give them a bag of faeces and some urine in a vacuum bottle. I'll even give them a few hairs from my head. But if they want to examine me whole, they'll have to kill me.

Ariadne is a worry. She is not awake yet. I am doing what I can to speed her revival.

If worst comes to worst I shall hold her with me in our sleeping bay. I will send them to inspect her long-sleep chamber. All her records will be there. If they are true medical people they will know that nothing can survive the long sleep except the organism that enters the long sleep. They can check the filters if they think I am wrong.

I will not pick a fight unless that is the last option. Chrono has advised me. And I very much want to stand on Earth again.

One last thing, I plan to hide this book of writing where no one will find it.

So, when and if I write again, we shall be bound for Earth. Either that or the pages will scatter in space to join the rest of the debris.

9

The medicos are come and gone. They didn't even want to examine us. They accepted my gifts and thanked me for my thoughtfulness. They were suspiciously polite in comparison with the first visit. I do not know what to make of it.

One of them said to me (a woman, it was), "You have done a great service to Earth in bringing Pioneer Murray back."

Well. Well.

I pressed her for more information but a technician with ANAESTHETIST stencilled on the top of his contact helmet bundled her out of the way.

They were gone within an hour of entering our ship and now we are free to drop down to Earth. Already it is larger in our view-screen.

Ariadne likes her red hair. She is dozy and silly, but she wears my little white stone between her breasts. She talks as though six months ago were only yesterday and that our ordeal with the contact crew were only a nightmare.

I think that the short sleep she has experienced is more disorienting than the leap which takes generations. She also wants to know whether I like her red hair. I have told her I do. And now she wants to read what I have been writing. I wonder what she will make of my tale about Jeupardi? I shall take charge of the landing and she can read at her leisure.

> Angelo you bastard,
> I love you.
> Ariadne

10

Ariadne is a woman of few words when it comes to writing. But what she does say has an enormous power. I wonder what her account would sound like if she were writing and not me. Like messages on a telegraph, I think.

Writing is far from her mind at present. She is asleep at last. I look at her, shivering under sacks and rolled up into a tight little ball to conserve her warmth. And I wonder, what has happened to this sad old ball, the Earth?

What I am about at present seems to me rather silly. I can't sleep. I am too cold, despite my furry insulation. So I am sitting on the floor of an overland transit with my back braced against the wall in the direction of our travel. Above me there is a bare light bulb in an iron-mesh cage which casts a dismal watery light. I have my book and pencil though I can hardly hold them. There is a window broken and through this whistles a bitter wind. Ice has formed on the inside of the glass. A thin white carpet of snow fans out from the broken window across the transit floor and has formed a little bank against my leg. Ariadne is tucked beside me on the other side. Her hands are inside my clothes, taking what they can of my body heat. But it is not enough. She sleeps, thank God. But she shivers and mutters to herself.

Indignity on indignity. We risk everything and are treated worse than cattle. Cattle would at least have straw to lie in.

Anyway. I don't think I have strength for a diatribe. I want simply to set down the details of our homecoming to Earth, then perhaps I can sleep. It has been so different to other arrivals.

We entered Earth atmosphere above Africa. Fire blazed round us as we burned away all the crap stuck to our spaceship. Then our engines cut in and slowed our descent. We glided sedately round the Earth, gradually losing altitude until we could see the peaks of the Andes and the mottled blue of the Pacific and a great storm that was hammering at the coasts of Old Japan.

Soon there was just blueness racing by beneath and a hard horizon in front. We passed over islands fringed with white breakers and then in front I saw the dark green, almost black, hills of Aotearoa.

They leaped towards us. We described a great arc, shearing the air above Rotorua and then plunging south. We would have been heard as great thunder and I am sure that Bonniface and Amsterdame reared up from their hot pools and waved to us as we roared above leaving a clear white line in the sky.

We registered the Taranaki beacon. The sky was clear and we could see every detail of the snow-covered shoulders of the old volcano. Wisps of steam rose from its crater and drifted over the deep green of the forests which stretched from the coast right to the heart of the land.

We followed the coast south, holding a steady controlled path until we could see the mountains of the South Island. Then we dipped low and passed over the abandoned city of Wellington.

There was once a great city here but now all that can be seen are a few towers sticking up through the dense dark bush.

Like so many cities round the world, Wellington was destroyed by the storms and tidal waves which battered the Earth after the Catastrophe. Now nature has reclaimed the land. Where there was once a bay there is now just a large muddy estuary where millions of birds paddle.

We flew over the mud flats and a low range of hills called the Rimutakas and finally made our landing at Master Town Space Station.

There was no one to welcome us.

Rain sizzled about us as we settled on to a vast concrete platform of the space station. We could not see the hills for the low billowing banks of mist. The grey curved roofs of the space hangar merged with the clouds.

I noticed immediately that the station was in a dismal state of repair compared with the last time I had seen it. Grass sprouted from cracks in the concrete. Most of the low buildings which had once housed the administrative staff were either razed to the ground or had collapsed. I remembered a garden of flowers which ran beside the main runway. That whole area was now a bowed forest of manuka trees. There were a few new buildings, domes mainly, but in none of their windows could I see lights shining.

Ariadne joined me at the view-port and we stood looking out waiting for something to happen. Finally there was movement in the dark mouth of the hangar. A low multi-wheeled cable tractor emerged and took charge of our ship and towed us slowly on to the eight sets of rails which curve into the hangar. I tried to make radio contact but no one was at home apparently. On earlier landings we have usually been asked to assist the final docking by using our tread engines to give greater impetus. Now, it seemed they wanted to use the cable tractor alone and we saw it labour and strain as it heaved our bulk into alignment.

Well, they could have it their own way. No one had informed me there was a change in procedure.

We could not see the driver of the tractor. Previously there would have been hundreds of people milling about calling orders into small transceivers. The arrival of a starship was a great occasion.

"Where is everyone?" asked Ariadne.

I shrugged, already suspicious. "Perhaps they've been told not to make us welcome."

"But why?"

Again I shrugged. "Who knows? Maybe we should contact the Space Council. Perhaps they have given orders. We have not been made welcome anywhere, so far."

Inch by painful inch we were towed into the hangar and positioned beside a great grey and black ship which we recognized as belonging to Bonniface and Amsterdame. Plates had been stripped from the side of it and its Worm lay extended on the ground like a dead silver snake. The main electrical connections were exposed like tufts of hair.

Only when we had stopped and all our systems had been closed down did we see our first human.

He came marching along a high gangway at the level of our upper airlock. When he activated the external control switch we were already waiting for him.

I have met such officials before. They speak like overseers and do not look at you but through you. He held a clipboard. Positioned in front of his lips was a pencil-thin microphone.

"Angelo and Ariadne?" he asked.

"Yes. Returning from the rescue of Pioneer Murray."

"I see. And where is your Pioneer?"

This question amazed both of us. "He . . . er . . . Well, he was off-loaded while we were in moon orbit. The Space Council took charge of him."

"Really?"

"Yes, really."

"Well, I was not informed. Do you have a receipt?"

Ariadne looked at me and then at the official. "You are being silly," she said. "If you don't believe us then contact the Space Council on the moon yourself. They took him from us and placed us in quarantine."

He whispered into his microphone and we could not hear what he said. He made some brief notes. "Then why were you delayed?" he asked, speaking between us as though to some third person.

"Because we were in quarantine," I answered. "Have you not been in contact with the Space Council?" He did not answer this question.

"Have you any damage to report?"

"Nothing significant," answered Ariadne.

"And *we* are both well," I added making my emphasis as ironic as possible. It washed over him.

"You will both remain aboard your ship until primary

112

detoxification has been completed. Then, when you receive the order, you will be free to disembark."

He spoke into his microphone again and immediately figures in white contact suits, carrying canisters on their backs and portable spray hoses, appeared on the gangway and entered our ship. We let them pass.

When the detoxification team got to work the official departed with no more than a curt nod to both of us.

A doctor arrived and I treated him with caution but all he was interested in was our gums and whether either of us had vomited blood. I diagnosed that his examination was more for form's sake than any real attempt to discover whether we were ill. But he at least was friendlier than the official who had greeted us.

The ship was closed again and we found ourselves alone. Through the view-screen I could see a small team of men who climbed about on the outside of our ship. What they were trying to do I could not guess but I was suspicious. I climbed back up to the control room and there spent a few minutes of consultation with the main systems computer. I set it on alert. I had never had to do this while on Earth before. I gave it quite simple instructions that no part of the ship was to be opened except by Ariadne or me, after I had closed it down.

Then we sat and waited. We waited while the dreary day wore on. Outside there was no movement. I thought we had been forgotten.

"They're probably checking with Moon Base," said Ariadne when she saw how impatient I was, striding up and down in our small kitchen.

"It doesn't take all day to check with Moon Base," I replied. "I think they are up to something."

Whether they were up to something or not I will never know.

Night fell and with it came wind and rain. We ate a meal. We looked out into the dark hangar lit by only a few lights.

"Remember how it used to be," said Ariadne. "Bands playing. People wanting to touch the ship. People wanting to

113

have their photographs taken with us in the picture. Women
with – ”

“Sh . . .”

“Sh what?” she whispered.

“There’s someone just opened the upper airlock.” Silently I
crossed to the cubicle where we keep our survival suits and
removed my small stun pistol.

“Angelo.”

I reached in and removed her gun and threw it to her.
“Better safe – sh. Listen.”

We could hear someone whistling. Whoever it was was not
making any attempt to hide himself. He came clattering down
the gangway from the upper levels in iron-shod boots. He was
a big human with curly blond hair and freckles. When he saw
us he opened his mouth in surprise and then grinned at us
revealing gap-toothed teeth.

“Hey, sorry. Didn’t know you was still here. Thought you’d
gone hours ago. You must be Angelo and Ariadne, right?
Strum me pink. First time I’ve ever met real Pioneer hunters.
Hey, is that thing real?” He pointed to my claw and I flexed it.

“Real,” I said.

“Wow.”

The man was no threat and neither Ariadne nor I let him see
the guns we were carrying. “And who are you?” I asked.

“Pedro,” he said. “I look after the ’ponics tanks. Me and my
kid brother. Have you seen him?”

“We’ve seen no one.”

“Well you can’t miss him. Mind if I get to work?”

We didn’t mind. We watched him clean the filters and check
the fluid levels and rub the leaves of plants between his thumb
and finger. He whistled as he worked.

Finally Ariadne said, “Well, I’m going to get changed. I
think it is time we went outside, orders or not.” Pedro watched
her go with an appreciative look in his eye which I recognized.

“Is anything happening outside?” I asked.

“Strum no. Quiet as the grave. They’ve all gone to the
meeting.”

114

"What meeting?"

"Fertility exercises," he said, as though I should have known.

"And why aren't you there?"

"I'm colour blind. Anyway, they won't let me in. They think my spunk's diseased. Any kids of mine might turn out like Kier. I failed the purity rites."

None of this made any sense to me. "Would you like to go to the . . . er . . . fertility exercises?"

He looked at me strangely. "Strum yes. Any chance to get out of a hole like this. But the quota's already full. Say, how long have you been away?"

"Over a hundred of your years."

His face dropped open vacantly. "Strum me . . . How'd you manage that?"

I didn't try to explain. "Your grandfather or great-grandfather may have seen us depart. We brought back a Pioneer. Do you know what a Pioneer is?"

"Yep," he said, and then quoted: "'Pioneers carry the spirit of the old world. Pioneers are going to save the world.'"

"Something like that," I said, thinking of Pioneer Murray.

"Have you brought lots of Pioneers back?"

"Quite a few."

"You must be pretty old then?"

I nodded, "Pretty old. But it doesn't work like that."

He nodded to the door through which Ariadne had departed. "She doesn't look too old."

I shrugged. "She is the same age as me," I said.

"You got children?" he asked.

"No," I said, "We can't – "

"Naw," he said before I could finish. "Kids don't get made anymore, do they. Least not down here."

At that moment Ariadne re-entered. She had changed into the kind of clothes we used to wear when we returned. Soft clothes with loose pleats. She had added make-up to her eyes which made them seem clearer and more widespread. It was a style from the time of our first departure . . . a style that had

115

disappeared from the face of the Earth centuries ago. There was perfume too.

Pedro took her presence like a physical assault. His eyes said everything.

This may seem strange but I felt sorry for him. It came as an awful realization to me that this young man had never looked on a woman in the simple richness of her womanhood.

"Well," said Ariadne, pleased by his obvious attention, "shall we go?"

We climbed up through the ship. At one place Pedro reached out and touched Ariadne's hair. He touched it as gently as though he was touching something spun from fine glass threads. Ariadne had taken all the words out of him.

We climbed on and I made sure that all the doors we did not want opening were closed and locked and registered by the system computer.

Waiting for us at the airlock door was a young boy with a face as pale as ivory and cropped white hair. His eyes were vacant and pinkish. He cringed away from us as though afraid he was going to be kicked.

"This is my brother," said Pedro. "This is Kier. Now do you see why I can't go to the fertility meeting?"

Outside I made sure that all the major safety docking procedures had been observed. Thick black cables festooned down from the high roof and were joined to key points on our ship. Blue safety lights glowed dully.

I looked across at Bonniface and Amsterdame's ship. Pedro followed my gaze. "That ship'll be going nowhere in a long time," he said. "Can't get the parts. All the spares are held on the moon. There's been orders in for months. We keep the old 'ponics working though, don't we?" he said to the boy called Kier and ruffled his hair. The boy did not reply.

We climbed down from our ship. Pedro helped Ariadne every step of the way. On an impulse I scooped up Kier and set him on my shoulders and felt him grip grimly into the fur of my scalp as I swung out from the ship and climbed hand over claw down.

116

There was no one. No guards. No attendants.

When I stepped off the last rung and lifted Kier down I heard Ariadne describing to Pedro what it used to be like when a Pioneer Rescue Ship reached home.

". . . and there were flowers. Always plenty of flowers and women with baskets full of fresh fruit and vegetables and new bread. You see they knew we'd eaten nothing except hydroponics food for generations. . . . Nothing that had ripened in the true light of the sun."

Pedro bent down and whispered something to Kier and the small boy ran off into the darkness at the end of the hangar.

I think Pedro felt responsible for us. He guided us to a path which ran beside the ship and then through a small door in the side of the hangar which led to a covered walkway. The sides of the walkway were open and the wind carried the rain in wet gusts right across the path.

Ariadne was not dressed for such weather and the rain plastered the clothes against her. Pedro walked beside her, trying to protect her. I stumped along keeping a wary eye open for guards. I concealed my gun on the inside of my arm. I was indifferent to the rain.

We came to loose swing doors which led into a prefabricated building. This, as Pedro informed us, was the main transit shed. It was here that the magnetic shuttle from Auckland and Rotorua docked. Pedro consulted a timetable pinned to a wall. "Hey, there should be a shuttle here in five hours. You're in luck."

This transit shed was new to both of us. It was a bare, dirty, unpleasant room. Ariadne perched on a case in the corner and spread her skirts to dry while I tried to fit my frame into a low chair that was too small for me. . . . Pedro pottered about and eventually produced two beakers of tea which he offered to us with the same flourish as once people handed us champagne.

I watched the young man closely. "Aren't you afraid of us?" I asked as I took the tea carefully with my claw. "Since we returned, most people seem to treat us warily."

"Well you're just a . . ." Pedro seemed to be searching for

117

words. "You're just a clever monkey, aren't you? Big but harmless."

"And her?" I said nodding towards Ariadne.

He looked confused. "Well she's a . . . she's a woman, isn't she?"

I shook my head. "No. We're the same," I said. "Both adapted, despite appearances."

He couldn't accept this thought.

"Angelo," called Ariadne, "stop trying to confuse the boy."

He looked from one of us to the other. Me, ginger and giant and with a claw as big as his head. Ariadne, like a dream on legs. I watched him struggle.

"Oh hell," he said finally, "the world is crazy."

"What are your plans, Pedro?" asked Ariadne. "Do you intend to spend the rest of your life here looking after 'ponics tanks?"

"Strum no. The only thing that keeps me here is Kier. But he's growing up. When I get the chance I'll head north."

"And what will you do then?" This from me.

"I'll join one of the reclamation teams and go into the forbidden zones. They need strong men who can make the earth grow. I'd like to go to Old South America and start a family. My family came from there you know. I'd like to start a colony."

"But surely you need women for that?"

"Yes. But I hear there are fertile women over there. Women that the Moon Colony hasn't found or is afraid to touch."

"Why not just escape into the hills round here? Find yourself a girl and head out for the hills. It could be a good life."

"There are no girls. Not fertile ones anyway. Not for the likes of me. They're all up on the moon."

He said this without bitterness but with sad resignation. An acceptance of the way things were.

"Why are they on the moon?" I asked, making my question as quiet and as casual as I could.

"The Fertility Programme," he said. "Surely you've heard of

the Fertility Programme. It's been going since before I was born."

"We've been away a long time," said Ariadne.

The swing doors flapped and a gust of wind raised the dust on the floor as the young boy Kier elbowed his way in. He was carrying a box which he dumped down in front of Pedro. Then he withdrew into the shadows and looked at us with large eyes. On the top of the box were flowers: dried helichrysum and a daffodil or two. Underneath I could see apples and vegetables. Pedro picked up the flowers. He seemed suddenly uncertain of himself. "We couldn't get any bread. But I hope the veggies are all right. Kier's just picked them. We grow our own. They're all right." He looked at the flowers in his hand. "We grew these too. Hope you like them." He thrust them towards Ariadne and she took them graciously by the stems and sniffed them.

"I think they are lovely. Don't you, Angelo?" I nodded. "And thank you both for trying to make us feel welcome." Then she kissed Pedro who stood stiff, almost to attention, and Kier who tried to shuffle away and wiped the kiss off as soon as given. But the intention was clear.

Kier spoke for the first time. "Got to go. Got a sick horse to see to. Threw a shoe and cut its leg." He nodded to both of us and then shuffled away.

Was it my imagination, or was there a hint of a swagger there? I hoped so.

"He's growing up," said Pedro. "Getting to that awkward age. You know. Guess how old he is?"

Ariadne shrugged. "Nine," I said, genuinely guessing.

"Almost fourteen and a half. Doesn't look it does he?"

"No."

"But he feels it. You know."

Neither Ariadne nor I knew what to say. I felt that the tragedy of what had happened to the Earth during our absence was epitomized in the pale, diminutive figure of Kier.

"So, I'd better be getting along too. Things to do. Chicks to feed. You know?"

119

"What about your parents?" asked Ariadne. "Do you help them?"

"Gone," said Pedro. "They took Mum shortly after she gave birth to Kier. Dad split off up north looking for her. Both gone. We manage. Don't worry about us."

For the first time I could feel a brooding anger in him, but he smothered it quickly. "Shuttle'll be here soon. You shouldn't have to wait long. And don't worry about your ship. Kier and me'll see she's right. So." He looked at his feet. "Hooray, eh?"

And he was gone quickly.

Eating an apple in the soft light, Ariadne looked at me steadily. "Do you think the ship will be safe? Do you think those two can cope?"

"The ship'll be safe enough. If anyone tries to break in there they'll need a bloody clever can opener. And as for Kier and Pedro, I think they'll look after the hydroponics better than me."

"Pedro seems a nice boy."

"Yes."

"You don't sound so sure."

"Don't I? Well it's nothing to do with him. I think he is a nice boy, as you say, but he hasn't a clue what is happening. I just keep thinking about the past."

"Mmm. Well, things have certainly changed. Why didn't Chrono warn us?"

"I don't think even Chrono knows how clapped out everything is. His main contact is with Moon Base, remember."

"Even so. Fancy there not being any women down here any longer. Men without women go mad."

"Some do. Some find it a relief."

"Yah." She threw the apple core at me. "You wouldn't last a month without me."

"I lasted six months while you were sleeping. Best six months of my life. I was able to do some thinking."

"Yes, but you missed me. Go on. Admit it."

"Yes, I missed you. I thought of activating the clone. All

120

nice and firm and innocent. But then I thought that two of you would be too much to handle."

"She wouldn't be me." Ariadne spoke with absolute conviction. "She might look like me, but she wouldn't be me."

"No, I suppose not," I said. I lapsed into silence. I couldn't keep the banter going. I was too preoccupied with the Earth and what was going on.

Ariadne stood up and crossed to me and sat down on my knee. "Come on, Chimp. You look so sad sometimes."

"Do I? I don't mean to. It's just that . . . do you remember what Pedro called me? A clever monkey."

"He – "

"No, don't worry, I'm not insulted. He meant no harm. But that is all he saw. He never thought to ask how, or why. And sure as hell no one has taken the trouble to explain things to him. Once we were part of the great adventure. We brought the Pioneers back. We risked our lives. Now we are just part of the luggage. I tell you, the only reason that Pedro was friendly was because he was ignorant. He's a nice young man. But ignorant. He knows nothing of the wider causes. He looks at you and thinks, Yum, yum, a real woman."

"And what is wrong with that?"

"Nothing is wrong with that in one way. Very natural. Very human. But you are not a woman. You are something that was made. Like me. We are . . . something else."

"Where it counts I am a woman."

"Then show me. Show me this 'where it counts'." I paused, surprised at how angry I was becoming. "What, as a woman, do you think of this Fertility Programme?"

"I think it stinks."

"Well so do I. Humankind have given away their humanity. They are treating one another no better than rats."

The argument had suddenly petered out. I suppose I had half expected Ariadne to take the human side, and when she didn't I was lost for arguments.

"But I am still a woman," she said and clapped her hand over my mouth before I could reply. "Wait until we get to

Rotorua. I know you have lots of questions. But perhaps Bonniface and Amsterdame will be able to answer them."

"Perhaps they will." I was quieter. "But let me finish my thought, Ariadne. I am worried about us. I am worried about what the full-humans think of us. Think about Lindis and Tui. Think about Larum and Silver. What is happening? Being Pioneer Rescuers is one thing. Being sent out on senseless expeditions is another. Think what they did to us up there. You bald as a frog. Me like a plucked chicken. Don't be surprised if I'm angry and want to ask questions. I'd like to kick some heads about.

"We brought that sod Murray back. *We* did it. He's alive and sane and well and screwing himself crazy by the sound of it, and *we* made that possible."

"They don't do it that way. They use syringes and sterile crucibles."

"Don't bet on it. Any woman who thinks she has half a chance of being fertile will do anything to get a shot of old-time, pre-Catastrophe sperm. And you know as well as I do that Pioneer Murray has a good pedigree as far as genes are concerned and he's as randy as a goat. He's probably peddling himself on the black market and loving every minute of it."

"Hush, darling."

"No, I won't hush. If humankind is saved it will be because of us and Bonniface and Amsterdame and our dead friends Lindis and Tui. We saved the precious genes for them. We deserve more than to be cowering in a dirty broken-down reception area with a basket of fruit."

"We're not cowering."

"You know what I mean. Where's the sense? Where's the justice?"

"They deal just as coldly with their own kind."

"Yes. That worries me too. Who is *they*?"

"The Space Council, I suppose."

"I'd like to know. And what is the Space Council anyway? The great-great-great-great-great-grandchildren of those who were lucky enough to get off the Earth when the Catastrophe came. Hell they're probably as inbred as mice now."

"That was always the danger. And they saw it. Hence the Pioneer Programme."

"But it hasn't worked."

"Not till now. Not till Pioneer Murray."

"That remains to be proven."

"True."

"For all we know the future of the Earth may be in the hands of idiots. There's probably more good blood in that poor lad Kier."

"You know your fur is lovely and silky."

"Eh?"

"Finer than before they shaved you. And it smells nicer too."

"Ariadne!"

"Angelo, I don't want an argument, I want a rest. For a few months I just want to be me. I don't want to worry about the Space Council or who might or might not be running things or who is screwing what or how. I just want to be me. Savvy? Come on, have an apple and relax."

"I don't want an apple."

"You'll have a bloody apple whether you like it or not. Or shall I ram it down your throat, you mangy great ape?"

"*What!*"

We started to fight, rolling over and over. Ariadne fights dirty and you know where that leads.

My only worry was that Pedro might hear our commotion and come running to the door. But he didn't. And when we were finished and lying close, I found that I was relaxed and I ate an apple.

The doors at the end of the transit lounge slid open to reveal the cross-country transit rocking slightly on its supports. Ariadne didn't want to move so I picked her up bodily and then scooped up our bags and climbed aboard.

With a greaseless dry squealing the doors closed and the transit lurched and we were on our way.

*

So here we are now.

Writing has had a bad effect on me. I am angry again and have no way of venting my anger.

All I can do is cuddle close to Ariadne and try to sleep. My fur is stiff where it is frozen.

I cannot sleep. Sleep seems irrelevant. Time to sleep when I am basking in a hot pool with my own kind. There is a greyness at the windows. I have been writing a long time. I am stiff and need to stretch.

I have looked out of the window. I had to breathe on the panes to soften the frost before I could brush it away.

I looked out and a mountain stared back at me. Its shoulders were covered in snow except where rock falls showed like black veins. The presence of the mountain seemed to invade the cabin. There is no snow or rain. Just a clear milky light in which I can still see the stars flickering. The sun is rising but there is no warmth. The wind is like cold flame.

Ariadne is awake again. "Are we nearly there? I'm so cold. So cold. Warm me, Angelo."

I lie down beside her. "Not too far now," I say. "We're just passing Ruapehu. It'll be downhill soon and then there is a breakfast stop. I think. There always used to be a stop at Taupo."

"Uhuh. I wish I had a built-in fur coat like you."

"The mountain is magnificent."

"Uhuh. Give it my regards."

She sleeps again and I stretch out beside her. I will sleep now. The worst is past.

11

Let me get this down quickly. It says so much about the full-humans. Opposite me is a little old man whose eyes glitter with hatred. He holds his arm gingerly, for I think it is broken. I did that and I am not sorry. Beside me there lie the remains of a pistol.

That nasty bastard nearly killed me.

We must have come down from the mountains. I woke up when the transit changed lines. I had to blink for the sun was shining full on my face and when I looked away I could see black and silver and a hard blue sky.

The air didn't seem any warmer, but I saw beads of condensation forming on the windows and the ice patterns were fading.

We dropped down into the deep green and muddy crater of Taupo. There was once a lake here, but an eruption after the Catastrophe drained it and, where there had once been trout, lava had flowed. Now the land was settled again but all the vegetation looked young and tentative. This land is always shaking.

Ahead were lights. The transit jumped lines again and we glided down to ground level. We trundled into a small station. This used to be one of the main livestock terminals and, pens for cattle and sheep stretched on either side of the transit rails. We drew up to a small hut and I was relieved to see that smoke curled from an old, crooked chimney.

As soon as we stopped a door banged open and an old man with a beard that came down to his belt stepped over to the transit doors. He peered in at us through squinting eyes and then threw open the lock switch and the doors slid open.

"Are you alive or dead?" he called when I waved to him.

"Dead," I said, "or as near as makes no difference."

He cackled. "Aye, she was a hard one last night. There'll be lambs gone in the high country." He looked round the transit chamber. "Why didn't you turn the heating on?"

"Heating?" It was Ariadne's voice.

"Aye. When it's human cargo we usually put the heating on. There's a switch back of there."

The man must have been short-sighted. I saw him squint at me and then I must have come into focus for he backed away with his arms up in front of his face. "You're one of them," he said. "You're not human cargo."

"Yes, one of them," I said and tried to growl. I swung down from the transit. Ariadne followed me. If I'd had any wit in that cold dawn I'd have started to beat my chest. But all I could think of was warmth and breakfast.

We entered his small hut and the first thing I saw was a fire of pine cones which blazed brightly. On the table was a basket of eggs. A side of bacon, brown and withered from smoking, hung from the rafters.

"We want food," I said. "Bread, butter, honey, bacon, tea. Better, beer if you have it. All we've had is fruit and raw vegetables since we landed."

"It'll cost you."

It was Ariadne who growled. She stood up, brushed the palm of her hands down her smock, and seized a frying pan. She cut butter into the pan, broke eggs, hacked thick slices of bacon straight from the side, and tore bread into hunks. Within minutes the room was filled with a thick, sizzling, mouth-watering smell. She served the food straight on to plates and dumped one down in front of the old man who had set himself down at the large central table. "This is on the house," she said. "You can send the bill to the Space Council. They'll pay."

By the time we had finished eating, an old black kettle was piping steam and we made thick tea.

"Do you have cigars? Angelo likes cigars."

The old man fumbled about and finally produced a pipe which he filled with tobacco and offered to me. I lit it with a

126

spill from the fire and enjoyed my first taste of tobacco for well over a hundred years.

"Now, you tell us why you were so unfriendly," she said. "Kindness doesn't hurt, does it?"

The old man looked at the floor. "No," he said finally. "But we don't see many like you. The last ones smashed my hut. And . . ."

"And what?"

"Well, you're not natural are you? You bring disease. Everyone knows that. You're dangerous." This was directed at me. I sensed his anger and a certain excitement as he spoke. And there was something more. He was hiding something. The old fox had something under the table.

I acted by reflex and knocked the iron tea pot with the back of my fist, sending the contents in a wave across the table. He was distracted for an instant and that gave me time to move. I reached over the table and grabbed him by the shoulder and twisted.

The gun, for that was what he had been hiding, an ancient pistol, went off and the bullet shaved my leg under the table and dug into the wood of the floor. He did not have time to fire twice before I was on him and gripped his arm in my claw. He screamed, for I was not gentle. I shook his arm and the pistol clattered to the ground. Ariadne picked it up.

"Have you any more tricks?"

"No."

"I think I'll dip your head in the fire just to make sure," said I.

"No. I haven't. I haven't – "

But I singed the hairs on his head all the same and then dropped him by the fireplace where he lay moaning and cradling his arm.

"Welcome home," I said to Ariadne.

So there we are. After the rudeness of officials we have the violence of a frightened man.

Ariadne dressed the thin wound on my leg and then tied the

127

man's arm in a splint. She was gentle. I was dangerous. I took his pistol in my claw and broke it. Then I picked him up and carried him out to the transit and set him down inside. Perhaps he could get treatment in Rotorua Mining Town. If not, he would have to travel on to Auckland. I knew there was a large hospital there.

Ariadne dowsed the fire, collected a sack of food and locked up the hut.

We set out on the last stage of our journey.

And we are nearly there. We can smell a change in the air.

I have kept careful guard but have seen no one. Not a single human being.

The transit is sweeping over undulating hills of dark pine trees. The valleys are filled with steam.

There is a lake of grey-green water. The pylons of the transit run along its shore.

In places the water simmers. Occasionally gouts of mud heave into the air and slop back. There is steam everywhere and the pungency of sulphur.

When the mist clears I can see across the lake. There are great geysers: columns of water and steam blast into the air with a noise like thunder. The water drifts in the light breeze like the plumes of a feather.

We can feel the hot breath of the earth.

We are almost home.

It is wonderful.

12

All I have managed to set down since we returned two days ago are random impressions.

It is harder to write here. There is too much to do.

Bonniface. I saw him even as the transit was angling down to the small station in the Pioneer Settlement. He was by the lake with his hand shading his eyes, staring at the transit.

He must have heard me or seen me waving, for the next thing I saw he was charging round the lake like a great black ape, kicking up the sand and waving his claw above his head.

Fast as he ran, the transit was faster and we slid into the station and found it deserted.

"Take care, old human," I said as the door slid open. "Your arm should heal. This – " I snapped my claw in front of his face – "doesn't sting."

He made no reply.

Ariadne threw our few bags out and we stepped down on to the dry scoria. Behind us the transit closed and, with a rattle, began to gather speed and slide up to join the main overland rail.

We heard Bonniface before we saw him. He was shouting as he ran, calling to Amsterdame to get out of bed. Then a bell started to toll. It had once been a mission bell and was used to call all the Pioneers together if there was an important meeting.

Bonniface came bursting through the swing doors into the station. There he pulled up short; huge and black and dangerous. "You mangy bastard, Angelo. Where the hell have you been? We thought maybe they'd got you."

Then he was on us. He swung Ariadne high and planted a kiss full on her lips. "Still as lovely as ever, Ariadne. Wow. Wait until Amsterdame sees your hair. She'll turn green."

Then it was my turn. I was ready. With Bonniface, friendship and fighting look almost the same to an outsider. We both swung our claws together with a smash and then punched and pummelled and finally locked like wrestlers. Bonniface is bigger than me and has more leverage, but I was fitter. We struggled, grunting and laughing and bunching our muscles and eventually fell over one another and rolled down a shallow bank and into a puddle.

That ended the first stage of our greeting. Bonniface sat up and spat out muddy water and with it a tooth. I could feel my right eye starting to close.

Up on the top of the bank, Ariadne and Amsterdame were in one another's arms. Then Amsterdame, ever mindful of the needs of a situation, uncorked a bottle of wine and sprayed us with its contents. We gulped the air, trying to drink, and then rubbed the wine into our fur and collapsed back into the puddle heaving and gasping.

"Welcome back to Aotearoa," called Amsterdame. Other voices joined hers. I looked up and climbed to my feet and walked up the shallow bank. The station was filling with Pioneers. Many I knew. Some must have arrived since our departure. The ones that were here were the ones that could move on land. I saw hairy faces and scales, spines and suckers, downy wings and leather cloaks. Wonderful really, the variety. Among these, Murray would have been the odd man out. All had one thing in common. Eyes. Eyes bright with intelligence.

And within minutes they were clamouring for news.

Random memories.

Ariadne, dancing on one leg by a hot pool she had dipped her toe into and found was too hot.

Me, lying on my back on a hillside and letting my gaze slide over the hills as the patterns of clouds changed. Then waking up in a shower of rain.

Amsterdame trying to teach one of the Pioneers to swim and the Pioneer swearing in an old language.

130

Bonniface beaming with pride in front of a mural he had made from scraps of old tile and shells.

It was all old and new at the same time.

I think we have been lucky. The Pioneer Settlement is its own place, different and changeless.

Once, many years ago, before the Catastrophe I think, this place was a holiday centre. It occupies an entire hill which I think is artificial and which sticks out into the grey lake. We have pavilions and gardens and narrow little paths.

No doubt the humans who lived here in the olden days would be shocked to see how decayed the once fine buildings now are. But the decay is ours. And decay has a kind of stability all its own. It is the effort to keep places in a pristine condition that is hard.

Our pride is a large terraced building which contains the hot pools. They gurgle on, year after year, changing their temperature slightly but always delightful.

Since returning we have spent a lot of time in the hot pools.

I stood on the side, on the broken tiles, above the clear, bright emerald water and raised my arms, and let myself fall forwards, like a man of lead, face down into the water.

The heat engulfed me, reaching deep inside. I swam for a few seconds, turning under the water like an otter, and then broke surface and lolled. The water opened my fur and tickled my skin making me tingle. I wanted to scratch but didn't know where to begin and so just floated, and soon the itching went away.

Now that is as close as ever I shall come to a definition of happiness.

The hot pools are good places for talking. While your body floats away in pleasure, your mind is free to think.

Bonniface needed to talk. Like every other creature, he wanted news. I told him carefully, methodically, everything that had happened to us.

He whistled when I described how Pioneer Murray had been

131

taken from us and how we had been treated by the medical officers from Moon Base.

"Nothing like that happened to us. Our Pioneer hadn't survived. We found what was left of his dome but that was all. The beacon had malfunctioned. I pulled it aboard and checked it. All that distance for nothing. Anyway, when I got back into Earth orbit I told them what had happened and they told me to land as normal. Master Town was like a tomb. Just a few officials and a gang of mechanics who didn't seem to know the difference between a crowbar and a spanner."

"Was your ship in a bad way?"

"Well, you know. A couple of rough landings. And the Worm was jerky. Nothing that couldn't have been fixed in a few weeks in the old days."

"They were still waiting for spare parts to come from Moon Base when we were there."

Bonniface shrugged as if to say, "Well, what can I do?"

"And we met a friend of yours," I said. "An old man who runs the Taupo station. He tried to shoot me."

Bonniface guffawed when he heard that and beat his hand and claw on the water. "I believe you, Angelo. He's a mean bastard. Did he tell you what I did to his place?" I nodded. "Yes, well, I should have killed him. Do you know what he did? Eh? He told me he didn't have any medical supplies. And there was Amsterdame sick as a dog and trying to throw up and dry retching every five minutes. I tore his hut to bits. You should have seen his face when I punched out a wall. He wanted me to stop. Offered me drugs, but my temper was really up by then and I didn't stop until I'd scattered the roof iron. Then I took what I wanted and booted him down the hill."

"And what about Amsterdame?"

"I got her temperature down. Pumped some antibiotics into her. She had eaten something rotten. I tell you Angelo, our hydroponics unit started to go toxic just after we'd come out of the long sleep. Something to do with filters. I don't know why it didn't affect me. I must have a stomach made of iron."

132

"Well at least I know why the old man was so difficult with me. I'm not surprised he wanted to shoot me after you'd bust his house up."

"No. That doesn't explain anything. Yeah, sure it explains why he was particularly mad, but it doesn't explain why he was so difficult in the first place. Hell, you come over the mountain, chilled to buggery, and he won't even offer a cup of soup or salt water for a sick stomach. That takes some explaining. I've thought about it a lot."

"And?"

"Well, I think it is all to do with fear. People do strange things when they are afraid. Fear makes people hard. It makes them look for something to attack, so they don't feel so afraid. Do you know that we were attacked the last time we were in Rotorua?"

"No."

"Yeah. Five kids who'd been brought in for the mining went for me with iron bars. They were after Amsterdame. She sorted three of them out like that." He snapped his claw together. "I cracked a couple of heads. I mean, it was nothing. You and I have fought harder. But why did it happen? In the old days it wasn't like that, was it? We used to be able to go for a party downtown and people'd come to our table just to hear the stories. We were accepted. Different, but part of the life."

"So why do you think you were attacked?"

"The Fertility Programme. It's been going for three generations now. There's strum all women down here any longer. Everyone's so afraid of mutation they'd kill their own granny to prove they had a good pedigree. They think *we* are mutations. I mean we look like mutations, don't we? You and I do. Amsterdame and the others look like regular women."

"Don't they know we're all adapted?"

"Pah. History. Who gives a monkey about history? As far as they are concerned we are thriving."

"But we're not thriving. Anyone can see that. We can't have children. We're all sterile."

"We don't look sterile. We don't fight sterile. And we have

133

women. Good-looking women. They know nothing of history. They see us depart when they are children and it is the great-grandchildren who wave when we come back . . . except there aren't many great-grandchildren any more."

We sat in the hot water regarding one another. We had reached an impasse. I broke the silence. "I wish we could have children."

"Yeah. I'd like a son to kick about."

"Has Amsterdame ever mentioned anything about children?"

"No, she's not much of a one for words, our Amsterdame. But after the last long sleep she spent hours feeling her breasts and rubbing her womb. She made herself a dolly out of one of the sleeves of my overalls. She used to sleep with it. Thing was a bloody nuisance. Then when she woke up properly she threw it away."

"Ariadne hasn't done anything like that."

"But you never know what she's thinking. I bet she thinks about babies."

Then we talked about Lindis and Tui. Bonniface knew more about them than I did. He confirmed our fears.

"That crash wasn't an accident. There's no way that Tui would crash. She was a brilliant navigator. They were fed the wrong coordinates."

"You mean Chrono . . .?"

"I don't know about Chrono. I only heard about it when we got back to Earth. One of the Pioneers down here had been monitoring the signals. He says he heard Tui fighting the computers, trying to reprogramme them. She knew what was happening to them. Then they passed behind the moon. That was it."

"But who would destroy a working ship, and a Pioneer and an expert crew?"

"You tell me."

"Crazy people."

"Right."

134

We swam for a few moments silently. "What was the Pioneer like that Lindis and Tui had on board?"

"It was a vegetable. Pioneer Sorenson had become some kind of clever cactus. Even Lindis and Tui joked about it." Bonniface spat into the water. "A plant. And Lindis and Tui lost their lives for it. I tell you one thing, Angelo. And I wouldn't tell anyone this but you, but if they do ever fix up my ship, I might just . . . I might . . ."

"Might what?"

"Take off. Find a quiet place for me and Amsterdame. There are some lovely planets up there. There are some nice places on Earth for that matter. We could be very happy and have no worries."

"You'd never get away with it. They'd order you down, and we always obey."

"Perhaps not. But I'd take the chance. Are you thinking that what we have now is better? Well it isn't."

There was a sudden whoop at the far end of the bath and Ariadne and Amsterdame burst through the doors reeling and laughing and half fell, half dived into the water.

"Drunk as newts," said Bonniface raising his eyebrows. Then his legs were pulled from under him and he disappeared downwards with his mouth open. I started to laugh and next thing I knew I too was underwater and fighting for air. When I bobbed up there were three faces grinning at me.

"Good news," said Amsterdame.

"Great news," said Ariadne. "We've just heard that Raven and Lattisbourne and Kingi and Elf are on their way home."

"We got word from Chrono. He managed to slip a message down."

"They've finished their survey up north. They'll be here soon."

"Barring accidents."

"Boy, are we going to have a party," said Bonniface.

135

13

Ariadne and I go to bed early these days. Reaction from our recent long journey has begun to set in. Our rooms are the same ones we have occupied ever since the Pioneer Centre was established here at Rotorua. And how long ago is that? Centuries. When we are not here, others occupy our rooms, but they still feel like ours.

At the back of the house is a small garden. In front, the rooms are built on concrete piers. Our bedroom looks out across the great steaming lake to the twinkling lights of Rotorua Mining Town.

The night is calm with a rising moon and though the night air is chill, we leave our windows wide. Somewhere we can hear the mud bubbling to itself.

Ariadne has spent a long time with Amsterdame. They have talked about many things.

"We talked a lot about you two men," says Ariadne. "I told her about your lust for writing everything down."

"You didn't."

"I did. She wasn't surprised. She said you'd always been an odd one. She said she was glad you were back as Bonniface always admired you . . . your calmness and thoughtfulness. . . .Ha. She said Bonniface was going out of his mind with boredom and bursting to talk to you."

"Go on. What else?"

"She told me about this Fertility Programme or whatever it is called. It sounds very strange. Desperate in some ways. She thinks the Moon Base people have abandoned the old races of Earth. They are trying to start afresh. Later they will try to recolonize the Earth. But they need new genetic stock."

"Well, well."

"That's why they were so keen to get hold of Pioneer Murray. He seems so close to the human prototype."

"What about the others?"

"Useless. Too far gone. She says there's a critical point in adaptation. Beyond that point the genes produce nothing but monstrosities. Children with exposed gills. Children with faces like lizards. I think they are getting desperate."

"I always thought they had the technology to cope."

"So did I. But apparently a lot of the old lore is lost. Amsterdame tells me they have text books that no one can understand any more. They're hoping that old Pioneer Murray will teach them some of the secrets of genetic engineering."

"He probably knows a trick or two."

"Do you think he'll help them?"

"He may."

"Mmm. It's a lovely night. I'm glad to be home."

We lay still, looking up at the stars. High above a shooting star cut a path through the darknes and disappeared.

"The others'll soon be here."

"Mmm."

"Bonniface talked about children. Do you ever think about children?"

"Mmmm."

Outside I can hear a scuffling in the darkness and now the clear raw call of a Weka as it settles for the night.

"Ariadne? Are you awake?"

"Mmmmm."

14

Ariadne says I am less introspective these days, and she says it approvingly. She told me that she was worried that I was starting to chase my own tail like the proverbial snake that started to eat itself.

Being here is making me feel better – much more relaxed. Perhaps it is the smell in the air or eating tomatoes that have been ripened under a real sun. Perhaps it is the presence of friends who are easy and uncritical. I think of us as castaways on an island. The Pioneer Settlement is very like an island. We are self sufficient in a simple, uncomplicated way.

At the same time I am aware that we are waiting in a complex way. We are waiting for Kingi and Elf and Raven and Lattisbourne. They are already overdue. We are also waiting to find out what is expected of us. We have received no orders. We have not even received recognition that we are alive and down here. We are lotus eaters in a prison. For the time being I am content but that will not last forever. I do not want to see my fur turn to mange and my claw get stiff while I languish in hot pools for the rest of my days.

Today Ariadne and I went for a walk through the Settlement, visiting. We visited the old Pioneers and brought them what news we could of their latest brother Pioneer Murray.

There were those who had known him; Indira for one. She lay back in her grotto where the steam rose like wraiths above the deep green water and regarded us with fishy eyes. She has relearned to speak since the last time we were on Earth and is smaller and much more compact. Ariadne sat at the water's edge with her ankles dangling down into the water while Indira turned and curled like an eel.

"Young Murray was a quiet boy," said Indira. "Much given

to reading, I remember. When they took us on tours he was always the first out of the transit or whatever. Do you get the picture? I can't remember what he looked like. Skinny, I think. Did he look a human when you found him?"

"Pretty much."

"Not like me, eh?" she cackled and stirred the water with her broad webbed hands. "But I am changing. Adaptation never ends, you know. In a few more hundred years I'll be a real mermaid. I'll get one of you to cart me over to the sea and then I'll take my chance in the broad Pacifico."

"Do you want to become human again?"

"Pah. What's human? I'm all right as I am. I'll find me a lazy sailor and I'll catch the fish and he'll comb my hair. We'll breed sprats by the thousand. They'll come from me like water squeezed from a sponge." She laughed again and then splashed water up on to Ariadne. "Away, don't look so serious, girl."

Mazeppa is quite different. He was one of ours. Our third rescue. He lives at the top of an old concrete building which can now only be reached up an old and rusty spiral staircase. This was once a place where full-humans stayed on holiday before the Catastrophe, I am told. When he hears anyone coming, Mazeppa climbs out on to the balustrade outside his balcony and spreads his thin wings and flaps them so that they catch the air. He can still fly, just, but he too is changing and soon, say in a few more generations, his wings will be no more than flaps of skin. For all that he is strange and has a face like a parrot and is no more than three feet tall, he is very human with a peculiar kind of vanity. He likes ceremony in all things and hates to be caught unawares.

We made a clattering and talked loudly as we climbed the rickety old staircase to his apartment. When we arrived he was ready and waiting. He strutted over to Ariadne and took her hand in his thin fingers and pressed his beak to her knuckles. I have no idea what this ceremony means but he always does it. Then he flapped once or twice and managed to rise a few feet off the ground and launched himself at my chest. He crashed against me and I held my arm out in front while he clambered up using his beak and talons in my fur, and finally perched himself on my shoulder.

"Welcome home, my loves," he said in a voice that is surprisingly deep. "We have missed you. Settle yourselves. Make yourselves at home. There are cigars in the barrel, Angelo. If you will light one for me I will smoke one with you."

The ritual is always the same and I always smoke one of his cigars though they taste as though made from cabbage leaves. His technique of smoking is unique. I hold up a lighted cigar which he then skewers with a long fingernail. I am sure he keeps it sharp just for the purpose. He tucks the cigar into the side of his beak and puffs quickly. When he sees that I am smoking comfortably he usually lets his own cigar drop discretely over the edge of the parapet. As I say, ceremony is everything with him. "Now tell me all your news. We shall have a new brother with us soon I hear."

"Perhaps not," said Ariadne. "Pioneer Murray may be the first *successful* Pioneer."

"Successful. Bah. I was successful. Wasn't I king of the trees when you found me?"

"Yes."

"Well then?"

"I mean successful in the new way. He may be the first Pioneer to return who remains genetically intact."

"Never. No way. He may look like a human but inside he will be as wild as me. Take my word for it." Here he flapped his leather wings and dug his claws into my fur. "Right, Angelo?"

"Whatever you say, Mazeppa. Now calm down."

"He would have been better if he had gone through a mighty transformation. Do you remember when they saw me? Ha, ha, ha. They couldn't believe it. Couldn't believe it. I gave them no cause for comfort. Do you remember I escaped and flew up to the rafters of the landing bay and shat at them whenever I could?"

"I remember," I said. "I had to climb up and bring you down. You bit my arm."

"I was frightened. Will you have some tea?"

We both nodded. Mazeppa is able to brew the best tea in the world. He grows it in one of the deserted penthouse apartments next door. The leaves are always bright green and he adds mint and lemon. "I've had a kettle boiling ever since you landed."

He flopped down from my shoulder on to the ground and strutted through to his kitchen. We heard a clattering as he busied himself.

"Can I help?" called Ariadne.

"No. No. You rest. It is my pleasure to serve."

"It is hard," said I to Ariadne, speaking softly, "to realize that Mazeppa and Indira and Pioneer Murray all come from the same human stock."

"Induced evolution rarely produces things of beauty," she said. "Remember Jinks on Jeupardi?"

"I remember. Have you been reading my – "

"Of course. I don't think you have been very wise writing all – "

"Here we are," said Mazeppa, shuffling out from his kitchen. "A different blend which I hope you will like." Mazeppa poured the tea carefully, pinching the dry green leaves into the cups and then adding the pale yellow water. "I have found that this helps with digestion and promotes a sense of well being. But you know, I still can't grow tea the way I once could on my world. That is one thing I shall regret until my dying day. The rest I have learned to live with."

The tea was delicious. We complimented Mazeppa and he nodded and shrugged. "We are also glad to see that you are well."

"I am well. But like all of us I am still changing. My evolution is slow now. If I had a proper challenge . . . a new planet . . . Perhaps when you speak to the Space Council you could mention that."

Despite everything, Mazeppa remains a Pioneer. He would like to have the chance to reform another world. When we

141

plucked him from the high trees of Christmas he had already transformed a large part of the forest into sizeable dwellings fit for humans. He had learned the language of the dominant species and transformed himself into a working tree dweller. I well remember his disappointment when he discovered that we had come to bring him back and were not the first of a new line of human Pioneers come to build on his work. He had adapted well to being back on Earth but part of his mind remained alien.

"Drink up. The first cup is for tasting. The second is for drinking and the third is for memory. Surely I don't have to remind you."

We dutifully drank our three cups and kept up a light conversation. As I drained my last cup leaving the dregs turning in half an inch of water, Mazeppa hopped close to me.

"Forgive me, Angelo, if I offer you a word of advice. I do not see much of the world from my eyrie. I am content to crack nuts and boil water, but this world is no longer a happy world. Some time ago a small boat came across the lake. I heard singing and laughter and then shots. I do not know if the shots were aimed at me but when they were gone I dug this pellet from my walls." He dropped a twisted bullet-head into my hand. "Times are changing. We Pioneers who gave up so much are now the target. I would not like to see either of you hurt. We go back a long way, don't we?"

I agreed and slipped the bullet into my satchel. "We do."

We made our goodbyes and then climbed down the narrow spiral staircase. My last sight of Mazeppa was of him standing on the edge of his balcony with his wings spread out to the afternoon sun. He looked frail and small.

Some minutes later Ariadne and I entered the dense scrub which surrounded his high tenement. When we were several hundred yards away we both relieved ourselves. (Mazeppa's apartment has no working lavatory.)

"Is that bullet like the one that that old man in Taupo fired at you?" asked Ariadne, squatting some few feet from me.

"Yes," said I.

"Could it kill?"

"If it hit the brain, or the heart or some other important organ."

"Then Mazeppa is right. We must be careful, Angelo. All of us must be careful."

During the rest of that afternoon we visited other Pioneers. There was April who had been brought back by Lindis and Tui. She is the only one of the Pioneers so far as I know who was able to breed with an alien population. She had lived in mountain pastures and had there established her queendom. She mated with one of the tall antlered creatures which walked there. Her world was very like the Earth and had followed a similar evolution. When Kingi and Elf found her she had a fine spread of antlers, the match for any of the males and a splendid house of interlocking stones. The quarefellas, as she called the inhabitants, were shaggy beasts much given to wrestling and sports and who were fine workers of stone and carvers of wood. They looked on her as semi-divine and under her direction had built many houses in the valleys and equipped them for the expected arrivals.

She was carried away stunned by Lindis and Tui and they endured a massive hail of slingshots and spears. I remember Tui saying that that rescue was the hardest task that either of them had ever undertaken. April never settled to life back on Earth.

For a time April was the great hope of the genetic engineers but she fought them every inch of the way and willed mutation upon herself as only the Pioneers can. Within a few years of her return she had taken to living in the wild and ate only what she could find or steal.

Eventually she was left alone and finally came to live close to the Pioneer Settlement but she never forgave Lindis and Tui, or any of us for that matter. She dreams of returning to her world, one day.

We found her sitting by one of the rare clear-water streams which tumble down in rapids and pools to join the great warm lake. She was majestic, clothed in one of the long red and brown gowns which she dyes herself from crushed berries and minerals. Her crown of antlers sprouted like the branches of a magnolia tree.

"Why have you come to see me?" she asked, standing up.

"To pay our good wishes," answered Ariadne.

"Have you any news that would interest me?"

"None, I think."

"Well then?" She stared at us with brown eyes that were curiously hard. Then she tossed her head to free her antlers from some small branches which drooped down. "I suppose you have heard that Lindis and Tui are dead?"

"Yes."

"I did not weep for them."

"No. But they were our friends, and we miss them."

"Mmm." Again the silence. "Well, I'll offer you some hospitality. Here is some clear spring water. Better than that filthy, stinking water down there. Are you hungry?" We both said no. "Just as well. I am fasting at present. That is one secret of youth. You should remember that. Sit down." We obeyed and she sat down upstream from us and let the hem of her gown trail in the clear running water.

"I gather that you have been successful and another sheep is returned to the fold."

"Hardly a sheep," I said.

She raised her eyebrows. "Rebellious then?"

"We don't know. He was a sad, difficult man. But Chrono tells us he is working with the Space Council on the moon. He is helping with the genetic programme."

"Ah that. What is his name?"

"Murray."

"Never heard of him."

"He was long before your time."

"One of the true ancients? Like Indira?"

"Yes, but he looks completely human. He never left his dome."

"And I never had to use one."

144

"No."

April seemed to drift off into a world of her own with her eyes fixed on the distant bank. Then, after a few moments, she roused herself. "Well, enough of that." She turned her gaze on us. "You two are a strange pair. You particularly." She inclined her head with its high crown of horns towards me. "You are so careful to be friendly and yet you are a perfect servant of the human masters. Don't you ever think to ask questions?"

"What kind of questions?" I asked.

April laughed as though she saw clear through my pretended ingenuousness. "Well if ever you *do* start to ask questions, *real* questions, you will know what I mean. As I see it we are all part of the same conspiracy. Even the late Lindis and Tui were part of it. I would like to know what their last thoughts were as they realized they were being sacrificed on the moon. They would not have thought kind thoughts about your human masters."

"How do you know they were sacrificed?"

"Because I am still sufficiently human in my mind to understand these things. They were killed in anger. Petulant, childish anger. But with sufficient cunning to make it seem an accident. They brought back a vegetable I am told. How that must have dashed the hopes of the God almighty Space Council. A plant! That is the most radical transformation I have ever heard of. Were the Space Council about to give comfort to a plant or to the fools that mindlessly brought it in? They would think they were being mocked. And meanwhile, all they could produce were weeds of their own."

"Maybe you are right."

"You know I am right. And I hear your return was not easy."

"How do you know that?"

"Informed gossip. We Pioneers take an interest in you homunculi who are often so much better than your masters. What we can not understand is why you insist on behaving like toys on a stick."

She stared at me. Her gaze was hard and mocking and at the same time, challenging.

145

I wanted to leave, I knew where this conversation was heading. I stood up. Ariadne looked up at me in surprise and Pioneer April reached across and gripped me by the arm. "One more thing before you leave. If ever you do start to think for yourself and ask questions and decide to take action, I want to book passage with you. Understand? You know my destination. I would even break these antlers off at my skull in order to fit into one of your sleep tanks. Can I say more? So, on your way. Remember my words, Angelo and Ariadne."

Ariadne stood up close to me and we took our leave. As we walked away down the hill I could feel Pioneer April's eyes on me. She is a powerful magnetic woman who can use magic I have heard. She made me feel awkward and clumsy.

When we reached the low hills where the grass was stunted by the sulphur in the soil, Ariadne stopped me with her hand.

"You know, Angelo. If ever it should turn out that . . . well, if ever our circumstances change and we are obliged to leave Earth for ever, we should honour that promise."

"What promise?"

"You heard her. You didn't refuse. You didn't blow up and protest that you were a faithful child of the Pioneer Programme. She understood that."

"Have you been talking to her privately?"

"No. Of course not. But I am a woman. And you are not a fool."

"Huh. I feel a fool."

"April is everything that human beings should be: passionate for love and justice. No wonder she makes people uncomfortable. We take her, you hear?"

We walked on in silence.

While the pale afternoon wore on we visited other Pioneers and the graves of those who had died since our last visit to Earth. We paid our last respects to Mohog whom we brought back. He was a great bear of a man. A huge lover of beer and laughter, but finally he found the gravity of Earth too much for his heart.

146

And Olympia who rowed her boat out on to the lake one evening and was never seen again, though her empty boat was found.

And Benjamin who always wore a mask because he found the air of Earth toxic.

And Astra who never believed that she had returned to Earth and who tried to climb up to the stars believing they were holes in a cloth.

And many more . . .

Then, as we walked back to our low, white pavilion, we heard a rumbling in the west that made the earth tremble. Bellying down through the low clouds came the black ribbed shape of a ship like our own. On its side were large white stencilled markings and we knew it was our friends returned from the far north. The ship slid sideways through the sky until it hovered above a wide salt flat. There it lowered with a great uprush of dust and stones and an audible creaking as its stubby legs dug into the ground. Finally, when it had stabilized and settled, its noise became a whine which faded to silence.

We began to run, jumping over the small meandering creeks and breasting our way through the low shrubs and manuka. When we were about halfway to the ship we saw its side door open and Lattisbourne stepped out. She was wearing her silver survival suit but without the helmet and we could see her black face. She waved to us, arching her hand above her head. Then Raven stepped out beside her and he was followed by a small woman that could only be Elf, and finally the powerful squat shape of Kingi.

They all waved as we ran towards them. We heard the war whoop of Bonniface who came bounding down a side path and joined us.

15

The Far North, Old Europe, is not inhabited, but it could be. We have heard tales of great forests and wild tumbling rivers and large blue lakes where there once were cities. There are glaciers too which calve into the sea and even the remains of harbours. To hear Lattisbourne talk you would think this was a promised land, a virgin tract just waiting the hand of a Pioneer . . . and I wonder why the Space Council hasn't thought of that. Now if the Pioneer Programme were redirected to tame Mother Earth, that would make sense. Some of these old Pioneers, given their head, would soon make the forests ring. And who would inherit them? Ah, there perhaps is the question. For a strong man with a will and an axe and a faith in the future could do just as well.

Tonight we are going to have a party. Bonniface insists . . . in fact all of us insist, and we have decided upon a bold plan. We intend to invade Old Rotorua Mining town just like in the old days. Some of the Pioneers have decided to come with us so it will be a rare and strange gathering. Amsterdame has taken charge of arrangements. She has promised us wild boar on the spit and beer to drown in. It will be a reunion for all of us and a proper farewell to Lindis and Tui.

We are all excited and Ariadne has insisted that I rub oils and herbs into my fur. My only worry is that there may be trouble for I remember the warning of Mazeppa.

"Trouble?" says Bonniface. "Don't you worry. If they want trouble, we'll show them what the word means."

That does not make me feel easy. I have seen Bonniface in this mood before and I would rather come between a hungry lion and its food than cross him.

16

We pushed off from our jetty in the long flat-bottomed barges which we use for short trips out on to the lake. I took charge of one, working the long T-ended pole down into the silt at the bottom of the lake and then walking the length of the boat. Bonniface manoeuvred the other. We had decided to race.

I should say that both Bonniface and I had primed ourselves for the contest and we were neither of us too steady on our feet. It was anyone's guess in which direction the barges would go. "Just so long as we get there before sundown," called Lattisbourne. "Amsterdame says the pigs will be crisp by then."

A sturdy Pioneer called Rollo, who was as agile as a monkey, was elected race master and he teetered on the front lip of my barge and when he judged that we were both about equal he gave the signal to start.

Bonniface and I dug in. We heaved and ran, setting our shoulders into the notches of the poles and then bracing ourselves to drag the poles from the water. We stirred up great muddy prints.

Each time we ran we charged down different sides of our boats while the occupants cheered and berated us. In this manner we made doglegged paths out into the steaming lake and in the general direction of Rotorua Mining Town.

The lake is not deep. Not more than a yard and a half in most places, but there are holes. Bonniface was the first to strike trouble. He plunged his pole in and, without waiting to see if he had found purchase, applied all his weight. The pole went straight down, and Bonniface followed it clean over the side.

By the time he was out of the water and back on deck I had a good two poles' worth advantage. I heaved and ran and heaved and ran, pausing only to refresh myself from a basin of beer which Ariadne held up for me.

Perhaps I was too confident, but on my sixth or seventh run I felt the pole snag. I heaved on it at the end of the boat but it failed to come free from the water. The pole stayed while the boat moved on and I, foolishly, held on to the pole. I was dragged over the end and found myself treading air and the pole tilted over and dumped me in the black rotting silt stirred up by my efforts. It got into my mouth and nose. God, it tasted awful.

Silly thoughts come to one at such a time. I remember thinking, so much for Ariadne's aromatic oils, and then I was on the surface and wiping the weed and muck from my face. The pole floated beside me. I gripped it in my claw and swam sidestroke after the barge. I could hear Bonniface hooting with laughter. But he wasn't watching where he was going. The two barges collided, pitching half the occupants out into the lake. Lattisbourne ended up in the water beside me. "At this rate," she observed, spitting out weed, "we'll none of us reach Rotorua before daybreak."

Finally, when we had all sorted ourselves out, a rematch was called. Rollo, dripping from head to tail, restarted us and Bonniface and I floundered about on the wet decks while we tried to propel our barges towards the distant, winking lights.

Bonniface at first made headway through sheer strength. But I was fitter and gradually caught up with him and began to forge ahead. Both barges sliced through the water . . . and suddenly the Rotorua wharf was close.

We were both at the front of our barges preparing to plunge our poles into the water when suddenly both boats slowed. Bonniface and I were pitched forwards and toppled into the water. It was only a few feet deep and we both sat up in the silt. We saw Pioneer Indira rear up out of the water behind the boats and roar with laughter. She held the trailing tiller ropes of each barge in her broad webbed hands.

A dead heat. That was how it was judged as the two barges ground up on to the shingle. Bonniface floundered through the mud over to me and we clashed our claws together. Then we threw our arms over one another and strode from the lake splashing as much water as we could over the occupants of our respective barges.

Amsterdame was waiting on the quay. She took one look at us and threw her hands in the air. "Have you no style? Here have I been working my fingers to the bone trying to get a decent party organized and you two clowns come wandering in looking like something that just emerged from the lost lagoon. Here, get yourselves dried."

Amsterdame loves organizing. There were not many taverns to choose from but she had found one proprietor who, for a high fee, was prepared to give us the run of his establishment for the whole night. It was a brightly decorated square building (new since our last visit to Earth) partly set out on poles over the lake. Private mineral pools were available and in the centre was a square floored with scoria. Here fires were burning and spitting as the oil from the roasting pigs dropped on to them. The smell was almost overpowering, a mixture of resinous wood and roasting meat. Bonniface and I went into one of the private pools and soaked. And when we were refreshed we dressed and went to join the others.

We are a strange people, we Pioneers and rescuers. In our work we are so careful and yet we don't know moderation in our pleasures. You can see that in our dancing. We go to extremes either sitting back with just a finger drumming or up on our feet trying to tear the air apart. The music matters hardly at all. In our dancing we are wild and lustful and dangerous. We smash tables and fall on our knees and bay at the moon. At other times, when the mood is on us, we dance alone, closing our eyes and ears to all company. We dance in a private world until we are sick and have to be carried out on to the grass.

Elf was feeling wild. I watched her. She danced like a goddess and everyone gave her space. She stripped off her shirt and the sweat poured down her arms and breasts. I think she was dancing to the memory of Tui and perhaps Silver. I expected to see Ariadne join her soon. I wanted to join her and nip the

151

moon with my claw and pull it down to earth. But later. Later. I am told that I am one of the wildest when I get going. I save my energy until I can flow.

Rollo was dancing, wagging his goat's beard and pumping his arms. Raven was on the floor too, upside down, supporting himself on his hand and beating his claw on the ground. Mazeppa fluttered. Lattisbourne wove her arms like black snakes. Bonniface, huge and glosssy and puffing like a steam engine, stamped his feet into the scoria and sent up clouds of dust.

The poor hotel owner did not know what to make of it. His mouth and eyes were wide open. I think he would have liked to dance with Elf. Who wouldn't?

I found Kingi by the roasting pigs. He was stealing what bits he could while Amsterdame did the basting, nipping them off the carcase with his claw.

"Is everyone having a good time?" he asked.

"I think so," said I and filled my jug with beer.

The Pioneers that had accompanied us were generally more restrained, as they have to be. Aldus had come for the outing. He still has long sharp quills of cartilage which rise when he feels angry or threatened. When he is quiet he looks as though he is wearing a cloak. Caesar and Vesta had oiled their scales and looked magnificent and wild like creatures carved from ivory. Mazeppa scurried and bobbed from table to table clutching a beaker in his thin-fingered hand.

All was well. I could see no hint of trouble though there were many faces pressed against the outside of the damp windows trying to get a glimpse of the activities within.

I forgot about them when the food was served.

Great slabs of pork with hard crackling and juice that oozed when you bit was all I thought about.

"A story. A story." It was Bonniface calling. He was up on one of the tables with a leg bone in his claw and he waved this to get attention. "What about a story like in the old times? Who wants to hear about Old Europe?"

This was greeted with shouts and a great thumping of feet. To many of the Pioneers, what we call Old Europe was still a living memory. "Tell us about Europe."

"Then I give you . . ." here Bonniface paused and looked round while everyone fell silent. "I give you Lattisbourne. Queen of storytellers."

Lattisbourne waved as if to say no. But a chant grew. "Lattis-bourne. Lattis-bourne. Lattis-bourne," and she found herself hoisted up and thrust into the middle of the assembly.

"Well, so long as you are all comfortable . . ."

"We are. We are."

"And have got plenty to drink so I won't be interrupted."

At this there was a general rush to the drinks table where the proprietor had just tapped his third barrel and lined up crates of resinous white wine.

Lattisbourne is the best storyteller amongst us and knows how to play her audience. "Then I'll begin."

"Tell us about the Mediterranean." This from Rollo.

"Is it wine-dark? And are there dolphin there?"

"The Mediterranean is as blue as Angelo's eyes." Here she winked jokingly at me and many faces turned to me. "If you dipped a brush in it you could paint the sky. We saw more dolphin than you could count in a week of daylight and red crabs as big as a rowing boat. We came in from the south and west flying low. There is a great delta not too far from the pyramids."

"I've been there. I've been there," said Rollo.

"And the delta is green with weed. It stretches right out like a hand. Then we swung west and started to fly over islands. We came to an old city with a high hill and pale buildings on it like the bones of a great animal."

"Athens. The Acropolis."

"Perhaps . . ."

"I've been there. I've climbed – " But many hands pushed Rollo down and he subsided muttering.

"We flew on over mountains and sea and islands. Everything is green and blue and white where the snows reach right down

153

into the valleys. That is where the forests begin. Mile after rolling mile of dark green pine. We came to a vast black lake with a high iron fortress which poked up through the weed."

"*Est-ce que la Tour Eiffel reste –* " began Mazeppa but many voices hushed him.

"We turned north and followed the coast. But it is hard to tell where the sea ends and the land begins. It is now a vast mud flat covered with low bushes which stretches as far as the eye can see. The waves from the north sea come sweeping in, in great arcs lifting the low branches so that they wave and then sink again. We flew on for miles and then turned inland towards a row of low hills.

"The trees were different here. Not the dark green of pine, spiky and unbroken, but the paler green of ash and elm with the occasional towering oak. There was grass too, cropped short by the wild deer which spread and scattered from our shadow.

"Flying over the hills we saw a light gleam for an instant among the trees and though the instruments told us there was nothing down there of interest, we turned in a large circle and lowered to investigate. The high branches scraped along the bottom of the ship and then a clearing opened and we were able to put down without uprooting trees or tearing a great scar in the soil.

"You should have smelled the air when we opened the doors and heard the birds. Night was falling. And with the night came a gentle rain. We watched at the doors for hours but no one came creeping out to see our ship.

"In the morning we decided to explore on foot. We drew lots and I became the leader. Raven was chosen to stay behind.

"As we stepped down from the ship something wonderful happened. Deer had gathered close to us in the night – perhaps they had felt our warmth. They raised their heads and stared at us motionless. Then their leader, a creature far taller than me, ambled over and began to snuffle at my pack. I offered it some dry food and it began to eat from my hand. That is one of the nicest things I have ever felt.

"When we moved away from the ship, the deer scattered with a great pounding of hooves. Within seconds they were gone, leaving behind them a smell of musk and of torn earth. We found a track – perhaps it had once been a driveway – that led down the side of a hill under the trees, and at its end was a house."

"A real house?" asked several voices, almost whispering in awe.

"A real house. Several storeys high. Built of stone, with windows set into it and a small gate. There were flowers round it. Autumn flowers of red and gold. It looked clean and neat and if someone had come to the door and waved to us I wouldn't have been surprised. But no one did come. We called and shouted, unable to believe that the house was not occupied, but no one came. I tried the door and found it locked and Kingi had to prise back one of the panels and reach in. But still the door wouldn't budge. It had set within its frame. Eventually we cut our way in and stood in the hall. The air was dry and still. There were carpets on the floor and paintings on the walls. There was even paper on the walls, but everything was brown. We entered a room that was full of books and another that must have been the kitchen for there were great bowls and saucepans hanging on wooden pegs. There was an iron range with ashes still in its pan. Do you believe in magic?"

"Magic?"

"Aye. Magic. For the embers in the fire were still warm. I put my hand in them and they were still warm."

"Was someone still living there?"

Lattisbourne shrugged. "Perhaps. Ghosts. Spirits that couldn't bear to leave the place they had loved and so lingered on. In another room with large bay windows which looked down the valley to a lake under the trees we found bones. They lay on a padded sofa and only the arm had become dislodged and was scattered on the floor. Upstairs were the remains of two children. That was all. But the house felt alive. It welcomed us. It spoke to us. It said, 'Welcome. Stay here. Bring back

155

laughter and tears. Make the corridors echo.' That night we did stay there. We shut up our iron ship and brought Raven down and he and Kingi climbed on the roofs poking out the nests and the sodden clumps of moss from the gutters and clearing the chimneys. We got a fire going in the kitchen and we cleaned out some of the old saucepans and cooked meat and vegetables. We ate off plates that were bright with pictures of flowers. And after we had eaten, we carried the remains of the humans outside and buried them under the trees. That night we slept in the room filled with books and heard the walls creak. And in the morning we left. We mended the door and reset the plugs in the old chimneys and tiptoed away.

"That was the only house we saw in the whole of our journey."

"There must be others."

"Perhaps, but we never saw them. We saw fields of rubble and lakes of ash. We saw spires that rose above the skeletons of buildings. We saw great pits of stone where the rock and concrete once flowed like water. But we did not see another house intact. If that was how you ancients once lived, what madness made you give it away?"

There was no answer to that. Except Mazeppa, who hopped up on to a table and flapped his loose leathery wings. "Not everyone lived like that in the old days."

"Perhaps not. But you had everything to lose and nothing to gain."

"True."

"And now look at us," said Aldus, speaking for the first time that evening. "Pitiful, aren't we?"

"I once lived in a house like that," said Rollo. "I was born there. But it was in a city. And no, it wasn't like that. But it should have been. I know what you mean. Mud hut or mansion. I know what you mean. Home. Why did we give it all up?"

"We were the lucky ones," said Mazeppa. "We are still here."

"Lucky? What's lucky?"

I watched the old Pioneers begin to argue among themselves.

156

They all had their own backgrounds, fancied or real. I found myself thinking about myself. My earliest memory was the academy on the moon where Ariadne, Bonniface, Lindis and Tui and the rest of us had all grown up together in a place of white plastic tiles. I am not sentimental, but I cannot pretend that that which we inherited is better than that which the full-humans lost. Lattisbourne feels this. She wants the permanence of hard rock bedded deep in the soil and time to watch the flowers grow and wilt. Ariadne too feels the pull of the tides. Little by little I believe we are all wanting to settle down. It is not a lot we ask after all. Time to build, time to grow old, freedom from fear and the harsh hand of authority. Are we so different from the full-humans?

Any further thoughts were suddenly interrupted by the shattering of glass above our heads. Someone had thrown a rock or a brick from outside and up on to the conservatory roof above the drinks tables. We stood, staring at one another. I don't think any of us quite understood what had happened. As though in a dream I saw blood begin to run in a curtain down Rollo's face.

That first stone must have been a signal, for the next moment, rocks and bottles began to thud against the walls and break through the windows. The spell was broken and suddenly we were all shouting.

We pushed the Pioneers, who were the most vulnerable, under the tables. "We're being attacked," someone shouted, though that was hardly necessary. I stole a glance outside covering my eyes with my arm and saw in the pale light from the tavern hundreds of faces and waving arms.

Bonniface, who had been under the window when the first stone came, shook himself and shards of glass flew from his fur. I saw him take hold of one of the tripods that had supported the spit and wrench it from the ground. Kingi dived and rolled and came up with one of the long skewers used to hold the meat. I had nothing, and then I heard Ariadne call and she threw to me from across the room a length of chain with a heavy padlock on the end.

157

Then a shot rang out and Raven, who was in the act of tearing a leg from one of the serving tables, stiffened and shook his head and then fell with a look of utter surprise on his face.

That we had not thought to bring weapons with us now seemed a ridiculous oversight. We had known what might happen. I had even mentioned my fears to Bonniface. I think we had all turned our eyes away from reality.

Now instinct, that most unreliable of all guides, took charge. We were attacked and so we counterattacked.

I saw Bonniface smash a door clean from its hinges. Kingi threw a table through the glass arcade. I picked up the small serving table that Raven had dropped and used it as a shield while I moved forward and began to swing the length of chain.

We advanced together. The full-humans were not organized and they began to fall back and we began to run. Wood splintered from the table held in front of me and I heard the loud bang of another shot very close to me. Any restraint left me then. I swung the chain into faces. I smashed the table forwards and trampled. Before my eyes was a misty redness and I did not know who I was or where I was. The only reality was the chain with its happy weight at the end.

The lust to kill was on me. It is an instinct engineered in me and hardly ever roused till then. I do not know how many times I was hit. I felt pain but it did not affect me like pain. It made me exult. I swung the chain like a sword and wrenched it free if it got entangled. I did not think of Bonniface and Kingi, but only of the vague fleeing shapes in front of me.

And suddenly I found myself up to my legs in water at the lake's edge. There was no more running and I felt cheated and beat the chain on the water.

Behind me there was fire. I turned and saw a dark red plume of fire and smoke rise from the small hotel where we had held our party.

Ariadne.

I came to myself with a shock and started to run, scrambling and slipping in the darkness.

When I was close enough to feel the fire Ariadne suddenly

158

reared up in front of me. I tried to hold her but I was slippery with blood.

"Make for Raven's ship," she ordered. "Quickly."

"The Pioneers . . .?"

"Most of them are on the lake. Indira is towing them. Now move, dammit."

She barged me from the side, tearing at my fur, turning me away from the fire. "Run. Run. Keep pace with me. There are too many of them."

But still I held back. "Lattisbourne, Amsterdame, Elf . . .?"

"They've already gone. I stayed for you. Now come on."

She began to run and I followed. We ran down a street. In the low street light we could see the evidence of Kingi and Bonniface's work.

We turned a corner and came face to face with a large crowd of humans. I think they were as surprised as us. They held burning torches and garden weapons such as rakes and slashers. A great cry went up and stones and broken bottles began to rain down on us. "This way," shouted Ariadne. "Out of town. Follow the lake road. We can outrun them."

We cut across an open square and then down a side road which led slantwise to the lakeside. Behind us there was a roaring like an animal. "Pace yourself. They can see no better than us."

I lumbered on but the recent fight was starting to take its toll. I tried to pace myself, but a raw pain was beginning to tear at my shoulder, and my legs were senseless as stumps of ice.

We came to a low mulchy creek of hot water and flopped across. I started to slip on the far bank but Ariadne seized my claw and dragged me up. "Come on, Angelo. Not too far. Fight man. Fight."

I ran like a machine. One foot in front of another. That was all that mattered. One step. Two steps. Three steps . . .

High above the lake, there was a sudden stream of fire in the sky and a massive roar as a dull ship passed close above us. "Is it Bonniface?" I asked, each word a gasp.

"God knows what it is. Keep running. Come on, love."

*

159

Time lost all meaning. There was only me, a ball of pain, and the woman who paced beside me. I wondered vaguely at Ariadne's strength.

Then there were other lights, the rim lights of Raven's ship, and we could see its blunt shape and great fins and a searchlight stabbed out across the lake, sweeping across the grey steaming water. It was still standing on the plateau just up from the lake and under the hills. We turned inland and as we staggered through the low manuka the searchlight found us.

We had only a few hundred yards to run and the landing ramp was down when a posse of men ran out of the shadows between us and the ship. They had guns and I saw flashes of orange, and then, just when I was almost on them, I pitched forwards into darkness.

That is all I remember.

No, not all. I remember two things more, but they hardly make sense. There was a seething redness like boiling smoke and men with faces like horse bollocks walked towards me spraying white lather from nozzles which they held in front of them. The lather spattered me and stuck. I tried to raise my claw but the straffin arm wouldn't budge. I wanted to reach and crush but the lather covered my head and face and I sank into darkness like I was buried in sand.

When I next came to, they were dragging me. Four of them had hold of my legs and I was scraping along on my back with my arms spread wide. I saw bare light bulbs jerking by above.

I thought, kick.

But there was no kick in me. No voice either, just a rattle, and then merciful blackness again.

When I woke up I was here.

17

Here is a bed in a cell.

I lie on my back and I can see a clear plastic tube which trails from my nostrils up to a bottle.

I seem to be well but cannot move . . . or if I do move, I hurt and so I stay still.

Occasionally I am visited by a man who moves my arms and inspects my bandages and listens to my chest.

I am not sure whether I am in a hospital or a prison.

How do I know these things? Well, in truth, I am bored and at the same time I am deeply worried about my friends. That is a strange combination. But when I try to think, I seem to drift off into sleep. Nevertheless I try to think. I try to memorize everything. I try as a matter of will to count the white tiles opposite me and stretching up the walls. By deduction, 32 multiplied by (estimated) 40 equals 1280 tiles. There. That is roughly how many tiles face me. But oh the effort. And where is Ariadne? Is she in a bed close to me, or in the next room or in the ship with Bonniface?

18

It is impossible to tell days and nights in this place. Day is when I am awake and night is the rest of the time. There are no windows. The only way I know that time is passing is by the fact that I am getting better. Today the doctor, in one of his rare moments of communication, expressed surprise that I was recovering so quickly. I am no longer fed by a bottle and some of my bandages are off. Parts of me have been shaved again, my arms in particular and I can see wounds like thick red lines, held together under pieces of shiny plastic. But my shoulders hurt, God do they hurt.

I can sit up and I have asked for paper and pencil. I did not expect to be given them but a whole plain-paged notebook and three sharp pencils arrived on the tray with my meal. I have set down everything I can remember about the party and the fighting and how I came to be here.

Though I have asked questions of the orderly who brings the food and clears my slops, and of the doctor, I have received no answers. I don't know where I am or what is happening. I don't know whether I am being made well simply so that I can stand to be executed. Certainly my last and most vivid memories are of the lynch mob that cut us off before we could reach Raven's ship.

Last night something strange happened. I woke up and the room was dark. I was just in time to catch the shrinking ribbon of light as the door closed. Someone had been in my room watching me. My guess was that when they saw me restless and waking, they departed. Who? Why?

There was a faint odour in the room too. A smell that I seemed to know but couldn't place. It wasn't Ariadne but someone had been there.

I found I couldn't sleep after that, and when the doctor came I asked him if he had visited me in the night. He looked at me blankly and then got on with dressing my wounds as if I had never spoken.

So that brings me up to the present.

And now I have decided to take the initiative. I have begun to exercise. I have taken my first walk. My legs are a mess but at least they support me. I have found my clothes all neatly washed and pressed in the utility closet in the corner of my room. If I ever get the chance I know I shall be able to walk out of here and I shall be on watch tonight.

I lay still in the dark. Occasionally I heard people walk by in the corridor but none of them paused. Then, after a long quiet in which I almost dozed and had to shake myself awake, I heard rapid footsteps getting closer and closer. I heard the handle of my door turn and then the rattle as a key was inserted and turned. A crack of light appeared and then widened.

I waited until my visitor had entered and closed the door and then I acted. I swept back the covers, swung my legs out and then reached for and hit the light switch.

The light flickered and came on full and I found myself staring down at a small monkey-shaped man in a white coat. He had neatly trimmed wavy hair and a beard. He danced back from me, well out of my claw's reach and then winked and grinned. "Hello, Chimp. Glad to see you are getting back to normal."

Someone walked past outside and he froze with his fingers to his lips. When the footsteps had passed he motioned for me to sit. I flopped back on to the bed. Surprise had knocked the stuffing out of me. Of all visitors, the person I had least expected to see was Pioneer Raoul Murray.

He checked the door and locked it and came back to me. Finally I found my voice.

"What the hell are you doing here?"

"Keeping an eye on you. Making sure you don't get into any more trouble. Trying to keep you alive."

"I'm alive. Where's Ariadne?"

"Sh, sh. Keep your voice down. No one knows I'm here."

"Was it you who came last night?"

"Yes. I've dropped in to see you whenever I could. Just to make sure everything was all right. Are you feeling better?"

"Yes . . . a bit stiff. Look. What the . . . What is going on here?"

"All in good time. Now listen. I know you are going to find this hard, but I only have a few minutes, so listen. Tomorrow you will receive an official visit. From me. I want you to play cold and dumb. Be the perfect Pioneer Rescuer, ready to go to the farthest stars to bring 'em back alive, as we used to say. Don't argue. Don't try to pick a fight. They'll kill you. All they want is an excuse to say your programming has gone haywire. Just be quiet and polite. Be pleased to see me. With luck I'll be able to get you out of here. Trust me, Chimp. I'll answer all your questions when I can. Here, I brought you this. I thought I was going to have to wake you up and I wanted something to calm you down."

He took from his pocket a silk scarf with a dark brown pattern stencilled on it. It was the scarf that Ariadne had worn round her neck on the night of the party. "Anyway, I thought you would like this. Keep it hidden. Now I must go. See you tomorrow after the second meal. Remember what I've said."

He stood up, crossed to the door and listened and then unlocked it and slipped out. He was gone before I really knew what was happening and I heard his quick steps retreat down the corridor.

Ariadne's scarf. I sniffed it, but it smelled of soap. What did it mean? Feeling more confused then ever, feeling again that the initiative was not with me, I switched out the light and then groped my way back to bed. I lay down heavily and pulled the covers round me.

Tears are not a sign of weakness, believe me. They are nature's release. Even dogs can cry, and that night I cried. For

164

loneliness, for want, for pity and fear, for my dead friends whom I loved, for myself. And at some point in that long dark night, I fell asleep.

The next morning the breakfast I received was a proper meal, not thin gruel and slim toast. The orderly seemed excited and busy. He plumped up my pillows. "Big day. Special day," he said nodding at me as though I should feel grateful.

"What happens today?" I asked.

"You'll see."

Then he stood to one side while I ate and when I had finished he cleared my tray and brought me a bowl of water and flannel and soap. "Now you wash special. Give that thing a good scrubbing," he said, nodding towards my claw. "Sometimes it smells bad enough to make me want to throw up."

That was the first time anyone had ever said anything like that about my claw.

When he had gone I washed slowly enjoying the water and I *did* pay special attention to my claw. I polished it and flexed it and sniffed it, but I could smell nothing.

I hid Ariadne's scarf among my own clothes and then hopped back into bed and smoothed the covers and waited for the doctor. He came bustling in a few minutes later with two attendants and proceeded to change all my dressings.

"Is today special?" I asked.

"Why?"

"You are dressing me up like a pharaoh."

"A what?"

"Doesn't matter. Is today special?"

"There is going to be an inspection. That is all. They want to know that you are well. That you have been well looked after."

"And have I been well looked after?"

"You have made a very speedy recovery. Your metabolism amazes me."

"That was not what I meant. Keeping me alone. No visitors. No information about the outside world. Is that what you call keeping me well?"

"My concern is with your physical wellbeing only. And I am extremely busy. In other wings, far away from this isolated little room there are wards and in the wards are men who do not have your inbuilt survival mechanism. They have been maimed, injured and traumatized by you and the other creatures like you. Each day some die. We don't have all the drugs we need, you see. But we still have sufficient professional honour to keep someone like you alive, and we hide you down here, so nobody knows. So that the hospital will not be attacked. Good day. I have other patients. I hope you enjoy your inspection."

He did not say it, of course, but I speculate that in my early days here, when I was vulnerable as a sleeping kitten, he must have been tempted to extend my wounds and open an artery. To his honour, he resisted. Silently he packed up his instruments and bandages. I watched him and then I called to him, "Cheer up, Mr Doctor. We all have to do jobs we don't like sometimes. Thank you for saving me." He didn't reply but hurried out and the attendants went with him.

I lay in the clean bed in the locked room and stared at the tiles and waited and waited.

Then there was commotion in the corridor outside my room. I heard orders and the tramping of feet. The door rattled and sprang open and two armed soldiers burst in. They took up position at the foot of my bed with their small laser cannon trained on me. I noticed dangling at their waists bulbous rubbery gas masks and I remembered the faces of the men who had captured me.

After the guards came the doctor who had tended me and then several officials each of whom was dressed up in some fancy uniform. I mean fancy. They wore decorations made from some cheap painted plastic. I recognized one face. Major de Beer.

Mindful of Murray's directions, I stared at Major de Beer dully. Then two women entered. One of them was pregnant and the baby stretching her womb made her uniform look ridiculous. They all stood to attention while Pioneer Murray

166

stalked in. He looked as though he had a bad smell under his nose. He too was wearing a uniform.

This monstrous and comic pageant gathered round my bed and stared at me. Then Pioneer Murray spoke.

"Angelo, are you feeling well?"

"Yes, Pioneer Murray."

"Have you been well treated?"

"Very well treated Pioneer Murray."

"Do you have any requests?"

"What is my next assignment?" I saw a gleam in Murray's eye and realized that I was going too far. "But before that I would like to be reunited with my mate Ariadne."

"That is not possible. At present."

I wanted to scream questions at him, but I resisted and settled my eyes on the ceiling above the two guards.

"Are you able to walk?"

"I believe so."

The doctor stepped in close to my bed, raising his hand. "I can see no reason why Angelo cannot walk though his motor reflexes have not been fully tested, for obvious security reasons." He stepped back. Oh, I could see the gist of his statement: I was somehow a security risk. Did they expect me to run amok?

Pioneer Murray stared at me for several seconds and then asked, "Do you remember what happened at Rotorua Mining Town?"

"I do not remember the details."

"Why did you begin fighting?"

"The Pioneers were under attack. I defended them."

"Why did you defend them?"

I paused and then began to quote from an early training manual which had been prepared for our guidance many centuries ago. "'The Pioneers represent the most developed genetic stock of the Earth. They must be protected at all costs, even if that cost be your own life.'" And in stating this I was stating the simple truth. The fight in me, the mindless will to kill that had carried me over many bodies down to the water's

167

edge, was triggered by that directive. The ancient and long-dead programmers had never foreseen that such a directive would ever be turned against humans. They had expected us to be pitted against Gorgons, against fierce predators, against creatures like the ants we found on Jeupardi.

"Did you know you were killing humans?"

"I was defending the Pioneers."

The officials conferred together. I could not catch all that they said, but I caught some bits. "He brought back Mazeppa who was there at the party . . . No evidence of preparation . . . no evidence of deviance . . . Test him . . ."

They drew back and Pioneer Murray faced me again.

"Do you call Bonniface a friend?"

"We grew up together. He is a fellow Rescuer. Ariadne is my friend of course."

"Bonniface has become unstable. He attacks humans. We are holding him outside. You must execute him. Do you agree?"

"If Bonniface can no longer fulfill the purpose for which he and I were created, then . . ." I let my voice trail away. "However, I would not like to be the one to kill him. We are of the same species. Adapted."

"That seems to me completely reasonable," said Pioneer Murray, addressing his colleagues. "We must remember that they were *created* together and that makes for close bonding. We cannot ask the impossible."

I knew that they did not hold Bonniface. I had seen him up aboard the ship just before I was taken. And in any case, he would have fought to the death. I knew that this was a question planted by Murray to allow me to demonstrate my loyalty.

The officers, or whatever they were with Murray, grunted their unwilling agreement. Then one of them faced me. "Are you ready to take up your next assignment?"

"When I am fit." I replied.

"I think you may leave him in my charge now," said Pioneer Murray. "He is no danger to anyone. He regards me as a father. I will see him through his convalescence." He looked

168

round his companions and they all, one by one, nodded their heads. "I will collect him in three days," said Pioneer Murray, speaking directly to the doctor. "See that everything is done to build his strength. But if you have any worries or see any dangerous wilfulness report directly to me."

"I will," said the doctor. And then the entire party departed. Last of all were the guards who held their rifles on me to the last moment when the door closed.

You can believe that I was a model patient for the next three days. I did not ask any questions. I ate the good food and at night, when all was quiet, I exercised. Pioneer Murray did not visit me.

And then on the third day, after breakfast, the orderly opened my cupboard and laid out my clothes. I pretended to be weak and he helped me stretch the zip shirt over my shoulders and ease my slab legs into the trousers. I had no idea what to expect from the future. I was watchful of everything. I was suspicious of what kind of game Murray was playing, but I had no choice but to play along. I had so many questions.

I sat in my clothes in my locked room while the minutes ticked into hours and then, just as my patience was reaching its limit, my room was thrown open and two armed guards wearing their disgusting gas masks beckoned me outside. They marched me down long corridors and up flights of stairs until we reached the daylight. I found myself staring at one of the back doors to the hospital. It was a service door through which vegetables were delivered. Waiting outside was a low flyer of the type which had once been used to skip from city to city. The ramp was down and I climbed up the steps and inside. Murray was waiting for me. He was lying back on a couch and close to him were his two female attendants. Languidly he motioned to a chair and then handed me a cigar. He snapped his fingers and one of the attendants hurried round and presented me with a light.

"Welcome to the daylight, Chimp. Keep your trap shut until we have lifted clear." I saw the staircase retract and the door seal and then heard the thrum, thrum, thrum as the rotor blades established their rhythm and lifted us.

The hospital dropped away. Within minutes we were above the city of Old Auckland and I could see the sunlight glitter on the sea. Then we swung in an arc and began to head south.

Murray slapped his hands and directed the two handmaidens to leave us. They weren't happy, but they obeyed and went forward to join the pilot.

And when they were gone, Pioneer Murray sat up. "Well done, Chimp. And now you are free."

"I've got questions to ask."

"Enjoy your cigar."

"I want some answers."

"I'm sure you do."

"Well then. Where's Ariadne?"

He sighed deeply and regarded me. "Oh Chimp . . ."

"Don't call me that."

"All right. Angelo."

"Where's Ariadne?"

"She's dead. She died defending you." Those were words I had not expected to hear and I gaped at him. "She died defending you. By the time we got down to her she had been cut to ribbons. She died quickly I think and we rescued her body. You will see her soon. I don't know whether it means much to you, but I loved her too . . . but it was you she loved."

"Dead?" Why had I never expected that? I suppose because *I* had been saved. I had assumed that everyone else was safe. I felt a sudden loneliness and fear. "Am I the only one left? Were the rest killed?"

"Bonniface, Amsterdame and Lattisbourne escaped aboard the ship. We couldn't have stopped them even if we'd wanted to."

"Kingi? Elf?"

"No, they were caught. There was nothing I could do. It was as much as I could do to save you."

"And how did you save me?"

"Your cigar has gone out."

170

"Damn the cigar. Talk."

"I was coming to visit you. I was coming to visit some of the old Pioneers. I had planned to come down close to your settlement and give you a surprise. But when we got close we saw the fire and the crowds. I was able to pick out Bonniface's ship and I saw him and a woman, Amsterdame I suppose, climb up on to it with a crowd at their heels. They got a searchlight going and started firing. They were trying to help you I think. Show you the best way. They can't have known there were full-humans waiting to attack. But when they shone the searchlight on you I saw you. You were a red man and you were staggering like a drunkard. I saw Ariadne pulling you and then I saw a small crowd of full-humans emerge from under the ship. I honestly don't think Bonniface knew they were there. I could see what was happening and I ordered my men out. They were firing even before they hit the ground. But they were too late. I saw you go down. And Ariadne stood above you, pulling at the fur round your neck. She was calling for Bonniface. Then two of the humans reached her and she kicked and chopped and bit. But that was all she could do. They had guns you see."

"I remember . . ."

"And there is no way fists and anger can repel bullets. By the time my men reached her she was already dead."

"And Bonniface . . ."

"He came down from the ship. He fired at anything that moved and I spoke to him from my ship. I used the loudhailer. I told him who I was. I told him I would look after you and Ariadne. I told him to get the hell out of there. But he still stood as if he couldn't move. And then another woman, the black one, Lattisbourne, came scrambling out of the darkness and collapsed. He picked her up and climbed back inside. And I saw the doors close and the ship rise. He flew straight across the lake and then opened up with the laser cannon: a carpet of fire unrolled. And when he had burned the buildings he tried to burn the lake. He must have been demented inside his ship. Then the cannon stopped and the ship hung still for a moment and then it roared away to the east. Your friend is safe and

171

there are two with him. But I think their career as Pioneer Rescuers is ended."

I glanced at him and saw that he had a resigned sad smile on his face. He nodded at me as though agreeing with something, and said, "It was a long, sad night. The fires were still burning at dawn."

"What did you do with Ariadne and me?"

"Brought you into my ship. You were breathing in great wet gulps and we managed to get a tube down your throat. I am quite good as a doctor remember. Your shoulder was open and so I cut away the fur and stitched you up. The hardest thing was to stop you shaking. Every time I got the needle in you'd give a heave and tear out the stitches. I finally gave you an old medicine called morphine and that stopped you. But I didn't expect you to live, Angelo. But when I had done what I could for you I turned to Ariadne. I cleaned her up and took her aboard the sick bay in my ship."

"Is that where she is now?"

"No. But you will see her soon and your old friends Kingi and Elf."

"How long have I been ill, recovering, in prison, whatever?"

"Almost eight weeks."

"So long?"

"Only an adapted creature such as you would have survived. It was a wonder your body held together. And you will have lots of scars to tell your grandchildren about."

"Shut up."

"Sorry, that was a saying from the time when I was a boy. But you are alive. That is the main thing."

"Is it?"

"You're not going to get silly are you. Listen, I've been alive a lot longer than you and I've seen a lot more . . . I've seen a lot more than you could stomach of life and death. Grieve for Ariadne, yes. Grieve for your friends, yes. But you will live to fight again. Do you think they would want you to give up?"

"Oh shut up will you. Don't start morali – "

"Only the Ariadne you knew is dead. You can make another."

He said this quietly and it stopped me. I thought briefly of the cold tanks in the back room of our ship. It was absurd, rude, insulting to the memory . . .

"Why you . . ."

He moved his arm and I saw the gun he held, glowing red, fully charged, ready to burn but not to kill. "I thought you'd react this way. Silly Chimp. Get a hold of yourself. Think. Damn you. Start to think. Go over to the window there."

I obeyed.

"Now look down. Read what you see. The history of the world is the history of bereavement. Think how many people have walked, and kissed and died down there. You should think yourself lucky. You at least had a woman who loved you. What do the rest of us have?"

I didn't answer him but stared down at the milky rivers that wandered through the dark bush. We were already close to the volcanic region. I saw pits of yellow sulphur and dark green lakes which opened like holes in the bush. Vaguely, though I could not have given clear expression to the thought, I associated the suffering of the land with the grief that was now beginning to work through me.

"And if ever you get thoughts of attacking me because I tell you the truth, remember that I am watching you and I will set fire to your fur, but I won't kill you. Only stop you."

He got up quietly and went to the door that led to the pilot's cockpit and slipped through, closing the door silently.

I found that when he had gone I couldn't settle. I wanted to grieve easily and steadily, but my mind was like a kitten that runs after one dancing string and then chases another.

Ariadne diving into water and laughing as she shook her hair; the strange grave woman April, with her spread of antlers; Bonniface waving a pig bone; the silver mountain; the dead-faced doctors who had shaved me; Murray, smug after love-making. . . . And below me the dark green hills moved past. I

173

felt older and different. I looked at my huge scarred hand and the joints that flexed. I felt still and dry.

Murray was right. Life goes on and all that Time achieves is to leave its mark on you. Suddenly I was thinking about our ship and the sleeping clone that waited inches below the surface. What would Ariadne do if she were now standing in my place? Ariadne would know what to do. That clear and thoughtful woman had all the right instincts. I remembered how she had made me bomb the island of the ants. Remembering her fierceness and her strength did something strange to me. I suddenly thought that she was not dead. She was close to me. Hell, she was in my mind and in my fur. I felt a strange kind of elation. And even as I felt that elation, I felt a hollowness and knew that I would have to face many dark hours alone.

The helicopter began to lower and I saw familiar landmarks. We flew round the margin of the lake and over charred stumps and gaping gutted buildings. This was all that remained of the old mining town. There were no people.

Then we span out over the lake and crossed the spit of land which used to house the Pioneer Colony. The buildings were still standing but I saw no movement there. We began to climb into the hills and I could see the path that Ariadne and I had followed when we visited April. We flew over the squat shape of a black moonship, Murray's ship I guessed, and then banked sharply and began to land.

The wind from our rotor blades beat the manuka flat and birds scattered.

We were suddenly down with a bump and a lurch and the engine cut to a whine.

"Come on Chimp, work to do," said Murray, banging open the door to the travelling chamber. "You've had enough time for thinking. Let's see you put those muscles to some good use. You carry me through the manuka. We're going visiting."

One of his attendants released the main safety catch and I

174

pushed the exit door open, forcing the manuka back so that it scraped under the door and then sprang back up again. . . .We faced a green sea of waving branches and there was no way we could lower the landing steps. I jumped out and found myself up to my neck in the sweet-smelling trees.

"You two stay here and keep the place warm," said Murray to his two companions. One of them leaned close to him and whispered something and Murray laughed. "Trust him?" he said. "Course I can trust him. Young Angelo is like a son to me. Aren't you, Chimp?"

I nodded from the branches and lifted my arm and claw.

He squatted down and then grabbed my hair with his hands and swung his legs over my shoulders. "Aeneas did the old Anchises bear through the smouldering fires of Troy. Come on Chimp, giddy-up."

I was glad of his humour. Though Murray had not mentioned it, I remembered the foal-like creature we had abandoned on La Plage. That also had been his son.

Murray was heavier now than during the days on La Plage, but still light. I settled him like a rucksack and began to break my way through the small trees. He had to guide me by tugging on my ears and steadily we advanced up a slope away from the helicopter.

I came to a pathway and followed this, zigzagging up into the hills. We left the manuka behind and came to a place of grass and the path ran steeply beside a stream. The water was cold and clear and I recognized the stream that ran beside April's small hut.

"Are we going to see April?" I asked.

"Yes. A fine woman, don't you think?"

I didn't bother to answer his question. "How come you are so God almighty powerful with the full-humans?"

"I am a full-human, remember."

"You know what I mean. We heard you were cooperating with the Regeneration Programme."

"I was. I am. My sperm is as valuable as old wine. I come

175

from the Golden Age. With a little bit of Murray in their veins, the children of the future have some hope."

"Are you serious?"

"Yes and no. This world you brought me back to is nothing like the world I knew. I feel sometimes as though I am trying to teach calculus to an ape. No offence meant."

"So?"

"So it is all touch and go."

"I see."

"No you don't. Up there on the moon is all that remains of the world I once knew. There are books, but many of them are in languages I don't know. They expect me to be an oracle and when I tell them I don't know the answers, they think I am being secretive. We have embryos up there, cultured from my cells, and any fertile women are already pregnant."

"Ariadne guessed as much. She said there were techniques of sperm implantation which – "

"I do it the old way. The way that Ariadne taught me. Steady Chimp, you have no fight with me, remember. And the worst crime you can commit is to try and rewrite history. I am an old man, growing into a boy."

I stumped on in silence.

"Keep talking," said Murray. "It is nice to hear your voice after all this time; and besides, talking helps. Ask me questions."

"Is the Regeneration Programme working then?"

"I don't know. I think the cell culture is useless. All we seem to produce is messes. The pregnancies may result in good healthy children and that means that one day we will reinherit the world. But we need girls, women. And there are so few now. Inbreeding has already taken its toll. There are strains of haemophilia which keep occurring. We can cope with that on the moon, but those children would die within days of reaching the Earth. Worst of all is the lack of will."

"I don't understand."

"Nor do I. Here, put me down. I want to walk. This is the purest air I have ever smelled."

176

I hoisted him off my shoulders and set him on his feet. He seemed very small, scarcely taller than my ribs, and he stood there in the sunlight and looked up at me. "You know, you are the ones who should be having children. You and Ariadne and Bonniface and what's her name?"

"Amsterdame."

"We are all too weak for this world."

"We are sterile remember. We were designed to cope, remember, with this," I held up my claw. "And we were patterned on the ape."

"I know, I know. But still I wonder."

He pushed ahead of me, stooping under the tree ferns and at times stepping down into the water. I let him lead the way.

"Ariadne would have liked children. You should have talked to her," I said.

"She still might," he threw back at me over his shoulder.

We came to the top of the path where the stream opened into a pool. April's hut was before us.

"Hello. Anyone at home?" called Pioneer Murray. "Come on out. We're friends."

At the doorway of the hut I saw something move and the long fronds of willow were pushed back. April stepped out. I hardly recognized her though it was only a few weeks since Ariadne and I had sat with her beside this very stream. Her head was shaved and her antlers had been cut away almost to the skull. All that remained were two stumps each of which was topped by a black scar. She gave no sign of recognition but stared at us with a cold level gaze. Then she beckoned us. "You have come for your prizes? Take them, I have had enough of watching over the dead."

Inside her hut the air was cool and sweet with the smell of aromatic oils. There were three beds. Laid out on one was Ariadne. I approached slowly, wondering what I would see. It was Ariadne's hair. It was Ariadne's face, what remained of it. When I drew back the cover I saw where April, or someone, had tried to mend the wounds. I touched her and it was like

177

touching cold marble. There was none of the electric resilience of flesh.

This was not Ariadne! It looked like her but it was not her. Where was the spirit? Ariadne was all spirit. Without the spirit this was just a sham. I covered the face and turned to the next body.

This was Elf, smallest of all of us, petite as a child. Despite the wounds and the cut marks, I did not doubt that this was Elf. She seemed to be sleeping. And the same was true of Kingi. I pulled the covers completely back revealing their bodies. Kingi had lost his claw. It had been hacked off. The fur had been stripped from his lower legs and one foot was twisted at a ridiculous angle.

I looked at them and tried to remember my friends.

Their necks seemed longer and I looked closer.

"The mob caught them. They hanged them," said Pioneer Murray, moving close to me. "Now you must bury them."

Outside, away from the stream I stamped flat a stretch of the bushes and then dug a hole. I made it as wide and as deep as I could before my spade struck stone. Then, one by one, I carried the stiff bodies outside and lowered them into the ground. I turned the soil over them and that was that. I could think of no words. No special ceremony. There was nothing to be done. Death is so final and so unreal. Yet it all seemed appropriate. Aotearoa was once a land of proud warriors. I could think of no better resting place for people of such rare courage.

April moved behind me and when I had finished she scattered seeds on to the dark earth. She spoke words which I could not understand, words from the race of antlered people with whom she belonged. Her meaning was clear enough. She was wishing the departed Godspeed in whatever adventures lay before them. For myself, I do not believe in an afterlife. I do not think that we adapted people have what the full-humans call souls. That may be one thing which marks us out as being not quite human.

178

Nevertheless, I was grateful for her words. Her ceremony provided an ending which I could not.

"And now what?" The question was mine.

"I would speak with you," said the tall graceful woman, and took my arm. We began to walk down the path away from the clearing and the small simple hut. Pioneer Murray followed several paces behind. "Do you remember my request?"

"Of course."

"I have shaved off my antlers."

"I am glad it was you. At first I thought that the full-humans had . . ."

"Bah. They never got up here. I protect this place with magic. And besides, I would never submit to that while there was life in me. No, I trimmed them when I heard what had happened down by the lake. I wanted to be ready." She walked on in silence. "So?"

"So, I don't know. I don't know what I am going to do next. I doubt if I shall make another trip out into space. I shall probably go and look for Bonniface and the others."

"If the Space Council will let you."

I shrugged at that. "Aye, if they let me. But it is either that or nothing."

We walked on for a few more moments and then she stopped in the track and faced me, squarely. "I order you to take me home." I could feel the pressure of her will in my mind and it straightened me. She did have magic, but something inside me made me shake my head.

She started almost in disbelief and then began to speak and then paused, and finally spoke on. "I believe that I am not unattractive – "

"Don't."

Pause. She breathed deeply. "No, I was mistaken. You are like them. Like Lindis and Tui. And there is no kindness in you, or pity. You deserve your fate. I do not. But mine is the tragedy." Then she turned away and walked back up the hill.

179

She never looked back though I watched her until she disappeared into the trees.

When she had gone I blew out my cheeks and looked at Pioneer Murray. "Well, what do you make of that?"

"She is right, Angelo. You do have a cold streak in your not-quite-human constitution. Why not take her back? What are a few more months to you or a couple more long sleeps?"

"Is that all you see? Do you think I can go through all this and then just blithely set out into space again? No. There are more important things now. I feel as though someone has dug a great big hole inside me and I have no mind to be the kind and gentle hero. I have not much kindness left in me."

"Shock. You'll come right. When you have lost as many loved ones as I have, you eventually begin to accept life as it really is. Not just as you would like it to be." He took my hand and we began to walk on down the hill. It was like walking with a child. "But, I hope you will make one more trip. If not for poor April with the shaved head, then for me."

I began to answer but he hushed me. "I don't want your answer now, Angelo. I want you to take your time. I have a present for you down in the helicopter. That's what we used to call them. It is an old word . . . from an even older language."

"What are you talking about?"

"Nothing. Just thinking about age. You know she's a fine woman."

"Who is?"

"April with the shorn horns. A man would be proud to have a woman like that beside him. But I wish she would smile once in a while, laugh a little. She has much energy, but she fritters it away on the past and in a sullen anger. Can you imagine her dancing with flowers in her hair?"

"What are you talking about?"

"Love, Angelo. Love. Do I have to tell you about love? It begins in respect."

"Are you saying you are falling in love with April?"

"Angelo. You have the body of an ape and the understanding

180

of a child. Let us drop this topic." We were now entering the low manuka. "Here, carry me."

We could see the helicopter below us as I hoisted him up on to my shoulders. I walked slowly downwards placing my feet carefully in the soft earth and pushing the dark stems of the manuka aside with my elbows. One of Murray's attendants was waiting at the open door of the helicopter and waved to us.

"I would like to see the old Pioneer Settlement," I said as I hoisted him into the craft.

"And so you shall. But food first I think. I'm hungry, if you are not. And, though you've made a swift recovery, you are still not yourself yet. You will probably eat like a glutton, and after you have eaten we can go and see the ruins."

And Murray was right on both counts. Once I had started eating I was ravenous and the old Pioneer Settlement was in ruins.

We picked our way carefully among the fallen timbers and broken glass. The old walls were breached and the plaster was scarred where fire had burned the timbers. The apartment where Ariadne and I had lived was completely gutted and the sky showed through fissures in the roof. Everything was damp or sodden with rainwater and heavy to move and stank of mould. I didn't linger long. Here were no good memories.

I carried my memories in my hands, in the notebooks. These were the present that Murray had promised me. Somehow he had managed to rescue them, and I knew that he had read them, though he never commented on their contents.

We visited the mineral pool where Bonniface and I had bathed. Its surface was covered with scum and muck. Water still bubbled in through the old clotted faucet and I tested it with my finger. It was still hot.

"How would you like to do this place up?" said Murray. "It shouldn't be too difficult. You could build yourself a palace. Hot pools, plenty of land, fine climate."

I looked at him, not certain whether he was joking or not. "I think this place is dead," I said simply.

181

"Places don't die."

"To me this place is dead."

"Ah, that's different. But you should be aware that an older spirit than you lives here."

"Perhaps." I didn't want to be drawn into this conversation. I could feel the drift of Pioneer Murray's thinking. Individuals may die, but life continues. I chose to change the subject. "Tell me, are all the Pioneers gone?"

"All gone. All dead."

I shook my head in disbelief. "But I thought they escaped. I thought Indira took them safely out on to the lake."

"She did. But that was a night of terror. They came after them in boats. They clubbed Indira to death in the water, and the rest put up no resistance. Then this place was burned. Now the only Pioneers left are me and April. What a waste, eh?"

"That is terrible. Innocent, gentle Indira . . ."

"We are not fighters like you and Bonniface and Lattis-bourne. We Pioneers are gentle. We are shapers of climate and soil. We adapt slowly . . . quick by human terms . . . but slowly all the same. We are not made for sudden catastrophes. Can you think how poor Mazeppa – he was one of yours wasn't he? – can you think how poor Mazeppa would defend himself when faced with an angry full-human swinging an axe? Well, he wouldn't, would he? Give him three or four generations and he could probably become the best axe-swinger in the world if he wanted. Well, Mazeppa was the most adaptive of all of us . . . and now he is gone and I'm sorry, but I can't even tell you where his remains are."

"It doesn't matter."

"No, none of it matters. History doesn't matter so long as you don't fall into the same trap every time a problem presents itself."

"Meaning?"

"Meaning that you and I are just about all that is left of viable life on this planet."

*

182

We wandered down to the lakeside and sat on the old jetty with our feet just a few inches above the slate-grey water. "What happened to the rest of the full-humans?" I asked. "The ones who attacked here?"

"We resettled them in Auckland. Many of them were in the same hospital where you were. Others are now growing fruit. Some are fishermen on the east coast. The mining settlement is closed. They are the last generation that will thrive on Earth . . . No, there may be a few settlements where life clings on."

"You paint a dismal picture."

"I am a realist, or I am nothing."

"Mmm. And what then is this last journey you want me to take?"

"I want you to look for Pioneer Rip. He set out before me."

"Why do you want me to find him?"

Pioneer Murray drew a deep breath. "Because I think Rip can help us. Don't ask me why."

"Don't play games with me. What makes you think that Pioneer Rip can help us?"

Murray picked up a handful of pebbles from the shingle that lay beside us on the jetty and threw them out on to the grey water. "Because I have dreamed of him. Because I think he has tried to contact me in my dreams."

"Is his beacon still flashing?"

"I don't know."

"Well for God's sake . . ."

"He is alive and will help us. I am sure of that, Angelo."

"How will he help us?"

"I don't know."

"You're mad, or senile, or worse. You want me to go out to God knows where because you have had strange dreams?"

"Yes."

"And if I don't?"

"Then we will dwindle, all of us. You and me. Into nothing."

"I won't go," I said.

*

183

That was the end of our conversation. The light was failing as we made our way back to Pioneer Murray's helicopter. Waiting for us at the door was one of his female helpers. It was the pregnant one. Her face was white as she welcomed him aboard.

"We've just had word," she said, "from the moon . . . a special dispatch. We didn't know how to contact you."

"Well go on, what was it?" said Murray irritably.

"Some of your children have been born there."

"Good, a bit premature. But they can cope."

"Yes, but the initial finding is that they are all sterile." Then she broke down in tears and we could get nothing more from her.

"Sterile," said Murray, and looked directly at me.

PART 3

Pioneer Rip

1

The overland transit slid down from the hills and connected with the bumpy ground rails that led into Master Town. It was night-time, perhaps two in the morning, and there were no lights showing in the small town.

The transit entered the dark station and came to a halt. The doors jerked and then opened to reveal the dingy departure lounge where Ariadne and I had waited. I was on my guard. Since Pioneer Murray delivered me from the hospital in Auckland I had avoided any contact with full-humans. During the entire journey south from Rotorua Mining Camp I had kept awake lest some fanatic with a gun were waiting to snipe at the transit. The small shack that served as a food-stop at Taupo was boarded up and the transit didn't even slow.

I had no idea what my welcome might be in Master Town. At worst the inhabitants of that small town might have gathered in a lynch mob. At best there might only have been Pedro and his strange small brother called Kier.

But there was no one. A single bulb burned in the ceiling and caused moving shadows as it swung in the gusts through the transit door.

Though I looked mangy and striped where my fur had been shaved for the operations, I was very fit. I swung down into the lounge and rolled as I landed. There were no shots.

Within seconds I had crossed the lounge and slipped outside through its loose doors. No sound. No movement. I sprinted down the path into the hangar and found myself staring up at the dark bulk of our ship. Along its roof glowed the bright blue points of the security lights.

I kept close to the wall as I worked my way round the ship until I was opposite the narrow metal ladder which led up to the side airlock. One bound and I was on the ladder and climbing. Now I was most vulnerable, and knew it. I doubt if I have ever climbed so fast. Minutes later I was standing on the small catwalk outside the airlock and pressing my palm against the security plate. It seemed an eternity before I heard the clamps release and saw the door slide silently open.

I dived straight in and banged the emergency close switch with my claw. After a moment's hesitation the door closed. I was in.

I waited, expecting the inner door to open automatically but it didn't. This was strange. Normally when we are on Earth there is an equilibrium between the two doors and they can be made to function together. While I had closed down most of the sensitive parts of the ship, I had certainly left the airlock functioning so that Pedro and Kier could get in to service the hydroponics.

Beside the inner door was a switch hidden under a small safety membrane. It is designed so that it can be activated by a blow from a human elbow. This is the emergency override switch. I jabbed it with the point of my claw. Still the door didn't move.

"Identity?" The voice was that of our main computer. I would recognize its peculiar nasality from a hundred similar voices.

"Angelo. Come on, open up. You can read my voice. This is an imperative." Then a thought struck me. "No, wait a moment. Delay." The door had unlocked, but not opened. "Why did the inner door not open when I came in?"

"Because it was on emergency."

"Who placed it on emergency?"

"Identity not known."

The conclusion I had jumped to was obvious. Whoever had placed the door on emergency was still on board. They had to be.

"There is someone on board." I said. "Can you tell me where?"

"Not certain. Just a moment." (Whoever had originally programmed the speech memory of our computer had given it

188

a certain conversational finesse.) "A lavatory in your living quarters was activated some hours ago. Does that help?"

"A bit." I thought for a few moments. "Has anyone tried to get into the doors I sealed before Ariadne and I departed?"

"Oh yes."

"And?"

"And what?"

"Oh for God's sake. And did they get in?"

"No, of course not. Only you or Ariadne can open them. Those were the instructions. Am I right?"

"Yes. Tell me, when was the inner door put on emergency?"

"Twelve days ago. Since that time the airlock has not been used."

"Has anyone tried to tamper with the inner doors since then?"

"No."

"Aha."

"Shall I open the inner door now?"

"When I say." I was forewarned. There could be an ambush though I doubted it. The pattern did not make sense. In any case I had no option but to take a chance. But I wanted to give myself the maximum advantage. "Close the door leading into the airlock chamber."

"Closed."

"Extinguish all lights in the airlock chamber."

"Extinguished."

"Do not bring any lights on until I call for them, all right?"

"Understood."

I placed myself well to one side out of any direct line of fire. "Open the door."

I heard the motor's hum and felt the inner warmth of the ship stroke me. The door was open. I growled, making the sound as low and menacing as I could. Still no answering sound. I dived and rolled through the door and came up with my claw advanced. I know my ship. I snarled and jabbed in the darkness and then called for the lights. When the lights came on I was not surprised to discover that I was alone in the small chamber.

So I closed the airlock door and reset the emergency.

Methodically I began to work my way down through the ship. I used the pull-poles so that I made no sound. A pattern began to establish itself. At all levels the lights were on in those parts of the ship which I had left accessible to humans. All doors which I had not specifically sealed were open. I smiled to myself at that. Those who have never travelled for months aboard a ship such as ours always feel frightened in the darkness behind closed magnetic doors.

Finally I came to the area where Ariadne and I had lived. I had still heard no sound of any human. I dropped from the pull-pole on soft feet and crept down the corridor until I was just outside the door. There a sudden thought occurred to me and made me quail. What if something had gone wrong with the life-system computers and they had awakened the sleeping clones of myself and Ariadne? They could be sitting at the table now, still sleepy and staring at one another without comprehension. What would I do if I found myself facing myself? Vaguely I was aware that too much imagination can hinder action and before I could think any more I slipped quietly round the door.

He was asleep at the table. He was not an ape-giant like me, but a small boy with white hair and pale skin. I recognized Kier. His head was resting on his arms and his face was towards me. He was bruised. One eye socket was livid and closed. There was a cut on his cheek which was healing into a scab and his arms were scratched.

What now? I did not want to wake him quickly. That might scare him out of his wits. I reasoned that if Kier was here then perhaps Pedro was close, perhaps in the hydroponic sheds or the kitchen or even the swimming pool. I tiptoed round the sleeping boy and entered the kitchen. No one.

I scoured the parts of the ship which had been available to the two of them. There was no sign of Pedro. And when I returned to the main living quarters, Kier was waking up. He stared at me blankly, perhaps thinking I was something in a dream and then I saw terror enter his face and his mouth opened though no sounds came.

I did not know what to do and so did the only thing I knew. I picked him up. I lifted him up to my shoulders and buried his face in my fur. I patted him gently on his back with my claw and said what words I could. He squirmed and fought and I admired his pluck but then he held tight to my fur and I heard him begin to cry.

Finally, when all the energy seemed to have drained out of him I held him at arm's length and looked at him and let him down on his feet and nudged him back to his chair.

He looked at me with large eyes. I suppose I looked a fearsome sight. My injuries had not improved my beauty. In Auckland the surgeons had been thorough but hardly cosmetic. The wounds had healed, but my arms and shoulders looked as though they were attached to me by giant zip-fasteners. Where I had been shaved my fur was growing back as a thick stubble. In some places my fur was no longer ginger but grey.

His gaze lingered on my claw which I opened and closed hoping to amuse him. But he did not smile.

"Angelo," I said finally, touching my chest with my claw. "Angelo. A friend." Still he said nothing. I reached across and touched him being careful to use my human arm. "You are Kier. We met you when we landed. You and Pedro. You brought us fruit and flowers. You have looked after our ship. Where is Pedro?"

That drew a reply. He shook his head. "Pedro gone."

"Gone? Gone where?"

If I had hoped for a flood of information, I was mistaken. Drawing information from him was like pulling teeth of stone. I brought juice from the kitchen. I prepared a rough meal. I lit one of the cigars which Pioneer Murray had given me and let him puff on it until his eyes watered and he spluttered. Gradually some trust was established. He began to talk. I was able to build up a picture of what had happened.

Pedro had run away one night. He had heard that they were calling for volunteers to join a breeding party in a place called Whakatane. The plan was to establish a colony somewhere in Old Peru though how they intended to get there no one knew.

191

Then news had come of our battle in Rotorua Mining Town and some of the people from Master Town had attacked our ship. They had thrown stones at it. Later they had stoned Kier because he was identified with us and that was when Kier moved inside and closed the outside door. He had pressed whatever switches came to hand.

They had tried to burn our ship by lighting fires under it. The rest I could guess. At an elementary level our ship is programmed for self defence. When a party climbed up on to it intending to smash the cables which gave us energy, the ship simply charged its skin and they dropped off like burnt flies. Since that date there had been no further attacks and Kier had lived inside as a hermit.

Kier had no belongings save a few things he carried in a woven flax basket. He stood up and fetched the basket from the sleeping cubicle which he had claimed as his own. He extracted a sheet of paper and spread it out on the table in front of us. It was a crudely printed broadsheet of the type that pass for newspapers in this wretched time. The ink was smudged but I could still read it. It said, "Killers Defeated". Below this headline were pictures of me and Bonniface and Amsterdame and Kingi and Elf and an account of the way we had attacked the peaceful citizens of Rotorua Mining Town. One picture showed the hanging of Elf and Kingi.

"It is not true," I said, but Kier only shrugged.

"I cannot read," he said. Then he pointed at my picture. "You write." He had a pen and pushed it into my claw. Carefully I signed my name and then I printed the names of each of my friends, pronouncing their names clearly. That pleased him.

When I had finished he folded the page carefully and put it back in his basket. "Did you kill many?" he asked.

"The killing was an accident."

"But did you kill many?"

"Yes." I expected him to shy back, but he didn't. His eyes gleamed.

192

"Good. Tell me how you killed many. Was it with this?" He pointed at my claw.

"Yes."

He nodded as though satisfied. "I wish I had a claw," he said.

Then I think I understood. This poor frightened boy with bleached skin and straw hair took delight in the slaughter. He too was an outsider, stoned for protecting our ship. Perhaps from his birth he had been derided as a living symptom of all that had gone wrong on Earth. He wanted revenge. He looked on me as a brother. Or if not as a brother, at least as someone on his side.

And he is right.

I have written all these words carefully. My notebooks and papers are growing into a library. I feel it matters that I write down things as they happen. I am no longer concerned with philosophy. Nor do I any longer worry about meanings. Ariadne would be amused by that.

Notebooks and papers! They are not much when compared to the life we have been living, but they are all I have. I consider them important.

Kier has his woven basket and I have my papers, each one carefully written out by hand. Ariadne once asked me for whom I am writing. At that time I had no clear answers. Now I know. I am writing them for myself and no matter if they burn with me in space or end up sodden and trampled. Something was said. Something was done.

Kier is asleep. I have tucked him up in the cubicle which once belonged to Ariadne.

And tomorrow I must open our clone chamber and bring Ariadne back to life. Only it will not be her. Cannot be her.

I am afraid of tomorrow.

At the same time I am excited. I suspect this is my genetic planning working again. I wonder what Kier will think when he sees me raise a woman from the dead.

I tried to tell him about Ariadne . . . about what she meant to me, but the boy fell asleep.

I wonder where Pioneer Murray is? Perhaps stretching out with one of his fertile women. I hope he is still alive when I return, if I return. For when I have woken up my Ariadne II I plan to seek out Pioneer Rip. And I will bring him back, if I can.

What alternative do I have? All alternatives are equally meaningless and thus all are equally hopeful.

Bah!

Tomorrow.

2

We ate a good breakfast, I saw to that. The boy Kier seemed more cheerful, the effect of company I suppose, and after we had eaten he insisted that I accompany him on a tour of inspection of the hydroponic troughs. He was proud of them, proud of his work. All the narrow gardens were filled with bright green foliage. I noticed he had added rhubarb and silver beet to our standard crops. New tomato plants were neatly tied up against a trellis and he explained in detail how he had pollinated each of the yellow flowers carefully by hand. I pretended to be stern and opened the filter cups and felt inside to see if I could find any slime. They were completely clean with all the pores open. I turned to find him grinning at me. "They were very mucky when I opened them," he said. "Looked as though they hadn't been done for months."

"Probably hadn't either," I said. "I was never a good gardener. But you have kept this place spotless. I'm very grateful."

Kier shrugged, "It gave me something to do."

More than that, I thought, but said nothing. Praise would have had no meaning. But I could imagine the white-faced boy bending over the green leaves, nipping out the dead ones, checking the ties to see they were not too tight, combing the gravel and vermiculite with his thin fingers, finding comfort in his work. "Would you like to help me with another maintenance job?" I asked.

He nodded seriously. "I'm pretty good with machinery."

"This might be a bit scary."

He shrugged as if to say, "So what?"

I led him from the hydroponics centre back to the kitchen and then down the narrow corridor to the hibernation chamber where Ariadne and I had fallen asleep and woken up so many times. This was all new to him as the hibernation chamber had been locked. He looked in surprise at the twin platforms with their cowls of clear silica. Perhaps to him they looked like peculiar greenhouses.

At the end of the chamber was the door which led to the cold room where the clones slept. I touched the lock, identifying myself, and then pushed the sliding door open. Inside it was gloomy as it always is. Pale blue lights gleamed in the ceiling casting an icy glow over all the sterile surfaces.

Kier shivered. "Nip back and find yourself an overall if you are cold," I said, but he just moved closer to me.

"This is how this chamber looks when we are travelling," I said, "but there are better lights. Cover your eyes." He did as I asked and I touched the main power switch and bright white lights blazed above us. They made the room seem small and revealed every detail of the twin coffins in which slept the clones of Ariadne and myself. "Go ahead and have a look," I said.

Kier tiptoed away from me, afraid for some reason to make a sound, and peered down into one of the clone baths. He gave a cry of surprise and then stared back at me. It is hardly likely that his albino face became whiter than it is, but he seemed to become paler. He was looking at my clone, Angelo II, fresh faced and innocent, asleep in his liquor. I smiled and winked. "Don't worry, I'm alive. But I told you it was scary."

"What's in the other coffin?"

"Have a look."

He glanced up at me and licked his lips and then stepped across the narrow companionway and looked down at Ariadne.

"Is she alive?" he asked.

"I hope so."

"How will you find out?"

For answer I pointed to the twin auto-nurses which cared for the two clones. Each auto-nurse had a face of dials and purred quietly to itself. "If anything was wrong they would be clamouring and there'd be red lights flashing and you'd have heard the computers telling you to get in here and see what was wrong. Not that you can do much if there is something wrong. There

196

are procedures . . ." I thought of the long list of instructions implanted in us on what to do if anything goes wrong in the clone chamber. "But it is very complicated."

"She's beautiful."

His simple words stopped me.

"Yes. Do you remember her?"

"I remember you had a woman with you, but I don't think she looked like this."

"She looked like that. Well, similar."

The moment was upon me. I realized I had been avoiding it ever since I had returned to the silent ship. I now had to look at Ariadne. Vaguely I also realized that I was glad that I had the simple young boy Kier with me. Hell, I was using him to help me. I do not know what I would have done if I had been alone. Perhaps I would have avoided the issue altogether.

I moved to her coffin and looked down through the clear surface. She lay, perfect as a newly drowned corpse, but with grace and dignity. She looked younger than the Ariadne I had known (which of course she was). She was a woman, but she looked like a child. No, not a child . . . pure as a child. . . . And when I woke her up, what would I find?

"What is the maintenance we have to do?" It was Kier again bringing me back to the present.

"We have to wake her up."

He frowned. "How do we do that?"

"Simple, we activate the auto-nurse."

"And what about this one?" he pointed towards my clone which lay in its large tub.

"We will leave that one alone," I said. "We don't want two of me running about do we?" He shrugged. The question had no meaning to him. But then he nodded. "I see, we might have trouble feeding all of us. Right? Shall we do it?"

I let Kier check each of the auto-nurse's dials and then I tapped out the wake-up code. I let him press the green activate switch.

He watched silent and round-eyed as the auto-nurse went about its programmed business. The liquid which covered

197

Ariadne II became milky as millions of small bubbles were generated to provide a gentle massage. Nerves came alive and recorded pleasure. The brain began to wake from its slow dreams. Blood flowed as the heart began to beat steadily. The body moved slightly and the face slid through a chaos of expressions. The auto-nurse was checking out all the muscles.

Kier and I stared in astonishment and then finally I took him by the hand and led him out of the chamber and switched out the lights. "It will take many hours," I said. "Possibly up to three days before she is ready to emerge. Come on, we'll check out the rest of the ship and make sure it is ready for space."

During the entire day I worked through the ship and Kier followed me wherever I went. He wouldn't say much and I guessed he was thinking about what was happening in the clone tank. But I was wrong.

In the evening as I prepared a meal for us in the kitchen he appeared holding his basket which contained his few pathetic possessions.

"Well, I suppose I'd better go now," he said.

I stared at him in surprise. "Go? Why?" It had never occurred to me that he would want to leave.

"Well, you're getting your woman back and the ship seems OK and I've done my job."

I saw he was close to tears but holding the tears back.

"Do you want to leave?" I asked, and he shook his head. "Well, then?"

I have never held any human being truly close except Ariadne, but now I found myself almost bowled over by the young boy who hurled himself at me and clung to my fur. I patted him, and stroked him with my claw, whispering words of friendship. "You are with friends now. You are part of the family." He clung to me and said nothing.

Looking back I wonder at what point I had decided to adopt him.

*

Adopt him I did. And so on that same night I gained a son and performed a strange, ritual killing which would have had my original programmers jabbering with disbelief.

When Kier was asleep, cosily rolled up in Ariadne's bunk, I made my way to the kitchen and thence to the clone chamber. Ariadne's coffin was full of activity. Her body was threshing about like a grounded fish whipping the fluids to foam. Her arms and legs churned and kicked as her muscles began to discover their strength.

I watched her for a few moments and then turned away. It was not her I had come to see. I turned to the other coffin and tried to ignore Ariadne's frantic movement. I stared down at my own impassive face. How complete I was in repose: my face unlined, my fur unsinged, my claw, glossy and open and unbloodied. Where was the kick that made Angelo? The body which lay there was both me and not me, and I conceived a deep loathing for it. I am Angelo. I am the scars and the passion and the hurt and this, the sum total of all the pages I have written. That thing is a dream of my makers. I realized that while it lived I could never be free and that therefore I had best dispose of it.

One by one I broke the seals which closed the tank containing my simulacrum. The alarm bell on the auto-nurse began to clamour and I ripped out its circuitry. For one horrible moment the body in the tank moved, half turning on to its side.

With the safety seals broken I still could not move the great silica lid and so I smashed down on it with my claw and at the fifth blow it broke. I began to tear the coffin apart. The syrup in which the body of my clone had lived for centuries slopped through the cracks and down on to the floor. The body lay exposed. I reached in and placed my hand and claw under its shoulders and levered it up into a sitting position. Hundreds of bio-crystalline fibres, each smaller than the finest hair, tore loose from the body leaving a stippled pink rash.

We were face to face, the clone and me, and my sense of humour saved me. "If he wakes up he's going to be terribly upset," I thought, and got on with my business with a laugh.

199

The body was heavy (I am heavy) and I had to pull and tug with all my strength until I finally had it slumped over one side of the coffin. Holding it steady with my claw I moved round the tank until I could get my arms firmly under its soft arms and lift. I half carried, half dragged it over the rim and set it down on the floor. It was greasy as a fish and awkward as a bag of wheat. But now at least I had room to move. I stooped over it, took it firmly by the arms and lifted. One heave and I had its head over my shoulder. One more heave and the body was evenly balanced and I could straighten my legs. Behind me I heard a thump as its claw landed heavily on the ground.

I walked out of the clone chamber and through the hibernation room. The corridor leading to the main living area was narrow but I squeezed through.

Moving as quietly as I could I climbed up through the ship. I used raw strength and it gave me pleasure to hoist myself and my burden up by the pull-poles.

At the main airlock I pressed the release mechanism and both doors slid open with a hiss. I was surprised to discover that in the outside world it was daytime. Sunshine blazed brightly at the end of the hangar and the air smelled crisply of early morning.

Standing on the narrow gangway I turned round and released the body. It fell with a thump and lolled half over the platform under the safety rail. One nudge with my foot and it toppled and fell. It struck the side of the ship and rolled down its rough metal until it came to the end of the curvature and fell into space. Seconds later, I heard it land on the concrete of the hangar floor.

That was all there was to it. Let anyone who found the body think what they like.

I closed the airlock and sealed it. During the rest of the morning I cleaned up the mess in the clone room and then showered, trying to wash from my fur the sticky fluid that had protected my clone and the smell of it.

Tired, I slumped still wet on to my bed and fell asleep face down.

*

"Angelo, Angelo." Something was tugging at my shoulders and trying to roll my head. "Angelo, wake up. She's stopped moving and the other one has escaped."

I opened my eyes and found myself staring into the frightened face of Kier. "What's escaped . . ."

"I've been down there. Down to that room. The woman isn't moving any more. She's floating on the surface. But the other one has broken out. It's smashed its tank. It might be anywhere."

I understood and nodded sleepily. "No worry, Kier. I sorted the other one out and threw it out of the ship. There's only us three here. And the woman isn't floating. The fluids are draining away." But still he wasn't satisfied. He was afraid. I shook myself and rolled on to my back and yawned, cracking my jaws wide and then snapping them shut. I suppose I felt like a great bear that had been awoken early from its hibernation. I was in none too sweet a temper either. I sent Kier to make a drink while I sorted out some clean clothes. I saw with surprise that I had been asleep for five hours. "Must be getting old," I mumbled to myself. Time was when five hours sleep would have seen me fully refreshed and fighting fit.

Kier was waiting for me in the clone chamber. He was staring down at the sleeping body of Ariadne II. What he was thinking I could not tell. Certainly he had never seen the body of a naked woman before.

"What are those?" he asked pointing at her breasts which were rising and falling as she breathed.

I did not feel like giving an elementary biology lesson at that moment. "For feeding babies," I said. "Now help me check the auto-nurse."

"Oh. I thought they might be to help her float."

I was impressed by his logic. "How old are you, Kier?"

He shrugged his expressive shrug. "Don't know."

"Pedro told me you were almost fifteen."

"Something like that."

"Well I'll explain things to you later. Just now we have things to do. She'll be waking up soon. But she won't wake up straightaway. It'll take time. Go back to the kitchen and make food." He looked at me in surprise but did as I asked without question.

Ariadne's waking up was taking place more quickly than I had expected. I wanted to be alone with her in those first stirring moments. I looked down at her. I remembered the torn body I had seen in the hills above Rotorua and tried to match that memory with the woman who lay before me. They were not the same. This was the Ariadne I had known years earlier when we began our rescue missions. My Ariadne had died saving me and nothing could replace that memory. And yet . . . and yet . . . My programming began to work. I could feel it. I could feel tenderness and care begin to flood through me. I was a creature torn in two. The past and the present both pulled at me and, so help me, the present was winning.

She sighed and turned her head and rubbed her cheek against her shoulder. Half a smile warmed her face and then vanished. It was Ariadne's movement, observed by me . . . how many times? "And what dreams does a clone have?" I wondered, trying to force some bitterness into my mind, a tribute to the dead Ariadne. "Ariadne's dreams," answered my mind, imperturbably.

While I watched, her eyes fluttered and then opened, completely unfocused. She blinked several times and shook her head and when she next opened her eyes she stared straight up at me through the clear roof of the tank. There was the start of a smile which slid into a frown and then into a smile again. As though that were the cue, the silica sides and roof of her cover slid back and she sat up and yawned.

How different, I thought, *the waking of a clone, from the dozy exercises we have to go through after the long sleep*.

She looked at me closely, like someone peering into a fish bowl, studying my face and my shoulders, my arms, hand and claw. "Who are you?" she asked.

"I am Angelo."

"Who am I?"

"You are Ariadne."

202

"Of course. Am I human?"

"Not quite, but almost." You will be glad to know that I said those words with a slight smile.

I left her for a moment sitting on the bright resurrection bench looking about. Something had begun to worry me. A memory. It was years since I had consulted the manual which dealt with the awakening of clones. Most of the instructions I knew by heart, but there were some things I had forgotten. I wanted to consult the paragraphs which dealt with the clone memory. I did not know how much the new Ariadne knew of her predecessor. While she explored the auto-nurse and looked into the chamber which had contained the clone of myself, I found the booklet and rifled through its pages. Concerning the clone memory I found this:

Special up-dating circuits exist in the auto-nurse. These are linked directly to the long-sleep chamber of the parent entity. During a long sleep, memories are fed directly from the parent to the clone. The clone awakes with a conscious knowledge of all events leading up to the last long sleep. However, these memories may be garbled at first. It is very important to realize that *the clone does not awake with an awareness of its condition*. Care must be exercised in smoothing the transition from sleeping clone to active entity.

There it was spelled out. I would not be dealing with a newborn woman, an Eve, but with one both complex and aware. She should, barring accidents, know pretty well what had happened up to the time that Ariadne took a long sleep while we were imprisoned in moon orbit. Still, I would have a lot of explaining to do.

My new Ariadne shook her head making her dark curls bounce. "I am glad that the shaving did not affect my hair too much. I feel as good as new." She looked closely at me. "But what happened to you, Angelo? Did they come back? Did they harm you again? I didn't know you had been so scarred."

"It is a long story," I said. "You have a lot to learn. I have a lot to tell you."

She looked round the room and seemed for the first time to take it all in. "Why are we in here and not in the long-sleep chamber?" Before I could answer she turned and stared down into the empty coffin where my clone had lain. When she looked back at me her eyes were wide. "Are you Angelo . . . the real Angelo, or have you climbed out of this?"

"I am the real Angelo."

"Then . . ." She looked across to the platform where she had woken up. I could read her mind. "No, that's silly . . ." she began.

I realized that I was failing to cope with the situation. The first thing an awakened intelligence does is ask questions. I should have got her out of the clone chamber and into the living area before she was fully awake. I had not expected her to wake up so quickly. "Come on," I said, trying to sound casual. "Let's go down to the kitchen. There's plenty of time for questions and answers. Would you like something to drink? Eat even?"

She screwed up her face the way Ariadne did. "Food. Hell no. What I need is a swim."

And that, I thought, was just as well.

So began a strange and difficult time.

Between swims and her first morsels of food I told her the truth about herself. She both believed me and disbelieved me. She read the clone manual from cover to cover though she knew most of it by heart. Finally I let her read the pages I have been writing. She read the last sections with great care and then set the pages aside. Her eyes were wild and haunted. I had never seen Ariadne look like that. "So, I died miles from here saving you?" I nodded. She looked round the room and her eyes settled on Kier. "And this child is a waif you found guarding the ship?" Again I nodded. "It is all very strange. I don't think I can be a proper clone. I don't think we clones are supposed to be so tormented. What did you do with the other one?"

"I killed it and dumped it outside."

"How could you do that? Your basic programming forbids you to kill except . . ."

"I don't think I am any longer quite what my makers intended. Any more than you are." She digested this thought for a while.

"Your Ariadne must have been a wonderful woman. Did you love her very much?"

"Very much indeed." She started to cry when I said that.

"And now all you have is – "

I stopped her before she could finish the thought. "And now I have you. And I am glad. You are Ariadne." I reached out my claw to comfort her, but she knocked it away fiercely.

"I am not Ariadne. I might have been Ariadne. I have her memories but I don't have her experience. Memories aren't experience." Curiously in her anger she was identical to the Ariadne I remembered. I hardly knew what to think. "You must not call me Ariadne," she said. "I am my own thing . . . And I love you as much as . . . oh, this is ridiculous."

She picked up a page of my writing and turned the page over and lay it flat on the table. I offered her a pencil. First she wrote ARIADNE (her writing was the same) and then she wrote the name backwards, ENDAIRA. "There," she said. "Call me that." I tried but the name was difficult and so we shortened it to Daira and finally Aira. That pleased both of us. I told her that the name reminded me of an ancient word which meant anger and she smiled. "Good. I am angry. Someone's going to pay for what I've been through. I want action."

We sat and stared at one another for several minutes and then she reached forwards and stroked my claw. "It's beautiful," she said, "but you haven't been taking care of it. I'll clean it tomorrow."

Sometimes I surprise myself with my tact. I didn't say anything. Instead I stood up and slipped my arm round her and lifted her gently. I told Kier to turn out the lights.

I suppose I shouldn't have been surprised, but I was, for later in that night, when we joined in lovemaking, I discovered that Aira was a virgin.

205

3

I have telescoped time. The events I have just described took all of three days to complete. But everything important is written. Now we have settled down happily and are getting ready to leave Earth. Aira is keen to go, but we are enjoying a kind of honeymoon. I find it hard to describe. We have all settled down into a quiet routine. But every moment is happy.

Kier has become something like a son and something like a younger brother. He has taken over certain jobs. He tends the hydroponics garden regularly and keeps our living quarters neat and tidy. He has begun to put on weight and that is no bad thing.

Today I took Aira for her first trip outside. The fresh air made her giddy. She ran along the top of the ship and I was frightened she would fall. I keep reminding myself that the body she wears has been asleep for many generations. It might still have surprises for us. But she was just enjoying her freedom.

At the bottom of the ship we found the remains of my clone. It had started to stink and animals had been at it. There were flies everywhere and Kier had the bright idea of covering it with oil. This we did.

We saw no humans. As far as we are concerned, the whole of Aotearoa might be deserted. The whole of the Earth for that matter.

There is no reason to stay.

4

Moon orbit.

And to use an ancient colloquialism, I have burned our boats.

A short time ago I was contacted by the Defence and Quarantine section of Moon Base. I found myself talking to Major de Beer. He was very angry. He demanded to know why I had taken off without orders.

I asked him what he was going to do about it. That silenced him. I guess that by now a very graphic report has reached the Space Council describing the way that Bonniface laid waste to Rotorua Mining Town. The settlements on Moon Base are very vulnerable. They will not be so foolish as to tempt me. So we are free.

Major de Beer asked me if we were setting out on a Pioneer Rescue Mission and I said, "Yes."

"Which Pioneer?"

"Rip."

"But Pioneer Rip's beacon has been dead for years."

"No matter. That is where we are going." And then as an afterthought, a vicious one, I added, "When we return, you will already have been dead for many years." That hurt him deeply. He jumped back from the screen with his fingers to his lips. A frightened child looked out through his eyes.

Once Ariadne told me that she believed the population of Earth was getting stupider. I believe she was right: stupider and more afraid. They no longer face reality.

I have matched orbit with Chrono and we have exchanged news. He tells me we are the only long-range ship still operating. He is not very optimistic. "I shall be waiting for you when

207

you return," he said. "Perhaps I shall be the only creature waiting. Bon voyage."

Now we are into the sleep programme. I have been pleased to see how easily Aira has adapted to the preparation. I thought there might be some psychic resistance as she has been awake such a short length of time. But no. She has begun the hypnotic countdown calmly and methodically.

Kier is not so easy. I have prepared the Pioneer cell for him. That auto-nurse is used to dealing with unruly and restless minds. It will treat him as though he were a Pioneer. I have decided to adapt the spare chamber in the clone room to receive Pioneer Rip if ever we find him. By rights it should have already started to grow another clone of Ariadne but neither Aira nor I wanted that so we cut those circuits. That phase of the programme is at an end and we adapted creatures now face our mortality like the humblest of humans.

The re-programming was surprisingly easy. One auto-nurse is pretty like another: the nature of the care is different, that is all.

What more have I to say? Yes. Our departure from Master Town was eventful and no ship will ever be able to land at that spaceport again.

As I worked our ship out from the hangar I found that a giant kahikatea tree had been dragged across the tracks in an attempt to block the exit. It was crude but effective. When I tried to nudge it out of the way, the branches dug into the ground and tore up the tracks. I could have burned it with the laser cannon, but instead I simply fed power to the main generators and we lifted straight up. We tore through the roof of the hangar and left it sagging behind us. The hangar caught fire and then the old service depot. There must have been liquid fuel stored there. We saw it explode and fire ran in rivers. Finally all we could see was oily black smoke which billowed. Tongues of orange flame licked up through it.

Kier loved every minute. As we drifted away from the port he pointed out to us where he and Pedro had lived. The wooden house burned like a torch. Then we were out over farm land and after that the dark blue sea.

I let Kier guide the ship for a few moments. He was amazed to see our shadow skimming over the waves. Then I took charge again. On an impulse I took us back over Aotearoa. We crossed the Ruahine range and later the Kaimanawas. Finally we came to Lake Rotorua. I hope that Pioneer Murray looked up and saw us if he is still there.

Then it was straight up into the darkness.

The computers have run a thorough check and all our systems seem fine. We seem to have suffered no damage from our brief stay on Earth.

We are on our way. Chrono is behind us and our next stop will be at Rip's planet which is called Barley. A merry sounding name I think . . . a robust name.

As the great ship accelerates and we slip closer to sleep, I am brooding on differences. I am thinking of Aira and Ariadne. Clones are supposed to be identical and in most things Aira is the same as Ariadne. But there are differences. Aira is more inquisitive. She asks more searching questions. She is like a woman awakening in the early morning. What I am saying is that she seems to have a different attitude to experience. Ariadne accepted that there were things that she didn't know and sometimes grew impatient with me when I asked questions. Aira likes me to ask questions. She stands by me in the darkness and we both look outwards.

Now Kier is stowed. The auto-nurse is soothing him. I have sat close and tried to probe his dreams but the boy does not rest easily.

I fed him a sedative for I could find no hypnotic suggestion that would bring him ease. With Kier, both Aira and I are at the limit of our programming. Kier is a full-human and very young. If he were a Pioneer we would know what to do. We would be ruthlessly efficient as we were with Pioneer Murray. But he is *not* a Pioneer, he is a boy, and we do not know how boys think.

209

This much I can say. He dreams of plants, beautiful flowers that can climb and sting. He dreams of *me* too. He wants to be as big as me and as strong. In his dreams he ports a claw like mine and side by side we fight incredible battles, very bloody battles. Kier both wants to kill and wants to be loved. He wants dignity and a sense of purpose. He wants to be normal.

At my prompting the auto-nurse is nudging him towards dreams about our ship. I want him to dream that he is captain of our ship, setting out on a voyage of great discovery. He will face difficult decisions, and in that way I hope he will come to accept himself more. Perhaps he will gain some hope.

I hazard the guess that in two generations when he wakes up, Kier will be a happier boy.

Good luck to him.

Aira and I are close to sleep. We seem to be laughing a lot and that is not quite normal; at the same time, I cannot feel that it is bad.

I think the presence of Kier has weighed heavily on us.

I am saying nothing against him, but sleep preparations require easiness and we could not be at ease while there was a third party.

We have been laughing about the rescue of Pioneer Bell many generations ago. It is a long story but I will tell it briefly. Bell's world was a clone world. On that planet the auto-nurse had gone rogue and kept reproducing clones of Pioneer Bell. When we arrived the world was populated with identical men each at a different age. So when we landed and they saw Ariadne, a real woman, for the first time they didn't know what to do. We found them friendly and charming and helpful and then suddenly they all fell in love with Ariadne. Finally they kidnapped her. Just like that.

It caught me off guard. I wasn't particularly worried about Ariadne – she could take care of herself – but I wasn't sure what *I* should do. Wherever I went there were moony men, and still the auto-nurse kept on popping them out every three months or so, fully formed at age twenty-one.

The air stank with frustrated men.

Eventually Ariadne came home. To satisfy one she would have had to satisfy all, and that, as she admitted, was beyond even her appetite.

We bopped one of the Pioneer Bells on the head and put him in the care of our auto-nurse. I was for taking off straight away but Ariadne wouldn't hear of it. She went back in to Bell's world and visited the rogue auto-nurse. She gave it cells from herself and adjusted its mechanism. It began to produce clones of Ariadne. We stayed until the first Ariadne walked out of the adapted clone chamber. Then she taught one of the Bells how to control the auto-nurse and determine what sex of creature was to be produced.

There being a definite shortage of females, I guessed that the auto-nurse would produce nothing but Ariadnes for the next several generations.

We departed.

The point being (and this is what Aira and I found comic) somewhere out there, there is a world populated with identical men and women. On the whole it is probably a happy world. Pioneer Bell was a fine looking man, an athlete and a musician. Ariadne told me quite clearly that she found him very attractive. Knowing herself, she knew that she would not lack for physical and mental satisfaction.

At the same time, as she pointed out to me when we made ready for the long sleep, each of those Ariadnes would have in the backs of their minds, an idea of a dream lover – a creature with a claw and a gentle mind and the body of an ape. How would they explain that to their lovers and husbands?

So we both have reasons for liking Bell's world.

Sadly, I have to say that the clone Bell we captured did not survive the journey home to earth. He died in his dreams.

Perhaps it is just as well.

I am the last to sleep.

The great ship mumbles to itself as our speed increases.

The sea is calling me.

211

5

I am eating a tomato and lettuce salad. The lettuce is brittle as scorched paper and I crunch it and swallow and drink glasses of ice water. I have experienced the gentlest awakening I can remember.

Kier has been awake for weeks and that is why the vegetables are so well advanced. He potters about taking care of me and I have even heard him singing. The boy is very different. He is more direct in his speech. He carries himself with confidence. All the effect of good dreams I think. I notice that his hair is a different colour. Where it was pure white and skimpy it now has red and gold lights in it. The auto-nurse has been busy. I did not know they could tinker so deeply with the human metabolism. He is firmly muscled too. The effect of years of massage and a healthy diet. Much to his delight and my amusement, he has the start of a beard and his pubic hair is bushy. The auto-nurse has allowed him to age. I would say he is about seventeen as such things are measured on earth. His voice is deeper, naturally. I wonder if he dreams of women yet. The only woman he can really be aware of is Aira. Hmm. I must watch that. I hope she does not take it into her mind to introduce him to one of the pleasures of being a man. I would find that very hard.

Despite the changes he has undergone, he would still look like a freak to other full-humans. That is something he may have to live with.

I have begun to teach him to read. There is an alert brain there though he is certainly no genius.

Aira is still asleep. She will be with us in the next few days. I recall how Ariadne was usually the first to wake up and I am not displeased with this change in our states. We will feed her lots of lettuce and tomatoes.

Rip's world is somewhere ahead but we have no way of seeing it. We are in a vast shoal of asteroids, each much bigger than we are. Our guidance computers are in a kind of heaven, I guess, making minute accelerations and side-slips, easing us through. It may take us a long time to reach Rip's world.

But it is there. I can feel it. And that is not all. Some hours ago, before the last sleep break, I was sitting at the table in our living quarters – Kier was swimming or messing about in the hydroponics chamber – and I swear I heard the door behind me open and close. So real was the impression that I spoke without looking. I assumed it was Kier. But I received no reply, and when I turned round there was no one there. But still I felt there was a presence. I am too old a hand at this game to dismiss such thoughts as fancy.

Space can play strange tricks. The waking process always has its strangeness. But I remember Pioneer Murray saying that Rip had spoken to him in his dreams and I have confused feelings about this neck of space. Perhaps in his own way, Rip is letting me know that he is aware of us. I don't feel anything dangerous, for the moment, just an awareness.

When I look out of the window I experience claustrophobia. There are so many looming shapes above us and below us and to the side of us. Our ship registers the impact of many particles. We are coated in dust and rubble. Occasionally the laser cannon vaporizes a chunk of rock the size of a house and our windows are shrouded in dust. Occasionally we glow as the guidance computers check our ship's inertia. Then, the windows clear.

The silence is strange. I am used to the silence of space and I have never been so fanciful as to imagine that the stars have voices. Yet I cannot avoid the thought that these mountain-sized slabs of rock, pitted and cratered and carved into fantastic shapes which float so calmly beside us, should make some

213

noise. A growling maybe. And why have they not clumped together? That I believe would be normal.

We are in a strange part of space.

Aira has rejoined the land of the living. She is very sick and I have told Kier to take good care of her. I don't think she has rested as easily as she should. When she was a clone she woke easily. Now she is a woman she has difficult dreams. That may be significant but I shall check her auto-nurse carefully before we return. For the time being she is content to doze in the pool, sip juice and cuddle up at night. How unlike Ariadne who was always so quick to come awake.

This is strange. It is not two days since last I wrote and I have just checked with the guidance computers to see if they know where we are and how long it might be before we reach Rip's world. They tell me that they are homing on his beacon! Apparently it is loud and clear to them. It is quite close, no more than fifteen lems. Barring accidents we should be there in a matter of days. I told them that I thought Rip's beacon was dead but they say it is deafening.

It seems that we are making our way crabwise through this belt of asteroids. When I feel our thrusts and the counter-thrusts of energy and look out through the window of the view-screen, I can make no sense of our progress. They say they will alert me when we are in visible range.

6

We came over a great asteroid shaped like the beak of a parrot and floated out into clear space. Immediately I felt depression lift from me as though I had been freed from heavy chains.

Stretching away behind us was a great grey wall of asteroids. At this distance they seemed piled upon one another like stones in a rough cast wall.

In front of us was a brilliant sun which blazed with a blue light. Round that sun moved a world. It was swinging round to meet us. Rip's world. There was nothing else.

We have begun a steady acceleration.

Two days and we will be there.

"Who were you talking to?"

"When?"

"Just now."

"No one."

"But I heard you. Was it Kier?"

"I wasn't speaking to anyone."

Pause. Aira looks at me shrewdly. "But I heard you. I'm not making it up, Angelo. You were talking about Pioneer Murray."

"What was I saying?"

"You were describing him. And then you went on to say that the breeding programme on the moon had failed."

"Are you sure?"

"Why would I make it up?"

That, to the word, is a conversation I have just had with Aira . . . and yet I have no recollection of speaking about or even thinking about Pioneer Murray.

Strange. It is all very strange.

*

Rip's world looks as sterile as the moon. It moves monotonously beneath us. We have gone round it twice and have seen no sign of life. The computers tell me that as we approached, Rip's guidance beacon suddenly stopped transmitting. How ironic if after everything we find that Rip died just when salvation was near.

We shall have to land, but the question is where. One place seems pretty much like another. I have ordered the ship to descend. I have decided we shall spend some time down there, perhaps hop about a bit . . . and then if we find nothing we will head back to Earth. That would be a great disappointment. I do not know why, but I had placed a great deal of hope on this venture, perhaps because I think this will be the last Pioneer Rescue Mission anyone ever makes from Earth. All our ambitions have shrunk. I like clean endings. I like bangs not whimpers. I realize also that I placed a great deal of faith in Pioneer Murray's dreams. Perhaps too much.

7

What I am about to write *you* must take on trust.

Ha! Trust. The only thing *I* trust at this moment is the cigar that I am smoking and that will burn my fingers in a few moments if I don't stub it out.

I am sitting in a mountain cabin. It is cold outside, so we have a fire blazing and chuckling to itself. Since I cannot explain what has happened today, I shall simply describe it.

We began to descend towards the sterile planet. I chose a wide-rimmed crater which seemed to have a flat floor. The sensors reported that the proposed landing site was firm and stable. We made a slow, controlled descent and were able to watch the shadow of the high rim creep across the crater floor. Both Aira and I were reminded of the approach to Moon Base. Then, just as we were passing below the rim line and swinging in a wide arc, it seemed that the sky became tinged with purple as though there was atmosphere there.

No, I will describe that another way. My first thought was that there was a purple fire blazing beyond the crater wall and that we could see the reflection of the flames on clouds. There were swarming movements in the sky. Looking out through the view-ports of our ship I could see our blunt shape alive with purple light and the light was sinuous like snakes. But it was not a reflection. The light ran like lather over our ship and dribbled down from our fins.

Immediately I ordered the ship up. But nothing happened. I spoke directly to the main guidance computers, but they ignored me. Apart from anything else, that fact alone is extraordinary. The computers are tuned to my voice. My voice is an imperative. They cannot ignore me. But they did. Something else, with a stronger voice than mine, controlled them.

217

This had been a controlled descent, but now I got Aira and Kier to set their couches in emergency position and checked that their magnetic clamps were securely anchored. Lying back we stared out into the roiling purple light. We were powerless. We could only watch as our ship was taken and turned and gently drawn downwards. Any sense of the crater or its floor was lost to us.

I remember Bonniface once describing to me how, on one of his missions, he had had to climb the steep snow face of a mountain. He lost his footing in the ice and began to slide. "It didn't hurt," he said, "but I had no control. I couldn't tell up from down. It was as though I was being sucked down the mountain side." I could use the same words to describe us.

Then came a gentle bump and we knew we had landed. The ship tilted slightly so that when I released the catches on my chair I rolled out sideways.

The computers did not seem concerned. I asked them, "Are we damaged?" and they assured me in their bland way that all was well. So much for artificial intelligence!

I released Aira and Kier and helped them down on to the sloping floor. I looked to see if Kier was frightened, but his eyes were alive with the light of adventure. I thought of his dreams and hoped he had been prepared for this.

Aira the practical began to check our support systems. Aira does not trust the computers any more than I do: she wanted to see for herself.

I moved to one of the external windows and looked out. There was nothing to be seen. Outside was pure blackness (if blackness can be called pure). Of the brilliant purple which had made the inside of our cabin glimmer like a cave there was not even the faintest tinge. The ship's lights were on. They glared into the blackness. They should have revealed half the crater floor or the shape of our ship, but they showed nothing. We should have seen the beams of light probing into the atmosphere. But nothing. The blackness pressed upon us like fur.

"So what now?" asked Aira, joining me. "You're not thinking of walking out into that are you?"

I shook my head. "No, well not immediately. Who knows what we might have to do eventually. But for the time being, let us just sit quietly. We haven't been damaged so far. Perhaps there is a plan."

Surprisingly she smiled when I said this. "You're enjoying yourself Angelo, aren't you?" she said, and led the way down to our living quarters.

And of course, she was right. I wouldn't have used the word "enjoy", but there was something churning round inside me and it wasn't just the chemical thrill of adrenalin. I think I would call it hope. We had faced a dead world and suddenly that world had transformed itself. It had responded to us. In that gleaming purple light that washed over us like breaking waves of the sea, I had sensed life.

If all had gone according to *our* plan, we should now be waiting on a dead world looking up at a roof of grey asteroids. That would have been hopeless.

We sat together in the kitchen and listened to the ship whispering about us. None of us felt hungry. There was not much conversation either. I busied myself with the survival suits making sure that all the power packs were charged and that the systems worked smoothly. Aira checked the guns. This had always been Ariadne's job. Kier, much to my surprise, settled down to the reading exercises I had prepared for him. Periodically we caught one another glancing at the blackness outside our view-window but there was never any change. Finally Aira closed the window down and it became just another part of the wall.

I do not know how long we sat together. I know I began to feel tired. Kier closed his book with a slap and gave vent to a body-stretching, wide-mouthed yawn. He muttered something and took himself off to bed.

Aira and I echoed his yawn. Minutes later we followed his example. There being nothing else we could do for the time being, bed seemed a good idea.

*

219

I had strange dreams, all about Earth. In my dreams I could see myself floating in the hot pool at the Pioneer Centre with Bonniface and Amsterdame. Next I relived the battle in Rotorua Mining Town and woke up at about the moment when Ariadne was killed. I was wet with sweat and panting.

Aira did not sleep easily either. She moaned and writhed and only became quiet when I stroked her and whispered to her and held her close with my arm round her shoulders. She held my claw, her fingers trustingly within its rough blades.

She woke up once and we made sudden love . . . a mingling of waters, like river meeting sea. Afterwards I asked her about her dreams and she was reluctant to tell me. But then she whispered, "I think I dreamed I was having our baby." That was all she would say and I let her sleep.

There was no more sleep for me. When she was resting easily I stole from our bed and made my way to the kitchen. I thought of waking Kier for I felt in need of company, but finally I didn't.

I was drawn to the window. I pressed the release catch and the shutters drew back. Light shone in on me. Sunlight.

I looked out on to a green and brown world. Ferns were pressing against the window. Beyond them was a lake of brown water. Small swampy islands covered with bright green plants raised their backs. As I watched, a flock of birds flapped down from the sky and settled clumsily on to the water. They began feeding, up-tailing like ducks and bobbing under the surface. A lizard (it would have been about as long as my arm) clambered on to our window with a curious high-stepping motion. Where its toes touched, suckers as big as my thumb opened and held it secure. It moved its head back and forwards hypnotically in the morning sunlight.

Some time later Kier joined me, stuffing his head up under my arm, and then Aira.

Together we watched in silence. Finally, with a start, Kier said, "Who's that man, Angelo, sitting under the tree watching us?"

*

The sharp eyes of the boy had seen what I had missed. There *was* a man with green-brown skin sitting with his back to a tree and his legs stretched out so that his heels rested in the brown water. He was as naked as the lizard.

He raised one arm slowly and waved to us, apparently aware that we were looking at him. I waved back and felt self-conscious in the gesture. It was hardly likely that he could see us at this height and through the foliage. Besides, our windows could not be seen through from the outside . . . and therefore . . .

"Is that Pioneer Rip?" asked Aira. "He looks as if he grew from the mud."

"Get the glasses," I said. "Let's have a closer look at him." The sudden appearance of the man (for so it seemed to me) had pushed into the background my wonderment at finding a swamp where I had expected to see an arid, airless crater. When many strange things occur together they tend to cancel one another out.

Kier brought the glasses from our equipment locker and I trained them on the man. I studied him from head to toe. His skin looked slightly mottled but for the most part it was the colour of forest moss. His hair fell to his shoulders and looked fair and at the same time greenish, like stained copper. The face was ageless with high cheekbones and a firm jaw. There was a hint of a wispy beard. He lay completely relaxed. He could have been asleep or dead except that his eyes were bright and concentrated and seemed to stare straight into me. I handed the glasses to Aira and she rested her elbows on the window support and began a careful study.

Two of the birds that had landed on the lake earlier paddled their way over to the man and waddled up on to the mud shore close to him. He raised his hand and fluttered his fingers and one of the birds edged in close and settled under his hand and hunkered down.

When Aira had looked her fill it was Kier's turn. He took the glasses keenly and adjusted them to his eyes.

221

"That must be Pioneer Rip," I said. "I suggest I go out and meet him."

"*We* go out and meet him," said Aira. "I'm not staying back here alone. And you can't leave Kier behind."

"OK. I suppose we have nothing to lose. So long as this crazy planet doesn't shift round again. I would not like us all to be stranded in that blackness."

"Well, it's all or none," said Aira. I had heard that tone before, from Ariadne, and knew that nothing would be gained by arguing.

"What is the atmosphere like?" I asked.

"Breathable. No problem. And gravity is about Earth normal. Come on, let's get our suits on."

As Aira said this the man stood up. For the first time I could get some impression of his height. He was very tall. Considerably taller than me, I judged, and firmly muscled. He stood with his hands on his hips and then he beckoned with one imperious motion. That seemed to end the discussion and we dressed as quickly as we could. We put Kier into Aira's spare suit. It did not fit particularly well but at least it would give him protection if there were any biting creatures about.

Dressed, we hurried up through the ship. I activated the Worm and guided it towards the island where the man stood. Fully extended the Worm was a hundred yards too short.

We could have broken out one of the small boats which we have at our disposal, but Aira didn't hesitate. She sat herself down at the control panel and began tapping out instructions to the guidance computers. They responded without a murmur. The Worm retracted and the great ship lurched and steadied itself and then began to crawl towards the small island. The man stood and watched us. There was a smile on his face.

After several minutes of churning through the mud we were close and within easy Worm-reach. The Worm snaked out and its airlock mouth came to rest just a few feet from where the giant stood.

We climbed down the segmented corridor. At its end we

could see through the clear silica airlock. He was still standing there.

"Me first," said Aira, "like in the old days. You keep me covered." Before I could protest she touched the airlock release and the main door irised open.

The man had stepped back. He *was* tall, a good head and shoulders taller than me. He stood with arms folded, staring at us.

"Hello," said Aira, speaking from within the airlock. "Are you Pioneer Rip? We have come from Earth. We have come to rescue you."

I remember thinking at the time that this was a silly little speech, not like Aira at all. It made me realize how nervous she was.

"Oh," said the man. His voice matched his size but was mocking, which made it unpleasant. "Then you'd better step outside and let me welcome you."

Aira tried to step outside but couldn't. There was something like an invisible membrane covering the airlock opening. I raised my claw and tried to push through but met a rubbery resistance.

"And in order to step outside you must remove those silly clothes and weapons. They have no place on this world. You come naked into this world or not at all."

It seemed we had no option. I was the first to react. I removed my helmet and unzipped my survival suit and let it drop to the ground. For some reason, the idea of closing the airlock and climbing back into the ship never occurred to me. So there could be no mistake, I opened my hand and claw to show that I was not armed and then stepped forwards.

I stumbled. I suppose subconsciously I was expecting to encounter resistance, and there was none. I did not exactly fall on my face, but I floundered and when I recovered my balance I was standing ankle deep in the mud.

Aira followed me, stepping delicately. She wore her nakedness like clothes, the way that some women can. But poor Kier was very embarrassed. He held his hands over his genitals and that made him seem very frail.

The giant studied us with equanimity. He paid particularly close attention to my claw.

"You are not human then?"

"I am adapted from human stock," I said.

"So am I," added Aira.

The giant mused, studying our faces. Finally he spoke again. "I can hardly tell." He turned to Kier. "But this is of Earth then?"

"Yes."

The giant moved close to Kier and rested his hand on the boys head and ruffled his hair. Kier jumped as though stung but didn't move away.

"Why did you bring a boy with you?"

"We saved him. From Earth. From the other full-humans."

The giant nodded and bent down and stared into Kier's eyes. He seemed to be looking right into him. Finally he straightened up. "I understand," he said. "It is not the Earth I once knew."

He seemed to come to a decision. "Come with me. I have prepared a place for you." He turned and ducked under the trees and began to lead us across the island. I held back. I was not happy about leaving our ship.

The giant paused and turned. Again he was smiling that supercilious smile. He stared briefly at our ship. Immediately the Worm flexed along its sinuous length and the airlock closed with a snap. Then the Worm began to withdraw its segmented compartments into the ship. When it was fully withdrawn the ship began to sink. I watched powerless as mud bubbled up round its sides and the vast particle vents filled with ooze. The sinking of such a large ship took little more than a few minutes and then all that remained was a slow whirlpool of chocolate-coloured water and some heavy ripples which washed up on to the island. "There, does that solve your problem?" asked the giant, facing me. His face did not smile, but I had the impression he was laughing. At the same time he seemed to be challenging me.

*

224

The island was little more than a mud bank topped with trees. We crossed it quickly. Waiting for us on the opposite side was a narrow flat-bottomed boat which had been dragged up into the reeds. The invitation was obvious: the three of us climbed in and the giant pushed the boat out into the water, wading beside it. He pulled himself aboard and stood wide-legged in the stern. A pole lay along the side of the boat and he hefted this above his head and then plunged it into the water and began to push us out into the lagoon.

I looked about. Perhaps for the first time since stepping out of our ship, I took full account of our surroundings. There was no sign of any crater walls peeping up above the trees. The landscape was a monotonous round of mud-flats and low islands.

"What shall we call you?" asked Aira suddenly. She had been very quiet for some time.

The giant stopped in his pulling.

"Yes, introductions," he said, seemingly to himself. "I had almost forgotten. Call me what you called me at first. Rip. That was the name I was known by." For some reason he found this funny and laughed, making the boat rock. "And you are . . .?"

"I'm Aira. This is Angelo and this is Kier." Pioneer Rip nodded but didn't say anything more. He applied himself to his pole again and the boat darted out over the brown water.

The sun was now high in the sky and its heat made twists of steam rise from the water. I had a hundred questions waiting to be asked but the steady poling of the giant made interruption impossible.

No. It was more than that. I felt constrained in a way that I am not used to. Several times I started to speak but he ignored me. I felt hostility in his silence though I did nothing to provoke it. So, finally I kept my peace and concentrated on the journey.

Once there was a commotion in the water close to our boat and a shoal of silver fish beat the surface to foam in an attempt to escape some predator. Shortly afterwards a giant grey back lifted and I had the impression of a leviathan paddling its way through the dark water. It raised its head, a scaly mask with

225

low-slung jaw and myriad sharp teeth, and swam beside us, eyeing us. Pioneer Rip paid the creature no attention until its shoulders bumped the boat and its head on its long neck hung over us. Water dripped from its jaws and splashed over Aira and Kier. I stood up attempting to shield them but the Pioneer barked at me to sit down. Then he swung his pole and cracked the beast on the head. It subsided quietly until only its eyes were visible above the water, cruising beside us. The giant continued to pole us along steadily.

He did break his silence briefly. Between strokes he said, "Don't worry, Angelo. You'll have plenty of opportunities to prove your strength and courage before you depart."

Finally, we approached what seemed to be the mainland. Dark wooded hills rose to meet snow-capped mountains. Rip steered us into a shallow bay. He gave one final push on his pole and the narrow boat ground its nose into the shingle.

"Up there," he said, pointing to the hills, "you will find a shelter. Wait there and see what happens."

We climbed out and he dug his pole into the shingle, preparing to depart.

"Don't go," I said, gripping the boat with my claw and digging my heels in the shingle. "I have many questions to ask you."

"I expect you have," said Rip, "but they will keep."

Then he dug with his pole and heaved and the boat slipped from my grasp. The last I saw of him he was far out in the bay poling away from us. Then we trudged inland. When next I turned to look out across the water, he had gone.

We climbed for hours. High in the hills, at about the place where the lowland bush gave way to deeper-rooted trees, we found a cabin. It reminded me of one of those mountain retreats I had seen in pictures . . . the kind of cabin that used to be popular in Old North America. The roofs sloped steeply. There was a porch in front with low easy chairs made of planks. The door was heavy and the walls were made of half trunks.

The door opened easily at my touch. Inside was a large living room complete with tables, a stone fireplace and a thick chunky rug on the floor. In one corner stood a desk on which were placed a neat pile of white paper, pencils and a box containing cigars. Pioneer Rip had obviously studied me.

A wooden-runged ladder, set against one wall, led up to an upper room. Kier scampered up this and his shouts of pleasure told us that he had found and claimed his bedroom.

A door led through to the back of the cabin and there we found another bedroom as well as a kitchen and toilet. Everything was made of deeply varnished wood. It was comfortable and plain.

Aira and I felt as though we had stepped back in time. The style of the cabin was probably popular when Rip was a boy . . . even earlier possibly. Aira loved it and immediately began changing things round to suit her taste.

What was my reaction?

Now as I sit at the solid wood desk and puff on one of the cigars, I have time for this question. I have sat for hours writing about what has happened to us. Kier is sleeping noisily above. Aira is stretched out in front of the fire with a book on the floor. She has draped herself in a curtain from one of the windows. She looks very beautiful and at home. I can see the fabric rise and fall as she breathes. The night is very cold. There is even a hint of snow.

What is my reaction?

I think I am more deeply afraid than ever before in my life. I do not trust anything. I do not trust the wood beneath my hand or the pencil I hold in my claw. I have no power to control anything here. The planet changed its nature before my eyes; the great ship which has carried us to so many worlds sank in shallow water; we are sitting in a comfortable cabin surrounded by a wild world and only the power of the Pioneer protects us. What can I do?

I feel a prisoner, and am only surprised that neither Aira nor Kier feel the same way. They seem to have accepted everything. They look to me to make decisions. Not that I have any decisions to make.

With Kier I can accept this. He knows so little. But Aira? I do not know why she is so passive. I expected questions from her, a fighting spirit, a refusal to accept, a canny female suspicion. But she is contented as a cat on a cold winter night.

What can I say about Pioneer Rip? This much. I am not afraid of him in a physical sense. The pain of a fight – death even – I can accept. I have faced such before. I simply do not understand him. I do not understand his manners or his attitude to me. He seemed to taunt me and yet I can find no reason for his malice. I wonder what Murray would make of him.

Perhaps he is insane. That thought has crossed my mind more than once. I have always suspected that one day we would meet a Pioneer who was unhinged. Maybe he is jealous of me, though why I do not know. He has shown no interest in Aira.

I have kept my thoughts to myself.

Aira has noticed his rudeness, but she does not feel it the same way a man does. She thinks it is just a matter of manner. I know different. There is something calculated about him. In comparison Pioneer Murray *was* a child, and I think I coped with him quite well. I do not know how I will cope with Pioneer Rip.

I am on my guard. Something is brewing.

8

Five days have passed and nothing has happened.

Five days and finally both Aira and Kier are becoming restless. We have climbed up to where the snow begins and down into a valley where we discovered delicious fruits in the trees. We lack for nothing and yet we lack for everything. We have started to argue about silly things.

Aira does not like my cigars. Ariadne never complained. So that perplexes me. To save any further argument I shifted my table outside and wrote and smoked and finally went for a walk alone.

I made my way down to a headland above the bay where we landed and sat staring out across the water.

Then something did happen. I saw a bird. It was high and flapping its wings lazily as it made its way home. I watched it pause and hover and then dive. It came straight towards me.

The attack was so sudden that I ducked only just in time. It grazed over me with its beak wide and screaming and I felt its wings slap against my shoulders. It banked in front of the trees and beat its way into the sky again. I watched it turn and dive again. This time I was ready. I let it approach and when it was almost on me and I could see its talons I struck upwards with my claw and tore its breast open. It crashed on the rocks a few feet from me and its claws scratched at the sky as it died.

When it was still I picked up the body and flung it as far out from the headland as I could.

This event may not be significant, but I think it is. It may mean that the Pioneer's protection has been lifted from us, in which case we must be ready for all kinds of trouble. It may be that the event is symbolic in which case I have shown my power to kill and that puts me into a particular class of creatures. No

229

doubt Pioneer Rip would have stroked it and the bird would have flown away peacefully to its eyrie.

We have all moved indoors and the doors are closed.

The night is again very cold. Flakes of snow have begun to fall.

I can stand no more of this waiting.

Tomorrow I will go down to the shore and begin building a raft. If Pioneer Rip will not come to us then I shall go hunting him.

9

I have woken up in the night aware that something is wrong. Apparently I am the only one who feels this for Aira and Kier continue sleeping soundly.

I got up quickly and searched round the cabin. The embers in the fire were still glowing and I kicked them into flame. The fitful light lit up the walls. Nothing seemed different yet something was different. When I tried to go outside I found that the door of the cabin was locked. Though I pulled and tugged and in normal circumstances could have ripped the door from its hinges, I could not budge it. Only then did I look outside.

The blackness has returned.

We are adrift in a sea of blackness and the light within the cabin dies at the window pane.

My desk is a refuge to which I retreat from that which is not known. Tomorrow may bring understanding. Even as I write I feel watched.

10

So I must write it.

Little Kier is dead and I killed him.

Aira stands behind me, her face white and unloving, and demands that I set everything down. I shall try, and in the manner which I have always adopted; I shall try to be objective. Others may judge. Others, if there are others, may judge.

Morning found me asleep at my table. Aira had placed a blanket round my shoulders. As I raised my head I saw that the windows were white in the sunlight. I rubbed my eyes and called for Aira and Kier, suddenly afraid that somehow they might have been taken away from me while I slept.

Aira was making breakfast and she came to me when I called and placed her arms round me and hugged me. "Bad dreams?" she asked. "I heard you get up. You were prowling about for hours."

"Something like that. Where's Kier?"

"Outside playing with the snow. He's never been in snow before. Have you seen outside? It's wonderful."

Feeling old and confused, I made my way over to the window and looked out. The whiteness which shone in through the windows was dazzling and made me squint. Despite this, I saw a figure, but it was not Kier. It was Pioneer Rip, naked as the day we first saw him, sitting halfway up a snow bank, staring at me.

It was a moment in which nothing outwardly happened, but I had the overriding feeling that I was facing my enemy. Such things cannot be explained. They are in the water of a person. I felt a deep loathing for him. I believe the fur on my shoulders rose. I experienced a black hatred.

This creature had played with us long enough.

What game was he involved in?

If he had harmed Kier . . .

Two strides and I was at the door. It opened easily but so great was the tug I gave it that the top hinge tore from the wood. Then I was across the porch and down on to the snow.

"Do you want to fight me, Chimp?" He stood up slowly, his body knitted and relaxed, after the manner of practised fighters.

"Yes I want to fight you."

"I'll kneel on your neck and make you squirm."

"I'll die first."

"You probably will."

He came down the snow bank in big strides, sinking up to his knees. I held my ground, trying to remember how he had poled the boat. My guess was that he was left-handed. That bit of knowledge was perhaps my only advantage. Then he was on me.

He came with reaching arms and I dived low. Height can be a disadvantage. I rolled grabbing with my claw for his ankle but he stepped aside neatly. Still I had surprised him. He wouldn't be so cocky now.

I let my roll carry me to my feet and stood with hunched shoulders. I was as broad as him. Plans formed in my mind, just as they are supposed to. If I could once get under his guard . . . get my arms round his back I could squeeze and lift. He could tear my fur but I would have him and I wouldn't let go until his face was black.

He feinted to my left, pretending to reach for my claw, and when I parried he zipped out a punch which hit me on the side of the head like a brick. Two more punches followed and for a moment my mind darkened. Then he had me by the hair. I knew what was coming, a kick with the knee tearing into my balls or solar plexus, jarring upwards. There is only one defence. I pushed forwards, jamming my head towards him, tipping his balance. As he tried to kick he fell. I rammed my head into his face and felt wetness as his nose broke.

We both fell into the snow and rolled over fighting for

233

advantage. He was like an eel. His fingers were in my face feeling for my eyes. My claw was pushing for his throat. Then he got his legs under me and kicked. The kick broke both our grips. It sent me backwards and I landed badly. Something broke. A rib I think. I felt an amazing pain on the side where my heart is.

He recovered before me and staggered to his feet. His face was a mess and I had torn him open at the shoulder. The snow about us was spattered with red.

Somehow I managed to roll though it was like rolling on spikes. But it gave me a yard or two more.

I was up on my knee when he attacked. It was a clumsy attack. An attempt to put me down by sheer weight. The advantage was open before me. I let him think I was stunned. I let his weight come down on me and when his stomach was exposed, I opened my claw and tore upwards. No scaly beast or slimy eel could have withstood that blow. I unseamed him.

And even as I launched into the blow I was aware of the transformation. There was a mistiness before my eyes. The creature that I killed was a small white-haired boy. I saw it happen. I saw the Pioneer transform. Time slowed for me but the movement was irreversible. Kier died with my claw buried deep in his stomach.

Oh trickery.

Hours later . . . it seemed like hours, but I know it was only minutes . . . I pushed the small body off me.

Someone else was pulling at me and beating at me with their fists. It was Aira and she had my fur in her hands. "What have you done, Angelo? What have you done?"

Then she was on her knees beside the small corpse, rubbing its hands, looking in the eyes.

She did not look at me as she lifted the body and carried it through the crimson snow and into the cabin.

Still I did not understand. I dragged myself up and followed her. I think the adrenalin was still pumping in me for I kept looking round for Pioneer Rip.

What was I expecting? Another attack?

Inside the cabin, Kier was laid out on the rug in front of the fire. Aira was by him and she was crying. I had never seen Ariadne cry. And now Aira was crying.

"Where is Pioneer Rip?" I asked, aware that my voice was choked and ugly. "I was fighting him. Where is he?"

She looked up, her usually beautiful face reduced to the simplicity of a tragic mask. "Pioneer Rip? There was no Pioneer Rip. What are you talking about. There was only Kier. He thought you were playing. Thought it was a game. And I saw you . . . " She looked down again.

You who read this may wonder.

Believe me, I have turned this matter round in my mind many times in the last few hours. I think Pioneer Rip *was* outside in the snow. I think I fought him. But that does not alter the fact that Kier is dead and it was my claw that killed him.

You may say, "You were confused. You thought you were killing Pioneer Rip. He misled you. If there is any guilt it is his." That brings no comfort. Ignorance is never an excuse. If the instinct is to kill, the victim hardly matters. The instinct is the illness.

All that Pioneer Rip let me do was face my instinct.

No matter that I feel cheated and used and worthless.

There, it is written, and now I must bury the body. Aira insists.

11

How dark and cold this cabin is. How lonely.

How awkward the marks on the page. I am using my right hand. The effort makes me concentrate.

I shall finish the narrative tonight.

Aira would not accompany me. It was as much as she could do to speak to me. She held the door as I carried the body outside. I knew without her having to say it that she would not be here when I got back.

Yet still she loves me. That I know. What can she do? She is at war with herself.

Outside in the crisp air I hoisted the body and held it firm in the crook of my right arm. My left arm I held tight against me to ease the pain as I walked.

I did not walk across the bloody snow but skirted round it.

Stepping as carefully as I could I set off down the hill. I did not know where I was going. Downward seemed the natural direction in which to travel. I wanted to bury the boy in open ground.

The snow was beautiful, wind-smoothed into tight curves. In other circumstances I would have taken pleasure in it. When I broke through the crust it was as light as feathers. The wind blew up to me carrying thin wraiths of snow which span and vanished.

I moved through the tall dark trees. Occasionally the way was so steep that I had to brace myself against them. I walked sideways, planting my feet flatly and firmly. If the cold got to me I didn't notice though my fur was glazed with frost and driven snow.

The snow ended in patches. The earth became boggy. Quick tumbling streams ran through meadowland. The air became gentler. And suddenly I smelled smoke. Somewhere below me there was a wood fire.

Protecting the boy as well as I could with my head and shoulders, I broke through a stand of brittle trees and found myself on the edge of a valley. The ground fell away before me. On the valley floor where a river meandered I saw a bright yellow point of fire. There was someone chopping wood. How can I explain that it seemed so natural that I should come upon someone chopping wood?

The climb down was difficult. I had to use my claw to hold on to the trunks of saplings and the pain made me dizzy. Kier was light, but each step down was like being touched by red-hot pokers. I remember thinking that before I could dig a grave I would have to strap up my side. I needed to keep moving so that I wouldn't stiffen.

The last few yards was down a cliff and I slipped and landed crouched in the cold, stony stream. Wading across brought me some relief, the chill water numbed the pain. By the further bank I sat down in the shallows and let the cold water run over me. It plastered Kier's hair to his face and washed his wound clean. I think I could have lain there for eternity.

But a strong brown arm reached down and dragged me up. I flopped on to the bank, still holding Kier, and found myself facing Pioneer Rip. He looked as strong as a bear; there wasn't a scratch on him.

"No, it is not over yet," he said. "You brought your cruelty into my world, now you must see it through to its end. Come on, Angelo, don't just lie there. You've got work to do. I've even helped you. I've dug a grave. But you must bury him."

He reached down and lifted the boy from me. I felt too weak to resist. Close to where I was lying was a mound of earth. The Pioneer jumped down into a hole and lowered the boy.

How long it took me to fill the hole I do not know. The earth was black and moist and clung to the shovel. But finally it was done. During all this time we did not exchange a word. At the end I drove the spade down into the soft soil and left it standing. I moved away, back towards the river.

"Where are you going?"

"I don't know. Back up there. Where else is there?"

"She won't be waiting for you. She's gone already."

The conversation seemed pointless. I wasn't prepared to engage in another round of folly. All I wanted was to be left alone. I moved on.

"Hey, Chimp. How if I make a bargain with you?" I paid him no attention. "How about if I bring the boy back to life? I can, you know. I am master of Life and Death on my world."

This I was not expecting and it stopped me. I turned and looked at him, vigorous and strong and holding his axe lightly by its shaft. His face had the same mocking smile that I remembered from when we landed. "Why do you torment me?" I said. "We came as rescuers. We offered no violence."

"Iron in flame."

"I don't understand."

"You will. Anyway, what say you, Angelo? A bargain. I will bring the boy back to life if you will do one thing."

"What is that?"

The giant lifted up his axe. "Chop off your claw."

"What?"

"You heard. Chop off your claw. There on the block. With this axe. And I'll bring the lad back to life."

"How can I trust you?"

The giant shrugged. "You have my word."

"No."

"So the claw is worth more to you than the boy's life."

"No. I don't trust you. You are playing games again."

"Games." He looked at me steadily. "Is that what you think I am doing? Well, you have a simple choice. A life for your claw. Watch, I will help you make a decision."

The giant looked at the mound of earth where I had buried Kier. The turned soil began to heave and convulse. It was the stuff of nightmares. I don't think I have seen anything more terrible in my life.

238

"Now what do you think?" he said.

"If I do this will you allow them both to leave this world in peace?"

"Yes."

"You give me no choice."

"There is always choice," he said and lifted the axe towards me.

The stump where the giant had been chopping wood was criss-crossed with cut marks where the axe had bitten into the wood. I got down on my knees and placed my claw on the block and gripped the axe close to its head. I raised it and then hesitated.

The giant smiled. "In your claw is all your pride, isn't it, Angelo? Where will you be without it?"

"Damn you," I shouted and brought the axe down.

I saw the blade sever the flesh and the bone and the heavy claw rolled and fell off the stump.

Blackness dropped like a cloak upon me.

How I made my way back to this cabin I do not know. No doubt I climbed by instinct. But here I am, writing with my right hand. All pain has left me. I sit like a man made of ice. What I shall do now I do not know.

I have been tempted to walk on up the mountain and there lie down in the snow. But I will not do that, nor anything like it.

Beyond reckoning I hold life to be precious.

Perhaps I shall sit here for a few days, watching for a sign. And if I see nothing I shall walk back down to the sea. After that who knows?

I doubt if much worse can happen to me. Perhaps some scaly beast will take me for breakfast.

I have reached the bottom of hope.

12

We climbed for hours.

High in the hills, at about the place where the lowland bush gave way to deeper-rooted trees, we found a cabin. It reminded me of one of those mountain retreats I had seen in pictures . . . the kind of cabin that used to be popular in Old North America. The roofs sloped steeply. There was a porch in front with low easy chairs made of planks.

Seated on the chairs and enjoying the late afternoon sunshine were an old man and an old woman. They looked like brother and sister or they could have been a long-time married couple who over the years have come to resemble one another. Their faces were older versions of the giant who had steered us here.

"You've had a hard journey finding us," called the old man, standing up. "Come on up and sit yourselves down."

I looked at the cabin. *Déjà vu*. Is that what it is called? I had the feeling that I'd been here before, but could not remember for the life of me how or when. I stopped in confusion, but the old woman held out her hands to me. "Don't get lost in your dreams, son. You've found us now and that is all that matters. Come on up."

At the steps to the cabin I reached up with my claw and she took it between both her hands. Why, I do not know, but that gesture of friendship made me wince.

Aira followed and then Kier. Gratefully we sat down on the rough planks of the porch and stared out over the water and islands.

It was later than I expected and already the sun was low. I was bone weary and surprised at myself. The most I had done that day was sit in a boat and then climb up to the cabin. Why should I be so tired?

"I expect you'd like one of these, Angelo," said the old man and offered me a cigar. "Enjoy it. Enjoy it. We've got plenty more." Even the cigar troubled me, but I smoked it just the same.

Kier sat cross-legged and fidgety. "Do you live here?" he asked.

"Sometimes. And sometimes we live over there." The old man gestured airily. "Do you want to explore? You can. I've been trying to grow some vegetables out back. Perhaps you can give me some tips. I understand you've a way with vegetables." Kier grinned and hopped off the porch and disappeared round the side of the cabin. It never occurred to him to ask how the old man knew all this.

But it occurred to me and to Aira. I could sense questions forming in her mind.

"Time for questions when the sun goes down," said the old woman. "Enjoy the evening with us."

We sat while the sun turned the sky to red and gold. As the sky darkened I began to see the great wall of asteroids which surrounded this world. It was hard to believe that just a few hours earlier we had been picking our way through that wall.

That thought led me to the memory of our ship, sunk now in a sea of mud. There were many questions I wanted to ask.

"Ay-yi," said the old man sitting forwards and standing up slowly, "time to move indoors. Our guests are getting impatient."

Kier appeared round the side of the cabin. He held a white rabbit in his arms. "Hey, look at this, Angelo. It's real." He rubbed his cheek against the white fur. "You can feel its heart beating. Honest."

"Keep it," said the old man.

"Can I?" Kier was excited, but then he checked himself. "No, I won't keep it," he said. "It would never survive the journey home."

He sounded so serious, so grown up in a way that we had never heard, that Aira and I found ourselves laughing. Aira slipped her hand into mine and squeezed it. "I think things are going to be all right," she whispered.

*

241

Stew. The old woman served it directly from an iron pot set in the middle of the table. And after the stew came apples baked in their skins and laced with cream. I don't think Kier had ever eaten so well. At the end of the meal he said, "Did you use to eat like this in the olden times?"

The old woman gave him what I think would be called an old-fashioned look – something between a reprimand and a smile. "Aye, this was how we ate. Do you approve?"

"Er . . . Yes." He began to blush, he had not expected to be addressed so directly or to be asked a question.

"Well, you can help clear the dishes then. Your mother and I have something to discuss and the men'll want their smelly cigars out on the porch. Then bed."

I doubt if anyone had ever spoken to Kier in this domineering yet friendly way. He beamed, and I could read his mind. He was accepted, he had a place in things, responsibilities. He stood up from the table and began clearing the bowls and plates.

Aira too was surprised but for different reasons. When the old woman called her Kier's *mother* she jumped as though pinched and then blushed.

The cue was obvious. The old man grumbled something about being bossed about and shambled about looking for his box of cigars. It was still on the porch. Minutes later found both of us sitting outside, lying back in the chairs, puffing out clouds of blue smoke and staring up at the grey crazy paving of the sky.

"How do you feel?" asked the old man after a few minutes.

"OK now. Rested. More at home than I expected. I didn't find the man who brought us here particularly friendly. He seemed to have something against me. He said *he* was Pioneer Rip."

"How does your claw feel?"

That was an odd question. The claw has been part of me ever since I can remember. Normally I think no more about my claw than I do about my head. And yet there was something strange about it. I *was* aware of my claw. Aware of its weight and its

242

strength. I flexed it, like a man who has been injured looking to see if there is any pain. The blades opened and folded together neatly, able to pick up a leaf or sever a bone. "My claw feels fine," I said. "Why do you ask?"

"Just wondering. It is a strange piece of equipment for a man to be carrying."

"I am not a man," I said. "I am not a full-human. I am adapted."

"Where it counts, you are a man. Take my word for it."

I did not know where this conversation was leading. As though by accident it seemed, the old man had touched on one of my main preoccupations, one that has worried me in all the pages I have written. Was it an accident? Could it be an accident? I didn't think so, but I didn't know how to frame the questions I wanted to ask.

We lapsed into silence again. Somewhere out in the darkness a bird called. It was a harsh repetitive keening. I have heard that call before on Aotearoa. A weka bird it is called.

"That sound carries me back," said the old man. "I was just twenty-one when I left Earth. Grew up in Taranaki in what you now call Aotearoa. When I was a boy I heard that sound every night, lying in bed in the dark. In the morning it was magpies, sounding like bells, that woke me up. I was luckier than most. I had a happy boyhood. Not like poor old Murray. We were classmates at the Pioneer academy. Did he tell you?"

"He has told me little about the early days."

"Well, we were. I was older than him by a few months. That's why I was sent out first. Anyway, we all studied together. We used to give him a hard time. We thought he was a bit of a lick-plate. You know? The kind of kid that always wants the teacher to praise him . . . always wants to be top. I think he's still a bit like that even now. When you get back, if he's still alive, tell him Rip says 'hello' and then give him a kick up the backside from me." The old man laughed.

"Are *you* Pioneer Rip then?" I said, remembering the way the giant had spoken to us earlier in the day.

"Yes, I am Rip, or a small part of him anyway. And so is the

243

old busybody indoors and the big fellow you met when you landed and many more. As many as you care to dream up."

"How can that be?"

The old man did not reply immediately. And when he did reply it was in a question: "What do you think of this world?"

"I don't know." A pause. I thought about my answer. "Friendlier than when we landed. I like the cigars. I haven't seen much. Not much of an answer is it? You seem more at ease than any of the Pioneers we have had dealings with and I suppose that says something about this world."

"Yes, well. . . . When I approached, centuries and centuries ago, I came through the same wall of asteroids as you. But what I found was a world without a spirit. Do you know what that is? It is a world where there is life but where life has no meaning. It was waiting for me. It sucked me in. Whoosh. Young Pioneer Rip died in his body when he was still twenty-one, but wherever you look you see Rip. I am Rip, the trees are Rip, the birds and the things that live in the lakes and the seas are Rip, the wind is Rip and he falls in the rain and snow.

"You came to rescue Pioneer Rip. Can you carry a whole world in your spaceship?" The old man laughed. "And you see there is one thing you must understand. This is a world where life thrives. Look at that young lad Kier. He *knows*, though he couldn't put it in words. Think what this world would have become if I had been a killer say, or wholly self-centred or angry because I had left Earth. The world would have a different mana. And we would not be prepared to help you. We would be jealous of you."

I grappled to understand. "You say you are Rip and does that mean that the woman who is now inside talking to Aira is also Rip?"

"Just that. She is what I would have been if I had been born a woman. I am what she would have been if she had been born a man. Don't be fooled, young Angelo, life is the common force. The differences between men and women are very small."

"But – "

"But the rest is politics. That is something that Murray could never understand."

I thought about Pioneer Murray and remembered how sad he seemed when first we rescued him. I remembered his creature and the dome enclosed in ice. "Will you help Earth?" I asked.

He thought for a long time. "Earth is an abstraction," he said finally. "I will help you and Ariadne or Aira as you now call her, and I will help Kier into his manhood. The rest will be up to you. You will deserve the world you make. You have learned a lot since you have been here. You don't understand me now, but you will."

I shrugged. He was right. I didn't understand what he was talking about.

"Now tell me about old Earth. Are there any new jokes? I haven't heard any jokes since I blasted off and that was a long time ago."

I couldn't think of any jokes but we started fresh cigars and I told him everything I could about Earth and told him about the Pioneers he had known as a youth. I described the battle at Rotorua Mining Town and the ways that affairs on Earth were managed.

I don't know how long we talked but at some point in the evening Aira and the old woman Rip joined us. They seemed happy and relaxed.

We sang songs; songs from the time when Pioneer Rip was young. Aira and I did not know the words but the melodies were easy to follow. Kier crept out and joined us. He kept very quiet and sat with his knees drawn up to his chest, watching everything.

I yawned a yawn that would crack the heavens and that was the signal for the end of the evening.

"You two go inside," said the old woman Rip. "You've a long journey in front of you. You need all the sleep you can get."

Though I was tired, sleep was not on my mind. Nor on Aira's either.

We made our goodnights as politely as we could and shooed Kier upstairs to bed.

"Don't worry about us," said old woman Rip, "we'll probably watch the night out. When you are old and can still see the night out, that's a wonderful thing."

In bed, later, both relaxed and drowsy, with my arm round Aira and her sprawled half across me, I asked her what she and the old woman had been doing most of the evening.

She kissed me and buried her head in my fur before answering. "We talked about having babies. She wants me to have a baby. She said that was the best way that Rip could help Earth."

"But we are sterile."

"I told her that."

"And?"

"And she just laughed. She said the cure was already taking place. That we were being renewed."

"What did she mean by that?"

"I don't know."

"Do you feel any different?"

"I feel . . ." she began and then stopped. "I feel different here, on this world. I feel that something has happened to me. Perhaps when we landed. Perhaps in that blackness, when the ship was descending. I can tell you this much, I've never talked to another woman so frankly. Not even Tui and we didn't have many secrets. It was a relief to talk to her and she told me about herself. You know that she is Pioneer Rip?" I nodded. "And that none of this world is real. No, how did she put it? 'It is real for the moment but not permanent.' They created it for us."

"Why?"

"She said it was a test."

"A test of what?"

"Us."

246

"Oh." I thought for a while and could not understand. "Did we pass?"

Aira squeezed me and I heard her laugh quietly. "I think so. Else why would they be so friendly?"

"Don't know. Perhaps they feel sorry for us."

In the night I awoke. The room was filled with a thick purple light which streamed in through the window. It was the same light we experienced when we descended. All I can say is that I was not troubled by it though it seemed to hang about me and make my fur shine like copper.

Aira was on her knees on the bed staring straight into the light. She was completely unaware of me.

Then what did I do? I do not know. I must have done something but I have no idea what. Very unsatisfactory. I don't remember. Perhaps I am not supposed to remember this much.

The memory of being there is all I have and it teases me.

I have written all this in the morning while everyone else is asleep. Apart from the memory of the events in the night, everything seems normal. It is just after dawn and the sea below is wrapped in mist with only the dark peaks of hills poking above it. In the night it has been raining and the leaves are dripping and the air smells clean.

I could not find Pioneer Rip (any of them).

Thinking about the events of yesterday, I find it hard to believe that this world which seems so tangible to all my senses is part of a dream spun by Pioneer Rip. That is what Aira told me. I wonder what the world really looks like. Perhaps there is no such thing.

Anyway, I sit and I wonder and hear my stomach rumble.

247

13

We are again in our ship and have entered the maze of asteroids. We have seen the last of Rip's world. As we soared above it and out into the blackness of space, we left behind a purple world where colours raced like ink in oil.

The purple mist, for so it seemed, descended even as we lifted, and obscured from our view the muddy water and the low hills and the mountains. I think that what I saw was the reality of Rip's world. A world without form, because it does not need form. A world of potentialities as shiftless as mind. I remember Pioneer Rip saying to me, "Think what this world would have been like if I had been angry or jealous." I know that we would not have survived the passing.

Even as I completed my last entry I heard steps on the porch and a shadow fell across me. I looked up and found the giant who had poled us here stooping to look through the window. He had an axe in his hand. He elbowed the door open and wedged it with a sliver of wood. Then he began carrying arm-loads of timber into the house and stacked them close to the open fireplace. Though he looked at me he gave no sign of recognition. It was as though I was invisible. Even when I spoke and wished him good morning he ignored me. If he wanted to ignore me, so be it. I decided to ignore him. The problem was his, not mine. Pioneer Rip is obviously a very complex being. Perhaps this giant is an incarnation of his crueller nature, but I don't really think that is so.

When the wood was stacked, the giant departed, kicking the wedge away from the door.

I was left alone. A few minutes later Kier climbed down from his bed still rubbing sleep from his eyes. "Who was that?" he asked.

"The big man who met us."

"Oh. What did he want?"

"He brought wood."

"Oh. Shall I light a fire?"

I could see he wanted to. Delight in lighting fires lasts well beyond boyhood.

"Why not?" The morning felt damp and chill despite the sunshine and there is something about a wood fire in the morning that always makes everything seem brighter.

While he was laying the fire and carefully placing the small pieces into a wigwam over the dry kindling, he said, "Angelo, I had a strange dream last night."

"Oh yes," said I. "We all had strange dreams last night. Do you want to tell about it?"

"I don't know. I've never had a dream like this before."

"So tell me. Bad dreams often go away when you talk about them."

"Do they?" He sounded relieved. "I dreamed I died."

"Many people have dreamed that."

"Have they?"

"Yes. And then they wake up and get on with living."

"It was so real."

"Some dreams are. Then what happened?"

"Well, when I was dead I seemed to be floating, or swimming in that blackness, you know, like when we landed. And there was a light in front of me. I swam towards that. And I swam into the light and landed on my feet and you were there."

"What was I doing?"

"You were chopping wood. And you said 'Make a fire, Kier.' And I did."

"Did it burn all right?"

"I think it did. I'd just got it started when I woke up."

"Well, it wasn't a bad dream was it?"

"No, I suppose not."

"And now you are lighting a fire."

"Yes."

I realized there was something more, something he hadn't said. He paused for a long time, fiddling with the fire.

"You see . . ."

"Go on."

"You see, it was *you* that killed me." There, the words were out. He looked up from the fire and straight across at me. There was something different about his face . . . A directness. "You killed me. It was horrible."

Despite the fact that he was halfway to being a man and might be embarrassed, I opened my arms to him as I would to a child. After a moment's hesitation he came over to me and put his thin arms round me and squeezed me and then stood back.

"I woke up afraid, but that's gone now. Thank you, Angelo."

I didn't know what he was thanking me for. I had done nothing but offer comfort. "Well you are all right now," I said gruffly and added, "I'll never harm you Kier."

"I know," he said. "Let me tell you a bit more. In the dream we were fighting. It started as a game and then you suddenly got angry with me. I've never seen you angry, Angelo. You killed me with this." He pointed to my claw. "It was frightening."

I nodded and opened and closed my claw, letting its blades slide together like a parrot's beak. I didn't know what to say. It *is* a cruel weapon.

Kier laughed briefly and punched my arm and turned away. "Well, the dream's gone now. Laid to rest. But I needed to get it out of me. I'm glad I told you."

"I'm glad you did."

"Well, I'd better get that fire started."

"Yes."

"Where's Aira?"

"Still asleep."

"Will she wake up soon?"

"I expect so."

"Good. I don't like it when we are apart."

It was a strange remark but I let it pass. Other thoughts were in my mind. While Kier had been speaking, I had been noticing the differences in him. His eyes for one thing. There was something about them that reminded me of Pioneer Rip. And his voice too. He was still Kier, still the boy who had protected our ship in Aotearoa, still the young man who had stepped out of the auto-nurse after the long sleep . . . but he was more than Kier as well. I watched him concentrate on the fire, wondering.

While we had been speaking, the new wood on the old embers had begun to smoke. Now he blew on them and a bright yellow flame sprang up. Soon the fire was crackling and he fed it strips of bark.

Minutes later Mrs Rip arrived at the cabin rubbing her hands. She saw the fire, just beginning to make its warmth felt, and smiled brightly at Kier. "Good lad. Just what we need on a morning like this. We'll cook pancakes on that. I imagine it is a long time since you have had a real pancake. You can help me. Go out back and find me some fresh eggs from the hen house."

How ordinary she made everything seem. I had to remind myself with an effort as I looked at her, perky as a sparrow, that I was looking at the spirit of this world.

She turned to me as though reading my thoughts, "Well. Did you sleep well, Master Angelo?"

"Well enough. I think I woke up once. We seemed to be surrounded with purple fire. Maybe I dreamed it."

She seemed amused. "Pay no attention to that, Angelo. Whether you saw it or dreamed it makes no difference. It was just us tinkering. The old man will be here in a moment. He has something for you. . . . Not a gift, something of yours that he wants to return to you. Where's Aira?"

"Still asleep."

"Good. Take care of her, Angelo. She is embarking on a great adventure. Both of you are. Now – pancakes."

I watched her bustle about. I was content just to watch. I felt very relaxed, as though I was on the first day of a holiday. Outside scudding clouds obscured the hills and it began to rain again.

251

A figure hurried, head down, across the grass outside the cabin. It clumped up the steps and stood for a moment shaking the rain from an old hat and struggling out of a heavy raincoat that looked like a poncho.

The old man entered. He was red-faced and puffing. "Morning, Angelo," he said. "Fine weather for ducks." In his hands he held a small package. He crossed straight to the fire and stood with his back to it. Steam rose from the backs of his trousers. "Got something for you," he said, and held out the package. "Keep it safe. I'd rather you didn't open it until you are up there, off planet. OK?"

"OK," I said. "Whatever you want." The packet was soft, a roll of papers I guessed. I was completely mystified. I was however surprised that he wanted us to leave so soon, and said so.

"It's not a matter of wanting, Angelo. In other circumstances you'd be welcome to stay as long as you liked. All of you. But you have accomplished what you set out to do. And it would be best if you left quickly."

"I take it you won't be coming with us."

He laughed at that. "No, we won't be coming with you. We wouldn't even if we could. Mmm, a bit of us will go with you and that is the main thing."

"Is there a message you want us to take back?"

"Remember to give Murray a kick up the backside." He laughed and then slapped his hands together. "Now breakfast," he said. "I'm hungry and you must be too. You had a long night."

And so we had breakfast.

Halfway through Aira arrived. She had fashioned a dress for herself from a sheet. It was knotted above her breasts. She took her place quietly and the old woman Rip fussed over her. I said "Good morning" and was surprised when Aira looked at me almost shyly. But she was not shy. She reached across and took my claw and squeezed it. It was an open gesture. An obvious gesture for all to see. A gesture of love, and when I glanced at Kier I saw he was smiling.

Something was different yet nothing was different.

I cannot say that either the old man or the old woman hurried us to leave. And yet there was a hurry. We finished our breakfast and then, as though it was the most natural thing in the world, I found myself at the door shaking the old man's hand and bending down to kiss the old woman goodbye. I felt, and this may make you smile, for you know that my origin was a calculated mingling of genes in a crucible, but I felt that I was saying goodbye to my father and mother. Perhaps what I mean is that I wish I had had a father and mother like that old couple. I was interested to observe Aira. She too said goodbye as though saying farewell to her parents. There were tears and gladness. How quickly they had grown into confidence! Kier stuck close to me. He was sad to be going but glad to be with us.

As he was saying goodbye to Kier, the old man performed an antique conjuring trick. He pretended to produce an egg from Kier's ear. (Both Kier and I had seen him pick the egg up from the table.) He insisted that Kier take the egg with him. And he said these words: "Carry this egg with you back to Earth. Keep it warm. If you are lucky it may hatch into a chicken. It will help you to remember us." Kier carried the egg clutched in his hand.

We descended down the hillside to the bay. Waiting for us was the shallow canoe. In its stern sat a girl who seemed not much older than Kier.

"Don't tell me," I said, as we climbed aboard, making the boat rock in the water, "you too are Pioneer Rip."

She wrinkled her nose and nodded. "'Fraid so. I'm going to take you back to your ship."

As she paddled us out from the bay and into the open water the heavy sky lifted and we could see the hills and mountains of the mainland. We could not see the hut we had left earlier.

Aira trailed her fingers in the water. Kier looked for fish. I

253

just watched as the islands slid past. No creatures rose from the deep to bother us.

We came round a low muddy island and our ship came into view. It was riding high. It looked as though it had never been submerged. The Worm was extended and reached right to the shore of the island. Birds, which were perched along its fin, flapped into the air as we approached.

The girl had not spoken during the entire journey. She seemed happy to paddle and I must admit that this return journey did not seem as long as the first. She jumped out before we beached and guided the canoe to the mouth of the Worm. She helped us alight, standing up to her knees in the muddy water. I shepherded Kier and Aira into the Worm and then turned to face her and said goodbye. Before I could speak she raised her arms and kissed me full on the lips. She tasted of earth and salt.

"Good luck, Angelo," she whispered. "Take good care of them."

Then I was in the Worm-lock and waving through its translucent plate.

The rest you know. I know.

And I am seated at the familiar kitchen table, the table where I have spent so many of my waking and dreamy days, the table where I faced old Pioneer Murray. I like familiar things. I like the table that bears the scratch marks of my claw. Aira and Kier are in the bathing pool. Both seem refreshed and very perky. I am enjoying my solitude.

Facing me on the table is the small package that Old Pioneer Rip gave me this morning (it seems like a week ago). I have not unwrapped it yet, honouring to the full his request. I am strangely uncurious about the contents. I doubt if the contents will elucidate the strangeness of Rip's world. That world is an enigma to me. We are all different for the experience of being there though nothing really happened. Oh well. I shall unwrap the package.

14

Papers.

Sheets of paper covered in my handwriting. And rolled up in the papers, two cigars.

I have read through the words and almost know them by heart. They tell a grim little story with a frightful ending. The pages have an air of truth about them that I cannot deny. Whether they be allegory or simple narrative I can't tell. But I recognize my own style.

But as I sit here, I have no recollection of snow, or a bird that attacked me or of fighting the giant or of killing Kier or finally chopping off my claw. Why, I can no more think of chopping off my claw than I can think of castration. And that of course may be the issue in a symbolic way. These are pages from an amnesiac's diary. Not knowing what to do with them I have wedged them among the earlier pages where they seem to belong. That something of a real and traumatic nature happened to me is obvious. I have checked with the chronometers aboard the ship which keep constant time. According to them we have been on Rip's world for the equivalent of nine days! I remember a day and a half.

The events happened. How then I am as I now am I do not know. Rip can manipulate reality, but I can't. Rip has tried to explain. Neatly folded among the pages of my diary was a square of paper. On it was a note in a different hand. The handwriting was characterized by loops and difficult to follow. I here write it out in full.

Dear Angelo,

Light a cigar and sit back. By now you will be well away from my world and no doubt you will have read and puzzled over the enclosed pages. Do not worry about them too much.

They tell about a part of your life which you lived and which is now no more than a dream. You put your humanity to the test and won and I am glad that I do not now have you wandering, lost and clawless on my world.

You worry too much about learning, Angelo. Let things happen. Wisdom grows without our knowing it and comes from the most unexpected sources.

You have a job to do. Take good care of Kier. I would not entrust him to you if I didn't now know that you are capable of that trust.

Kier is the fertile one among you. There is now something of this world in him. He will sire many children and has the power to overcome barrenness. He does not understand this, nor does he need to. The women he meets will recognize the truth. Ask Aira if you do not understand for her womb is now open and active. She is complete, and if she is lucky she will give birth to many children. Aira can do what Ariadne could not, so perhaps there is providence in the fall of a sparrow . . .

For you, Angelo, I have the cruellest words. You will be the father of many children but you will sire none. There was nothing I could do to help you except try to make your mind ready. To make you fertile I would have to have un-made you and then re-made you. You would no longer be Angelo. And I am not God. The same fate awaits any of your colleagues who are still alive.

Here is the simple truth for you to chew on. Your makers did not complete you. We who were manipulated to be Pioneers shared the same fate except that we were given the ability to evolve rapidly. If you were to live a million years you would never achieve fertility. Here is the cause of your worries. You have worried about what it means to be human. Let me tell you that where it counts, you are more a human than many I knew and better than most.

Be of good cheer, Angelo. I have done what I can. The rest is up to you. You are the guardian.

Rip

I understand the words. I can't help it but I understand them like a death sentence. I would like to climb up through the dark ship and open the airlock and push out. In my mind that is what I am doing. And yet I will not. I know I will not.

Programming, you see. Bloody programming.

Later I will show Aira this letter, but not for a while.

Not for a while.

They have returned from the swimming pool.

Aira asks me what was in the package and I tell her, "Just some papers that I left behind." She is content with that. There is a lightness about her. A bright roguish quality. Tonight we will make love like hammer and anvil, we both know it and delay is sweet.

Kier is simply tired. He has stretched and yawned. Now he is attending to the hydroponics, talking to the tomatoes and cabbages. He has no knowledge of his awakened body. His potency lies within him like a sleeping cat that soon will stretch and yawn and show its teeth.

That is the wrong way for me to think about things.

They leave me alone to do my writing. They think I am absorbed.

I have reached a decision. When Kier is abed I will show Aira the letter. Why delay? Delay would be simple cowardice. I may be a fool of fate, but I am not a coward. Let any who call me coward face me, be they ant or giant or Pioneer. If there is one person I would like to kill at this moment, it is my maker and if black hatred can reach back through the ages to the time I was cobbled together, I pray that it touch that white-coated creature who conceived me in a crucible.

Kier has gone. Aira looks at me strangely.

"What is the matter, Angelo? You are restless and fidgety. Why won't you look at me? Have I done something wrong? Are you upset?"

I don't answer. Instead I open the letter from Rip and slide

257

it across the table to her. She reads, and I see she is as puzzled as I was at first. While she reads, I see her press her hands against her womb and rub as though massaging a hidden ache.

"What does it mean, Angelo?"

"It means that if you want to have a child you must apply . . . sorry, wrong word . . . you must make love to Kier, and as many times as necessary until *it* is accomplished."

She is round the table to me: crouched, small beneath my shoulders and head, taking my lumpen killer claw in her hands and squeezing it. What words? She says nothing except "Angelo", and I do not know what that means.

"Murray," I say, my mind running on by association, "knew nothing of this, you may be sure. In his own way he is as marred as I am, and Bonniface." From somewhere, from some seat of the ridiculous in my mind, I feel a smile tug at my face. "How does it feel," I ask, "to find yourself the future mother of the human race?"

But she does not smile back at me. "I can't," she says. "This is not like it was with Murray. I will not hurt you again, so much. Let the old world die with us. After we return there will be no more flights. We will age normally. Let it be."

"You can. You will."

(Why am I suddenly so wise?)

I stand up; I want to kiss her but I don't. I cross to the cubicle where we keep our survival suits.

"Where are you going, Angelo?"

"Chimp's going for a walk outside."

I am trying to make a joke of it, but I see that I have streaked her face with pain. "Go to it," I say, and begin to pull myself up through the ship with my suit over my shoulders. "Don't worry. I'll be back. We'll sort things out then."

258

15

So here I am. Outside.

I have liberated one of our plastic survival tents and inflated it against the ship's hull just behind the deflector shield. All the seals have bonded with the ship and short of a direct hit from a lump of rock, I am safe. I am even snug, anchored to a security ring.

Despite the fact that it is absolutely *verboten*, I have taken off my survival suit and am smoking a cigar. I am thumbing my nose at fate. If millions of miles away there is a peaceful pebble with the name Angelo written on it, well so be it. But there isn't. I feel an uncanny security. If I am careful, I am safe. There is a life of difference between a calculated risk and a mindless gamble.

I am strangely at peace, lolling here. I have my notebook and pencil, water and chunks of food that I can chew for hours. What more do I need? How simple life is when reduced to its necessities.

We have left the asteroid belt far behind us. We seemed to be through it in no time. More of Rip's cleverness perhaps. Now I can see the stars through the plastic walls of my tent. They are like lights seen through rain. They flicker and slide as our ship turns.

My sense of the ridiculous is my best ally. I do not dwell on the thought that at this very moment Aira and Kier may be locked in fierce tenderness: he startled, and gasping slightly in pain, as his virginity is stripped from him. I do not dwell on that thought though I am aware that my words are passionate. Instead I think about myself. Perched on the outside of our vessel like a shipwrecked mariner. The last time I was here, Ariadne was busy introducing old Pioneer Murray to his manhood. How many more times will I have to crouch out here? Me and the stars. Does it all matter so much? Of course it doesn't. *We* determine what matters and if I choose to be un-jealous, I can be un-jealous. It only matters that I recognize my feelings for what they are.

Aira will not love me the less (I hope) and if she does, well, I will cope with that too. Me and the stars. Many men and women have suffered more. I think of the millions who have lived and died since the world began. They are sparks in the fire, and the fire is nearly out. I fear that the earth, when we return, four generations after we left, will be a greatly changed place. Rip was right. I will have a part to play. I will protect. I will teach. I will help to establish a world I believe in. But poor Kier will have to work hard too.

That is my sense of the ridiculous.

How long will I stay out here? I have not decided. Long enough. Proper lovemaking can not take place when the constable is at the door. It is all a matter of time, tide and rhythm. I will give them plenty of space. Perhaps several days. Soon our ship, under constant acceleration, will begin to eat into the time for our sleep preparation. Ariadne will know this. (Ach . . . I feel like an old man with a young mistress. Let me begin that again.) *Aira* will know this. Then I will have to go back indoors or the ship will have to slow. Perhaps Aira will come to fetch me. Then I will have to face Kier. He will not know what to make of things. If he is cocky I will clip him over the ear. If he is embarrassed I will laugh at him. If they are moonstruck and full of secret glances and touchings I shall leave them to it and make the speediest preparations for a long sleep. I just might do that anyway. I'll think about my sea, green as bottle glass and fathoms deep and I'll bask in it and roll . . . and plunge.

A thought has just struck me. Despite our long sleeps which retard our ageing, we still age slower than full-humans. It may be that I will see Kier into his grave. I shall certainly (all being well) outlive his potency. He will find that hard to cope with. It may be that I will stand shoulder to shoulder with my grand-children. They will say, "Who is the grey ape with the heavy claw? And why don't I have a claw like him?" There will be no answer to that.

I have slept a full round.

The last few hours I have spent clumping round our ship looking for odd jobs. The computers know I am out here but they don't know why. They switched the main searchlights on and I have been busy cleaning the grime off the lens plates. I have also cleaned and filled a couple of score marks. Routine stuff mainly. Non-essential maintenance.

I have been careful to avoid the windows near our living area.

It is only when you clamber about the surface of our ship that you realize just how vast it is. We occupy a small area. Most of it is grey featureless metal concealing the generators, pumps, auxiliary jet systems and the powerful engines that can move our ship across an ocean bed or up a steep hill. Although I only managed to cover half our ship I discovered some interesting things that I had never seen before. Graffito. Who was A.H.? A vacuum welder perhaps, for our ship was assembled in space. A.H. scratched his or her name in the year 2095, shortly before our maiden voyage. A long time ago.

Now I am back in my tent and wishing I had a cigar. I am tempted to sneak inside and steal a cigar or three from my secret supply. But I would be sure to be caught. That would be bad. I am starting to itch a bit too. I would like a shower and a swim.

There is a beautiful constellation out there. In front of us and above. I have called it the Fern. A blue star stands at its tip and two reddish stars make up its stem. It will change as we accelerate and spear our path through the Galaxy. Everything changes.

Day Three.

I have completed my survey of the ship. Nothing to report

except that while I was out there I did something foolish. I scratched my name on the side of the ship on one of our fins. I wrote "Angelo was here". I was going to add the date but suddenly realized that I had no idea what year it is relative to the year our ship was built. The question has little meaning, really. So finally I wrote "Last voyage", and left it at that.

I have decided to spend one more sleep and one more activity period out here and then I shall clamber back inside.

The grime of space is appalling. The inside of my tent is covered in a thin film of dust. When I try to wipe it, it is like oil and everything gets smeared. I suppose that when we jump everything will be scalded from our surface and we will emerge like a bright new pin, ready to be sullied again.

The meat I am chewing tastes like sour tripe. I have a feeling that the filtration unit is not as good as it should be. The air does not smell clean. One more round and that is it.

Day Four.

Today when I climbed back into my tent Aira was there. She had brought me cigars but stood holding her nose. "This place stinks," she said. "I brought you these but you can't smoke one now. I can hardly breathe in here. Come on, back inside. And take that silly look off your face. Everything is all right."

Together we collapsed the tent. I tore the chemiseal free from the side of the ship and then braced myself securely and threw the flimsy tent out into space. It was an impulse, and I felt better for it.

As we clambered round the ship and down the side to the airlock, Aira said, "Did you have a good holiday?"

I replied with what I think used to be called a raspberry.

Then we were in and I stripped the top of my suit off and breathed deeply.

Aira climbed into my arms and oh it was sweet. Together we drifted down through the levels to our living quarters.

Kier was there. "Hello, Angelo. Everything all right outside?"

262

I grunted. I was suddenly aware how dirty I was and how matted and dingy my fur.

"Got some food here if you want it." He lifted a plate and revealed a salad. "Fresh from the garden. Plenty more where that came from. You must be hungry."

I believe I grunted again. Then, pulling myself together I said, "I think I'll wash first."

He shrugged and then grinned. "Well, I'm turning in. I'm tired out." There wasn't a flicker as he said it. "Just stayed up so I could welcome you back. The place has been quiet without you."

Aira accompanied me to the shower. She must have been aware that I didn't want her to leave my sight. She cleaned my fur, gratting in it with her fingers. Then we swam.

I plunged and dived and banged from one end of the pool to the other. Though space is tiring, it does not really give exercise. It is a thankless tiredness.

Aira sat at the side of the pool with her feet dangling down into the water. Once I tried to speak to her but she stopped my mouth. "No questions, Angelo. It is done. I enjoyed it. I am very happy. I don't know whether I am pregnant or not. But I am glad to have you back. Kier may have provided the seed. But you are the father. That is how I see it. Now swim and get all that dirt out of you."

I swam and Aira slipped into the water with me and we made love and then I swam again. All like that, in one sentence.

Afterwards I ate and we retired.

There is really nothing more to say.

Tomorrow we begin the sleep sequence.

Aira says she does not know whether she is pregnant or not. Well *I* do. She *is*.

How do I know? I don't know. I just do. It is there, something in her manner, something in her movements, something in her hair even.

I know. I would stake my life on it.

263

Here I write it down. Aira, a clone, the erected form of Ariadne, herself an adapted woman, has, for the first time in the history of the world, conceived a child.

That is wonderful.

16

Everything is normal.

So normal I can hardly believe it. We accelerate second by second. Our sleep preparations are heavy upon us.

Kier is already in the arms of his auto-nurse. What he dreams I do not know. We have talked a bit, him and me, and I will write about that later perhaps.

Aira drifts about in a daze. She will go to sleep with the full knowledge that a baby is forming inside her. She will curl about that knowledge. What will the auto-nurse make of it? It will cope, of that I have no doubt.

I have had some problems. My old dreams of the sea don't seem sufficient any more. I am worried about Earth and I want a good life for all of us. I want my friends with me. I feel like an old soldier who has survived a battle . . . and the greatest moments of my life were in that battle. The future belongs with others. They can build on us. I hope that somewhere I will find Bonniface and Amsterdame and Lattisbourne alive. Even old Murray. We are all part of the same blighted club. But I am not bitter. That is very clear. I am however tired in spirit. Pioneer Rip's news is responsible for that. I am not pessimistic. I believe that the world has a future and, without question, I will do what I can to help that future. But it will not be mine. Have I made myself clear? Well it is clear to me.

Kier wanted to talk. He knew what Ariadne . . . (dammit) Aira wanted of him and he responded. (Who wouldn't?) He felt used, poor boy, and he asked me if lovemaking was always like that. I told him no. Simply no. I let him read the letter I had received from Rip and helped him decipher it. That made him feel better. But what he wants, what he craves for, is a woman of his own. Someone who will be his and no one else's.

At the same time he desires Aira, again. My philanthropy is limited. He won't have her. He is very confused.

It is an ancient confusion, between love and sex.

"Can the two ever come together?" he asked me.

"Yes. I think so." I said, and left it at that. I am beyond my depth. I cannot distinguish programming from simple emotion.

I keep reminding myself that in Kier's eyes, Aira and I seem only eight or ten years older than him. Yet we have seen so much more than him of love and death that we are worlds apart. I used to think of him as a son. He thinks of me as an elder brother, perhaps a replacement for Pedro. I know that he is the new generation. He does not know what that means. It is all very simple.

At all events, he went to sleep easily.

Aira will soon be asleep.

I shall be the last. In my solitude I shall live with my memories. Now I shall put my book away. I have nothing more to say, for now.

PART 4

An Ending of sorts, and a Beginning

1

No Saturn.

No special effects. Just a normal re-entry as I have experienced it many times before.

I am the first one awake and am putting myself together in my own way. Soon Kier will join me and later (much later, judging by her present progress) Aira.

I have tried to contact Chrono and there is no answer. That is bad. For the first time we have no advance news about how things are going on Earth and the moon. I face the possibility that Chrono may be dead and there may no longer be intelligent life on Earth. That is an incredible thought. More likely is that the means of transmitting intelligence through space have been lost and that what we shall encounter are moon-struck savages or roving bands of nomads on Earth.

But Chrono is the greatest loss. I have never seen him. None of us have. I only know his voice. He has welcomed every Pioneer Rescue Mission home until now. Chrono is one of us.

I have already spoken to the guidance computers and arranged for them to match orbit with Chrono's satellite if it is still there.

I can see Earth. I have looked at it under extreme magnification and it is still brown, green, white and blue. That alone is hopeful.

Kier is back from the dead. All he wants to do is swim. I showed him Earth and he nodded. My impression is that one world is as good as another to him. A phrase I heard centuries ago comes to my mind, "History is bunk."

For the last two days I have spent my waking hours sitting by the tank that contains Aira. She is alive. The auto-nurse tells me she is well. Her figure has not changed much. Obviously the auto-nurse has delayed the development of our foetus. That baby when it is born will be already sixty years old.

I want Aira with me but the auto-nurse has its own schedule. The baby is alive. I have seen its heart beat. For the time being I am content with that. I sit and watch as the fluids drain slowly away.

Not much more to report.

Oh yes there is. The egg. How could I forget it?

The egg which Pioneer Rip gave Kier has survived. Not only has it survived but today it hatched. Two fluffy yellow balls came out of it. Kier has set up a warm plastic enclosure in the hydroponics chamber. I said I doubted if this was wise but he told me I knew nothing about vegetables or livestock and stood with his arms folded when I tried to interfere.

So we have our first new arrival. I think it is a first for the entire Pioneer Programme. Kier takes great pride in them.

He wants me to make a regular chicken report.

2

Aira has woken up. She had a much easier awakening than last time. I would even say that she is brisk and business-like. I am guessing, but I think she feels she has a definite purpose and she can't wait to get back to Earth.

Still no word from Chrono. I keep his frequency open and we transmit our call sign to him every hour. So far as we can detect there are no signals emanating from either Earth or the moon. So we shall just have to wait.

As the days slip by, the pinprick of light that is Earth grows stronger. We are still moving fast but decelerating steadily. We should be close to the orbit of Mars in a matter of weeks. To pass the time I am again teaching Kier to read. There are no books, other than technical manuals, aboard our ship and so I have let him pick his way through the pages I have written. He is very slow. Painfully slow. And none of it means anything to him anyway. It is a fantasy to him. He cannot believe that there once was a world populated by millions of people who loved and hated and lived and died. I do not know whether that is good or bad. I who am a bridge between past and present ache when I confront my own ignorance. To me it is terrible that the wisdom of whole civilizations should be lost. How foolishly humankind has squandered its birthright. But Kier, if I understand him aright, believes that history begins with him. His memory of the old world is a memory of violence and exclusion, of meanness and frustration. He wants none of it.

Maybe he is right. Perhaps nostalgia is a hindrance when one has a world to build. I don't know. Perhaps I will have a better chance when it comes to teaching his children. I don't want to hinder them. But I don't want them to fall into the old pitfalls either.

271

I have made a private decision. When we reach Earth, no matter what we find, I will burn up our last bits of energy trying to save what I can. The paintings are gone. They were destroyed in the Catastrophe. But there may still be books.

How quaint. I think I am the last of the romantics. I wonder about my father. I know I had no father in a literal sense, but the genes that formed me, and which were altered to make me furry and big and clawed, came from somewhere. Once there was a man who gave his sperm or had it taken from him and who thought the way I do. That imprint, coded mysteriously, lives on despite the test tube, crucible and clever splicing. I am not human, but it does not matter. Where it counts I am very human. I think that is what Rip was trying to tell me. But I have had to find it out. You can't tell people wisdom. Wisdom is earned, not given.

I have come full circle in my thinking.

I will save what I can. I will help where I can. But the use that is made of the knowledge I save will depend on the quality of mind of Kier's children. The choice will be theirs. I will give them that choice. Is that not the way it has always been?

The chickens are doing very well.

We think that one of them is a cock. I have observed that that would fit well with Pioneer Rip's scheme of things.

I have told Kier that I want to see fresh eggs. I have a great lust for those old-fashioned things called pancakes.

3

The computers are happy. They are trying to work out our new inertia values and power ratios etc. You see, I have taken Chrono's entire satellite aboard. And Chrono, I am pleased to say, is alive, albeit a bit giddy, and is with us now. Our next stop is the moon.

We matched orbit with Chrono's satellite and the first thing I saw gave me hope. There were lights on, shining through the windows. But there was no hint of movement behind those windows and the radio remained dead.

I adopted standard docking procedure and took over manual control of the ship. We edged closer until the satellite was a small ball of light directly in front of us. Then I released the Worm. It sensed round the satellite, nuzzling it until it found the main airlock and there it anchored. Looking out I knew why we had not heard from Chrono. The satellite had been vandalized. Though I had never seen Chrono's home before, I know satellites well. It should have been bristling with antennae and fragile box-like grills for taking measurements. All the antennae were broken. Some remained close to the satellite held by wires that had been wrenched from the innards. Only the great fans of black solar panels remained intact. That too gave me hope. Whoever had savaged the satellite had not destroyed its life system.

I did not waste time speculating. Aira remained in charge of our ship while Kier and I donned our survival suits. I told Kier to be ready for a shock. Chrono was only a voice to me. I did not know what we would find. It was even possible that the entire satellite was now toxic. It might even be booby-trapped. It occurred to me that leaving the satellite brightly lit like a welcome lamp might be Major de Beer's dying attempt at having the last laugh. However, we have ways of coping with that.

I swung the great deflector shields round until they hid the satellite from us. Now, if it blew up all that would be severed from us was the Worm. I closed the Worm's airlocks and ordered the central computer to open the door into the satellite very carefully by remote control. I was able to watch the entire operation from the security of our main control room.

My caution proved wise. The computer began the open sequence and then stopped. The computers hummed and wittered. Apparently they had managed to open a dialogue with the simple machines that managed the affairs of Chrono's station. The circuits which opened the main airlock had been tampered with. New circuits which seemed to lead nowhere had been attached. The satellite's computers did not know what those circuits were. My bright lads and lasses got to work. Computers that can manage the affairs of a ship like ours, taking it from Earth to space to hyperspace and back safely, and can pinpoint a star system on the far rim of the galaxy, are not about to be fooled by a few stray circuits.

In effect, our ship took over all the functions of the satellite. They accomplished the transference without even a flicker of lights. Then they nosed and probed and twittered to themselves.

Our ship is programmed for survival. Within seconds our master computers knew everything about the running of the satellite. They isolated and closed down the entire airlock system. Then they destroyed the contacts which led to the stray circuits. The entire operation took only three or four minutes and then I saw the open sequence begin again. The airlock swung open. Revealed inside was a crude fission bomb.

What did they think we were, idiots? Later we threw the bomb into space in the general direction of the sun.

With our way clear, Kier and I set off down the Worm.

The first level of the satellite was a mess. Kier and I walked round past the windows in the glaring lights. Equipment whose function I can't even guess at had been ripped out and sometimes abandoned. All the pressure doors which led down to the inner parts of the satellite were sealed. If Chrono was alive, he was beyond these doors.

I checked and was assured by our computers that there were no more booby traps. Even so, I was nervous as I began cutting through one of the doors. I must have triggered some mechanism for the door suddenly hissed and slid open. We were in.

We looked down into a garden. That was my first impression. Creepers climbed up the walls and bright flowers hung at impossible angles. Suspended in the middle of all this greenery was a grey and wrinkled bag of protoplasm. But it had a face of sorts. Eyes on stilts. A beak for a nose. A fleshy gap for a mouth. And it expanded and contracted regularly as it breathed. There were no legs, only arms, eight of them. Nimbly the creature reached up to one of the creepers and pulled and released so that it floated directly towards us.

Kier wanted to run but I held him firm. In my mind I had no doubt what we were seeing. I have faced many Pioneers. This was Chrono.

The creature spread its arms when it was close and held itself steady on a vine.

The fleshy lips moved and a voice I knew well greeted me.

"Who are you?"

"I am Angelo. I have returned from Rip's world."

"So soon. I had not expected you for many years. But then I have no way of telling how quickly or slowly time is passing. Welcome home, Angelo. And how is Ariadne?"

"Well."

"And is this your Pioneer?" One of the hands darted out and pointed at Kier.

"No. He is a full-human who accompanied us."

"Oh, so you take passengers now. I thought he was Rip. He has a look of Rip about him. I saw him, you know. Met him. He visited me before his departure. Some of the very early Pioneers did, before everything became routine. So, if this is not Rip, where is he? Is he dead?"

"It is a long story."

"I like long stories."

"Yes, well, now is not the time. Perhaps later. We thought *you* were dead, Chrono. We have come to rescue you."

"From what?"

The directness of his question surprised me. I had no ready answer. "From isolation," I said finally.

"Ah." There was a croaking sound. It was the first time I had ever heard Chrono laughing. "I have been alone," said Chrono, speaking very distinctly as though to a child, "ever since the first of you blasted off. I don't think I know what to do with company. I am as you can see, unique. They broke the mould after they made me. I do not want to leave my flowers. Where would you rescue me to?"

"Earth."

"I would die on Earth. Look, no legs. And the gravity would crush me."

He. She. It. Chrono was right, of course. And I felt curiously foolish.

Thinking the matter over now, I realize many things. During the time since my awakening I have assumed that Chrono was a prisoner, like the rest of us adapted beings, and that he would resent that state. He was always willing to help us with information though when I think back, his manner was always cool and detached. It never occurred to me to think that he was happy.

He was made for his job. He had a brain and a stomach and arms aplenty to enable him to get about in the weightlessness of space. He had his garden which he loved and which he would die for in the same way that men have died for liberty. He was content in his job and he did it thoroughly; guiding us out, welcoming us home and overseeing all the vessels which moved from Earth to moon and back again. Perfect adaptation.

He is king and guardian to his own small world and asks for nothing more.

He and I have few points of contact.

I realize one other thing. I have become too zealous about

saving things: books, people. The residue of my programming! I am in danger of imposing my zealousness on others such as Chrono. He is indifferent about the fate of the Earth. Oh he doesn't want it to blow up as that would destroy his orbit, but he really does not care whether humankind survives or not. He was our protector when we were within the solar system and he felt the loss of each one of us, but beyond that nothing. A strange creature who now asks for nothing except to be left alone.

So Kier and I faced him and he looked calmly back at us. I am sure we looked as strange to him as he did to us.

"When did they come and damage your satellite?" I asked.

"Let's see. It would be shortly after you departed for Rip's world. I knew they were coming. Picked up their signals. But there was nothing I could do."

"Did you know they had set bombs in the outer gangway?"

"Yes. I suggested that strategy, Angelo. It was the only way I could save the satellite. They wanted to destroy it so that you would have no proximate space guidance. Silly really. They didn't know much about you or your ship and they seemed to think I was terribly important. I also suggested that they strip away all the unnecessary aerials so that I couldn't contact you. Don't look surprised, Angelo. I made a calculated gamble. All gardeners who plant seeds know what it means to make a calculated gamble. And if you don't believe me, look in the mirror. Look at your scars, look at your bald bits of skin, look at your eyes. You are built to survive. I do believe that of all the creatures now alive on Earth and moon and probably beyond, there is not one less likely to fall into the trap than you. The bait was reasonably obvious wasn't it?"

"Yes," I said.

"And even if you didn't spot it, Ariadne would."

A voice crackled in my ears. Aira was following the conversation from the control deck of our ship. "Better tell him about me," she said.

"Ariadne is no longer with me."

277

"Oh? But I thought you said . . ."

"She died before we left Earth. I activated her clone."

"Then Ariadne is with you."

"No, not quite. She is no longer Ariadne. She is now Aira. The same but different."

This information seemed to please him. "Good. Good. I have long maintained that even in the horticultural world there are no such things as identical plants. It is all to do with experience, isn't it?" He didn't wait for an answer. "Any more bits of information that would interest me? Pioneer Murray still with the living?"

"I do not know."

"That must have been a vicious fight you had in Rotorua Mining Town."

"It was." I paused briefly and looked at him . . . more alien in some ways than many of the Pioneers we had rescued. Then I said slowly, "Aira is having a baby."

How can I describe his astonishment? His eyes grew out longer on their pseudopodia, his mouth opened and I swear I could see down into his stomach and then with a twist of his wrist he turned a complete somersault.

"Well, well. This I must see. Obviously there have been strange goings-on on Rip's world."

The topic was too vast and too important for a casual conversation. We both knew it. He took a little persuading but finally he agreed to come back to our ship.

He agreed also to allow me to move his satellite away from the moon and into Earth orbit. "Safer," as I pointed out, "and at least we will be able to see you up in the sky, and perhaps contact you if I can fix up some of those aerials." Implicit in my remark is an understanding that the days of our ship are numbered. There is a limit to what on-ship maintenance can accomplish. There comes a time when even the most self-sufficient ship needs a well-stocked workshop. We are close to that time.

We got him into our ship with some difficulty. He squeezed

278

himself as small as he could. Even so, he almost filled the diameter of the Worm.

While he talked with Aira I manoeuvred his satellite under our ship and into the cargo bay. To make room for it I jettisoned some of our old Pioneer Rescue equipment.

And this is where Chrono's satellite now is. I have climbed about on it a bit and reckon with the help of our computers I can repair the main communiction system. Inside the satellite life goes on as normal. The plants seem happy. The actual communication chamber in the very hub of the satellite is spotless. Chrono has maintained it carefully.

Chrono can tell me nothing about Amsterdame or Bonniface or the affairs of Earth. He has been out of contact as long as we have. He wants to know all about what happened on Rip's world and to answer his questions I have read him my account.

He makes no comment. He does not understand really any more than I do. But he marvels at Aira. He asked to be allowed to touch her belly and she let him. Different though he may be from us, he is in all the important respects our brother. I remind myself of that. A little older than us, but a child of the same technology.

Poor Kier can't make sense of what is happening. He hears Chrono's voice and can understand but all he sees is the bloated body. He is fascinated and repulsed at the same time just as some people are with large spiders. . . . No, a better comparison would be with a toad for in repose there is something toad-like about old Chrono.

I tell Kier, and hope that I don't sound too pompous, that all life is to be respected. I also tell him that his kind created Chrono. He does not like to feel responsible nor do I press the point, for he is not responsible. He was rejected by his own kind. Yet he is a full-human.

We are drifting closer to the moon. We expect to be above Moon Base in a matter of hours. How cozy the solar system seems after the vast distances of galactic space. What we will find at Moon Base we have no idea. Not Major de Beer, that is certain.

There is a distinct smell of chicken droppings in our living quarters. Kier is very secretive.

Omelettes tomorrow, I think.

4

Moon Base was in the long lunar night.

We cruised low over the saw-toothed craters and the dirty pock-marked hills until we were only a few miles from the base. Then I switched our landing lights on. The lunar surface was revealed in an arctic brilliance. We saw the long lines of guidance beacons which stretch halfway round the moon. All were dark. There were roadways too along which surface tractors had once churned and lurched, throwing up clouds of dust. There were no tractors now. Nothing moved except the cone of our lights which crept over the surface like a bright amoeba. It climbed the last crater wall and slid into the flat crater which housed most of the domes of Moon Base.

I have said it before, but the parallel is irresistible: Moon Base is like a cluster of eggs, half buried in the sand. None of the eggs glimmered with light.

We were not expected. No one had responded to our approach signals. This could only mean that Moon Base no longer took any interest in movements in space. Either that or all the inhabitants were dead.

I took us right down on to the old landing platform. If any guard was on duty he could not miss the brilliance of our lights or the dust storm that we caused. I had the deflection shields in place just in case someone was foolish enough to take a pot-shot at us.

Such was my mood when I saw this place, remembering Lindis and Tui, that I half hoped we would be attacked so that I could use the laser cannon to puncture the surface domes one by one. But nothing happened. Moon Base was like a grave. The great hangar doors, which used to open like the jaws of a trap to receive visiting ships, remained closed.

Poor Chrono began to fret in the mild gravity of the moon

and I assured him that we would not tarry there for very long. But the visit had to be made.

I insisted on going alone. I carried a life beacon with me implanted in my survival suit. I made a solemn agreement with Aira that if my life beacon went out she would bomb Moon Base into oblivion, just as we did with the ant hill on Pioneer Jinks' world.

I advanced the Worm as close as I dared to one of the surface airlocks between two domes and stepped lightly out on to the moon's surface. For some reason, prestige perhaps or security, the airlocks on Moon Base and those on our Worm were not made to match. I loped across the last few yards feeling very much the chimp and activated the airlock mechanism with my sheathed claw.

The door irised open obediently and I stepped through into darkness. Be sure I had my particle pistol in my hand. After a few moments the door closed again and I registered an increase in pressure. At least the automatic circuits seemed to be functioning normally even if the human inhabitants were asleep. In the darkness I switched on all my body lights filling the small airlock chamber with light. I waited. I did not remove my helmet though the air pressure recorded Earth normal. I did not trust the air on the moon.

Finally, the inner doors lurched and ground open, squealing under protest. Facing me was a corridor lit with dim green lights, emergency lights by the look of them. The air seemed murky. In front of me the corridor curved down steeply under the surface of the moon. On either side of me were metal sliding doors which led, I guessed, into the side domes. I ignored those doors.

I am not very familiar with the modern layout and geography of Moon Base. It has changed so much since the days when we Pioneer Rescuers were engineered here. I know that most of the surface area is used for storage and the vast workshops which used to service the moon fleet. The living areas and hydroponics gardens are below.

So I set off.

On the moon everything is deceptive. It is like a Pioneer dome. Distances are foreshortened. You think you have to walk a hundred yards and you find it only thirty. Within moments, it seemed, I was already deep, and when I turned round I could no longer see the airlock door. It was beyond the hump of the path.

I met no one. The only sound was the soft padding of my own feet on the dusty floor. How dismal and dreary. I remembered a story I once read about a creature that visited the underworld in search of his wife. He found her. But what was I looking for? I was satisfying my curiosity, that was all. Now I was reporting back. Since the Space Council would not come to me, I was going to them. But more than once I was tempted to turn and walk back to the surface. Why bother with a dead world? But I didn't. I walked on and my body lights, shining on my head, my shoulders, arms and legs, drove the shadows in front of me.

I came to a place where the corridor widened and there were many doors. All of them were closed and dark and locked. Where I touched them I disturbed the dust. They had not been opened for many years. I swear, there is no dustier place in the universe than the moon.

Side corridors appeared and all of them were dark. I avoided them. I could tell that no one had passed that way for many years. The dust at my feet was like untrodden snow.

Finally the corridor bent round to the right and I found myself facing great double doors which were closed and completely barred my path. They were an old type of security airlock of the kind that was once used to seal off sections of Moon Base. I have seen such before. There was a wheel set out from the centre of one of the doors and I gripped this and forced it to turn. Once this wheel would have been power-assisted and turned easily. Now it took all my strength to crank the doors open. Beyond the doors the lights were brighter. I forced the doors half open and walked through. I closed them behind me. Security is a deeply ingrained habit.

There were windows in one wall and through them poured a hard green light. I looked through, cautiously, and stared down at straight rows of hydroponics troughs. I saw my first humans. They were tending the plants. They looked tall and spindly and very frail: figures made from matchsticks and dressed in white smocks.

One of them looked up, attracted by my lights no doubt. I saw it shout and point. All the others stopped and stared.

I began to run. I raced down the corridor until I came to wide double doors wich gave access to the hydroponics garden. I ducked, for the doors were surprisingly low, and charged in. The attendants were still standing, open-mouthed, and only when I approached did they try to flee. I suppose I looked a frightening sight, more solid than them by half and ablaze with lights. I trapped one of them between rows of fleshy looking beans, and held it by the arm.

Boy or girl, man or woman, I couldn't tell from the body. I caught it in my claw and drew it close, and made it look at me.

"I am Angelo," I said. "I have returned from a Pioneer Rescue Mission. I want to speak to someone from the Space Council. Do you understand?"

The creature wailed and looked up to the roof so that all I could see was the whites of its eyes. "Do you understand?" There was no reply but the wailing so I squeezed harder. "Do you understand?"

"No understand. No understand," came a thin voice. At least some communication was established. I relaxed my grip.

"I am An-gel-o. Who are you?"

"April Twenty-six."

I wanted to ask why, but realized this would be a useless question. Presumably a date of birth. I remember thinking it was a silly name and typical of the Space Council that they should choose such a name. The Space Council was always conservative. They even referred to Earth as home, long after they had abandoned it.

"Where can I find members of the Space Council?"

The figure squirmed in my grip in an attempt to point round the hydroponics chamber.

"No understand. No understand. Hurting. Hurting."

I set the figure free and it ran away and joined the others rubbing its arm. "Do any of you know?"

They just stood and stared at me. It was a mindless, vacant gaze. Flowers communicate more. I turned and left them. In frustration I tore up some of their plants and threw them across the hall.

Outside the hydroponics chamber the corridor descended for a few more yards and then levelled off.

Groping their way towards me was a line of women. They were naked from the waist up. They seemed to be blind and held one hand on the shoulder of the figure in front and felt about with the other. They were in the charge of a tall man who called orders and walked behind them. He stopped open-mouthed when he saw me.

I ran up to him. "Space Council," I said. "Where?"

He didn't answer. Just shook his head as though I was speaking a foreign language. Then he backed away and I saw him reaching down to his side.

My response was by reflex. I struck him low and he slumped and fell in the lazy slow motion typical of all movements on the moon.

The women set up a keening and I knew I had done a foolish thing. I could have disarmed him. Now anyone with ears would know that something was wrong. In those few moments I made some important decisions. Although I was beginning to feel that my visit to Moon Base was pointless, I decided to press on. I decided not to go back the way I had come. I decided to leave my body lights on as they made me more frightening. If I was attacked, I would fight. I decided to move quickly. Whether I was right or wrong is not in issue now. Those were my decisions.

I ran. I came to a place where the corridor divided and I chose the right fork. The path sloped up steeply for a while and ended in a wide, low-roofed chamber. That was the end. I was

285

surrounded by dark doors. I stopped. The only sounds were the ones I made. If there were still security forces on the moon they were either very inefficient or very subtle and I doubted that. I decided to explore. The doors were locked so I began breaking them open. In one room were piles of tables and chairs untidily heaped. The room had once been a classroom of sorts. Curled up in one corner were the remains of a human being. The flesh and soft inner organs were long gone but the skin remained tight and dark across the eyeless skull. Tacked upon one wall was a faded picture. I wiped the dust from it and recognized the smiling face of Pioneer Murray.

Another room contained boxes of shoes. They were of the light cover-all type favoured on the moon. Filling one entire wall were racks of clothes covered in plastic sheets. They were children's clothes. They looked as though they had never been worn.

The third door opened into a narrow passage lined with white tiles. I decided to follow it. This passage sloped steeply down and entered a large chamber. My lights shone back brilliantly from the white walls. The floor area was taken up by a multitude of blunt clone chambers similar to the ones we had in our ship. Most of the lids were open, but not all. Above each coffer was an auto-nurse and some of them were active.

I had heard about this place. I was in the experimental hospital. I checked the clone tanks one by one. Three contained the dry remains of half-formed bodies. There were stains on the floor where the vital fluids had been allowed to seep away. The alarms in the auto-nurses had burned out.

In the last tank, I found a simulacrum of old Pioneer Murray. He had certainly left his mark on this place. The clone bore evidence of crude surgery round the abdomen. I had no idea what had been attempted. It looked like a half-completed experiment on a living body. The clone seemed stable. I checked its registration record. It had not been visited for over ninety years. There was no automatic wake-up time indicated. My immediate guess was that it had been forgotten, over-looked, like a goldfish left in a house when the owner departs.

286

It had no future. To wake it up I would have required more power than was flowing in the entire room. But I doubted if it would ever wake. At most it might have a fleeting moment of consciousness before a quick slide into death. I thought of Pioneer Murray who might already be dead and who, even if he were alive, I would probably never see again.

My dilemma was immediate and in front of me.

I did not think or rationalize. I reached up and switched the auto-nurse off. An alarm bell clattered tinnily and I snipped its circuits. The body in the tank moved once, drawing its knees up to its chest, and then it moved no more.

What was I doing? Playing God, as they say so easily. I think I was being kind but I am still not sure whether what I did was right. I will never know. Perhaps I took the easy way out. Others who are wiser than me may tell me. I wonder though, what I would feel now, if I had left that helpless creature to eke out its days while the auto-nurse aged. Could I have faced Pioneer Murray and told him that I left a small part of him to die slowly?

Beyond the clone chamber I entered a maze of corridors.

I was lost. I blundered into empty laboratories and operating theatres heavy with dust. I came into a long room filled with cots. Nothing. No light. No life. No people. The tragedy of what I was seeing on the moon struck me at its fullest then. I picked up children's toys; soft shapeless things and bright balls on string and stuffed them in one of the vacant pouches of my survival suit. I would not leave empty-handed, and such things would not be in ready supply on Earth. Perhaps also in taking these things I was giving the moon a use.

In front of me were glass doors and beyond them a greenish light. I dimmed the lights on my suit. Someone passed and paid the doors no attention at all. I had a clear view of him. It was an old man in frayed clothes. No, not old. How shall I say? I think it was a young man in a prematurely aged body. He was too small for a man and the moon does not breed dwarfs.

287

I waited. I listened as well as I could at the door. I could hear nothing and so took a chance. I broke open the door, bending the lock out of its socket, and dragged the door closed behind me. The lights seemed brighter in this corridor, but if this was a main thoroughfare it was deserted. The floor sloped and I started to climb.

There were more doors and more corridors and no people.

But I heard singing. Children's voices by the sound of them. I followed the sound. I took a side alley and was able to peer over the top of a window and down into a classroom. I found myself looking down into a square box of a room. The light was brighter inside but even so much dimmer than the class-rooms I remembered on Earth. There were children there, about ten of them. They sat on a mat and faced the teacher who was a man not much taller than they were. I was disturbed to see that the children all looked similar. No, they were not clones, but they were similar, the same general shape, the same colour of hair.

Here is part of what they were singing. I set the words down. They are nonsense to me.

"*Ee aye en-ti-o-o*
The farmer wants a wife."

A farmer! On the moon!

The song ended and the children stood up. The teacher spoke to them but I couldn't hear his words. I guessed they were all about to leave and so I slipped across into a darkened room. I heard the door open and the children leave. They seemed to be walking in step. I wanted to follow them but knew that I might be the stuff of nightmares to them. Besides, it was already well past the time when I should have returned. Aira would be worried though she would know that I was alive. Chrono would be fretting and hurting.

I re-entered the main corridor and ran. I ran upwards. There was a curve in the corridor and suddenly I met a group of twelve or so old people walking down. They were walking in single file, holding on to one another, hands on shoulders. They hardly seemed to notice me. Strange. I was past them in a

288

moment. I didn't hear shouts behind me. Perhaps people do not see what they don't expect or what is impossible. A giant in a silver suit with body lights glowing! I was a wind in the air more than a presence.

I came to double doors similar to the ones by which I had entered and began to crank them open. Within minutes I would be back at the surface.

Then I heard a wailing. That is the word for it. The sad crying of many voices.

The sound came from a dark opening to my left. I crept in and encountered the inevitable locked door. I could hear the wailing coming from beyond it. It seemed to come from far away. Carefully I broke the lock and inched the door open. I found myself in a gallery high above a circular conference room. The gallery was deserted. This must have been the main meeting hall in the days when the Space Council on the moon managed the affairs of space. Even in decay it was grand.

Stealthy as a ghost I crept down the steps between rows of seats until I could look over the edge of the parapet. The wailing was coming from the floor below me. People were assembled. Stragglers were still entering. In sum there must have been about 300. All were kneeling save one, an old man with a beard. He stood with raised arms and conducted the ululation, defining its peaks and troughs. However, that was of little interest. What caught my attention, and held it, was a globe with lights inside it which hung above the assembly. It seemed the main object of the wailing. It was an image of the Earth. Blue, brown and streaked with white, just as I have seen it many times from space and just as it looks from the moon.

They were worshipping the Earth.

I crept away. I did not know what to think. I had too many thoughts. I believe that if I had stayed longer I would have switched my lights on and blinded them and perhaps tried to . . . I don't know.

I crept away. With the sound of the wailing in my ears I

cranked the stiff airlock open and climbed through, and closed it again.

I switched my lights on and ran.

Within minutes I was out on the surface of the moon and staring up at the brilliant stars. The Earth was just rising above a crater wall and bathed me in its pale light.

What had I discovered about Moon Base?

Everything, I think. I crept away from it like a robber that had stolen its secret.

I could see the high shape of our ship, ablaze with lights. It was no more than two miles distant. I started to bound towards it.

Aira must have seen me for she broke radio silence. "Welcome home, starman. We were beginning to worry. Are they after you?"

"No," I panted and ran on.

"Well, we have you covered just in case. Chrono's glad you're back. He's been complaining since you left. You look very beautiful. You're bright as a firework. It looks as if your feet aren't touching the ground."

I was pleased with her chatter. I loped up a small hill and jumped and turned a slow somersault.

Soon I was under our ship and coming round to the Worm. Seconds later I was inside and the mouth of the Worm closed behind me. I darted like a fish up the segmented corridor.

The final airlock into the control room closed behind me.

Aira and Kier helped me strip out of the survival suit.

"What kept you?" asked Aira.

"Nothing kept me."

"You stayed longer than we expected."

"I had a good look round."

"And . . .?"

"And nothing. I'll tell you when we're up there." I nodded towards space.

I couldn't cram what I felt into a few words.

I did not take time to shower or swim. Sweaty as I was I fed power to the main generators and we lifted smoothly and

290

gently. Chrono groaned and I kept our acceleration as low as I dared. I wasted power.

Calmer now and with the moon nothing more than a pocky disk in the distance, I can list a few things. I feel free. I feel released. I feel pity for those poor creatures hymning a long-lost Earth. Within one generation I guess, they will all be gone, and the moon will be as lifeless as it ever was.

Maybe one day a new generation of man will set foot on the moon again. Maybe not.

It is a dead world, not worth the bothering.

But will someone please explain why I can still hear that awful wailing in my ears. Goddammit, have I not earned some rest?

Programming. Bloody programming.

5

Never was a creature more glad to see his home than Chrono. He settled into his satellite and began fussing about. Some of his plants had collapsed during the time we were on the moon. They had never known what it meant to have weight. Chrono darted about, uncannily like a spider, and pegged them up and rubbed their leaves and made sure that all the capillary tanks were filled with fresh water.

I had managed to repair his main aerial so that he could both receive and transmit. We searched the wavebands used by both Earth and moon and received only a whispery hiss. But when Aira spoke from our ship, her voice boomed in the satellite. He would be able to receive us from no matter what place on the Earth we ended up.

Chrono made it clear that he now wanted to be left alone. We said brief goodbyes. Considering that this was the last time we might ever see one another, there was a notable lack of ceremony.

"Take care, Angelo. Look after Ariadne . . . no, what's her name?"

"Aira."

"Yes. Look after her and the young one."

"Will you be all right?"

"I'll be fine. Now on your way. You've a lot to do before the sun sets, as my mother used to say." What a startling thought! Chrono's mother. But Chrono would have had a mother once, just as Murray did and Rip. "I hope you find Bonniface and Amsterdame and Lattisbourne. Brave people, they deserve to survive. Anyway. Thanks for mending my aerial. We'll keep in contact."

He didn't exactly shoo us out of his satellite, but the effect was the same.

292

Kier and I climbed back into our ship and released the Worm and began retracting it. Our ship drifted gently away from the satellite. I had made sure that the satellite was in a stable orbit. It would circle the Earth almost twice a day.

So now Earth.

Now that I am actually facing the Earth and it is our next stop, I am not sure what to do. I know I must find whether Murray and our friends are alive. From the depths of space Earth is very small and such a quest seems easy. Close to, Earth is huge and the quest seems impossible.

We are already skimming the atmosphere. I have made a decision. For want of a better idea I have decided to seek out old Rotorua Mining Town. Someone may be there.

Aira is very quiet. Very absorbed in herself. She smiles a lot. She seems fine.

Kier is restless. I have not paid him much attention of late but when I do look at him I notice that he looks even more like Pioneer Rip that before. His body is hard and strong, the result of all his swimming. I asked him, "Do you remember Pedro and the old days?"

He replied, "I remember everything."

6

Four generations is a long time in the affairs of men: almost nothing to the Earth.

We approached Aotearoa along the old landing path. The Wellington bay was as I remembered it, a sharp blue fringed with dark green bush. The Rimutaka Mountains had snow on them, a sure sign that we had arrived in the winter months. Then we were over and dropping down to the plain where Master Town Space Centre once flourished. There was still grassland here but the bush was making steady inroads, climbing out of the river valleys and down from the mountain slopes. Master Town was almost completely lost under a canopy of giant trees. We could see clearings where once there had been wide open spaces of reinforced concrete. The hangar which we had torn through when we departed could not be seen. Wind and weather had no doubt destroyed it. There was no smoke. No suggestion of habitats or cultivation.

"Do you want to go down?" I asked Kier. He shook his head.

So we swung north. I took us up over the Ruahine Range and we travelled over mountains until we could see the pale mirror of Lake Taupo. It was fuller than last time we were here and was now an inland sea. The three mountains, Ngauruhoe, Tongariro and Ruapehu stood white and solid, just as I remembered them except that Ngauruhoe was smoking. There were stains on the snow. Sometime earlier it must have erupted.

We cruised on. In the control room, the computers were at full alert. I was using every part of our Pioneer Rescue equipment to detect any sign of civilization. They remained silent.

For a few moments I held us still over Tarawera and we

looked down at the pattern of lakes and hills. Lake Rotorua was already in sight.

We drifted over the lake, about half a mile high. If there was anyone about they would surely see us. But to make sure I fired our laser cannon briefly at the shoreline. We heard thunder rumble round the hills and a small smoky fire started and blazed brightly before going out.

Nothing. No answering flame or detonation. The birds that had risen when I fired flapped round the lake and then returned to their perches in the bush.

"So where now?" I wondered aloud.

"Be patient, Angelo," murmured Aira. "We have come a long way. There is no rush now. And if we missed someone because we hurried . . . well."

People who are right all the time and state the obvious can be very irritating, and I told her so.

"Mangy old chimp," she replied, in good spirits.

"Shut up. Go and cook something. Pancakes. You know how to cook them, don't you? Use up some of the eggs that Kier's chickens keep laying. Afterwards we'll land for a while. Perhaps we can find a hot pool that is the right temperature. Tell Kier. He's never been for a swim in a hot pool. There's nothing like it."

"Nor have I," said Aira as she departed.

Without much hope I switched the main view-screen to half magnification and began to study the hills. Quite suddenly I saw what I was looking for and nearly missed it. Smoke, rising in a still column from the top of a hill buried deep in the bush. I brought the screen to full magnification. The smoke was obvious, but there were too many trees hiding the ground.

"Smoke," I shouted. "Smoke."

Kier bobbed his head up into the control room. "What's wrong. Do you want a cigar?"

"No. Yes. What? Smoke. There, behind those pine trees. Tell Aira I'm moving the ship."

"She's just started . . ."

295

"I don't care. Tell her to hold the pan. I'll be careful."

And I was careful. I turned the great ship on its axis and edged us towards the hills. Our shadow crept in front of us.

I must explain. Apart from the smoke which was exciting enough, I had recognized the place from whence the smoke had arisen. I had spoken with the strange Pioneer woman called April there. I had buried Ariadne there and my friends Kingi and Elf. I had last seen old Pioneer Murray close to there. So that gave the place a special excitement.

We were almost over the clearing when I stopped us. I saw two figures, a man and a woman. They looked wild and hairy and I could not recognize them. But I knew it was not Bonniface or Amsterdame. They were glad to see us. They were dancing, jumping in the air in excitement.

I cast about and found a landing place further down the hill in a shallow valley where a stream wandered through dense stands of manuka. I put down quickly, leaving it to the guidance computers to make sure we were stable.

Aira and Kier joined me in the control room.

"Shall we send down the Worm?" asked Aira.

"No," I said. "Let's do it the old way. Out through the main airlock and down the ladder. Or they can climb up to us."

Aira had the airlock open even while the ship was still adjusting its trim. Together the three of us stepped out on to the narrow balcony. The air was surprisingly chill. Very clean. Very pure.

The two figures came pushing through the supple manuka and reached our ladder and began clambering up hand over hand. By their movement I would say they were in their twenties, strong and lean.

They reached the balcony and jumped up and stood looking at us. Then I recognized them. I suppose I should have known.

"Hello, Chimp," said a voice I had heard so many times before. The young man parted his hair with his hands and held it back behind his ears. I can say that at least his eyes were the same. "What kept you? We expected you years ago."

"Hello, Murray," I said. "I didn't recognize you." Then I

walked towards him with my claw extended as though to shake his hand. He reached up. Quickly I grabbed him and span him round and then booted him on the backside.

He spluttered and I landed another kick.

"What the hell . . . what the . . . what was that for?"

"That," I said, enjoying every moment, "is from Pioneer Rip. Personally delivered."

The woman behind him began to laugh. Her masses of hair, the colour of copper, shook in the air. It was April, of course.

Then Murray's face crinkled and his lips pouted. He looked like a little boy that wants to laugh and cry at the same time. Laughter won. And while he was laughing he punched me as hard as he could.

"You two," said Aira from behind us. "You two behave."

The laughter subsided. "And this is Ariadne returned from the dead," said April.

"No, her name is Aira," I said. "She is very different. We have a lot to tell you."

"And who is this?" asked Murray, pointing at Kier.

"Kier," I said, "a full-human who accompanied us."

"Ah. He has a look of . . ." began Murray. "I thought perhaps . . ."

"You can call me Rip," said Kier. "If you want."

I have moved the ship to a more stable landing site close to where Rotorua Mining Town once stood.

We have been talking for hours. We have told our story, most of it anyway, the bones of it. We avoided the parts we could not explain. Both Pioneers listened intently, especially when we explained that Aira was pregnant. I noticed that April became restless. She reached out and squeezed Aira's hand and the two of them moved close together and talked quietly. Aira must have explained about Kier for I saw April glance across at me in a knowing way. Then she looked at Kier and her look had a totally different meaning. She is a fine-looking woman, very direct in her eyes, broad-shouldered and full-bodied. I found myself envying Kier and then I caught Aira's eye. Kier, by means of whatever chemistry such things are communicated, knew what was happening too. He looked very grave, very strong and singular, and the aura of Rip was all about him. It was like authority. One did not have to be a clairvoyant to know what was going to happen, and soon too. Set a pot on the fire and it will surely boil.

I think Murray was the only one who wasn't aware. He found my cigars and we sat in the kitchen smoking just as we had in the days after we rescued him from La Plage. He told me his story.

After we parted on almost this very spot, he returned in his ship to Auckland. He had some explaining to do to the officials there, but such was his prestige that he was able to explain and justify why I had been set free. Then he returned to the moon.

That was where the trouble started. The sterility of his children robbed him of status. As if that wasn't bad enough, the news then broke that I had taken off from Earth and defied orders.

"I thought they were going to kill me, Angelo. They would have, I think, except I was still the only hope. I really got to work then. I did everything I could, Angelo. I tried everything I knew about genetic engineering. And I had some successes. But nothing long-term. Nothing lasting, if you know what I mean. The people about me aged quickly and died. For every advance I made, I slipped two steps back. You need good stock to start with, Angelo, and the inbreeding on the moon had been going on for years. I even experimented on myself. I built clones of myself. I didn't want to. I didn't like the idea of two of me running about. But I could see no alternative."

I stopped him at that moment. "I found a clone of you on the moon, Murray."

He looked aghast. "Was it alive?"

"After a fashion."

"What did you do?"

"I killed it." There was a long pause.

"Thank God," he said finally. "It would never have lived. Problems with digestion. They all had the same problem."

298

"All?"

"Yes. All. At one point there were thirty clones of me growing. I thought I had killed them all before I escaped."

"Well you missed one."

"Yes, either that or someone else was trying experiments. Anyway. The whole situation was desperate. It was ridiculous. Ships stopped coming from Earth. Chrono was silent. He'd been silent for years. I didn't know what had happened to him. I could see that if I didn't do something definite I would be stranded out there on the moon. I would outlive the lot of them. I'd be the only man on the moon, eh? What a fate. So I decided to escape. I said I needed special parts from a clone chamber on one of the old ships. I was the only one who now knew how they worked, so out I went. They sent a guard.

"I poked about in the hangar. Found one ship that looked as though it might still make it through space. It wasn't a Pioneer Class like yours. Just a small transporter. Anyway, I bopped my guard on the head, closed the airlock and took off.

"You can bet I had my fingers crossed. And anything else that'd cross too. I didn't know whether it would make it through acceleration or whether it had been grounded because damaged. I didn't really know how to fly it. But anyway, I've always been lucky. The next thing I knew I was out in space . . . heading straight for the sun. I swung round the moon. The bloody guidance computers kept saying 'Need reference. Need reference.' Do you know what that means?"

"No."

"Well, it's the old system. That's what Chrono used to do. He worked out the guidance coordinates to give the safest and most economical flight in case there was a lot of traffic. He provided the reference. Without it the silly computers didn't know where to go. It took me hours to work out what was wrong. Then I took over. I got one of the computers working out a decent trajectory. On the basis of this I calculated our fuel needs. I had just enough to get me home and slow me down. One mistake and it would have been *finito*, as we used to say." He slapped his hands together for emphasis.

299

"Hell, it was terrible. And I didn't have much food or water either." Young Pioneer Murray smiled. He was enjoying the memory.

"Well, you survived anyway," I said.

"Yes, but only just. I got close enough to the Earth and sat in an easy orbit. It felt like home. Then I set an automatic landing programme. The ship had different landing programmes depending on the cargo. I set it for fragile perishable goods. Me.

"Well, we were coming down nice and smooth. Outside was not too hot. No shuddering. And then we sprang a leak."

"Never." I suspected the true story was expanding into a yarn.

"True. As true as I'm sitting here."

At about this moment in the telling I noticed that Kier and April had quietly left the kitchen. Aira was still with us and when I glanced at her she put her fingers to her lips. She was quietly filling a pack with food. Murray saw nothing. He was too busy insisting on his tale.

"So what did you do, Pioneer?" I asked. "Stick your thumb in the hole?"

"Only one thing to do. I had one of those old survival suits on – not like yours, an earlier model, more bulky – I closed it down. Don't ask me why we didn't burn up. I don't know. All I do know is that we decelerated and lost air at the same time. By the time we'd achieved cruise height I was sitting in a near vacuum."

"And the ship still worked?"

"Well, not very well. I thought I was going to crash in Old Brazil, but then I made it over the Andes and set course for Aotearoa. Just made it. I used the last of my power to bring me down on the coast."

"Whereabouts?"

"A little place called Maketu."

"Is that where it is now?"

"No, it sank. I was about a hundred yards from shore."

"So you swam the last bit of the journey?"

"Floated. I didn't know too much about it. I think the survival suit saved me. When I woke up I was on the beach with the waves pushing me about."

"Good job there weren't any sharks around," said Aira. Pioneer Murray looked at her and caught the twinkle in her eye.

"Look, what I'm telling you is true. Heightened a little, that's the art of storytelling. But true all the same."

Both Aira and I nodded. "So what happened then?"

"Well I didn't know where I was. I found a stream and drank. I gathered mussels and got a fire going and ate mussels until I was bursting. Then I settled down into the sand and slept. The next morning I woke up with a dog licking my face.

"The dog seemed friendly and knew its way about. I followed it up a track and eventually came to a small camp. It was a man's camp. Men only. No women. They just seemed to be wandering. They didn't know what to make of me but they weren't unfriendly either. One of them told me they were looking for the valley of women. 'Where's that then?' I asked. 'Not far from here,' he said. 'Place called Peru. You heard of it?' I told him I hadn't. 'Where you going?' he asked me. 'Rotorua Mining Town.' 'Ah, not far from here. We've been there. Not much there now. You got friends there?' 'Don't know now. Might have.'

"I stayed with that band of men for a few days while I got my strength back and then I headed inland. I reached Rotorua Mining Town in a couple of days. I scouted about a bit and then found my way up to April's place. I've been here ever since. It's been the happiest time of my life. She's a wonderful wom – "

This was the moment Aira and I had been waiting for. Murray looked up and glanced round. For the first time he registered that April was no longer with us. "Where's she gone?"

Aira reached out and took one of his hands. "She's busy making a baby."

"Eh?"

Aira looked at me. "Angelo, you tell him."

I said it as nicely as I could. I said, "She's making love to Kier."

"She's . . ." Words failed him as he stared from one of us to the other. His youthful face became red and then blotched with white. I saw the primitive emotion rise in him – protection of property, jealousy, betrayal, insulted pride – all of these and probably more. He stood up and I reached over and took his upper arm in my claw.

"Now, you're not going anywhere. Leave them to it."

"But . . ."

"No buts. In fact you're coming out with me. We're going out to find a decent hot pool and I'm going to explain a few things to you. You've a lot to learn young man, though you're old enough to be my grandfather. Aira, pack us up some food will you. Enough for three days."

"Already done."

"Right then."

Pioneer Murray twisted in my grip but couldn't escape.

"You bastard. You slimy . . ."

"Be careful," I said, lowering my face close to him and nipping him in my claw. "Don't think I don't know what you are going through because I do. But if there is another peep out of you before we are outside I'll boot you up the backside again and I won't be so gentle this time. I'll boot your arse into your mouth. Now move." He might have tried to say something more but I didn't give him the chance. I pushed him up the stairs by the pull-pole.

Aira watched and laughed. Then she rubbed her belly which was already becoming prominent and kissed me. "Find a nice hot pool, Angelo. I might come and join you tomorrow."

So that was that. I will not bore you or myself with the details of the next few days' conversations. They were *very* boring. Eventually Murray came to accept the inevitable. . . . Indeed, what alternative did he have?

I located a hot pool which was very pleasant and where we

302

were able to swim back and forth. It was a natural deep hollow filled with clear emerald green water. We set up camp beside it.

Aira joined us on the third day. Murray tried to flirt with her while I was gathering kindling wood and she pulled him into the water and held him under until his arms were flailing. After that he was altogether more sensible.

That evening we spent round the fire while the night grew chill. Murray was more relaxed than ever I have seen him. Some crisis had passed in him. I think the ducking had helped. He wanted to talk and we let him.

He rambled for a while and then got down to what he really wanted to say. "We tried you know . . . to have children. We thought we'd succeeded several times. But we didn't. I don't know what was wrong. Perhaps . . . it was me. April seemed fertile enough. Hell, she'd had children to aliens. It became quite a burden . . . wanting so much."

"Were there any other people?" Aira's question.

"A few, at first. Roving bands. Men mostly. Ageing men. I had several fights. I wished I had a claw like you, Chimp. Sometimes April would go off into the bush on her own for several days. She never let me go with her. I don't know what she did, but I could guess. But she always came back. Then there were less people. We took in one group and tried to form a community for farming. But they died off over the years. That hill up there is quite a little graveyard. Suddenly there was no one else. Just us. We set out from here. We travelled up and down this island. We found a few communities. Not many. Where there were women, they were worshipped. April was treated like a divine. It was a good journey. Sleeping out, catching food. We both felt stronger for it."

"When did your bodies become more youthful?" asked Aira.

Murray thought. "I believe that started to happen shortly after I teamed up with April. Body programming. It happened naturally. We didn't will it. Survival, you see. We're tuned to survival. We began to evolve again in response to this natural world. Survival does not favour the aged except in civilization.

303

I think April worked some magic too. She is a very powerful woman."

"When did she stop growing horns?"

"After I arrived. It didn't happen immediately. It took years. When I first joined her she had a tremendous spread. Then one morning I woke up and found that she'd cut them off. Just as she did that time before Angelo's departure. They used to grow quickly enough. But this time they never grew back. I think she'd finally accepted that she was never leaving Earth again. I was there. We made a useful couple and we survived easily enough." He paused and poked the fire for some time, rearranging the embers. "But, you see . . . I can't pretend that I know all that goes on in her mind. I think she is the kind of woman who can only love one man at a time. I don't know what she's going to be like when we go back aboard the ship." He lifted his eyes from the fire and looked across at Aira and me. "You see, in this, you are the lucky ones. We Pioneers were adapted to survive, that is all. You were programmed to love."

I must admit, I had never thought of it that way.

Later that night, when Pioneer Murray was asleep, Aira and I lay together. Murray's words about April had stayed with me. "How was she?" I asked.

"Didn't see much of her. But I think Murray is right. There is a single-mindedness about her, something competitive. She was even a bit strange to me."

"Did she ask about Murray?"

"No. She was wholly preoccupied with Kier."

"Mmm."

"What are you thinking?"

"I'm thinking that if she becomes possessive we will have difficulties."

"Kier will take it hard."

"So will Murray."

"Yes."

I rolled over on my back and stared up at the stars. "Ah

304

well. Murray will just have to cope. They've both got a lot of learning to do. I don't want to spend the rest of my life babysitting Pioneers." Then I laughed, though I wasn't really amused.

"What's so funny?"

"I'm wondering if we'll ever find Bonniface and Amsterdame and Lattisbourne."

"We might. We still have fuel and they know how to survive and are hard to kill."

"Yes, but how are we going to cope with Bonniface when Amsterdame gets a whiff of Kier? He was even more territorial than me."

Aira laughed then. "I hadn't thought of that," she said.

When we returned to the ship we found the atmosphere quiet but tense. April resented our return. Kier was pleased to see us.

April took every opportunity to be close to Kier and to touch him and demand his attention. Her meanings were obvious; I have never seen such abandonment in a man or woman. I felt pity for poor Murray.

He took in the situation quickly. It was as he feared and he quickly retired to the privacy of the control room.

Kier came to me only hours after our return. He didn't understand. He said, "What did I do wrong, Angelo? I did my job. What more does she want?"

I tried to explain as well as I could. And when I couldn't explain I took the coward's way out. I said, "Talk to Aira."

It may have been the coward's way out, but it was the right thing to do. We are Pioneer Rescuers and each know the limits of our strength. Broadly speaking, I can crack heads but Aira knows what is going on inside them.

I realized one thing though. We needed action. We needed to try and find our friends. If we did so April would begin to see the larger picture. She would have to sit at the tent door. And besides, action can defuse tension.

I made plans for us to set out the very next day.

305

7

Murray helped me.

He was glad to help. He said it gave him a purpose. We sat together in the control room during most of the night, planning.

Now how do you set out to find three people when you have a whole world to search? Here briefly was my thinking.

We knew that Bonniface, Amsterdame and Lattisbourne had escaped after the fight at Rotorua Mining Town. How hurt they might be we did not know. But they had a ship, not unlike our own, and that was very important. I put myself into Bonniface's fur. Knowing Bonniface, what would he do after he had strafed Rotorua Mining Town?

Well, knowing Bonniface, I guess that his first thought would be to attack Auckland and any other human settlements he could find on the way. After that, if he had power enough he would probably try to attack Moon Base. In the words of a once famous king, he wanted just to kill, kill, kill, kill, kill. That is the blood lust. It knows no quarter. It is a state of mind, and Bonniface more than the rest of us was capable of a sustained fury.

But he hadn't attacked Auckland. He hadn't attacked Moon Base. He and his ship and the two women with him had simply disappeared. Murray, in all his wandering round Aotearoa, had heard nothing of them. So if they were alive, they were somewhere out there.

It was possible that they had set out from the solar system to some other world they might have come across while acting as simple Pioneer Rescuers. But I doubted that. I doubted whether any of them had the stomach for a long sleep. What could they hope for in the end? A gradual ageing to nothingness.

Here is where Murray helped me. I asked him, "Would Bonniface know that I had survived?"

"Yes. Certainly. I told him."

"Did he know that Ariadne was dead?"

"Not certain. He could have seen her go down. There were lots of people on her. He might have thought she was still alive. He knew your strength."

"Would Bonniface have trusted you . . . I mean believed you?"

"I don't know. But blood is thicker than water. He knew who I was. I said I would save you. And on balance you and the Pioneers you rescued remained closer friends than ever you were with the full-humans. I think he believed me. At least he didn't try to fire at me."

"Did Bonniface know what had happened to Kingi and Elf?"

"No. Certainly not. They were captured and killed the next day."

The picture was beginning to look more hopeful. As far as Bonniface was aware, after the fight at Rotorua Mining Town there might still have been four of his comrades alive and an armed rescue ship commanded by a Pioneer available. That settled one question. Amsterdame and Bonniface would not have set out for space while there was still a chance that some of us were alive. So, if they were still alive, they were still on Earth. Where should I start looking?

"Was there any part of the Earth they favoured?" asked Murray.

"The only place we knew well was the Pioneer Centre near Rotorua Mining Town. That and Master Town."

"Well they must have had a plan. They were Pioneer Rescuers after all. They knew how to cope in an emergency."

"Yes." I began to think hard. Thinking back. "They might have gone looking for Larum and Silver," I said. "We never knew what happened to them. They went south I think."

"Yes. South. But they would never have found them. Larum and Silver died under the Ross Sea. Didn't you know that? Their ship needed repairs. They should never have been sent out. They thought they were landing on ice. They came down in water."

"They could have survived. Our ships were built to survive shocks. Look at the world where we found you."

Murray shrugged. "You may be right. In which case, let's assume that Bonniface and his crew found Larum and Silver. Would they settle down in Antarctica?"

"No."

"No. Then rule out Antarctica. But they might now be five people. Where would they go?"

I was at a loss. "I don't know."

"Let's start to think. They wouldn't settle in any parts still affected by the Catastrophe, would they?"

"No."

"Well, the world is healing itself quickly now. Perhaps all you need to do is start quartering . . ."

"Just a minute," I said. "You've reminded me. On that last night, Lattisbourne told a story . . . a place they'd found. Where was it?" I was on my feet in an instant and jumping down the steps that led to the living quarters. I was looking for my papers. It was all in there. I had written it down. For the first time my habit of writing down things that happened had a real purpose.

I came barging back up into the control room holding my papers in my claw. I rifled through them. They are not easy to follow. And then I read my own words. "The Far North, Old Europe, is not inhabited, but it could be. We have heard tales of great forests and wild tumbling rivers . . ." I turned on. There was a story somewhere that Lattisbourne had told. Here, yes. "We turned north and followed the coast . . ." This was it. Together Murray and I read the pages. We read about the deer that gathered close to the ship, the stone house, the embers that still seemed warm to the hand, the fire and the cooking. And then the sentence, "If that was how you ancients once lived, what madness made you give it away?" I knew with a certainty beyond proof that I had found the place where Bonniface would have gone.

308

"Lattisbourne was on that search ship," I said to Murray, almost shouting. "She would know the way. Tell me if I'm wrong."

"Calm down," yelled Murray, grabbing the fur on my neck and shaking it. "You are not wrong. I think you are right, I want to go there. You're a clever bloody chimp."

Aira arrived up in the control room. "What's all this shouting about, you two? Don't you know what time it is? Leave you together for five minutes and you start rowing."

"I think," I said slowly, "that I know where Amsterdame and Lattisbourne and Bonniface are. You remember that story that Lattisbourne told . . ."

"Before my time I think," she said.

"No matter. You read my journal. Well, it's all in there."

She nodded slowly. "I remember reading it."

"In Old Europe. They found a place, a house. If they are not there, they'll be close to it. Tomorrow we begin searching."

"It is already dawn," said Aira, nodding towards the windows. "What say I cook some pancakes, and we begin looking straightaway."

8

And so the long search is over.

I look down at my old friend Bonniface. He does not move. Once he was black as a panther and you could feel the heat radiate from his body when you were near him. Now he is grey all over and his face is lined. He is the first of us Pioneer Rescuers that I have ever seen aged. He is very cold but warming I think.

I look across from him to Amsterdame. She is plump and blond and wholesome. She smiles in her sleep. Lattisbourne is here too. She occupies the chamber reserved for Pioneers. She looks as young as I remember, but I can see scars on her arms and legs. Though her eyelids are closed I believe she has lost one eye. I can see where her nose was broken and her cheekbone is depressed.

All are waking up.

I sit with them, my book on my knees. As far as possible I have given them a slow awakening as requested. Aira is with me.

I found a note pinned to the door of their long-sleep chamber. It was brown and faded with age but I could just make out the words. It said, "Angelo, if you are reading this then we are safe. Wake us up slowly. We have had trouble finding easy dreams." It was signed Bonniface and was written in his untidy hand.

Finding them was easy. Bonniface had done what I would have done. He left their beacon on automatic.

When we left Aotearoa we flew over Australia, and then north by west over India and paused to take our bearings when we saw the pyramids in Old Egypt. They alone among the things of Earth seemed completely unchanged, basking in desert sun.

Above the pyramids I brought our computers to full alert and activated the same search programme as I would have done if we were searching for a Pioneer.

I talked to Chrono. He seemed happy and at ease. Apart from calls from us he had received no other transmission from Earth or moon and could not help us.

We cruised slowly, two miles above the Earth's surface. We flew over forests, mile upon mile of forests broken only by the peaks of high mountains. I pored over the account I had written of Lattisbourne's words but there were few details. This whole part of the Earth was new to me.

When we came in sight of a large sea I turned us back inland.

Everyone was in the control room. Though we knew it might be a long search, no one wanted to miss the moment of discovery. And it came. A faint signal at first. It was a coded reference which our guidance computers seized upon. They changed our direction. We came to a place of many lakes and dropped lower. Then we paused in the sky. We were, so the guidance computers informed us, directly above the beacon.

We used the view-screen to look down. The terrain was a mixture of grassy hills and small forests. I could see no sign of a ship and a ship as large as ours is hard to hide.

"Land," I ordered the guidance computers, "but be very careful. Take us well to the side of the beacon."

We came down in trees. The beacon was broadcasting from a small wood only a few hundred yards from us.

Aira and I wanted to investigate alone but Kier insisted on coming with us, and we understood why. We left Murray and April alone to sort out their problems.

The wood was dense and overgrown with thickets. It was hard to penetrate. Past the outer edges the way became easier and we entered a quiet region of tall trees. There, rearing out of the ground and reaching up almost to the tops of the trees I saw the blunt fin of Bonniface's ship.

311

I ran towards it and heard Aira's call of warning, too late. I felt the ground give way beneath me and I slid and fell through a tangle of fallen branches, bramble and pale onion plant. I fell through the air. I bumped on rock. I tried to get a grip but the rock crumbled and I fell the last few feet into thick black water that smelled like the quintessence of decay. I could barely see, but I knew that in front of me was a solid black shape. I scooped my way close to it and reached out and touched it. It was, unmistakably, the side of the ship.

I do not usually record luck. But on this occasion I will. Luck was with me for as I banged my way along the side of the ship I came to the iron runged ladder which leads up to the lower airlock. I held on with my claw and spat the foul water out of my mouth and wiped my face. Then I began to climb. The rungs were slippery with moss and ooze. I heard voices above me. They sounded far away, almost in another world. "Angelo. Angelo."

"I'm all right," I shouted. "I'm climbing up to the airlock."

When I reached the narrow balcony in front of the airlock I paused and looked up. I could just see the dappled sky through the high canopy of trees. Opposite me were smooth sides of rock. I was still very deep in the dark hole in which Bonniface's ship rested.

As quickly as I could I cleared the spongy forest litter from the platform. I scraped moss from the airlock control mechanism and revealed the depressed handle. I prayed that the circuits were still alive and that years of neglect had not wasted the drive mechanism. Only one way to find out. I took the handle in my claw and gently turned it. Immediately a red light blinked on and seconds later a green one beside it. A few seconds passed. I knew that sensors aboard the ship would be testing the relative pressure values, the moisture content of the air and taking a hundred other readings. In a crude way it would also be evaluating whether the airlock had been triggered by accident and whether I was an alien trying to get in. It took a long time making up its mind. Bonniface would be cautious, I reasoned. Even so, I was not prepared for the voice which

312

greeted me. It was Amsterdame's voice, but distorted somewhat. It said, "State your name and business."

Clever old Bonniface I thought. A last defence. I knew that locked inside the ship's memory would be a sequence of acceptable responses. Failure to give the right response would probably mean that the ship would activate its surface defences just as our ship had done at the Master Town Space Centre.

"STATE YOUR NAME AND . . ."

"I am Angelo," I said, my voice rising to a shout. "Friend of Bonniface and Amsterdame and Lattisbourne. I've come to set them free."

There was a pause and then Amsterdame's voice spoke again. "Enter friend," it said, and the airlock doors slid open.

I did not enter immediately. I called up to Aira and Kier who were standing on the edge of the hole above me, and told them what had happened.

"We can't reach you," called Keir. "Shall I go back to our ship and fetch a ladder or something?"

"No. No," chimed in Aira. "Angelo, shall I go and move our ship closer? It can crawl up to here easily, then we can use the Worm."

"Not yet," I said. "Get well out of this wood. Go back to the ship. I'll talk to you from there."

"What are you going to do?"

"I haven't had a chance to check yet, but if everything is fine aboard, I'll try to lift the ship out. If not we'll use the Worm."

"Don't take any risks." This from Aira.

"Don't worry. I haven't come this far just to become a martyr."

"You fell down the hole. We can smell you from here."

"Get going."

"Aye, aye."

I could hear them depart, breaking through the undergrowth. Then I went in.

Though the Pioneer Rescue ships are built to a pattern, no two are quite the same. I mistook my way several times but

313

eventually found myself at the place I wanted to be. It was not the control room. I climbed down into a living area similar to ours. Everything was neat and stored. I noted with amusement that the table bore scratch marks similar to our own, where Bonniface had rested his heavy claw.

I went down the passage to the long-sleep chamber. There I found the note from Bonniface. The door opened easily to my touch and I saw immediately that the auto-nurses were active. I had guessed correctly where I would find them.

I checked them carefully. All was well, though I was astonished at Bonniface's greyness. He must have stayed awake much longer than the others.

On an impulse I opened the door into their clone chamber. I was not surprised to discover that both clone tanks were broken and their contents gone. That single fact made me feel very close to my sleeping friends.

Then I was climbing up through the ship. I came to the control room. Its door was closed. One of Bonniface's last acts would have been to pump it to vacuum to protect the computer outlets. I fed air to the chamber and when the correct pressure was established the door opened easily and the lights came on.

"I am Angelo," I called. "You may not know my voice, but I am a friend of Bonniface and Amsterdame. Will you work with me?" For answer the lights of the guidance and control computers blazed and I felt the ship come to life.

There was minor damage. The computers told me that. Some slight deformation of the tractor mechanism and one of the external sensors had been damaged when a giant tree fell on it during a storm. The ship could not face the rigours of space, but it informed me it could certainly lift out of the slimy pool and fly for a few hundred yards and land again safely.

I took control. I put the ship through the lift sequence without using any power, and let it explore its own strength. Other faults came to light: a leaking seam under the water line, some seized-up hydraulics, clogged filters. Nothing serious. The ship became warm. It was ready to move again.

Only then did I contact Aira. "Watch for me," I said. "Everything's fine. I'll be lifting in a few moments."

"And Amsterdame and . . ."

"All safe."

Then I fed power. I heard the great generators grumble as they started to spin. We shed inertia as the ship began to battle the gravity of the Earth. There was a sliding movement and I felt us strike rock. Then we shifted backwards. Outside there was smoke and steam. I left the view-windows clear and saw us begin to rise. We cleared the lip of the hole in which the ship had been buried and tore up the vegetation.

Aira described it to me later. She said it was as if the whole wood started to quake. Trees twitched. Some fell. Others rose into the air, riding on the back of the ship. She saw their roots burn and they fell with a crash back into the small wood.

When the ship was no more than a hundred yards above the ground I guided it in a gentle curve and set down in open meadowland.

The entire journey from first lift to landing took no more than five minutes.

And now I am waiting.

We have moved the ships together.

For want of something to do while our friends wake up, I have begun a whole repair sequence. Kier is up on top of Bonniface's ship shovelling muck away and locating any damaged sections. Young Pioneer Murray is tinkering down below sealing up cracks and drying out the filter system. April has gone wandering out into the woods. I think this part of the Earth reminds her of her long-lost world. She is communing with herself, sensing out her chemistry. I hope she comes to happy conclusions.

Aira is with me. She longs as much for the return of Amsterdame and Lattisbourne and Bonniface as I do.

Now all we have to do is wait.

I have seen movement in Lattisbourne's tank and the fluids around Amsterdame and Bonniface are draining away.

I give them, let's see, about another two days before they again face the world.

Chrono sends greetings. He wants us to keep open transmission as they wake up.

And we have found the house that Lattisbourne described. It is a tumble of bricks now and burnt rafters. Trees are growing up through it. I hope she is not too disappointed. I hope the place was mainly of symbolic importance to her: an image of what could be accomplished, of civilization in a cold climate.

9

This will I think be an ending . . . of sorts.

So much has happened since I last sat down with my journal that to record it all would be like a new beginning . . . and that I don't want.

I have discovered something that seems to me profound though it is very simple: there are no such things as endings. I used to see our departure to rescue a Pioneer and our returns (with or without our prize) as single adventures, part of a larger venture, granted, but complete in themselves. Now I know that every return was really a new departure. Simple, eh? But simple things are often the hardest to grasp.

At this moment, even as I write, I am aware that we are pushing out on a great new adventure and none of us knows where it will lead. The past seems like a prelude. That is why I find it difficult to bring things to order.

Still, there are loose threads.

Bonniface, Amsterdame and Lattisbourne woke up to order.

It took Bonniface a long time to establish that we were real and not just part of a waking dream. Finally he looked at me and his eyes had some of their old vitality. "Well, Angelo," he said. "I'd hoped you'd be as old as me. But it seems that I'm the grandfather." Grandfather or not, he was still impressive in his size and strength, and if he was feeling some anguish because his body was no longer quite as quick as it once was, or because he thought twice before committing his muscles to some task, well, that is an accounting all living creatures take.

I asked him how come he had aged and he explained simply.

"I was worried, Angelo. I thought that after what I'd done to Rotorua Mining Town, they would come hunting us." He grinned a craggy grin and flexed his claw at the memory. "I was

317

going to attack Moon Base you know, but Amsterdame hit me on the head and when I woke up the anger had left me. That woman of mine packs a wallop. Near killed me. Anyway, Lattisbourne said we should go north. She said she knew a place where we would be safe. And that is where you found us.

"I knew what was happening with you, Angelo. I was able to pick up your signals on the radio. But I couldn't broadcast. Some fault. I spent hours bellowing into the microphone. And by the time I'd got the fault fixed you were gone. You wasted no time. I tried to contact Chrono but he was silent as the grave and I didn't like that. I guessed they were out looking for vengeance so I lay low. I dug us in.

"We knew it would be four generations before you got back. So we had a choice. Either we could sit around and hope to survive, or we could take a long sleep. We decided on the long sleep. But I fooled the women see. I pretended I was all dopey and that my wounds hurt and that I was half asleep before they were. I even lay down in the tank. The hardest thing was to stop myself laughing. Eventually Lattisbourne drifted off. I though Amsterdame was staying awake deliberately, but eventually she came stumbling in.

"When they were both asleep I got up.

"See, what worried me was that the Space Council still might come looking. I wanted to stay on guard. I had the laser cannon ready. I had plenty of food. The only problem was boredom."

"How long did you stay on guard, Bonniface?"

"Fifty years. And when I looked at myself in the mirror, I'd turned to snow."

"Fifty years. And did anyone come looking for you?"

"Don't know. If they did they never found us. But it was worth it, Angelo. See, I don't think I'd have got to sleep for worrying right? We're the protectors, right?" Then he threw his arm round my shoulders and squeezed. "You'd have done the same, Angelo. You know you would."

Perhaps he was right.

Taking my time, I told Bonniface about our adventures on

Rip's world and I told him about Kier. His eyes opened wide and his brow furrowed when I told that Aira was pregnant.

"Oho," said Bonniface and stretched his jaws wide and growled. "Well, if that kid tries laying a hand on Amsterdame I'll bite his head off."

I groaned. It was as I feared. Bonniface aged was still Bonniface. I began rehearsing my arguments in my head, and then Bonniface grinned and banged me with his claw.

"Still the old Angelo. You never had a sense of humour. Good luck to the kid. Amsterdame'll strip his threads. And do you think a few wild nights are going to split us up? No way. That woman's crazy about me. I couldn't get rid of her if I tried to. And if the kid's able to do something for her . . . mmm." He mused for a few moments. "That Pioneer Rip must be a clever bugger. She's always wanted a baby. She's got all the right instincts."

The news that Amsterdame might be made pregnant by another man seemed to have put Bonniface into a good humour. You never really know people, do you? Not even your friends.

We began building. Luckily most of the Pioneer Rescue equipment was still intact in Bonniface's ship. We made an impressive camp. I don't think any survivors ever began with such an advantage as us.

I *did* go gathering books. But whether anyone will ever use them I cannot say. I also brought back livestock: goats, cows, pigs. Pioneer Murray insisted.

I can tell you that April is pregnant and that she and Murray live apart. That is the way of things. Murray has thrown all his Pioneer energy into building our new world. I have never seen anything like it. I am seeing the Pioneer Programme working fully and for the first time: it is good to see. He has fields planned and livestock pens built. The rest of us supply the labour.

We have tried to make Amsterdame, Lattisbourne and Aira take things easy for they are all with child, but they will not hear of it. That is a lesson in itself. I think we men feel a little left out. Their adventure is the greatest of all. Aira is due to give birth in a couple of months.

A short time ago a small band of humans, three men, two women and a little girl, appeared at the end of the valley. They approached us cautiously and we took them in. They are the only humans we have seen. We cannot understand them and they are certainly baffled by us. Bonniface and I come in for the greatest stares. Perhaps they think that the ape has been domesticated. But who ever heard of an ape with a claw?

I was particularly glad to see the humans. One problem has been weighing on me and I could see that it was also preying on the mind of Murray. If we are starting the new population of the world (and it gives me great pleasure to write that sentence) then we are starting from a very restricted gene stock. Surely, I reasoned, our fate will, in the end, be the same as the fate of those poor creatures on the moon.

I think though I have solved that dilemma. The genes of our women will be in the children. And what after all has made them fertile? I must not think of Kier as a man or a boy. That is his outward appearance. In his essence he is the spirit of a whole distant world and of this world. That was Rip's gift to us. Its variety will never run out. The children will be human but they will not be of Earth . . .

So we await that first birth eagerly and with patience.

As for me I am not quite at my ease though I do not talk about it. I shall end my journal and when I have placed the last full stop I shall write no more. I shall try to be simple.

But of late I have been troubled by memories.

That wailing I heard on the moon will not leave me. It was like the crying of babies. And I can't ignore that.

Perhaps, if I am allowed, I will take the great ship up for one more journey.

Programming, you see. Bloody programming.

320